ORPHAN HERO

ORPHAN HERO

A Novel of the Civil War

JOHN BABB

Skyhorse Publishing

Skyhorse Publishing books may be purchased in bulk at special discounts for sales promotion, corporate gifts, fund-raising, or educational purposes. Special editions can also be created to specifications. For details, contact the Special Sales Department, Arcade Publishing, 307 West 36th Street, 11th Floor, New York, NY 10018 or arcade@skyhorsepublishing.com.

Visit our website at www.skyhorsepublishing.com.
Visit the author's website at http://www.johnbabbauthor.com

Skyhorse® and Skyhorse Publishing® are registered trademarks of Skyhorse Publishing, Inc.®, a Delaware corporation.

10 9 8 7 6 5 4 3 2 1

Library of Congress Cataloging-in-Publication Data is available on file.

Cover design by Erin Seaward-Hiatt
Cover photo by Ivan Zanchetta, courtesy of Creative Commons

ISBN: 9781510725638
Ebook ISBN: 9781631580598

Printed in the United States of America

ORPHAN
HERO

One

The Belt Of Orion

Jeffersonville, Indiana 1848

On the day he learned he was a murderer, seven-year-old Benjamin Franklin Windes had been cutting purple-topped clover and orchard grass with a two-handled scythe which was, like his name, too big for him. It was already hot that May morning, and the humidity in the Ohio River bottomland didn't make things any better, as a continuous drizzle of perspiration ran down his forehead and stung his eyes. He had cut and raked at least six bushels, and the sweet-smelling stuff was sticking to every sweaty inch of him when his stepmother found him.

"I hear you been cuttin' grass fer Abbie, so's she can stuff them mattresses she sells."

"Yes, ma'am."

"How much she payin' you?"

Quickly, Ben considered the ramifications of his answer. If he lied, his stepmother might already know the answer, and she'd be only too happy to make use of a stout switch. In fact, it had seemed to him in past circumstances that she could be pretty enthusiastic in her use of timber where he was concerned. But if he told her the truth, he feared for the ownership of the small bag of coins he had buried in the chicken house.

His stepmother read the hesitation, snorted under her breath, and decided this was the day to tell him. She'd been wanting to for a long time, and now he was old enough for it to really sink in. "Y'see, I figure you owe it to us, what with you killin' yer ma and all. And the hard times yer pa has had ever since. For sure he woulda died too—that is if I hadn't saved him."

Ben stood stock still. All of a sudden it felt like he couldn't hold himself up. He pushed the blade of the scythe into the ground, bracing his weight against it to keep from falling.

"You was too big when you was born, and you just broke yer ma down. She was pale as a ghost from then on, like she didn't have no blood left in her body. And she couldn't keep up with all yer squallin', always wantin' more and more milk and keepin' her awake all hours of the night. She didn't have the strength to hold up, and you stole ever last drop of life she had in her. You finally kilt her when you was about four months old. You kept her up all day and night fer over a week runnin'—and that last mornin' she just fell over dead while she was totin' a bucket of well water." She paused briefly, her thin lips a straight line, to see what effect her words were having. "She'd be alive today, warn't fer you and yer selfish ways."

Although it was said in a voice with no inflection whatsoever, he would remember the almost triumphant look in his stepmother's eyes for the rest of his life. And from then on, whenever he smelled fresh clover, he couldn't avoid the jolting recollection of his crime.

She leaned toward him with a breath that took the sweet smells of spring out of the air. "So what about that money? Yer pa is headed back up the river to Pittsburgh tomorrow, workin' fer that same steamboat outfit, and he needs to fill out his kit at Riley's store."

Ben wanted to run off and be by himself, but he knew she wouldn't allow him the luxury of having private, uninterrupted feelings. He pulled himself back to the present and remembered he had three quarters tied up in a rag in his pants that he hadn't had an opportunity to add to his stash. "I've got six bits left, but I already spent the rest of it," Ben sniffed, hoping he'd hit the right tone and wanting to cry again when he thought about the two hard weeks he'd worked for those three quarters.

His stepmother looked at him, seeking a clue in his voice. "Yer sure that's all you got? Don't be lyin' to me."

Ben almost squirmed as he struggled within himself to keep from telling her to just go straight to hell—straight to that fiery pit that Pastor Swinson kept on about every Sunday. He couldn't think of anyone who deserved it more! He ached to say it, but his Aunt's voice clicked magically inside his head, *Remember that silence is sometimes the best answer.* So he packed away those hard thoughts in the place in his heart that was already too full, reached for the rag that was tied inside his pants with a piece of string, and pitched the little bundle to her without a word. When she untied the parcel and saw the coins, he knew by the glint in her eye that he was in the clear.

"You be sure you bring me anythin' else you git. Don't let me hear you been wastin' no more money." Her cold gray eyes made it clear—there'd be the devil to pay if he did.

"Yes, ma'am. But Aunt Abbie said just yesterday she hadn't sold many mattresses lately, so she might not need any more stuffing any-time soon."

She suddenly grabbed him by the hair, lifting his feet clear off the ground, and shook him hard before letting him go. He tried to make his face a mask and not give her the satisfaction of seeing him cry, for she seemed to take special pleasure in seeing him hurt, and he had finally discovered he felt much worse afterward if he allowed himself to give in to crying. But if he managed to not show any reaction to her meanness, he not only felt better about himself, but it also seemed to somehow disappoint her. Today he forced a blank look in her direction.

"Just be sure you bring me the money when you get paid." In the absence of the response she sought, his stepmother was already walk-ing off. "And by the way, you kin stay with Abbie all you want whilst yer pa is up river."

Ben watched her cross the field in her short-stepping, pigeon-toed way. His whole life he had known his ma died when he was just a baby, but this put a new perspective on everything. All the sadness he had felt because he had no mother—all the nights he had lain awake in the dark, wishing for her affection, imagining what it would be like if she was still alive—could it be it was his fault all along? What did his pa think about what he had done to his mother? Did he hold a grudge against his son? Here he was seven years old, and he guessed it was true that he had killed her. Surely, nobody would lie about a thing like that—not even his stepmother.

He stuffed a bushel of hay into each of his two potato sacks and began dragging them the half-mile back to his Aunt's house. She lived beyond the end of Market Street, where it petered out to a rutted dirt lane halfway between Jeffersonville and Port Fulton, Indiana.

He had gone to live with his Aunt Abbie after his mother died, because his father couldn't take care of him on his own. Abbie lived with her three-year-old daughter, Sue, on the edge of town and was glad for the extra company. She called herself a seamstress, but as far as Ben could tell, she mostly just washed clothes and mended holes for people in town.

Abbie had caught the smallpox when she was a girl, and though she survived, her face still bore the evidence. The bottom lobe of one of her ears was completely gone—taken by the pox, as well as a piece of her nose—and this unilateral imperfection gave the impression that her head was always cocked to one side. Sometimes Ben tried to see past the scars to see what she really had looked like.

He asked Abbie about his mother—her sister—all the time. The stories about the two girls growing up in Pennsylvania, moving to Ohio with their family, both of them getting married within a month of each other, and finally locating in Indiana, he could almost recite by heart. By luck, the smallpox had missed his mother. Both sisters had jet-black hair, which Ben had inherited, as well as what some of the women in town described as the blackest eyes they had ever seen. No likeness of Ben's mother existed, and since his pa never spoke of her, he had to rely on Abbie's description of her to draw a picture in his mind. No doubt she had been beautiful.

After he made three trips with the cut clover, Ben carefully spread it out in the backyard, unrolling a large fish net to cover the grass so it could dry in the sun. Abbie liked using flowering clover because it was so much softer than most hay, and it retained something of its sweet scent for months after it was cut. It was popular with her customers too.

Ben told Abbie about his stepmother's visit and giving her the money he had earned. But he kept it to himself that he had found out he was responsible for his mother's death. Maybe he didn't want someone else to confirm it as being true, or perhaps Abbie didn't know the real story, and he couldn't bear the thought of her finding out the terrible thing he'd done. Anyway, he had to think about it by himself for a while before he was willing to talk over what he had just learned with anyone else.

Abbie put her hand on his shoulder. "Well, with the clover you cut this morning, and what we have already, I can make at least ten mattresses when I need to. So for now, you can stop cutting and hauling grass. Besides, I've got another idea." Ben looked at her. "You and I are going into the soup business." She answered his confused look:

"You see all those steam boats and rafts stopping on our side of the river? I figure the crews will all be hungry for a decent meal, as well as the men who work on the docks. If I make a big pot of soup every day and a couple of skillets of cornbread or some of those soda biscuits, you can take it down to the riverfront and sell it for maybe ten cents a bowl.

"If we're lucky, we can sell twenty or thirty bowls a day. I'll give you two cents for every bowl you sell, but you've got to promise me that you won't spend a penny of it. I'll bet Mr. Riley was running his mouth to your pa or his wife and told them about you having money to spend in his store. You can't take a chance on that happening again, or she'll be back to get your soup money too.

"I'll do the cooking, but I need you to be the one to sell the soup down on the dock. I just don't like having to deal with people in town if I can help it."

Abbie turned her distorted face to one side as she spoke, while Ben's head was spinning with the financial possibilities of making forty to sixty cents a day. That would make him the richest kid in town—maybe in the whole state!

Abbie could see him figuring. "You can't tell anybody you're making any money. This town is too small to keep a secret—particularly from that stepmother of yours. We'll need to make our garden twice as big as it is now so we can keep making soup and still have something left for us. If you're willing, we'll start plowing this evening."

Ben asked, "Do I need to ask Mr. Finnerty for his mule?"

"If you can hold the plow steady, I can handle the traces. Even if he is my neighbor, I don't care for the way that man looks at me. He reminds me sometimes of a washtub full of wet laundry—like he's completely wrung out. It's almost as though he's plumb used up— maybe empty is a better description—with hardly any life left in him. And the way he keeps up that shack of his is a disgrace."

Ben thought this might be a good time to pose his question, as he needed to make sure he had a place to stay, "Is it alright with you if I stay here while Pa is working on the river?"

Abbie smiled grimly to herself, thinking about the real motive behind his request. "Sure you can. That'll give us a chance to get our soup business started without you having to walk back and forth every day and get anybody's suspicions up."

From Ben's perspective, Abbie was as tough as anyone he knew. She had raised her daughter by herself since her husband Albert had disappeared over two years earlier, when he headed out west to find a place where they could set up a trading post. Albert had begrudgingly moved with Abbie to Jeffersonville the year before Ben was born at the urging of Ben's father. It was true that there had always been employment along the river, but what Albert really wanted to do was move out to the very edge of the frontier, despite his wife's lack of enthusiasm for life away from the conveniences of a town.

He figured that a trading operation would allow him to connect with the wild land out there beyond Jeffersonville. Indiana was just too crowded with people and towns for his liking. Apparently, he had not considered the impact a constant stream of settlers on the Oregon Trail might have on any feeling of being away from the hubbub of life. Naively, he had headed west.

Abbie's last contact with him had been a letter he sent her from Joseph Robidoux's Trading Post in the township of St. Joseph, Missouri. She had read his short letter a thousand times.

> *Dear Wife*
>
> *I am up the Missery River, an I heared thet they was a fin plac fer trade up on the North Platt. Don worry none. The injuns has been pacyfied fer a couple years. I'll be sendin fer u an Sue afore ye no it.*
>
> *Yers, Albert P. Grimsby*

That was all she knew. However, twice since his departure, she had seen newspaper articles that warned people to travel only in large wagon trains on Crow and Pawnee land. Albert's letter had not mentioned that to head very far up the Platte meant traveling into the hunting territories of the two tribes, which were said to be among the most ferocious and merciless toward small parties attempting to cross their land.

Some people in town said, without too much effort to speak quietly, that Albert probably just ran off to another life. For months after that last letter, Abbie spent long minutes every afternoon staring down the road, wishing, and praying he would just walk back from wherever he had been. For the better part of a year, she continued to tell Sue that her pa would send for them one day when he found the right place. Ben realized it had been some time since he last heard Abbie make that promise. It also dawned on him that Abbie no longer spent any time looking down the road. But he continued to catch sight of his little cousin from time to time, standing at the front door, gazing down the lane and off toward the horizon for her pa.

Unlike most women of her generation who lived along the river, Abbie could read and write. And after teaching Ben those skills last year, they spent at least a half hour reading to one another at the close of every day. He loved the luxury of being read to, of dreaming about the characters, the scenes, and the heroic struggles without having to hit and miss on some of the words. Most of the time, he and Sue sat with each other while Abbie read. But for at least a portion of every night, he was the reader. After hearing all of Abbie's seven books read to him at least twice, he no longer had problems with very many of the words. But next year he was going to have to go to school. She insisted that he needed a real teacher if he was ever to be somebody.

When Ben lay down on his pallet in the loft, he had no intention of going to sleep as he had something he had to take care of. He waited silently until the sounds behind the curtain at the back of the cabin, where Abbie and Sue slept, faded completely away.

When he was satisfied that Abbie was asleep, he slipped the latch on the door and stepped out into the yard. The night was cool, there was no moon, and the sky was literally awash in millions of stars, but he spent no time admiring the sight. He looked off to the southwest, about forty-five degrees above the horizon, where he knew he would find his mother. When he was just three years old, Abbie had explained to him that heaven could be found directly on the opposite side of the three stars that made up the belt of the constellation of Orion the Hunter. And whenever he had a need to talk with his mother, he should look directly toward that exact area of the night sky, where she would be waiting to hear his voice.

It was a hard thing to do, but he had to apologize to her—to tell her how sorry he was that he had been the cause of her death. Always before, the conversation had been to tell her how much he missed her or describe one of the vexations of his young life. But after what he had learned that day, it seemed somehow wrong to talk about his small troubles. Now every time they talked, he would need to apologize for being the reason they were apart.

Abbie stood at the window, watching him there with his face turned to the sky. She could tell that he was upset, as several times he appeared to be wiping tears from his eyes with his sleeve. Maybe he would tell her what was bothering him when he was ready. But she had discovered he was a boy who usually kept his deepest thoughts to himself. When he finally turned to come back to the cabin, she hurried to get back to her bed before he re-entered.

Two

I Don't Wanta Get Hung

Jeffersonville, Indiana 1848

The morning they launched the soup business, Ben let the chickens out in the yard and sprinkled a couple of handfuls of grain on the ground for them. But when the pigeons in the barn loft swooped down to feed with the busy chickens, as was their daily custom, Ben was prepared for them. He clubbed two greedy pigeons that got too careless, cleaned them, and cut them up into small chunks. Abbie got a hot fire going in the woodstove, put a bit of bacon grease in the iron pot, and browned the meat. Then she filled the pot half full of water and added vegetables. By mid-morning, they were ready.

Ben was instructed to pull his wagon down close to the dock and get a small fire going. He would have to keep the soup warm and keep another pot on the fire in which to dip the bowls after they were used. They only owned five bowls and six spoons, so if they were successful, he would have to continuously keep his dishes wiped clean. As always in Abbie's kitchen, the corn muffins were done to perfection.

He knew there was no available wood at the dock to burn, as workers were always building fires to stay warm in the early morning, so he had to haul dry firewood in his wagon as well. Just before he left, he put a shovelful of dirt in the wagon and then placed a hollow bull horn on top of the dirt, with burning embers inside to make it easier to start his fire. Abbie handed him a jug full of well water.

"When you get to the dock, add this to the soup. If I add it now, the pot will be too full, and you'll slop soup all along Market Street from here to town."

Ben scouted the dock, picking a spot along Front Street so that the smell of his soup could drift over to where men were unloading boats and loading wagons. Front Street was the virtual center of commerce in the town. The north side of the street had recently gotten wooden sidewalks installed so that men conducting business could stay out of the mud and manure near the riverbank. Ben counted eight warehouses stretched along the street for almost a quarter mile. Oftentimes, merchandise had to be temporarily stored before space could be found for it on another ship headed in the same direction. Sometimes there was scarcely room for an additional wagon or buggy on the street in front of the warehouses.

Ben soon got his fire started, and shortly after the coals burned down enough for him to put the soup on, two men walked over. The smaller one of the two had a permanent tobacco stain on the side of his chin, a wispy red mustache, and eyes that were so close together there was barely room for a nose in-between. His friend was a full head taller and displayed a bushy black beard. Ben couldn't help but think of a bear when he looked at the bigger man, and that was only reinforced when he noticed the thick hair on the backs of his hands and the nasty, long fingernails. For a fact, they almost looked like claws. How in the world he worked on the dock with those nails, Ben couldn't fathom.

Both men were wearing clothes that were various shades of gray, having long since lost any sign of a former color. They had been sweating from their work that morning, but the smell emanating from them had at least a month of heredity behind it.

The smaller one spoke through no more than a half dozen teeth. "What you doin' here, boy?"

Ben felt the stirrings of uneasiness, but he had not come here to be scared of his first potential customers. "I'm about to sell stew and cornbread as soon as I can get it warmed up. It's ten cents a bowl."

A sharp laugh escaped from Beady Eyes. "That's way too much. We'll give ye two cents a bowl." The man reached for a bowl.

"I'm sorry, but this belongs to my aunt, and her price is ten cents." Ben didn't figure on this happening.

Beady Eyes reached for the dipper, "I said 'twas two cents."

Almost instantly the sharp "crack" of a whip rent the air beside Beady Eyes' head. It happened so fast, Ben literally jumped a foot.

"Put the bowl down, Red, or pay the boy what he asks." The voice came from a short, stocky man who wore a beaver cap with a turkey feather cocked to one side. Ben couldn't tell how old he was, but his grey hair didn't appear to be a factor in his willingness to mete out a dose of punishment if it was called for.

Red's hand immediately went to the knife on his belt, thought better of it, and said, "We was just funnin' with the little shite, Jeremiah."

"Don't be swearin' now. You know I find it distasteful."

"Sorry, Jeremiah. We meant no harm."

"I'm real glad to hear that. If you've got ten cents, pay for your soup. Otherwise, you and Butter get back to work."

Butter Simpkins turned to his smaller friend, vigorously bobbing his head up and down. "I shore would like some soup, Red. I shore would."

Something in the big man's manner made Ben realize he wasn't quite right mentally. His speech was childlike in its animation and inflection, and his hands were in continuous motion, as though he had no idea what to do with them if they were not at work. But his physical presence was so imposing it was hard to see past it to the damage beneath the surface. Perhaps once upon a time the man had come by his nickname because he was pudgy and soft, but nothing could be less descriptive of the huge man now than "Butter."

What a way to start a business, thought Ben. But he was even more surprised when both Red and his friend produced their coins. They greedily ate their meal and brought the bowls back. Butter spoke to Ben. "That was fine soup. Better'n they serve in town. You gonna be here tomorrow?" He turned to Red. "We can come back, cain't we Red?"

"I'll be here every day," Ben said. The two men moved off and Ben turned to the man they called Jeremiah, "Thank you, sir. I didn't exactly know what was going to happen next, but I wasn't going to run off and leave my soup."

Jeremiah grinned, "Glad I could help. Red won't hardly pick on somebody less'n he's bigger than they are."

"Do you suppose they'll give me a hard time every day?"

"Not likely. I'll keep an eye out." Jeremiah held out a dime, "Could I try that soup? One of the saloons in town sells what they have the gall to call chicken soup, but for all the chicken in it, I expect they only put in a rooster's shadow."

So the full-bodied soup and the comments of his first customers were great advertisements among the workers. In less than two hours, Ben was out of business, having sold twenty-three bowls of soup. He found Jeremiah and gave him his last corn muffin for free before heading home. He just couldn't help keeping one hand in his pocket, jingling the silver as he walked. Tomorrow promised to be just as good. Almost all the men had wanted to know if he would keep coming to the dock.

He only told Abbie selected parts of his first day. He had to tell her about his new friend Jeremiah, but he considerably understated the "teasing" he had received from Red and Butter. With Jeremiah around, he felt like he would be safe enough at the docks.

Almost every morning he was able to put a rabbit, squirrel, or a pigeon in the pot. More vegetables became available in the garden. Abbie bought more bowls. Then townspeople began to drop by for soup. They had to buy another pot. Jeremiah always seemed to be around, but after a milder harassment incident, Ben was treated fairly well by everybody. He tried to give Jeremiah his soup for free, but the man wouldn't stand for it. Every afternoon Ben was able to hand over three to four dollars to Abbie.

In 1848, the Ohio River was bound by the states of Pennsylvania, Ohio, Indiana, and Illinois on the north bank and Virginia and Kentucky on the south. It was also the geographic separation between northern "free" and southern "slave" states.

Jeffersonville was located along the Ohio, across the river from the big port at Louisville, Kentucky.

Ben had asked Jeremiah why so many boats stopped in Jeffersonville. Jeremiah explained, "Most of the year, these boats cain't travel all the way from Pittsburg to where the Ohio meets the Mississippi without stopping and unloading their cargo right here or across the river at Louisville. Then me and my men move their load overland some two miles and then reload it on another boat headed on west. The Falls of the Ohio—that's those wild rapids just downstream of here—are too dangerous for boats most of the year."

"Both sides of the Ohio River compete for the business of unloading boats headed both upstream and down, portaging the load to the other end of the Falls, then reloading onto another boat bound in the same direction to complete the journey. Louisville is a fine port, but because of the tight bend in the river, Jeffersonville and Clarksville can move their loads quicker 'cause of the shorter distance on the north side of the river's bend. We all depend on lots o' riverboats stoppin' on this side of the Ohio. All these dockworkers and draymen, not to mention the whole town, rely on a constant stream of watermen and boat passengers to keep their businesses alive."

June and July passed, and August came on hotter than ever. Abbie gradually paid off her bills at Riley's Store and Doctor Salyer's office. She even bought some material to make Sue a new dress, Ben a shirt and pants, and a pair of shoes for each of them. As for the rest of the money, half went into the bank, and the remainder went into a jug underneath the floorboards of the cabin. She explained to Ben, "You'd best keep skunks and bankers at a distance. They're too slick for my liking."

Ben kept his promise. Despite the fact that he could almost hear the licorice jar calling to him from Riley's Store, he buried his share in the chicken house at the end of every week and didn't spend a cent.

The third Tuesday in August started out just like every other sweltering summer day in a river town. Ben arrived at the docks around eleven in the morning, got set up for business, and started selling at a pretty good clip. Twice that morning, he looked down the street and thought he saw Red looking at him, but whoever it was disappeared quickly behind the Fambrough Warehouse. When Jeremiah dropped by, Ben remarked, "Have you seen Red and Butter today? They usually never miss, and I'm about out of soup."

"I saw them early this morning. They both said they were too sick to work."

"That's funny. I could swear I saw Red about an hour ago. Did they look sick to you?"

"Not no more than they usually do."

For some reason he couldn't really explain, Ben was uneasy that morning and finished his business, heading for home with still three or four bowls of soup left in the pot. The closer he got to the house, the more he hurried. Finally, he pulled his wagon into the bushes on the side of the road and began to run.

Abbie had finished picking vegetables for the next day's soup and was cutting them up on the plank table, while Sue played on her pallet in the corner. She heard a dog bark from across the road, wiped her hands on her apron, and went to the door to see what might be getting the dog's attention. There were two men on her front step—rough men.

The smaller one said, "You the soup lady ain't ye." It really wasn't a question.

Abbie tried to keep her voice firm, but something wasn't right about this. "Yes, I make soup and my nephew sells it in town."

"You got any made up? We done missed our meal today." He grinned at her. No wonder he liked soup—he lacked enough teeth in his head to chew anything more substantial. She tried to push the door closed, but his foot was inside the frame, forcing it to remain open. She could smell the applejack on his breath and see it in his eye.

She stood her ground. "No, I make it up fresh every morning."

The small man looked down toward the road in both directions. "Let's all go inside so's we can talk." He pushed the door out of her grasp and walked in.

Seeing that her only companion was a small girl, he spoke again. "Now let's have us a discussion about all the money you been makin' all summer. We figure you took in over two hunert dollars this summer. You'd best give it to us if you know what's good for ye."

Sue began to cry and Abbie looked over at her, finally getting her attention, then looked at the door, hoping her daughter would catch on and make a run for it. "What little bit I had left over is in the safe down at the bank." Abbie was backed up against the kitchen table, and the shorter man was just inches from her face.

"I gotta say, Missy, that you got brass. But it jest don't sell. Scarred up as yore face is, another cut or two won't make no matter. But if you don't tell us where you keep yore money, I'm gonna slice you good." He pulled his knife from his belt and nonchalantly thumbed the edge.

The big man spoke. "Please don't do that, Red. You promised this time."

"Shut up, Butter!"

Abbie felt behind her on the table, found what she was looking for, and aimed her big vegetable knife at his chest. He reacted quickly, moving just enough that the knife sunk into his left shoulder, deep enough so that she couldn't easily pull it out to try again. He screamed and hit her with the butt of his own knife on the side of her head. Abbie went down like a rag doll, and the man was right on top of her with his blade. Little Sue picked up a piece of firewood and hit him on the side of the head before he backhanded her, knocking her clear across the cabin.

The big man was wide-eyed. "Red, I think you done kilt the woman and mebbe the little girl too. You said there warn't gonna be none of that. If they catch us fer this, they'll hang us sure. I don't wanta get hung, Red." He shook his head slowly from side to side, and repeated himself. "Please, Red. Don't wanta get hung."

"The wench stabbed me! Cain't you see that?" He had blood all over the left side of his shirt. "If she ain't dead, she's gonna wake up without no nose." Red spit on his knife blade and wiped it off on his pants. "She'll be breathin' through two holes in her face when I finish with her."

At that instant, Ben burst through the door, swinging his firewood axe. He hit Red on the right hip, cracking his pelvis and leaving the axe in the man's flank, as blood poured out of the gash. Red screamed again but still managed to grab the boy by the throat. Ben felt the hand squeezing, could just barely hear the man cursing him, and was quickly becoming very dizzy. He could get no air at all and had no strength left to struggle.

A tremendous explosion went off behind his head and then another, and another, and another. Blood was everywhere—all over the floor—all over Ben. He was on his knees, coughing, and trying to catch his breath. His ears were ringing so badly, and he was so disoriented that at first he thought he was the one who had been shot and that all the blood belonged to him.

Someone picked him up and brought him outside. "You're OK, son. You're OK. I'll be right back." He returned in a minute with a hysterical Sue and laid her down with Ben. It was the neighbor, Mr. Finnerty! "Watch after her, son. I need to see 'bout Abigail."

Mr. Finnerty appeared again, this time carrying the limp Abbie. Both of them were covered in blood. He listened to her chest and got up. Ben looked at her, scared to know the answer to his question. "Is she dead?"

"Her heart is still beatin'. Can you ride a mule?" Ben nodded his head.

"There's a bridle on a post just inside my barn. Get to the doctor's office first and tell him to get out here for Abigail. Then go fetch the sheriff. I believe I kilt both them boys in there."

Mr. Finnerty was already holding a cool, wet rag to Abbie's forehead, talking to her, and trying to wipe all the blood from her face when Ben took off. He had never been on a mule in his life, but desperation was a strong teacher. Clinging to the mule's neck for dear life, he and the animal made fairly quick work of the trip to town, and Ben found the doctor where he generally was, playing checkers on his front porch. Thankfully, the doctor was losing, so he was only too happy to call the game on account of a medical emergency.

The citizens of Jeffersonville eyed Doc Salyer with a measure of uncertainty, never really quite trusting his medical abilities. It was easy to speculate that their lack of confidence was related to his funny accent, but the man had a dreadful tic in his right shoulder, and was liable to jerk vertically on one side every few minutes. Nobody relished the thought of him sewing up a wound with needle and thread.

Ben was able to get the doctor started for the cabin in his buggy then headed to the center of town to find the sheriff. The lawman was sitting in his office with his shoes off, picking at a huge blister on his big toe. His horse had come up just as lame as he was, so the only way to get him moving was to put him on the mule while Ben ran along behind.

Both the doctor and Mr. Finnerty were kneeling over Abbie when Ben returned, and he could see that she still was not responding. The doctor was looking in her ears and nose while Mr. Finnerty repeatedly whispered, "Abigail, can you hear me?" Sue had quieted down, but the side of her face was already purpling, and her lower lip was badly split.

The sheriff limped into the cabin for a few minutes, then came back outside and asked a question. "Would somebody explain to me how one of them boys has a kitchen knife halfway through his shoulder, an axe stuck in his side, one ear almost ripped off—reckon by a piece of firewood, cause there's a chunk of bark inside his ear—and half the other side of his head is plumb shot off. Who in the world used all them weapons on that man?"

It took no small amount of deductive work for the sheriff to find out what happened, since none of them had seen the whole thing. "What kind of guns was used here? I count at least four bullet holes in them boys. How many shooters was there?"

Mr. Finnerty pulled a pistol out of his front pocket. "This was the gun that done all the shootin'. After I shot the red-haired man that had hold of Ben, the big man came for me. When I shot him the first time, he got his hands around my neck. He was squeezin' so hard I thought he was gonna shake hands with himself. I had to shoot him twice more before he'd let go of me."

The sheriff's eyes fixed upon the large barreled pistol. The Dragoon Pepperbox, with its six barrels and walnut grip, held his interest far more than the chaotic aftermath of its power. "I don't think I've seen a weapon like that afore. It's shaped sorta like a derringer except for them six barrels. Where'd you get it?"

"Louisville. I took it off a mule driver that was threatenin' to hold up a friend of mine."

The sheriff looked at the skinny Mr. Finnerty with a new respect. He sent Ben back to town to fetch the mortician, who worked on healthier days as a carpenter, and to go tell Jeremiah Sledge that two of his dockworkers were dead.

Abbie was still unconscious, and her house was slippery with blood. Mr. Finnerty volunteered to put her in his house and agreed to help Ben clean up the gore in her cabin. Sue sat with Abbie with instructions to holler for them if Abbie stirred. About every hour, Ben and Mr. Finnerty paused in their cleaning and came over to the house to see how she was, even though there had been no sign of her awakening. Abbie was on a pallet on the floor, since Mr. Finnerty didn't really have a proper bed. And his redbone hound had to be chased out of the house twice, as he apparently was accustomed to lying on the pallet too.

By late afternoon, they were satisfied with their cleaning job and hoped Abbie would be too. She had roused up enough to drink some water but had a throbbing headache and was terrifically dizzy, so they decided to leave her where she was for the night. Little Sue finally went to sleep, while Ben and Mr. Finnerty sat up watching Abbie.

The candle flickered and finally went out some time after midnight, yet there seemed to be quite a bit of light coming through the window. When Ben walked outside, the full moon appeared to be bigger and closer than he could ever remember. His aunt had told him of the special power that was afoot on such a night, so Ben stepped away from the cabin and the two cottonwood trees in the yard to allow the moon to shine full upon him. When he knew he was completely illuminated, he turned his back on it and gazed at his full shadow displayed in the dew-covered grass. Abbie had told him that a wish on your moon shadow would generally be granted, unless of course it was a selfish wish. Ben whispered a plea from his heart for his aunt to be made whole again. With this accomplished, he knew he had done all he could for Abbie, but he still had one more thing to do.

Orion was barely visible because of the bright moonlight, but when he found it, he had a hard question to ask. "Ma, you probably know that Abbie was attacked today by two men from the docks. When I saw one of them hurting her, all I could think of was to try and kill him. I wasn't just trying to hurt him. I truly wanted to kill him. Ma, is there something wrong inside me? Do I have a murderer's heart? I don't want to be that way, but is that just who I am?" He stood there for a long time with his questions, then tossed and turned in his sleeping pallet for at least a couple of hours before he was finally able to get to sleep.

Ben quickly remembered he had missed supper the night before when he awoke to the smell of biscuits, beans, and coffee. Mr. Finnerty was conflicted between keeping an eye on Abbie and tending his fire. She had also wakened, and Ben moved to her side. She had no memory of the day before and listened intently when Ben explained to her what had happened during and since the attack.

When Mr. Finnerty came over to the pallet, Ben almost didn't recognize him. Gone was his scruffy, sparse beard. He had two good cuts on his chin, so Ben suspected it was a fresh shave by a seldom-used razor. He even had on sort of a clean shirt. But the shave really only served to accentuate his most noticeable feature. His eyes appeared to be set too low on his face. Although he had an extremely high forehead, it seemed as though he had no cheekbones at all, because his big eyeballs sat where his cheeks ought to be.

Abbie was quick to tell him how grateful they were for his help. He placed a hand on Ben and Sue's shoulders and told Abbie how brave they were, and that he had just been neighborly. Ben noticed he called her "Miss Abigail" and put his arm around her shoulders as he helped her to the only chair in the cabin. His aunt self-consciously covered her damaged nose with her hand and replied with a wavering smile, "Thank you, Sean."

Things began returning to some degree of normal. Abbie insisted on going back to her own house. Ben stayed home for a couple of days but soon went back to work with his soup. Apparently, the story had been spread all over the dock and in town as well, because almost every customer patted Ben on the back and asked how his aunt was doing. Jeremiah came by and told him he was a "young man of real courage." Ben didn't feel that way at all. Frankly, he'd been scared to death when he ran into the cabin with that axe. He hoped no one would find out just how full of fear he had been.

Three

The Boy In The Cage

Jeffersonville, Indiana 1848

I n late October, most of the crimson leaves of the Indian Paint Brush had fallen, and Ben was still going to the dock every day to sell soup. It was on one of those frosty fall days when he was hurrying to get his fire started and his soup heated up that he saw a familiar figure walk down the gangway of a steamboat and saunter up the dock. With a big grin on his face, Ben waved as hard as he could.

His father had returned from Pittsburg and certainly was surprised to see his son situated there on Front Street, but he was even more taken aback to witness Ben's sales operation and the way the boy easily interacted with the dock workers and other people from the town. He leaned against a big white oak tree to watch his son for a minute.

Daniel Windes was not a tall man, but the way he carried himself—straight as a ramrod, hands swinging at the sides, and sort of a side-to-side swagger in his walk—gave the impression that he was bigger than he really was. His clothes were worn thin with a half dozen places that had been crudely sewn back together. His skin was browner than Ben had ever seen it. His hair and beard were a good deal longer than Ben remembered, almost the color of sand rather than the usual brown. He obviously had been in the sun almost constantly these past months, but for the first time, Ben noticed flecks of gray in his pa's hair. Could it be that he was getting to be old? Ben felt his pa's hands on his shoulders—they reminded him of rough pig iron they were so calloused and hard.

"Who might you be workin' for here on the dock?"

"Abbie makes this soup every day, and I come down here to sell it."

His father suggested that he needed to come live at his house again so he could give up his soup job and then he could go to school full time, "After all Ben, you never even been to school before." As much as he cared for his pa, living in a house with his stepmother was the last thing Ben wanted to do.

"This soup business is the only way Abbie has to make any money. I don't know what she'll say when I tell her I have to start school." Besides, he really enjoyed what he was doing. He loved hearing the rivermen tell stories about what they had seen and done on the river. Many had been to St. Louis, others all the way down the Mississippi past Memphis to New Orleans. One told of a huge catfish he had caught (almost as long as a man and as big around) from a keelboat. In fact, the man claimed that the fish had actually towed the boat a couple of miles before he could land it. Several spoke of the wild Indians they had seen at trading posts in Missouri. With all the strange places to see and the tales of adventure shared by the rivermen, it was easy to begin to think of himself working on the river too, right along with his pa.

In the autumn of 1848, Ben's father had been remarried for five years. His new wife brought two girls to the marriage, both a few years older than Ben, as well as her younger brother, Arthur, who she had inherited after her mother died of apoplexy when the boy was just fourteen.

It must have been a terrible experience for Arthur to see his mother die so suddenly. One minute she was alive, and the next blood was pouring out of her nose and mouth as she lay on the floor, staring intently at her son, saying nary a word for some half an hour, until she finally quit breathing. So the boy moved in with the newly married Sarah and Daniel. He was quiet and kept to himself, but Sarah explained to her husband, "The boy seen too much for his own good. He'll be alright one of these days."

Daniel didn't think much about the boy's strange actions at first, but it was hard not to notice Arthur talking to himself all the time. Over the next several months, he quit communicating with the family all together but always seemed interested in his private conversations with himself. Sometimes Daniel had caught him staring in his direction with what appeared to be dark, threatening looks. He thought about punishing the boy, but realized he really had not done or said anything to be punished for.

When Arthur was sixteen, he went out to the barn one night and killed their three milk goats with a butcher knife. At least this was the only rational conclusion when Daniel discovered his goats in the morning and found Arthur's nightshirt saturated with blood. Although Ben was only five years old at the time, he remembered the confrontation well.

Daniel's voice was filled with rage. "What have ye done to my nannies?" And he was further infuriated when Arthur did not answer him but simply offered a blank look. "Did ye not know we'll have no milk in the house? Explain yourself!" Again, there was no answer, and he had no choice but to whip him as punishment and threatened to throw him out of the house if he did anything like that again.

At this, Sarah pleaded for her brother. "He's just a boy. He cain't make it on his own."

"The boy ain't right, I tell ye." But he relented. Even so, Daniel was more uneasy than ever around the boy.

A week later, he awoke to a noise, followed Arthur out of the house in the middle of the night, and just barely was in time to stop the boy from killing his bull calf. Knowing they could not continue to live this way, Daniel was ready to send the boy away, but Sarah again begged for leniency. Daniel left the cabin and returned at mid-morning with thirty stout oak poles he had cut.

"What are ye doin' with them staves?"

"If he's gonna act like an animal, he's gonna live like an animal." And Daniel spent the remainder of the day constructing a cage six feet long and four feet wide in a back corner of the cabin. "He's gonna stay in there 'til he can behave like a normal human."

Arthur's cell had no furnishings save a pallet to sleep on. His meals were passed to him through a narrow slot, and twice a day the slop jar in his cell was emptied. The hoped-for signs of improvement had not come, and the boy was now nineteen. He had not been allowed outside the cage except when he was attached to Daniel with a stout rope and taken out to the well for a bucket bath. He had only spoken to himself during the past three years, and the language he had begun to use was unintelligible to all of them.

Ben knew, beyond any doubting, that it was wrong to keep a boy in a cage. Certainly, nobody in the household had spoken out against the situation. Arthur himself had not spoken at all for the entire time he had been confined, except to the unseen beings he now communicated with. But to look in his eyes, it was not difficult to translate his quiet into pain and betrayal, compounded by what seemed to Ben to be a plea for understanding.

Ben understood his pa's side of the problem. He had simply reacted in the only way he knew to the unpredictable threat that Arthur posed to his farm and his family. Surely there was another way, but it escaped Ben, no matter how often he thought on it.

That evening, Ben told Abbie about his conversation with his pa. She looked at him and then turned her face away. Ben had a premonition that this conversation wasn't going to go where he wanted it to.

"Ben, you know my Albert disappeared three years ago, and nobody in this town believes he's coming back home. I've prayed over him so many times I've lost count. In the last couple of months, I've come to realize that a good man lives right across the road." Ben tried not to look shocked, but was astute enough not to remind his Aunt how she had described her neighbor just a few months earlier.

"Sean Finnerty asked me to marry him three times this month. Just yesterday, I finally decided to say yes. We'll live here in this house, as I couldn't stand to live in his. That'll mean Sue will have to move out of my bedroom and sleep in the loft. Both Sean and I care about you, and he said he would be willing to build a lean-to on the side of the cabin so you can live here. But if your pa wants you at home, I doubt you should defy him."

"What about our soup business?"

"Your pa is right that you should be in school. Sean can take over the soup selling now. Maybe you can help during the summer."

So there it was. His stomach felt like he had a rock in it. He realized he was about to cry, but knowing he was too big to give into that, he bit his lip to keep from it. Despite his best effort, his eyes seemed to be watering. Abbie found something to do on the other side of the kitchen. Ben gathered his few belongings, thanked Abbie for letting him stay there, and hugged Sue for a long time.

It was dark when he left. When he stepped inside the chicken house, the birds were all on their roosts and set up a stir when he entered. Needing no light to uncover his bank, he found what he was seeking within a couple of shovels of dirt. Shaking the tin box, he was reassured to hear the coins rattling. He didn't need to count it, knowing very well there was forty-seven dollars and twenty cents in the can—all in dimes. He'd counted it in his head every night before he went to sleep, but now he decided to find a hiding place tonight, before he went to his pa's cabin. He just couldn't take a chance on Mr. Finnerty accidently finding his cache.

He walked into the woods, heading northeasterly rather than taking the road. Every now and then people got robbed on the thoroughfare, and he was determined that was not going to happen to him, particularly tonight. Although the moon was only a couple of days past the first quarter, he knew the woods well enough that he was not particularly worried he might get lost. He made his way downhill to the creek but did not even consider a hiding place near the water, as there was always traffic up and down the stream. He crossed at a shallow gravel bar and stopped about fifty steps beyond the creek, listening for a good five minutes to be sure nobody crossed the stream behind him. His pa had taught him how to use water when they were hunting deer—listening for the sound of them crossing a creek as an indicator of their approach. He began to carefully pick up his feet with each stride rather than taking a normal step and dragging his heel.

His pa had shown him a few things about tracking too, and he knew any good woodsman could follow the trail of someone who wasn't being careful.

There was almost a total absence of wind—all the more reason to be watchful. Stepping on a dead twig could sound awfully loud in those circumstances, and anyone following from a distance could easily figure out where he was if he moved too quickly. Hearing a hoot owl off on the next ridge and a coyote answer, he moved forward slowly, feeling a bit panicky when he failed to identify the landmark he was looking for at the place he reckoned it might be. But just about fifty steps further, he saw the outline of what he was seeking silhouetted against the night sky.

The old tulip poplar had broken about thirty feet above the ground. The bottom half of the tree was hollow and stood in a thicket of briars. He chose not to put the box inside the trunk but wanted to be sure it was in the briars, which should prevent anyone just happening on his spot. The dirt at the base of the tree-top was gouged out and loose where the jagged end of the poplar had hit the ground when it fell. He silently dug a shallow hole to the side of the downed tree, covered his box with the loose dirt, then carefully added leaves and a few dead branches on top. As a final touch, he pushed briars over the top of his spot in what seemed a natural fashion.

He heard what sounded like a foot on a stick and froze against the ground. It could have been his imagination, maybe a deer, a coyote—anything. The tin box not only contained an entire five months of work, but it represented his hopes for a chance at a better day—particularly now that his future was less than certain. He laid there for fifteen minutes, briars sticking him from every direction. Finally, he moved away fifty steps, watching and listening. Satisfied, he walked toward his pa's cabin, crossing the edge of the Negro cemetery before he reached the new Plank Road that ran between Jeffersonville and Port Fulton.

He figured most people would avoid the route he had just taken in order to stay clear of the cemetery. He'd heard stories about ghosts coming out of the grave during a full moon to torment people who had done them wrong. In fact, there was no doubt that his stepmother was one who was convinced those stories were true. He turned right on the road and reached his Pa's cabin in another five minutes, deciding he would go back in the woods early the next morning to be sure the location gave no hint of his hiding place.

Four

A Surprising Talent

Jeffersonville, Indiana 1848

There was still a light in the cabin, so he hollered from the front yard. People had been known to get shot at if somebody thought they were sneaking up on a house at night. His pa came to the door, wearing his union suit. "I'm surprised to see you this evenin' Ben. Come in here and we'll make you a pallet in the house. And whilst yer at it, tell me about that fight over at Abbie's place. Soon as I walked in Riley's store today, people was tellin' me my son had been in a big shootout."

His stepmother was already in bed, and when she saw Ben, she said nothing but rolled over to face the wall. His stepsisters were probably already asleep, as he heard no sound from their direction. And Arthur—well Arthur hardly ever slept as near as he could tell. It seemed like he even stood in one place, leaning against the inside of his cage both day and night.

After hearing the short version of the fight, his stepmother spoke from her bed. "Pastor Swinson done started a prayer chain for us, what with Abbie and that hermit across the road killin' them two men," she raised up from the bedding to point at Ben, "and you bein' right in the middle of it all."

Ben remembered his first run-in with Red and Butter and how Jeremiah and his whip had come to his aid. He also would never forget what he had seen them do to Abbie and Sue through the window of the cabin. He was tempted to say he didn't need their prayer chain but bit his lip.

He didn't have much of anything of his very own at either house. It seemed like he was always visiting no matter where he slept—that he really didn't have a place to call home. And when he stayed with his father and stepmother, the woman always seemed to find a way to make it clear that he was eating more than his share—"takin' food from the mouths of my girls"—as she put it. He was suddenly so bone-tired he just wanted to sleep.

Like most mornings, he awoke to the sound of his stepsisters' voices, picking at each other and arguing over the few chores they had to perform. He rose, waved a hello at Arthur, and went out to the well and the necessary.

The girls were out in the yard feeding the chickens when he re-entered the cabin, but he was almost sure that his small bag of belongings had been rearranged. His stepmother was at the fire—had she rummaged through his clothes, already looking for something worth taking? She noticed the attention he was giving his bag and said, "Oh, I moved yer kit out of the way so's I could git to the fire without trippin' over yer clothes." She went on, "Yer pa and I was talkin' yestidy. He's gone to town to see if he can find work over the winter. If yer gonna live here, you can earn yer keep by doin' some things I couldn't do this summer. That firewood rack needs to be filled up. They's lots of downed trees in them woods west of the house. You can get busy and cut our wood then see that rack stays filled this winter."

Ben started to say that his aunt had managed to cut firewood, keep up a cabin, care for her daughter, plus run her soup business. But he knew he'd pay if he did. Unsatisfying as it was, he held his tongue.

"Then you can lay our garden by for the winter. Since you'll be livin' here, you'll need to make the garden bigger to account for all that food a growin' boy eats. The barn has a leak and some of the hay is wet that yer pa cut afore he went upriver. The roof needs fixin' and that hay needs to be turned if it's not ruined already. You'll need to bank the fire at night and get one started soon's you get up in the mornin' before you go to school. I'm wore plumb out from all these chores around here. About time you done yer part."

Ben didn't mind work. In fact, he preferred it to sitting in the cabin with his stepmother and her two girls. Sometimes he sat by Arthur's cage, and if there was an extra biscuit, he'd share it with him. But the communication was only one way. Arthur never responded, although sometimes Ben did believe he saw a flicker in his eye.

It sounded like there would be little time for school with the arrangement described by his stepmother. He picked up a cold biscuit from the Dutch oven and walked outside to get an idea of what needed to be done. He had not visited the cabin during the five months his pa had been gone, so he was surprised to see the state of the place. Weeds and high grass covered the yard. What a contrast to the neat, swept yard at his aunt's house! The sheer weight of honeysuckle and poison ivy vines had just about pulled down the rail fence by the barn. It appeared that at least a quarter of the hay was moldy and not fit to feed to the cow this winter. He would need to talk to his pa, as he wondered if there would be enough usable hay left over to last until spring.

When his stepmother said the firewood rack needed to be filled, she wasn't kidding. There were four sticks of kindling in the rack and nothing to cut in the wood yard. About one more meal and she would have been cold at night. He thought about his hiding place and considered going there this morning but knew he was expected to immediately get to work, so he put that off until later. The last thing he needed was to raise her suspicions, not to mention stoke her temper.

Ben picked up the axe that was sunk in a large stump in the yard, noticing that the head was covered with rust. She probably hadn't touched it the entire time his pa had been gone. He pedaled a large whetstone wheel for ten minutes to sharpen the blade then walked into the woods. Several limbs had broken off trees—probably the result of a strong wind storm that had passed through—and he went to work dragging the limbs back to the yard. By noon, he had cut what he figured was about three week's worth of firewood. He sharpened the axe again, rubbed some coal oil on the blade, hung it on two pegs in the shed, and went back in the cabin to see if there was anything to eat.

"We only ate twice a day all summer long." Ben heard one of the girls whine in front of the fire. "Maybe we'll have more to eat if your pa finds a job in town." Ben went back outside, drank a dipper of water at the well, and fished around in his pants for the last couple of bites of salt pork, which required more water. He decided to go back to work.

The fence surrounding the garden was as vine and weed-covered as everything else on the place. Ben used a hand scythe around the fence then started on the garden with a hoe. Not much had been done to keep the weeds out during the summer, and it was a wonder the vegetables hadn't been overwhelmed. After a couple of hours, he realized this was not going to be a job he could finish in an afternoon. To break up the monotony, he decided to clear a small area with the hoe. Then he would shovel a wheel barrow full of manure from the chicken house, spread that on top of the cleared garden area, and mix it in the soil with the hoe. It was near dark when he heard his pa coming up the lane. He had only finished clearing and fertilizing about half the plot.

He and his father cleaned up at the well and went inside, facing a supper of turnips, cornbread, and buttermilk. Although he wouldn't pick turnips as a favorite food, Ben generally didn't mind eating them, but these were so pithy that they were hard to chew. He remembered all over again how much difference there was between his stepmother's cooking and that of his aunt.

Ben made his pallet near the fireplace, and thankfully, he remembered one of his new chores before he went to sleep, so he went back outside and brought in two armloads of the wood he had cut. Then he laid two big pieces against the back of the fireplace, stoked what was left of the hot coals, and put enough wood by the door to rejuvenate the fire in the morning.

When he awoke the next morning, it was all he could do to pull himself out of bed in time to get the fire going again and get ready for the day ahead. The school was on Seventh Street, and consisted of what was a simple dog-trot house—two distinct rooms separated by a hallway that ran the length of the building. Students in the first six years were on one side of the hallway, and the last six were on the other side. They sat on backless benches that were not much more than split logs. Some of the smallest kids' legs wouldn't touch the floor, and it didn't take long in the school day before they were squirming with discomfort as the circulation was pinched on the backs of their knees. Only the teacher had a real chair.

There were twenty-eight children in the grammar school and eight in the preparatory school. Most of them would only finish grammar school, or maybe eighth year, before leaving to begin a daylight-to-dark working life on the farm or to find other employment to help support their families. Only the kids from the most well-to-do families were able to stay through preparatory school.

Since Ben had never had any schooling, the teacher started him off in first year that morning, but by afternoon he had been promoted to third year. She told Ben that as soon as he could become as proficient in arithmetic as he was in reading and spelling, that she would put him in fourth year.

He couldn't help but smile in appreciation of his new academic status as he walked home from school, but then he remembered the list of chores waiting on him, and that sort of took the joy out of his step. He resolved to spend an hour on the woodpile and an hour on the garden every afternoon until he was finished in the garden plot, then he could devote more time to building up a substantial supply of firewood. It seemed to him that his stepmother burned twice as much wood as Abbie—particularly once cooler weather began to set in. So he had trouble staying very far ahead of her appetite for firewood.

He worked on his arithmetic after supper; but when he asked for assistance with a multiplication problem, his pa couldn't help, and he didn't think his stepmother had ever been to school. If only he was at Abbie's house, he was sure she could explain it to him.

After Daniel stared helplessly at Ben's arithmetic primer for several minutes, his wife declared that if he wanted a haircut, he'd better quit acting a fool. Snatching a lock of Daniel's curly hair, she told Ruth to fetch her sewing box. Inside the wooden box, lay what may have been her most valued possession—a pair of scissors—carefully wrapped in muslin. She then retrieved her comb and a looking glass that normally hung on a nail on the wall.

His stepmother had a talent after all! Abbie had given Ben haircuts with a bowl and a pair of scissors for as long as he could remember, but this was a whole different way of cutting hair than he had seen before. First she wet his pa's hair, then set about trying to comb out the curls and tangles. Once that was accomplished, she combed tufts of hair, grabbed the hair with two fingers, and clipped off the ends of the tuft with the scissors. She moved slowly around his head, combing and clipping. In less than a half hour, his pa looked like a completely different person. Then she basically did the same thing with his beard and mustache—combing and clipping until it was short and even across his face. When she was finished, there was enough hair on the floor to reconstitute a small dog.

There were a few men in town with well-trimmed hair, but none looked as slick as his pa. He realized he had just seen something worth keeping in his memory. He would like to have had his own hair cut like that but just couldn't bring himself to ask his stepmother for a favor. He also wasn't sure she would have agreed to do it, even if he had requested it. Ben would just continue to ask Abbie for a haircut every couple of months, but he also made a point of watching closely when his pa received a haircut from then on. He also paid close attention to where she stored her instruments.

After school the next day, Ben lost no time in getting to Abbie's. He told her about school and described the unkempt status of his pa's farm. She helped him with his multiplication until he understood how to do it and told him to come anytime he had problems that he couldn't answer. He noticed there was only about a half hour of light left, and he wanted to check on his hiding place while he could still see.

As Ben walked into the woods behind the chicken house, Mr. Finnerty was standing at the window. "Now why in the world is that boy walkin' through the woods at this time of an evenin' instead of takin' the road?"

"It's shorter to go that way rather than back toward town to get to the Plank Road, and he's done it so many times he could probably do it with his eyes closed," Abbie replied.

Sean Finnerty said nothing.

Ben's stepsisters, Martha and Ruth, were eleven and thirteen years old, respectively. Both of them had hair the color of carrots. Despite the bonnets their mother made them wear every time they walked outdoors, in the summertime both girls were covered with freckles. Ben decided it was highly unlikely a fly could land on their faces without treading on a freckle. One thing he was sure of, there was no possibility that the freckles were related in any way to the sisters actually performing physical labor out in the sun. Both did a few menial household chores, but manual labor for them or their mother seemed to be out of the question. Ben figured they each needed about a month with Abbie to change their perspective about what "women's work" really meant.

Both girls were rail thin, despite their efforts to eat everything they could get their hands on. Ben couldn't help but compare them to a girl about their age who was in fifth year at school. Alice Mabry was one of the nicest girls in grammar school, and he could not help but notice that she had already begun to take on the shape of older girls. But as far as Ben could tell, neither of his stepsisters had shown any sign of those same physical changes.

One thing that particularly bothered him was their feet. Each of the girls had very narrow, exceptionally long feet. Their toes were long and bony too. And because they were barefoot for much of the year, this particular feature was hard to ignore. Perhaps it was an inherited trait, as he had noticed the same characteristic in his stepmother on those rare occasions when she didn't wear shoes. In fact, hers were all the worse due to the red, shiny bunions on the side of each foot. To see those six feet all splayed out in front of the fire at the end of the day was enough to take away Ben's appetite.

Neither girl made an effort to be nice to Ben, or Arthur either for that matter. Ruth, in particular, delighted in finding ways to torment them both. The girls called him Bennie Frank at every opportunity. He had tried asking them to call him Ben—or even Benjamin—but that seemed to make it worse. He decided the best policy would be to ignore them, and maybe they would tire of it. However, he didn't put a lot of store in that approach.

They took special enjoyment in humiliating Arthur. From time to time, they brought a kid home with them to show off "Wild Arthur" in his cage, and there was no attempt to hide their snickers and remarks, as though Arthur couldn't hear what they were saying.

Once the sisters had used a knife to carve "BEN" in letters four inches high into one of the cabin's logs near the hearth. When Ben was confronted by his stepmother, of course, he denied it. But she slapped him so hard—"for lying"—that he had a mark on his face all day. When he met his pa in the yard that evening and told him what had happened, he went inside for a few minutes. When he came out, he told Ben both Martha and Ruth said they didn't know anything about it—and why would they want to carve his name into the side of the cabin anyway?

"This cabin don't belong to you, and you got no right carvin' yer name into anythin' here. Mebbe you need to spend the night in the barn if ye cain't act civilized in the house." In addition to spending a cold December night in the barn, Ben missed supper, but it hurt worse to know that his pa wouldn't believe him.

In the following weeks, he made it a habit to sneak a biscuit from the breakfast skillet, keeping it in his pocket all day in case he was sent to the barn with no supper. Many times this strategy paid off, as he seemed to spend more nights in the barn than in the house.

The girls knew how much Ben liked to pick up his pa's musket and walk into the woods to hunt—particularly during the fall when the passenger pigeons were migrating south. It was a dramatic sight to view thousands upon thousands of the birds darkening the sky from September into November, and it was common to see the trees behind his pa's cabin literally filled with the roosting birds almost every morning. So most days during the early fall, he had been able to bring at least a couple of pigeons home to the pot.

He prided himself on being extremely careful, and on those days when he found nothing to shoot for dinner, he emptied the gun into the base of a sycamore tree while still in the woods. The old flintlock could not be unloaded in any way except to fire the weapon. Shooting into the tree also gave him an opportunity every few weeks to dig the lead out of the tree so that it could be melted down, poured into a bullet mold, and used again.

On this particular morning, Ben found no squirrel or rabbit and came back empty-handed. He fired the musket into the sycamore, went into the house, hung the gun over the door, and left for school.

When he finished his chores that evening, he came into the house to find his pa as angry as he had ever seen him. He grabbed Ben by the shoulders and shook him so hard his teeth rattled. "What do you mean leavin' my gun barrel plugged with mud? If it's still got a ball in it, whoever pulls that trigger on a plugged gun would prob'ly be kilt or blinded, because the barrel would blow up on 'em. I can see right now that you ain't old enough to be trusted with my musket. 'Til I say different, yore huntin' days are over."

Ben was dumbfounded. He knew he had fired the gun into the sycamore not five minutes before he entered the house that morning, so there was certainly no mud in the barrel then. And he was positive that he had not accidentally allowed the gun to hit the ground after that. In fact, it was his habit to carry the gun over his shoulder rather than at his side. He tried to tell his pa all this, but he was angrily waved off. He was accustomed to being believed whenever he said something—certainly that was his experience at Abbie's house. But to have his own pa not trust his word was a hard thing.

He saw Ruth looking at him with her arms folded and just the trace of a smile on her face. Could she have had something to do with this? He looked at Arthur to see if he would give any indication of what had happened, but unfortunately, this happened to be a time when Arthur was in a far off place where only he could go.

The thought began to form in Ben's mind that his pa was two different people. When it was just the two of them, they seemed to have what Ben thought was a good relationship. But with his stepmother in the picture, his pa was not the same. It was almost like he was doing everything he could to please her, even if it meant striking out at his own son.

He remembered something Abbie had said to him—that meanness doesn't just happen overnight. And he couldn't help but wonder if his stepmother were slowly turning his pa into a mean person. The realization of this was new information for Ben, and he didn't really know what to do with it.

Five

I'm Purty Hot To Go

Jeffersonville, Indiana 1849

In January, Ben turned eight years old, and that same frigid day a steamship arrived from Pittsburg carrying over a hundred passengers who were bound for California. Ben saw a worn newspaper carried by one of the adventurers that quoted President James K. Polk's December State of the Union message. The President's speech included the verified communication from the Military Governor of California, Colonel Richard Barnes Mason, that there was a huge gold strike along the American River in California, and that "extensive and valuable" mines had been discovered. Elsewhere in the paper was a report of "lumps of gold the size of a man's hand." If the President said it was so, didn't it have to be so?

All sorts of men from Jeffersonville immediately started their own preparations to head west. That evening, Ben's pa spoke excitedly about the President's speech. "Half the men in town are headed to California. I have to say, Sary, I'm purty hot to go." He paused to judge the look on her face then quickly continued. "I figger I'll mine gold for a year, make my fortune, and come back here so's we can all live like royalty. Shoot, we could probably buy one o' those big houses over to Louisville!"

Ben could almost see the twin demons waging a battle behind his stepmother's eyes. She wanted to cry out and curse her husband for even considering leaving a defenseless woman, three young'uns, and her poor idjit brother to go off on a wild adventure. But on the other hand, the idea of living like a queen was an argument that had to be considered. After all, she had always wanted to be a queen!

Daniel had spent the whole day talking to would-be prospectors, and learned that there were only three ways to get from the eastern United States to California. All of the options began by water. The first involved an ocean transport to the Isthmus of Panama, followed by a dangerous and arduous journey by foot or on horseback through a tropical jungle to the Pacific Ocean, and then another ocean voyage up the western coastline of Central America and Mexico to the port of Yerba Buena (some now called it San Francisco) in California. However, there was no regularly scheduled steamship travel along the Pacific coast, so the traveler sometimes waited on the west coast of Panama for several weeks, before being picked up by a California-bound vessel.

Also, it was an expensive proposition. He calculated that the trip down the Ohio, then down the Mississippi to New Orleans, and then on an ocean-going ship to Panama, would cost at least thirty dollars. Then he would have to travel across land to the Pacific and then pay for another ticket on a California-bound steamer. Nobody seemed to know how much that ticket might cost. And then he'd have to buy his prospecting gear and a supply of food. Even if he sold his forty acres of marginal pasture land and his calf, he couldn't raise that kind of money. And what if all the claims were taken? What if he failed to find gold? It's not like he had any mining experience. It might be all gone by the time he got there. Then he'd be coming back home to nothing but a cabin and a couple of acres.

The second choice was entirely a river and ocean voyage, requiring the traveler to round the southernmost tip of South America—the "Horn"—before sailing up the Pacific coast of South and Central America, then Mexico, until reaching California. This involved a sea voyage of seventeen thousand miles and commonly took five months or more. This option required the least struggle and pain on the part of the traveler, but it was the most expensive of the three, and subjected one to what were described as terrible dangers at sea. One fellow said a steamer ticket from New Orleans to San Francisco was a hundred and fifty dollars. Also, ships would only begin that voyage from September through February because of the horrendous weather around the Horn from April through September.

The third option was to travel by boat down the Ohio to Cairo, Illinois, then up the Mississippi River to St. Louis, followed by a trip up the Missouri River to a trailhead in Missouri, then overland—joining other travelers in a train of wagons to California. The overland portion of the trip was also projected to take about five months. Again, the traveler had to consider the time of year, as the trip could not be undertaken during the winter. No wagon master would agree to lead a party if they wanted to depart from Missouri after the middle of June. The preference was to begin the journey in April or May.

Of all the choices, this one involved the most significant physical demands on the part of the traveler. It was also very dangerous—wild Indians, crossing deserts, mountains, raging rivers, and maybe even starvation. But, as it was the most economical, it was overwhelmingly the preferred method of travel among the men from Pittsburg.

For a man traveling with a family, the trip would require purchasing a wagon and a team of oxen. But for a man traveling by himself, he could buy a lightweight wagon—maybe just a buckboard. Or perhaps he could just go on horseback. But the men from the steamship advised that each traveler would need several hundred pounds of food and supplies just to support his needs on the trip. Therefore, he would also need at least one, and maybe two, pack mules to carry that kind of weight.

Daniel's biggest problem was his lack of financial resources. He didn't have a dime in the bank. He earned four dollars a week in Jeffersonville and six dollars a week when he worked in Pittsburg. But his family spent the money as fast as he made it. He considered going to the bank to see if they would loan him some money. Maybe he could offer them a quarter of any gold he found. But he knew they'd want his farm to secure any loan. And until he actually found gold, how could he make payments on such a loan? The only other solution was to work his way to California. He certainly knew his way around a steamship. All he needed to do was hire out on the trip. It seemed to be the only way.

The first week of March, Ben went with his pa and his stepmother to the dock in Clarksville on the morning of departure. Looking out across the roiling river, Ben was amazed by the power of the rapids that held travelers hostage between Jeffersonville and Clarksville. He hoped there would only be smooth sailing from Clarksville downstream.

He had told his father goodbye many times—in fact, every spring for the last five years Daniel had gone upriver for months at a time. But this was different. At least in all those previous departures, it felt like the Ohio still connected them somehow, and he always knew his pa would come home every autumn. The trip to California seemed to be more final. It was too far away. If his pa was successful in his prospecting, he might well be gone for a couple of years. Then again, he might be hurt badly or even killed by Indians, and Ben might never find out how or when or where.

Daniel had indeed found a job on the steamship downriver, so he had to get aboard, for it was his job to make sure the boiler was constantly fed. Ben saw his pa hold and kiss his wife with tenderness, tell her not to worry, and that he would be back with bags of gold. Ben then stepped to his pa, but there was no touch, and his tone was no longer tender as his stepmother stood by watching. His pa looked at his wife, and she seemed to give him an approving nudge. "Ben, I expect you to help Sarah with chores around the cabin, and don't be no burden to her. You need to quit that school now so you have more time for chores. You kin start back up again when I get back. You'll need a big garden to keep all of you'ns fed. Be sure you do as she says, understand? I don't want to hear no word about you disobeyin' her, or there'll be hell to pay when I get back."

Ben nodded mutely as his pa turned away and stepped on board. Daniel turned and waved once then was gone in the crowd of passengers and crew. Ben felt like he had been kicked. It seemed to him that his stepmother's meanness was reflected in his pa's voice. Ben understood his pa's order, but at the same time, he had every intention to only go to the cabin when absolutely necessary. If only he could have gone with his pa!

Six

Run For Your Lives

Jeffersonville, Indiana 1849

When Ben awakened the next day, his stepmother told him they were all going to the Baptist church where she had been raised. Ben cringed at the memory of his last visit to Sarah's church, as he was much more comfortable at the Congregationalist Church in town. "Can I just go to church with Abbie?"

"We're all a goin' as a family—thet means you too. Pastor Swinson says he believes thet Arthur is possessed by the devil. He says if'n we'll bring him to services this morning, he promises the whole congregation can get the devil out of him."

Ben had not thought about that particular solution to Arthur's problem. "Since pa is gone, how are we going to get him there?"

"You and me are gonna tie ourselves to the ends of that hemp rope, and then tie Arthur in betwixt us."

"I'm not sure we can hold him. What if he decides to run off?"

"Well, one thing's for sure—I'd never let go of the rope, and you'd better not neither! Besides, he ain't never run off before. No reason to think he would now. Hurry up so's we won't be late. Pastor wants us on the front row."

As they began their two-mile walk to the church, Ben couldn't help but compare his tall, thin stepmother to a stretched-out earthworm. Once he thought about it, she was even just about the same color. He chuckled to himself when he thought about Mr. Finnerty saying that it might be a good idea not to take her to any funerals, as it was likely she could be confused with the corpse.

As they walked, Ben kept expecting Arthur to try to get away. But he was surprised at how docile the young man was. In fact, he just ambled along, seemingly happy to be outside and free of his confinement. Although Sarah had put one of Daniel's old shirts on Arthur, it did very little to improve on his appearance. The poor fellow was in terrible need of a bath, his hair and beard were matted and in complete disarray, and his only pair of pants was stained with urine and who knows what else.

They were one of the first families to arrive, and true to his word, Pastor Swinson seated them on the very front row, asking the deacons to give up their usual spot and sit behind the family on the second.

Sarah couldn't help noticing the Dyer sisters—the old biddies were looking at Arthur and undoubtedly sharing some sort of uncouth comment about her poor brother. Likewise, the Mathis family, who always normally sat toward the front of the church, retreated to the back when they caught sight of Arthur.

Although Arthur sat quietly when he first arrived, it seemed that he grew increasingly apprehensive with the arrival of more people. Apparently, the pastor had advertised the morning's events very well, as the small chapel was completely packed with not only traditional church members but a goodly number of just plain onlookers by the time the service began.

Who could have known that a packed church would not have required a full armload of firewood for the stove, but the Spirit was indeed at work among the faithful who—in their efforts to save Arthur—generated enough heat to run Satan himself out of the small church. Jackets and coats were shed, as the sweaty business of Salvation was obviously at hand.

Finally, with the last chorus of amen, the pastor asked his three most sanctified deacons to come down to the front. Each of the four men held a lighted candle in each hand, and they moved together to stand in a tight semi-circle directly in front of Arthur.

Pastor Swinson began by calling upon Jesus and all his angels to drive the devil from inside the body of their poor brother, Arthur. Then he called on every member of the church to chant together, "Devil leave us. Jesus come in." The congregation continued their remonstration over and over again. At the same time, the preacher and the deacons were each thrusting one candle forward, then another, toward Arthur's face.

For a couple of minutes, Arthur had no reaction, save jerking his head back away from the flames each time a candle was pushed toward him. Then a sheen of sweat appeared, first on Arthur's brow, followed by a growing perspiration stain on his shirt. His head began to rock back and forth, and a gob of spittle formed on his lips.

Pastor Swinson sensed success and increased the volume and the tempo on the chant as well as the speed of the moving candles.

When Arthur fell forward on the floor, Pastor Swinson hollered. "Come on brothers and sisters. Praise the Lord. We're almost there. Devil leave us. Jesus come in." The pastor handed one of his candles to Deacon Grey White and bent down to finish the job by laying his hand on Arthur's brow.

It was at that moment that Arthur finally responded to the loud noises, the heat, and the thrusting candles and was overcome with a fit. Pastor Swinson interpreted this for the congregation. "Hallelujah, the devil is leaving him!" And every member of the church leaned forward to see—in case the real devil, with horns and all, would suddenly appear and turn tail to flee from their little church.

But as the seizure became more vigorous, the pastor's right shoe was situated directly in front of Arthur's face, and as he convulsed again, Arthur's teeth fastened around the preacher's ankle and sunk right to the bone. The pastor screamed and attempted to jerk his foot away, but the clonic phase of the seizure was almost continuous at this point, and Arthur bit his ankle seven or eight times so rapidly that it was impossible to remove his foot.

"Jesus wept!" The Pastor hollered as he tried to hit Arthur on the head with his candle. "The devil's still got him, and he's got me too. Run fer your lives!"

The stampede started with the Dyer sisters, whose nephew Ralph leapt over the pew behind him as they tried to grab his ankles. Little Ray Stubblefield took the long awaited opportunity to grab Clara Beecham's chest as he escaped; and old Granny Copeland choked on her last dip of snuff, as she hobbled out the door declaring "Hit was a sight in this world how Pastor Swinson could cuss!" The pushing, shoving, and kicking, which then occurred in the melee inside the Twelve Disciples Baptist Church, would forever be regarded in the future as a moment the church would never speak about again.

Ben was still attached to Arthur, and as he got down on the floor with him, he looked for help from his stepmother. But rather than his stepmother sitting there in the empty pew, there was nothing but the other end of the hemp rope. Arthur's elbows and knees were convulsing along with the rest of his body, so Ben, dodging the flailing appendages, tried to keep from being hit or kicked while he repeated Arthur's name beside his head. The Pastor was still hollering, but the strength of the individual contractions was beginning to reduce, and within a few seconds, he was able to extricate his foot. Noticing that his flock had completely emptied the building, he then immediately followed them as fast as his mangled leg would allow.

As soon as Ben realized that Arthur's seizure was over, he told him he was going to be all right, and to just lie still for a while. He used Arthur's shirtsleeve to wipe the blood and saliva off his mouth and face. Ben thought for a minute that Arthur was going to go to sleep, as he appeared to be completely exhausted, but after a few minutes, the two of them stood up and walked out the front door with the empty end of the rope trailing along behind. Although he was still scared, Ben had no idea whether the devil had left Arthur or still had a hold on him, but he tried to act like everything was back to normal.

The pastor, his deacons, and Sarah Windes were speaking together in a small circle until Sarah shook her finger at them and walked over to where her daughters were standing. Pastor Swinson cleared his throat and addressed his members. "I made a mistake today, thinkin' that we could win this here battle with evil. But there ain't no cure for the wickedness in that boy. Satan hisself has got a firm grasp on him, and us innocent men and women of the church can't hope to do battle with the devil in this here situation. I'm gonna ask that Sister Windes and her family not come back to the Twelve Disciples Baptist Church until such time as there ain't no devil in her house."

Sarah stalked off, followed close behind by her two daughters (both of whom were threatening to die of embarrassment), while Ben and Arthur brought up the rear. Ben kept looking sideways, wondering whether Arthur might have another fit in the next few minutes, and gradually he came to the conclusion that the safest place for the boy was probably back in his cage.

After they arrived home and got Arthur settled in again, Ben told Sarah he wanted to go to Abbie's. "All you want to do is go over there and make fun of my poor brother."

"No. I need to tell them what Pa told me about quitting school." Surprisingly, he got no argument.

Before he left, he spent several minutes standing beside Arthur's cage with his hand on one of the timber cross pieces. On the other side of the barrier, Arthur stepped over and placed his own hand on top of Ben's hand—not in a threatening way at all—but rather just possibly as an attempt to acknowledge his thanks. They stood there looking at each other for a minute or so, before Arthur backed away and began a conversation in earnest with himself.

Seven

The Going Away Gift

Jeffersonville, Indiana 1849

Ben found Abbie, Sean Finnerty, and Sue at home. Mr. Finnerty was getting ready to pull his soup wagon into town. He told them about quitting school, then he reminded Abbie of their conversation wherein she had said he could help Mr. Finnerty with the soup business when school was out. "I can easily sleep in the shed when the weather turns warmer. There's no need to build a lean-to. I can help with some of your chores too. But I have to tell you that my pa told me I'd have to work over at his cabin too."

Abbie hesitated, but Sean was quick to say he had lots of work to be done across the road in his fields as soon as the weather broke, so Ben's offer to assist with the soup sales would help him a lot. If Sean had been completely honest, he would have confessed that he hated going to the docks every day. Ladling up the soup and passing out the cornbread made him feel as though he was no better than a common slave to the rivermen. The only reason he kept it up was because the money was so good. "And as to how much time you spend at the other cabin, we can play that by ear. I'll have to admit that just hearin' Miz Windes' voice is enough to curdle milk in the churn. But I got a feelin' she's always gonna have a long list o' chores for you. Dealin' with that woman is a tough stump to jump."

He spent the night at his pa's cabin, and the next morning was up early, determined to spend no more than a couple of hours working there before he headed to Abbie's for his soup run. He used a hoe on the garden, gradually expanding it for the planting that would begin in April. Then at about ten o'clock in the morning, he washed up at the well, picked up his belongings, and hollered to his stepmother that he would be staying with Abbie and would be back in the morning to work on the garden some more. He was determined to take off before she had a chance to stop him.

When he was high tailing it halfway across the front yard, she screamed at him, "Where do you think you're goin'? Yore pa told you to do my chores whilst he was gone."

He didn't slow down, "I'll be back tomorrow. I've got to go help Abbie."

He escaped into the woods with the sounds of "You come back here or you'll be sorry you didn't," ringing through the treetops. He couldn't help but laugh out loud as he ran through the woods.

Ben actually liked school and truly regretted not being able to go anymore, but he looked forward to going back to the dock. All the talk was about going to California. His friend Jeremiah complained he had lost almost half his crew. "All them boys caught the 'gold fever.' Some calls it the 'Great Itch'—and they just cain't bear it 'til they scratch it. In fact, the town must've lost fifty men in the last few weeks. I don't know who's gonna be left to do the work around here."

Ben told Jeremiah his pa had gone to get rich too. Jeremiah responded, "The only people that get rich during a gold rush are the ones selling something to the miners. The miners end up spending all their gold on food or whisky or women. Me and about four thousand other fools spent six months in Lumpkin County, Georgia during the rush of 1829, and I can tell you the one who probably took the most gold out of the state was Miss Annie O'Shaunnessy. Miss Annie ran a boarding house that had a little saloon downstairs and two real pretty barmaids. Most all the miners spent every night they could afford it at Miss Annie's. She had a scale in the place and exchanged gold dust for paper script. No telling how much she was worth by the time the gold played out."

"There was an Irishmen who set up a business sellin' a hot bath and a shave. Miners get filthy dirty, and they'd spend money just to get a bit cleaned up before they went to Miss Annie's place." A wistful look slowly appeared on Jeremiah's face. "Reckon I did the same thing myself. Anyway, the Irishman made his own pot full of money too."

While Ben was in town, Abbie got an unexpected visit from Sarah Windes. Abbie could tell she was hot under the collar but nonetheless invited the woman inside. Sarah looked around the cabin, seeing curtains at the two windows, the well-made oak table and four chairs, the wash stand with the porcelain washbowl and pitcher, all of the cooking implements neatly lined up at the hearth, the cleanliness of the place, and the smell of sour dough rising. It just made her madder. Abbie was rubbing her nose in it, for sure.

Self-consciously, Sarah tucked greasy stray strands of hair behind her ears but was determined not to lose control. "You know how special me and my girls think Ben is, and we are doin' our dead level best to have a happy family. But the boy has a stubborn streak that he musta got from his ma."

Abbie forced herself to smile as she replied. "Ben is truly like his mother. But I would say he knows very well where he has a family and where he does not."

That was enough for the pretense of manners to disappear. "Where you got my stepson? He told me he was comin' over here. He ran off afore he finished his chores at my place."

Abbie replied that Ben had gone to town and was doing something for her on the dock. Sarah knew exactly what was going on. "I need that boy over to my place all day long now that Mr. Windes has gone to Californy. You worked him all last summer fer your benefit, but that's not gonna happen now. He's either comin' home with me to work or you're goin' to pay me fer his labor. I'd say he's worth at least a half dollar a day. Jest remember, this ain't the south side of the river. They ain't no slaves over here."

Abbie looked at the skinny, hardscrabble woman in front of her. She was tempted to say that it sounded very much like Sarah was suggesting that she owned Ben lock, stock, and barrel. "I believe Ben told me that he would continue to perform his chores at your house when necessary. But he wants to stay here with us while Daniel is prospecting."

Sarah hated Abbie's uppity language. Here she was again, putting on airs despite her pockmarked face. She'd have none of it. "I got a legal right to that boy. His pa left him with me and ordered him to do as I say. So what's it goin' to be—Ben or Ben's pay?"

A small smile crossed Abbie's face. "I'll need to discuss this with Mr. Finnerty and Ben this evening." She went to the door and held it open.

The meeting at Abbie's house that evening was frustrating. Mr. Finnerty said, "Son, life is simpler when you plow around the stumps. Unless we're willing to admit you're bein' paid wages for your work, Miz Windes can say we're making you earn money for us. But if we say you're being paid, the woman will lay claim to the money you make plus whatever you might have saved. If you stay with us, she can claim that we're using you."

Ben had no good options. He realized that if he stayed with Abbie, his stepmother might cause problems for her. She had been far too kind to him for something like that to happen, but he couldn't stand the prospect of living under the same roof with his stepmother, let alone Ruth and Martha. He knew they would make his life miserable just for the pleasure of it, and doubtless it would be much worse with his pa so far away.

It was cold outside that night, so he laid his pallet by the fireplace. He slept very little but began to think about a plan. It seemed impossible, but the more he considered it, the more he came to the conclusion that his plan was his only choice.

The next morning he reported to his stepmother's place and began working on increasing the size of the woodpile. Having heard the sound of an axe at work, in a few minutes his stepmother came out of the cabin. "I see you decided to get smart and do what yore pa told ye to do. One more trick like that and I'm goin' to set the sheriff on Abbie."

"I don't think there's a law against helping your aunt." Ben turned his attention to the woodpile.

He was surprised when a bony hand grabbed him by the hair and turned him around. The slap was so hard it actually knocked him to the ground. "Don't force me to do somethin' you'll be sorry for, ye little shite. Just one more smart mouth out of you, and you'll find yerself in that cage yonder with Arthur! Maybe ye can keep each other company. Seems like you'ns belong together anyways." She glared at him, hoping to see him bawling his eyes out, but when he stood up and simply squared his jaw, she turned around with the flicker of a smirk on her face and stalked back into the cabin.

Ben suddenly realized that being put in the cage might be a very real possibility—that it might even be her plan with his pa gone. He knew she wouldn't dare say something like that if his pa were around, but he had no doubt whatsoever that she was capable of doing it in his absence. That kind of punishment truly scared him. As the morning progressed, he realized he needed to speed up his planning before he ended up in the cage and couldn't do anything about it. If only there were a way that he could talk to his pa. He shook his head in frustration.

Rather than the oak and elm that he usually worked on to build the woodpile, Ben exclusively began cutting cottonwood and pine. Those woods were much softer than oak and a great deal easier to cut. The problem for the final user was that the wood burned very fast and would not sustain heat for any length of time in the fireplace. It wouldn't take long before his stepmother and her daughters exhausted the pile. After he was gone, it wouldn't be more than a couple of weeks before his stepsisters would be forced to cut wood in order to stay warm at night. He couldn't help smiling grimly at the thought of it. He'd almost like to stick around just to see that happen.

At around midday he switched to working in the garden, and he quickly realized the ground was too hard to make any real progress in digging it up. However, he really had no desire to truly expand their garden space, so he simply used a hoe to cut away the visible vegetation at ground level. By dusk, it appeared that he had made some headway on increasing the size of the plot, but in reality the ground had not been turned over at all, and would quickly fill with weeds in the spring.

He spent a few minutes at the well cleaning up, and when he entered the cabin, he could tell that they had already eaten supper.

There was a bowl sitting on the table with half of a cold potato, a few brown beans with congealing bacon fat floating on top, and a biscuit. He realized his dinner was simply what was left over from theirs. He couldn't help but compare the happy atmosphere and good food at Abbie's house with what he saw before him, but he'd learned to keep his mouth shut and eat what was before him. The thought sprung involuntarily to mind. *The woman would make a wart grow hair on it.*

He knew the best way to get up early was to drink extra water right before bedtime. He calculated a couple of dippersful from the well would do it, and he was right. His bladder woke him about an hour before sunrise. He couldn't help but notice Arthur standing in his cell, watching him, as he slipped out of the house with an old tow sack. The ground was hard and crusty under his feet, so he decided to take a hatchet with him in case the earth over his little bank was frozen. Ben walked down the lane, turned west up the road for a quarter mile until he had passed the cemetery and then entered the woods. The moon was about four days past full, so it was still up above the tree line and provided some illumination. He preferred doing this on a black night, but it couldn't be helped.

A gray fog began to descend in the woods, and he had to be careful that he stayed on course. Despite the poor visibility, he was still cautious in approaching his cache, stopping twice to listen before moving on. He found the downed tree just as he remembered it, pulled away the briars, and tried at first to dig with his hands. There was more moisture there in the woods, and the ground was frozen, so he used his hatchet to knock away the top couple of inches of hard soil and then finished the job with his hands. His money was just as he left it. A smile of relief crossed his face.

He laid a handkerchief down beside his tin can and counted out exactly 370 dimes then tied them up as securely as he could in two kerchiefs and stuffed them in his pockets. He left the remaining coins in his bank, put it back in the hole, and covered it up so that it wouldn't look any differently than it had when he started. He pulled the briars back over the spot and stood up. The fog was thinning, and daylight was now coming fast enough that he needed to get away from there as quickly as he could.

As he moved away, he failed to see in the early light that everything on the floor of the woods was covered with a light frost—except for the imprints of his footsteps and the area where he had been kneeling and working on the ground. Dawn was already breaking as Ben emerged from the woods behind Abbie's chicken house, heard the hens stirring and clucking as he passed by, and hollered out to the house. Meanwhile, back in the middle of the woods, a figure was trying to follow the trail in the frost before the sun rose high enough to remove the evidence.

Abbie came to the door, wrapped in a blanket, and invited Ben inside. He asked if they could talk in private, and Abbie replied that Mr. Finnerty had gone squirrel hunting with his dog, so they could talk inside, out of the cold.

Ben got her fire going and told her what he wanted. "I need to ask you a big favor. I'd do it myself, but it would cause too much talk, and word would get back to my stepmother. I need you to take this money," he handed her the bundles of dimes, "and go to the bank today. Exchange the dimes for five of those five-dollar gold pieces and twenty of those Liberty half-dollars. And don't tell anybody that the money belongs to me."

"My goodness, Ben. What are you going to do with all that money? Why don't I just get a couple of dollars for you and you hide the rest?"

"Abbie, please don't ask me just yet what I aim to do. I promise I'll tell you before I spend a nickel of it. And one more thing—I've heard that some people hide money in their shoes or their boots. I've got two extra dollars here for you to buy me an extra shirt and a pair of stout leather boots. Get them a little bit big for me. I can stuff the toes with something until I grow into them. But I need you to sew a cloth pouch on the inside of those boots that's big enough to hide this money in. I have another ten dollars in dimes that's still hidden, but when I get it in a couple of days, I'll keep that in my pocket."

Abbie looked at him hard. "Where are you planning on going, Ben? I know that's what you've got on your mind. But where is an eight-year-old boy going to go?"

He knew there was no point trying to evade the direct question. "I aim to catch up with pa on his way to California." He hurried to explain. "When it's just him and me, we have a fine time, but I can't abide the thought of living with my stepmother 'til he comes back."

They heard steps on the porch outside and Mr. Finnerty came in. "Ben, I figured you might be here. I think you'd best come with me. You've got a problem!"

Abbie spoke up, "What do you mean, Sean?"

Mr. Finnerty saw the money on the table. "Did you leave any of your money in the woods? If you did, I don't think it's there anymore."

Ben jumped up. "How do you know about that?"

"Me and my dog saw you buryin' something in the woods back in October. We been keepin' a lookout on the place ever since. But this mornin', you was coming out of the woods just as me and my hound was going after a squirrel. I was afraid you'd been out to your hiding spot, so the dog and I decided to slip on over there. The more times you go to a secret place, the more likely it is that it ain't gonna stay no secret. You left tracks in the hoarfrost, so it was easy to see that's where you'd come from. When we got there it looked like the briars were pulled aside and some digging had been going on. There were two sets of tracks coming from the cemetery, and one set headed here to the house. Then there was a set of tracks headed back in the direction you came from. Let's eat ourselves a biscuit and then we'll walk down there and investigate."

"Shouldn't we go now before the frost is gone?"

"You needn't worry. My dog can track whoever it was after the frost is long gone." When they walked up on his hiding place, Ben immediately knew he'd been found out. He dug into the ground a second time that morning and quickly found his can. He knew it was going to be empty, but he shook it anyway. It did not rattle.

He saw something shiny in the dirt and uncovered a lone dime. He dug some more, hoping others were there. They weren't. One dime was all that remained of the ten dollars he had left in the can earlier that morning. He berated himself for being so stupid that he had not taken all his money when he had his hands on it. What made him think it was a good idea to come back a second time for the rest? He would lose money on other occasions throughout his life but would never forget this ten-dollar theft as long as he lived.

Mr. Finnerty called to his hound and led him a few steps to the north, where he had seen tracks in the frost earlier. The dog's long ears hung almost to the ground and waved rhythmically, providing an updraft that allowed him to sort out evidence with his nose. Mr. Finnerty spoke again, and the red bone enthusiastically sniffed and snorted as he worked the area. Quickly he barked, moving toward the cemetery at a fast pace. The dog cleared the west side of the cemetery, crossed the Plank Road, and turned right.

Confirming Ben's suspicions, the dog went straight down the road, turned left at the lane into the yard of the Windes' cabin, stood at the front door, and barked. Mr. Finnerty held back, not wanting to get in the middle of the fight that was about to occur, but willing to stay close enough that he could rescue Ben if things got out of hand with his stepmother.

Ben went into the house with a seething fury, but it only took a second to realize that only Arthur was at home. He saw a bonnet on the floor with three briars embedded in it. He thought it was Ruth's, but really couldn't swear that it didn't belong to the younger girl. He picked it up and took it outside to show Mr. Finnerty. "I guess this proves your dog knew what he was doing. These briars probably got stuck in her bonnet when she was stealing my money." He bent down, let the dog sniff and snort over the bonnet, and gratefully scratched the hound behind the ears.

Ben went back in, looked in all the spots that seemed like logical hiding places, and came up empty. For some unexplainable reason, he was suddenly able to look at the place with new eyes. The cabin was very plain, possessing none of the woman's touch he saw in Abbie's home. Instead of a decent table and chairs, there were two backless plank seats, and the table consisted of three boards nailed to an upright pickle barrel. The cabin was just dirty. The two windows were so smudged that it was difficult to see anything outside clearly. He couldn't really remember ever seeing it looking neat and bright. Discarded sleeping pallets were always in a disheveled pile on the floor, and as usual, dishes were sitting all day in a pot of once hot water. There was a small bit of butter on the table, with what appeared to be the eager footprints of a mouse tracking across it.

He realized there could be no delay in his departure now. The morning's activity had served to convince him there was no turning back. Then he remembered the barbering equipment—the comb, scissors, and looking glass. They were exactly where he recalled that she kept them. He picked up his blanket from the corner where it had been thrown aside and wrapped the barbering equipment and the few clothes he still had in the cabin inside. He retrieved an iron skillet from the hearth and a sturdy knife from the table, putting them in his sack.

He felt guilty when he realized Arthur was watching him and almost decided to open his cage. Instead, he retrieved a gallon of molasses from the almost empty pantry and placed the entire jug inside Arthur's cell. At least he could make him happy for a little while!

He walked back outside. "If I know those three, they've gone to town to spend that money just as fast as they can."

"Ben, you might as well forget tryin' to get that money back. Missus Windes probably thinks they got all the money you had. Maybe you're ahead of the game to have her think that. If she figgered you had more money, she'd try and take that from you too. And since you live with her, 'tis likely the sheriff would have to side with her. Be sure you ain't giving them any real good reason to figure out you been back home this morning. It'll probably be tomorrow sometime before she gets curious enough to come lookin' for you, and by then it'll be hard to find where you might be."

And so, Ben Windes walked away from his pa's home with his birthright—a hatchet, skillet, knife, mirror, comb, and a pair of scissors.

As he heard his sister, and the din of the bickering voices of her daughters approaching the cabin, Arthur cowered in the back of his cage, protectively holding his jar of molasses close and noisily sucking the last sweetness from his grimy fingers. His long hair and beard, now gummed with molasses, stuck to his ragged shirt, and his eyes flashed wild with pleasure. That boy, his only friend, had shoved the large, wide-mouthed jug into his cage, and left. Arthur wanted to thank him, but like other times, he forgot the words.

Arthur knew the others would want his jar, so he ate quickly. As his sister and the girls opened the door to the cabin, a puzzled look crossed his face, and his bowels growled with an oncoming rush of pain. Immediately, a smell greeted them that would remain fixed inside the closed walls for days, as Arthur—grinning as he stood half naked over the pot—relieved himself of his burden.

Eight

I Forgot What I Looked Like

The Three Rivers 1849

Abbie was back from town when they arrived at her cabin. In addition to Ben's coins from the bank, she had purchased flour, sugar, beans, coffee, and salt for him. She added several generous slices of smoked ham from the pork shoulder hanging against the back wall, one of her soup bowls, and a fork and spoon. Then she added a pound each of dried peaches and apples to his larder. "You'll need to try to find fruit from time to time so you won't get the scurvy. Eat this dried fruit when you can't find anything fresh. Put all your gear in this bag, and don't trust anybody with it. Here's your boots. I put a hiding place in each shoe, behind the tongue. Don't ever let anybody see you getting to your money. If you do, it won't be yours for very long."

Ben tried on the boots, took them off, stuffed a scrap of yarn in the toes, tried them again, and pronounced them just right. He hadn't meant for her to go to all this trouble, but she had assembled much more that he would need than Ben had thought of himself.

"I have something for you that was to be your present when you finished school. It looks like there won't be any more school this year, so you might as well have it now." She reached behind her and brought forth two books, handing him the first one. "I don't think you've seen this before. It's *The Three Musketeers* by Mr. Alexander Dumas. It will help you to keep your learning sharp, and maybe you'll think of us when you're reading."

The second book was a bit smaller and had a red cloth cover. Ben noticed it didn't seem to have a title on the front as Abbie handed it to him. "I want you to start writing in this journal. Try to do it every day. You're going to see things that none of us have ever seen before, and you need to keep a record." She opened the book, and every page was blank, just sitting there waiting on him. "By the time you fill this journal, you'll have a story for your children to read some day."

Mr. Finnerty spoke up. "Recollecting how to read and write don't stay with you unless you do it on a regular basis. 'Tis kinda like taking a bath. You oughta do it every Saturday night whether you think it's necessary or not."

Abbie half-smiled and elbowed her husband. "When you get wherever you're going, you write us a letter. In fact, you write to us regular. And don't go getting yourself hurt." There was a catch in her throat and she turned her face to the side.

Ben hugged her. "Thank you so much for the book and the journal." He floundered for something to say, but nothing was adequate. "I won't forget you." Then he went to Cousin Sue. He promised he would write to her, and someday they would be back together. Sue hung her head down and sobbed silently. Then there was a tear in his eye too. He shook Mr. Finnerty's hand, "I'll keep up with my reading and writing. Thanks for all you've done for me, trying to watch out for my hiding place and all. That was mighty fine of you." He grabbed his traveling bag, walked out the door, and was gone. He didn't dare turn around for a last look, for fear of losing his nerve.

Skirting the river, he avoided the town area of Jeffersonville. It took a full hour for him to reach the docks in Clarksville, and the lower end of the Falls of the Ohio.

My story. On March 20 year of 1849
Abbie says I must tell my story and I don't kno where to start but already I feel diferent and hope to find my pa soon. Together we are free of that evil woman and will find happynes just the

*two of us in search of adventure. Here I go only a boy and already
see strange sights and mostly strange people. All are bound for
Californya with hopes to find gold and happynes forever just like
pa and me. The rough men of Lehigh Coal Company from the
state of Pennselvania say they picked up their pay and walked off
never to look back, which is what I have done too.*

*For myself I am small, though there is hardly room to lie
down at night, and must keep my bag close by from these
rough men who look to take what doesn't belong to them. Last
night was awful cold with frost on my blanket this morning.
The fare took 2 of my half dollars and I hope I have done the
right thing.*

Going downstream on the Ohio River to the Mississippi was a relatively easy trip. The riverboat captain was comfortable with traveling
during daylight but didn't dare take a chance on challenging the river,
with its hidden and shifting gravel bars and floating logs, in the dark.
Before dusk of the second day, his steamboat, along with six others,
was tied to the dock in Cairo, Illinois, less than a half-mile upstream
from where the Ohio joined with the Mississippi.

What Ben failed to discover was that one of the boatmen traveling back upstream on another steamship—back toward Jeffersonville—was his pa. Daniel Windes had made it all the way to
New Orleans but soon discovered that everybody headed to the
gold fields was trying to convince the steamship captains that they
should be allowed to work their way on the voyage rather than pay
the price of a ticket from New Orleans, around the Horn to San
Francisco. Daniel was one of at least a hundred men who were trying to compete for every job that would allow them to avoid the
fare.

When Daniel asked Captain Lige Sunday about the prospects
of working his way to California, the boatman made him a different proposition. "Every man on my steamship is trying to be a gold
miner. Nobody is interested in going back upstream. What do you
know about working on a riverboat?"

"Well, that's really all I know. I spent the last four years workin' fer Captain Sprague out of Pittsburg. I worked aboard his steamboat on the run to Louisville and back, and some at his warehouse too."

Captain Sunday looked at him with a different eye. "I'm paying two dollars a day, plus two meals a day from the kitchen if you'll work the boat from here to Louisville and back. I won't tolerate drunkenness, and you won't be paid for the time we're in port in either New Orleans or Louisville. And one more thing, if you do jump ship in New Orleans to go off searching for gold, I'll hunt you down and beat the tar out of you for not holding up your end of the bargain."

Daniel looked at the stocky captain, started to tell him he might have something to say about a beating, but clamped his mouth shut. He was amazed at the offer—it was more than double what he had been making in Jeffersonville. He was also very hungry, as it had been a day and a half since he had eaten, and there didn't seem to be a meal in sight except for the captain's offer. Also, working all the way back upstream to Louisville would allow him to get back to his wife on a regular basis. He was already missing her in a terrible way, and besides, he wanted the chance to talk to his son again. That last conversation just didn't come out the way it should have, and it had been eating at him.

He quickly changed professions, from prospector back to waterman, and said yes to the offer. Thus, he found himself in Cairo at the same time as his son, but traveling in opposing directions. Neither of them would ever know they had passed this way.

The deck passage fare up the Mississippi to St. Louis was two dollars, entitling Ben to no more space than was required for him and his bag to lay on the main deck, along with a couple of hundred others. This compared to the second deck fare of twelve dollars. But the second deck not only offered the traveler a bed of sorts to sleep in and a chair on the bright and airy upper deck but access to the exorbitant fare in the dining hall.

The main deck was another matter. Passengers there were mixed with the crew, and no one had enough room. It was bad enough that two hundred men were crammed into a deck less than 140 feet long, but they shared that space with much of the cargo—bags of grain, crates of clothing and shoes, tools of all kinds, and assorted gear that was sought by settlers and miners heading west. The hold below the water line was packed as well, but there was barely enough room for a short man to stand upright in the hold, so there was very little space below decks, and at least a portion of the hold contained bilge water.

Going against the current on the Mississippi to St. Louis was not only more expensive, but it was considerably slower—and far noisier—than his downstream passage on the Ohio River. The sounds on the main deck were coming from all directions. The gigantic paddle wheel was approximately thirty feet in diameter and comprised of twenty-four separate paddles, with each one measuring six feet across. The sound of those paddles smacking the water and exiting the river dripping with gallons of water about four times a second was like a constantly repeating dull thunder. This combined with the rattling of chains on the gears, the constant pumping of the stroke, and the roar of steam escaping. It was an assault on one's senses, and there was no getting away from it on the main deck. Normal conversation was out of the question. Only shouting in someone's ear was effective.

Each evening the crew lit torches composed of a bundle of sticks dipped in whale oil, hanging them from iron fire-baskets that extended six feet out over the water. In this way, work could be done at night as the crew loaded firewood for the boiler from bank to boat.

On the second morning out, the boat captain announced that they would be in St. Louis the following evening. There seemed to be much anticipation among the crew and the male passengers that various businesses in St. Louis promised every customer a considerable good time. There was also a great deal of conversation regarding comparisons of the various attributes of one young lady versus those of another in the city.

That same day, Ben made the acquaintance of a former shopkeeper, Mr. Thadeus Green, from Washington City. Ben estimated Mr. Green at no more than thirty years old. He was a short man with hair that didn't seem to go with his face. His skin didn't have a wrinkle on it, yet it appeared that his hair was almost entirely silver. He combed his hair straight back from his forehead. It was quite wavy and had enough pomade applied to make it glisten in the sun like a wet rock. Ben also thought he could smell lavender water when the man passed him by.

Mr. Green walked with an obvious limp, and the first time he sensed that Ben had noticed the disability, he was quick to pull up his pant leg, point to a terrible scar that ran the length of his deformed calf, and exclaim, "I almost cut my leg off with an axe. That's why I ran a haberdashery. When people saw my limp, they weren't too interested in letting me work at most jobs, so I sold hats for a living. However, I don't think my leg is going to interfere one bit with me finding gold. President Polk himself says there's gold in California, and I aim to get enough of it to never have to stick a hat on another man's head for as long as I live."

Ben had put it off until now, but he just had to start sometime, and the steamboat seemed like as good a time as any to try out his idea. Particularly since this man apparently had some money. He spent a few minutes working up his courage, then, "Mr. Green, how long have you been traveling from Washington City?"

"I left there about a month ago."

"I couldn't help but notice the length of your hair. It appears that it's been a while since you've gotten a haircut. It seems a shame to go ashore in St. Louis with all the pretty girls they talk about there, without putting your best foot forward."

The man pushed his hair back on his head. "Maybe I can find a barber in St. Louis."

"Well," Ben replied with as much confidence as he could muster, "the captain said we wouldn't get there until tomorrow evening, so probably you won't find one that's still open for business at that hour. I happen to know how to cut hair, and I don't mean just trimming around a bowl either. I could do it right here on board for twenty cents."

Mr. Green looked dubious. "How'd a young boy like you learn to cut hair?"

"I took lessons while I lived in Indiana. I can do a real good job, too." Ben tried not to hold his breath.

Mr. Green was torn, but he did want to look his best the following night. "I guess it can't be too bad. Anyways, it grows pretty fast. And if it looks too rough, I'll just wear my hat. Let's give it a go."

Ben retrieved his tools and seated Mr. Green out of the cold wind, but in a prominent enough position on deck that lots of passengers would see him working. He had been practicing the evening before using the comb and scissors but only on a frayed burlap bag full of seed corn. Mr. Green would have shuddered to know that his pride and joy was about to be subjected to the skills of a complete novice, and Ben hoped he didn't accidentally poke a hole in his customer like he had the burlap bag.

He wet his hands several times and ran them through Mr. Green's hair. There was enough grease on the man's head that he had to wipe his hands dry before beginning so the scissors wouldn't slide through his fingers. He started tentatively, remembering as much as he could about his stepmother's technique, then began to gain a bit more confidence as he moved around the head. It was quite a spectacle, with the puffed up storekeeper sitting there on a box, along with a high opinion of himself, and the young barber standing on an overturned bucket, yet still just barely able to reach the top of his customer's head with one hand and cut his hair at a straight angle with the other.

By this time, he had an audience of ten or twelve men who were surprised to see the way Ben was cutting. Many had undoubtedly only been the beneficiaries of a bowl-cut previously, so they were convinced they were watching someone who knew what he was doing. Ben took special care to cut the sideburns at exactly the same length, standing in front of Mr. Green and sighting at his ears before making a few adjustments. Relieved that he hadn't drawn blood, when he thought he was finished, he combed the hair straight back, made another few corrective snips, and presented the mirror for Mr. Green's inspection.

He had dubious help from the audience. "Thadeus, you look like the south end of a northbound possum. You'd best stay on the boat in St. Louis. Ain't no woman gonna give you a second look less'n you put a flour sack over yore head."

"Before ye look in that mirror, just remember every road has a few puddles."

"Did anybody see that injun what scalped poor old Thadeus?"

"Looks like somebody stuck an old silver-backed badger pelt on top of yore head."

Mr. Green paid them no attention whatsoever, held the mirror in his left hand, re-combed his hair with the right, patted his hair on both sides, and handed over a full quarter. "All in all a good job. Thank you."

"I don't have a half-dime for change."

"It's a quarter haircut. That's what you should charge."

Ben tried not to show his relief but couldn't keep himself from grinning. "Anybody else want a haircut?"

It had been quite some time since his second customer had been to a barber of any kind—with or without a bowl. The man's hair hung below his shoulders on the sides, and when he removed his hat, the hair in the front fell down past his nose.

"I aim to look every bit as good as the feller that just got off'n this box, as I figger on havin' a real good time in St. Louis." Several in the audience laughed, but Ben went to work with vigor. The man's hair not only had not been cut, but apparently, he did not own a comb. Most of the tangles were simply cut away and dropped to the deck, but those close to the scalp had to be combed out, with accompanying yelps from the customer.

Even worse, when Ben parted his hair, he saw two red circles with raised bumps on the man's scalp. Ben had seen this before. He leaned over and whispered in the man's ear that he believed he had ring-worm. The man jerked his head around but was immediately appreciative that Ben had said this in a voice that was not heard by the audience. "Sir, my aunt used sulfur and coal tar on ringworm. If you'll apply it every day, it should be completely gone in about a week."

Upon completion, the man was very white on his forehead and neck where the sun had not been able to penetrate for several years, but he too was a happy customer. At least one person told him they had no idea he looked like that. Ben decided it would be best to wash his comb and scissors after he cut someone's hair. He didn't know if ringworm or other maladies could be transferred to someone else, but he decided not to take chances.

After that, a line formed. He was busy until the call for supper. Other than a fiery red blister on his right thumb, Ben was thrilled with the results of his new occupation.

> *My story. On March 25 year of 1849*
>
> *It is true. I am now a barber who took in sum of two and one half dollars today, and hope to do more of same tomorrow. The foulest of these travelers improved their looks considerable thanks to my new found barbering, and claim to be ready to meet up with the ladies of Saint Louis. I feel some easier now altho the frozen air torments us. I note ice along the ropes as the torch light allows me to pen this entry. Tho tired from my day as a professinel I remain better at ease with my decision to set out on my own. It is hard to write, as the steamboat is taking quite a beating on our way up river.*

With his thumb wrapped in a rag, the next day he was busy until the lights of the city came into view. After they docked, his last customer was the ship's first mate. "Boy, everybody on this boat knows you've taken in quite a bit of money these last two days. And several of these fellers would cut yore throat for four or five dollars. They're all gettin' off the boat here, 'cause we're turnin' back around tomorrow. I really liked seein' you workin' so hard the past couple of days. I hope my own boy has as much gumption."

"You might think about findin' a place out of sight to sleep and mebbe stayin' on this here boat 'til mornin'. Then around sun-up, you get off the boat and make tracks for one of the steamboats gettin' ready to head up the Missouri. You'll find 'em around the bend about a half mile south of here, where the Missouri strikes the Mississip. Everbody what was on this boat'll probably still be sleepin' off their good time, and you can git outa here with all yore money and all yore gizzard."

Ben was beginning to realize that having money was not an easy thing. He had been ready to step right off the boat with everybody else and see the sights. It hadn't occurred to him that someone from the boat might knock him in the head and take his money. "Thanks for the advice. I don't have much money, but I aim to keep what little I've got. And Mister, if you'll let me sleep on the boat, your haircut is free."

His last customer had been right regarding the status of the steamship's passengers and crew. When Ben walked down the gangway at daybreak the next morning, he didn't see a soul moving around, including the first mate. But the absence of people was overshadowed by the size and the numbers of warehouses along the riverfront. Not only did they almost stretch out of sight, but they all appeared to be some three or four stories in height. What manner of place was this St. Louis that there could possibly be so much commerce?

He spied a sign advertising breakfast about a block away from the dock and spent one of his haircut quarters on bacon, eggs, and biscuits, realizing it might be the last hot meal he would have until he reached Independence.

His traveling bag felt like it was getting heavier by the minute by the time he reached the Missouri River docks. There was certainly plenty of activity there. Horse-drawn wagons and Negro stevedores pushing two-wheeled drays and barrows were everywhere you looked. When he inquired as to the price of a boat ticket to Independence, the agent said he couldn't sell a ticket to someone his age without an adult along, as they were headed into wild and dangerous country.

"Why, sir, my father didn't get back to the hotel 'til almost morning, as he is a man that enjoys strong drink." Ben glanced sideways at the ship berthed in front of him. "He told me to be sure and get on the *General Jackson* packet boat if he wasn't here yet. He'll be along before you set off, but please let me go aboard so I can stop carrying this heavy bag around. If I have to carry this back to the hotel, my arm might fall off."

The agent looked at the size of the bag and the size of the boy. "All right, but be sure your pa reports to the captain soon as he comes aboard. You wantin' the main deck or the second deck?"

"The main deck is all we can afford."

"The trip is three dollars for you. Your pa'll owe four dollars."

A ride on the river was not without risks. Although rare, it was not altogether unusual for someone to fall overboard. Depending on the speed of the current, the undertow, the temperature of the water, the amount of clothes the victim had on, and whether or not they were strong swimmers, only a few survived a plunge into the river.

The Missouri was full of trees and stumps, and this was especially true during the spring thaw when the water was high and fast and had a tendency to wash away portions of the riverbank. Many a steamboat pilot ran his ship up on an invisible large snag, holed the hull, and lost their boat. At least one boatman was always stationed on the bow to watch for snags and measure the depth of the ever-changing river channel. Despite these dangers, steamboats and their passengers continued to make the journey.

The second day of the trip, Ben rolled out his barbering equipment again. He offered to cut the hair and beard of one of the wildest looking trappers on board, and within a few minutes, an audience assembled to watch the man's transformation. Once again, Ben had to stop his procedure and whisper a diagnosis. "Head lice." He repeated his prescription advice, remembering that his aunt had used sulfur and coal oil for almost everything.

One of the trapper's friends sat down in front of him, mesmerized by the man's shoeless feet. "Skinner, I don't believe I ever seen feet as dirty as yorn. They ain't no way them feet will freeze with all that dirt on 'em."

"Ain't you never heard of insulation? With this here layer of good Missouri soil, I don't need no boots like the rest of you girls." Finally, when his customer looked in the mirror at the close of his procedure, Ben noticed a tear in the man's eye. "Boy, I didn't hardly recognize my own self! I reckon I forgot what I looked like. Ain't had no haircut except what I could accomplish myself in at least eight or ten years."

Ben made sure he washed his equipment and his chair was full, with no letup even for a meal, until dark, when the steamboat made landfall on the south side of the river. A light was visible high up on the bluff, and a man who was obviously new to the frontier questioned Skinner. "Say, what place is this? We're not in Independence yet are we?"

"Naw. This here is just a little settlement, name of Rocheport."

The man had a look of anticipation when he asked, "Any excitement hereabouts?"

"Rocheport ain't got but two stores, two whores, and a fat German with a grape farm."

"Are they fine lookin' specimens?"

"The grapes or the women? I reckon it depends a lot on how picky ye are."

Thankfully, there was a much higher level of anticipation over the next three days for the excitement awaiting them in Independence, and Ben's scissors stayed busy, as all wanted to look their best when they arrived. Once again, he began to worry about too many people knowing about his money. Despite paying for his meals and three steamship fares for the last ten days, he actually had more money now than when he left Jeffersonville.

A full day out from Independence, a boatman on the bow shouted out, "Big log comin' downstream on the port bow." A few seconds later, "Cap'n, you better look. It appears to be a whole smokestack in the water off the port side."

Everybody crowded to the rail, including the captain. One look and the captain bowed his head. "I sure hope the passengers and crew are safe. I wonder if the stack is off the *Algoma*? Captain Greenlee left St. Louis about three hours before we did, and his was the only boat ahead of us. He's as solid as they come. I hope it's not his ship."

Another cry from the bow, "Another stack off the port bow."

This had to be bad trouble. But despite an order from the captain to look sharp for people in the water, there was no further sign whatsoever of a wrecked steamboat.

In less than an hour, boatmen began to point out an occasional chunk of ice floating in the river.

As the day wore on, the chunks were bigger and more numerous. The steamship captain assembled the passengers on board. "We're about two miles south of Lexington, Missouri on the south bank. I'm going to try to make it to Lexington so you folks will have a place to get out of the weather until this ice clears, but going on to Independence or West Port Landing right now is out of the question. This ice may have been what caused us to see those two smoke stacks this morning."

"How far is Lexington from Independence, Captain?"

"It's about forty-five river miles, but I don't know exactly how far by land. There are plenty of facilities available in Lexington. For about ten years, it was the jumping off point for the Santa Fe Trail. Lots of that traffic is now departing from Independence and West Port, but there are still several hotels and entertainment emporiums in Lexington." The captain paused to look upstream. "If you'll excuse me."

The boatmen were now very busy. Two lookouts were posted to advise the pilot about the location of ice coming downstream so that he could attempt to steer clear of it. Four men were stationed on the bow with long, stout poles. Their responsibility was to push any ice well away from the steamship.

The passengers began to realize they were in grave danger, and all were apprehensive at the sighting of every ice floe. Most realized if they were thrown overboard in a violent collision with ice, they could not survive the frigid water, let alone the powerful current.

The men at the bow possibly saved them all from disaster at least five times in the next twenty minutes. Once they were able to just barely push aside a huge piece of ice that was at least eight feet long and was as high as the main deck. That one would surely have torn a terrible hole in the hull if it had struck the boat. The passengers watched it intently as it slid silently past the boat. There was no doubt in most minds that this ominous white monster could have killed them all.

Finally, the captain barked to the pilot to ease the steamship behind a cut in the bank that would allow them to avoid any ice coming down with the current. With a skillful maneuver, the ship was throttled in behind the embankment while ropes fore and aft were made fast to three sturdy trees. A cheer of relief went up from all aboard, including the crew. About that time, pieces of ice completely filled the main channel of the river. It would have been impossible for the boatmen to avoid all of them had they still been pushing upstream.

The sight of over a hundred chunks of ice at one time in the river had an immediate effect. The captain called for quiet, but already a hush had fallen over the boat as they all stood watching on the starboard side, mesmerized by the thought of what had almost happened to them. "We all need to have a prayer said over us. Is there a reverend on board?"

No one stepped forward until a diminutive woman spoke up, "I am a deaconess in the Episcopal Church in Lexington. My name is Prudie Rice Ingram, and my husband, John Ingram—rest his soul—was a deacon." Missus Ingram moved in front of the people, paused for a moment, and raised both her hands high above her head.

"Dear Lord, thank you for protecting us in our time of peril. Thank you in your wisdom for sending us a wise captain and a brave crew. May all of us be made better for this experience. Help us to find our way to your church and to your side, and glorify your name. Today we all learned the truth of your hymn—A Mighty Fortress is our God—a bulwark never failing. Amen."

Those who had not been particularly religious earlier in the morning all found themselves fervently adding to the chorus of "amen." It was downright convenient to be able to quickly find one's religion when the situation demanded it.

The captain apologized for not tying up at the dock directly below the town, but his intention was to keep his boat safe from the sea of ice that was now sweeping past down the river. A gangway was placed across to the bank and made fast, and passengers began to gratefully ease their way over to dry land. Ben positioned himself near to Missus Ingram. He was worried about the safety of his money, but he knew if he could stay close to her, he would likely be able to reach the town without being in danger.

Nine

Not Bad For A Boy From Indiana

Lexington, Missouri 1849

She was dressed all in black, with a black hat and ribbon tied under her chin and a long black dress. She couldn't have been an inch over five feet tall and probably didn't weigh a hundred pounds. She wore wire-rimmed spectacles, and it was impossible not to notice the reddish, dried skin on her cheeks. It made her look like she was sun-burned, but only on her cheeks and the bridge of her nose in what appeared to be a butterfly pattern.

There was a long hill of at least three-fourths of a mile from the steamboat up the riverbank to the town. Although Missus Ingram was undoubtedly close to fifty years old, and carrying a bulky travel bag of her own, she was a strong walker; and it was all Ben could do to keep up with her with his own smaller bag. About halfway up the incline, she turned to him. "Are you following me, young man?"

"Yes, ma'am, I guess so. I'm traveling by myself, trying to catch up to my pa at the head of the Trail before he takes off for California. I heard you say you were from this town, so I was hoping you could tell me who to talk to."

"Maybe I can help you, but first I'm going to the church to say another prayer. I've never been as scared as I was on that riverboat! I don't know how to swim a lick, and I just knew we were all going to end up in that frigid river."

"Yes, ma'am. I know how to swim, but I don't think that would help much in that river."

The track from the steamboat gradually turned into Tenth Street, and they passed by a number of warehouses and granaries. By the time they reached the top of the hill, they began to walk by a line of substantial homes. Ben was surprised, as he had expected something like frontier shanties instead of examples of fine Georgian architecture on almost every street. Coming into the business district, he sighted two hotels and at least three saloons on the right and a large courthouse on the left. They turned south on Franklin Street, and within a block had reached Christ Church. It was a large brick edifice with an eight-sided steeple tower. Again, Ben was not expecting the church to be so well constructed.

He and Missus Ingram entered through a side door and stepped into the sanctuary. A man, not much taller than she, entered the room from behind the elevated pulpit. She turned to Ben, "This is my brother, Reverend Rice. But I don't believe I caught your name."

"It's Ben Windes, Reverend. We just got off a steamboat from St. Louis. Missus Ingram was nice enough to bring me here with her."

"Ben is hoping for some information to help him get to West Port to meet his father. I'm afraid our steamboat is marooned here because of all the ice on the river. Can you suggest someone in town that he can talk to about getting to the trailhead?"

"Normally I would suggest that he travel with one of the wagon trains headed toward Santa Fe and simply separate from them when they get to West Port. But I haven't noticed any trains forming up yet this spring. It could be dangerous if you travel alone. The trip is about fifty miles by land. I don't suppose you own a horse do you?"

"No, Reverend. I don't. But I believe I'm in the market for one."

"It's probably a good idea to buy a horse here rather than wait until you reach West Port. I hear that prices out there are quite a bit higher than what you can find here. Do you know anything about trading for horseflesh?"

"No, Reverend, we didn't own any horses back in Indiana. Do you know someone who can help me? I sure can't afford to pay very much."

"Let's find some supper first. You spend the night here in the church. Tomorrow we'll go see a friend of mine—a farrier—over at Tinsley Crowder's place. They buy and sell horses and mules every day. If Joshua doesn't know how to buy horses, nobody does."

> *My story. On March 31 year of 1849*
> *My last day on the steamboat was a God fearing one that showed what a coward I truly am to find ourselves in the middle of the Missouri River surrounded by large chunks of ice. My fright was hard to hide as the boat narrowly missed being struck. A fate that would surely left us all to an icy grave at the bottom of that fearsome river. When my feet touched soil I was truly grateful and aim to buy a horse and strike out for the town of West Port Missouri where I hope to find my pa at last.*

Early in the morning, Ben and Reverend Rice left the church and walked over to Main Street. Ben had his traveling bag in tow. The Reverend was dressed in a black hat and a long black coat that almost reached the ground, and it was hard to keep from noticing that he had a strange way of walking. He extended both of his hands in front of him at about chin height and held his fingertips together, as though he was prepared to pray at the drop of a hat. Indeed, the only movement left to him was to simply close his eyes!

They passed a large frame building that proclaimed, Russell, Majors, and Waddell—Suppliers of the Western Pioneer. The store was busy, and Ben noticed several customers that had been passengers on the steamboat. The Reverend pointed (with both hands). "This store has been in business here for about ten years. The settlers heading out on the Santa Fe and Oregon Trails have made the owners very wealthy men." He spoke wistfully, and mostly to himself. "I surely do wish they believed in tithing."

Directly behind the store there were at least twenty factories and warehouses on both sides of Commerce Street, almost all engaged in business directly related to the Trails. In the low-lying river bottomland just north of Commerce were four large corrals for horses, mules, cattle, and oxen. All of the corrals seemed to be only partially occupied with animals. The annual settler push would not begin in earnest for another month or so.

The reverend entered a door that was simply marked T. Crowder and Sons. A very large Negro man stood up quickly, holding a curved-blade farrier's knife and a whetstone. "G'mornin' Massa Reverend. How you do today?" A boy about Ben's age stood behind him, peering from around the man's huge legs.

"Hello, Joshua, my friend. I hope you and Merriweather are doing well today."

"Yas, suh. Mistuh Crowder prob'ly won't be here t'day. His wife, Missus Charity, jes' had nuther little one last night. Dat be number fifteen, I reckon."

Reverend Rice shook his head. "Fifteen children—what a blessing! I'll get out there and see the new baby in a day or two when things have quieted down. But it's you I wanted to see anyway, Joshua. I have a young gentleman here, Master Ben Windes, who is out to find his pa, and he's in the market for a horse to ride from here to California. I'm afraid he doesn't have much experience in dealing for horses, so I was in hopes that you could help him find the right animal at a fair price."

"Well suh, long about ten year ago 'twas easy to find a good ridin' hoss for 'bout six or seven dollars around dese parts. But since t'everybody started headin' out to that Oregon, a reliable hoss is mebbe twelve dollars."

The reverend turned to Ben. "Are you prepared to pay that kind of money?"

"Well, I didn't expect to. Would that price also include a bridle and saddle?"

Joshua winked at the Reverend. "It peers this boy already know how to hoss-trade. We got three hosses back here in the stable I shod yestiddy. They ain't for sale, but I kin show you some things to look at on these here animals when you trade for one you want."

Ben followed Joshua and Merriweather through the back door. He had seen lots of Negroes back home in Indiana, as well as working on the steamboats up and down the river, but he had never really carried on a conversation with one. The man was almost as tall and wide as the doorframe, and in fact ducked his head and sort of turned sideways just to pass through easily. He was not sure of Joshua's status. After hearing all the political talk on the riverboats, he knew that Missouri was a slave state, but it appeared to him that Joshua acted like a freeman rather than a slave. As far as he could tell, Joshua and his son were the only people in the business, and certainly, there was nobody watching over them in any way. He decided to ask the reverend about it later.

Joshua stopped in front of a stall. "How much 'sperience you have in ridin' a hoss? Dat is, kin you ride a spirited animal, or you lookin for one dat's well broke?"

"Well, I've only ridden a mule before—and that was just a few times. I guess I need one that will let me stay on."

"Den make sho you ride de hoss afore you make de deal. If you get one what's got a lot o' zip, you might end up walkin' to California. Take a look at this here chestnut mare. She not too big, but you'll still need some help puttin' a saddle on her. De hoss here gentle as kin be. But if you look at her teef—see how they's all ground down on the sides? This hoss close to mebbe twenty-two year old. She might have a real problem lastin' all the way to Californy. I'd pass on dat mare.

"See de paint pony in the next stall? From the way his ribs is showin', if I was guessin' I'd say the owner didn't put by enough hay for de winter, and this pony been tryin' to get along on too little feed. This paint hoss a good size fo' you. His teeth in good shape. Paints is usual purty sturdy little hosses. But if he start out on a terrible long trip lookin' this poor, he might not make it de whole way. He need about three or fo' weeks of good feed first. I'd pass again."

Ben interrupted, "Just so I'll have an idea, what would a pony like that cost, considering his current condition?"

Joshua continued: "Now dat's where the tradin' comes in. De man what owns this hoss will tell you what a fine animal he is, and most likely ask twelve dollars. But dat's when you have to point to de weak spots, an' say he ain't worth a dime over seven. Den if he give you any guff, you say he not what you really wants. Take a look at this here bay. Sorta medium size—a little bigger than de paint. Got plenty flesh on his bones. But this hoss either been rode by a big man, er mebbe used as a pack hoss. He be all broke down. Nuther thing, it look like somebody been whuppin' this hoss way too much. See all them quirt marks on his flanks? I doubt dis hoss got much spirit left in him.

"They's one mo' thing you got to watch. You got to look at de hoofs. I cain't show you no troubles on these hosses cause I takes care of dem. You best take Merriweather along with you. He knows what to look for.

"Merriweather, you take Masta Ben down to dat Chadwick stable t'other side of de Courthouse. Mistuh Chadwick got hosses for sale. I member dey was a young black mare in his corral, so look close at dat one. But be sho you don't look at her first. An' Merriweather, don't you be triflin' along." He put his huge hand on top of the boy's head. "Dey's some mens in this town what might snatch you up and take you out to they hemp fields, and if I cain't find you, I cain't get you back."

Ben held out his hand. "Thank you for helping me. I'll try to remember everything you've told me. And I'll make sure Merriweather gets back here."

The reverend stepped to the door, "I'll go with them, Joshua. Don't worry about your son."

The two boys walked down the street, confident in their mission, and believing they were ready to wheel and deal, while behind them strolled the black-frocked reverend, always at the ready to spring into prayer. Passing the courthouse, Merriweather pointed to the right, down Eleventh Street.

Chadwick's Livery Stable sat just beyond the Trailhead Hotel. Chadwick's place was far busier than Crowder's had been. There were several men in the store, and it seemed to Ben that everybody immediately turned to stare intently at the three of them. He didn't know if it was because they recognized he was somebody new, or that they were trying to puzzle out the mysterious relationship between a young Negro boy, an Episcopal reverend, and him.

Merriweather nudged him and pointed, "Dat be Mistuh Chadwick."

Ben waited until the man finished his conversation with two men. "Mister Chadwick, I'd like to buy a good horse."

Chadwick's voice quickly gave him away. "Now whut in tarnation would ya'll want with a horse?"

Ben had heard the accent all his life. "Sir, you sound like you might be from Caintuck."

The man grinned behind his greying mutton-chop whiskers. "I shore am. I come out here five years ago from Louisville. Sounds like you might be from somewhere close to there yer ownself."

"From across the river in Indiana, sir. I need a horse to catch up with my pa. He's headed to California."

Ben spotted the black mare as soon as they walked back to the corral, but forced himself to pay no attention. Instead, he asked about a bony Palomino. Mr. Chadwick had a helper get a rope on the horse and walked him over. Ben realized it would be a good idea to show that he was no fool. He looked at the horse for about a minute, and said, "This horse won't do. Could I see the bay with the white spot on her forehead instead?"

Mr. Chadwick looked at him. "Whut's wrong with the Palomino? He's a fine horse."

"Well, sir, he's not been fed well. I aim to ride him to California, so I need a horse in good shape to start with."

"All he needs is a couple of weeks on green grass and he'll be good as new."

"I don't have a couple of weeks to waste if I'm gonna catch up to my pa."

Mr. Chadwick nodded to the stableboy and pointed at the bay. While they waited, he pulled out a clay pipe and filled the bowl with Yellow Bank Tobacco, then inserted a pipe stem and fired up his smoke. Ben looked at the horse for a couple of minutes and realized the horse looked pretty good, but he remembered Joshua's advice not to make a deal until he rode the animal. "Could you put a bridle on the horse, sir?"

The stableboy struggled for a couple of minutes to get the bit in the horse's mouth. The bay kept tossing his head and avoiding the bridle. When he was successful, the stableboy walked the horse over to Mr. Chadwick. Ben took the reins and turned the horse over to Merriweather. He whispered to him, "What about his hooves?"

"Wa'll, dis hoss gots some feet what looks like he ain't been shooed 'til just recent. His hoofs awful chipped up, and de bottom of he feets don't look too good."

Ben walked over and handed the reins back to Mr. Chadwick. "This horse won't do either. His sore feet will never hold up for a long trail over rough ground."

Mr. Chadwick looked over Ben's head at the reverend. "Reverend, tell this boy he's bein' too picky." The reverend smiled and nodded his head.

Ben spoke up again. "Sir, do you have anything else I can look at? I saw a paint pony down in the bottoms that looked pretty good. Maybe I should go back there."

"I've got twenty good horses for sale right here in this corral." Mr. Chadwick sucked purposefully on his pipe and began to blow a series of smoke rings, which hung lazily in the stagnant stable air. He looked sideways at Ben to see if he was paying attention.

Having seen his stepmother perform the same maneuver hundreds of times to amuse herself, Ben ignored Chadwick's efforts and shook his head. "I don't see one that looks right." Then as an afterthought, "How old is that black mare with the one white stocking that's got dirt all over her? She seems a little young for this kind of trip."

Mr. Chadwick held his hands palms up in front of him. "I'd say the horse is at least two years old, and saddle-broke to boot."

"Can I take a look, sir?" Ben looked at the mare. Looking past the fact that she had been rolling in the dust, the horse was a beautiful animal. She was admittedly small but had plenty of meat on her bones. He led the horse to Merriweather and whispered to him, "Don't say where he can hear you, but what do you think?"

Merriweather lifted each foreleg as though he'd been a horseman for twenty years. He pulled on the bridle until the horse's mouth was at his eye level and looked at her teeth and gums. He felt of the forelegs. "You'd best ride this hoss."

Ben turned back to Mr. Chadwick, "I don't know, she seems pretty young." He turned toward Merriweather. "I told you we should have bought that paint."

"Yas suh, you did."

Ben could have hugged him. "Just to be sure," Ben said, "could you throw a saddle on this horse so I can see Merriweather ride it round the stable here?" He realized that showing what a poor rider he was would be the wrong move at this point.

Merriweather walked, then trotted, then cantered the mare. Ben knew he couldn't have pulled that off if his life depended on it. He handed the reins back to Mr. Chadwick. "Just for comparison, what do you want for this little horse?"

"Eleven dollars for the horse. The saddle and bridle are three dollars extra."

"That's too much. Until that horse grows another six months, I don't think you can sell her. I'll give you seven for the horse and two dollars for the saddle and bridle."

"I'll take twelve for the lot."

"I'll give you ten dollars if you throw in the blanket."

"Eleven dollars and that's my final offer."

"I've only got ten dollars and a half. That's all I can pay you."

Mr. Chadwick laughed. "Ya'll didn't do too bad for a boy from Indiana. You got yerself a deal." Ben had already been into the stash in his boot that morning. He dug into his pocket and pulled out a five-dollar gold piece, four silver dollars, and six quarters. Mr. Chadwick and the reverend stared at the gold coin. "Where'd you get that piece of gold, boy?"

"I worked for it back home in Indiana. That's all I've got left, so this pony has to get me to West Port pretty quick." Reverend Rice disappeared back into the front of the stable. Ben shook hands with Mr. Chadwick. "Thank you, sir. I appreciate you making a deal with me."

Ben got up behind Merriweather on the saddle and they headed back toward Crowder's. As they passed by the courthouse, Merriweather pointed across the street at a familiar figure entering the Sheriff's Office. "Lookee yonder at Massa Reverend. He sho' don't look to be too worried 'bout makin' sure I don't git snatched off this here street. What you 'spect de Reverend doin' wit de sheruf?"

Ben felt the hair prick up on the back of his neck. "Let's hurry and get you back to Joshua. It looks like the reverend is about to tell the sheriff about me. Maybe he thinks there's more gold where that came from."

Merriweather slid off the horse a block from Crowder's. Ben pulled a quarter from his other pocket and flipped it to him. "I owe you that for the job you did. Thanks for your help. If anybody asks, I took off along the river bank, headed west to Independence."

Merriweather struggled to take his eyes off the quarter. "You best hurry, Masta Ben."

Ten

A Brand New Person

The Trail, Missouri 1849

Ben glanced at Merriweather, then down at the horse, and nodded briefly as he turned the animal down the embankment into a thick growth of small pines and cottonwoods as branches slapped his face. Shielded from the town, and plagued by doubt, he tugged unevenly on the bridle. As Ben attempted to manage the reins, the horse felt his uncertainty, shook her head, and stopped abruptly. Perplexed, Ben decided to treat her just like he treated Mr. Finnerty's cantankerous mule as he leaned over to pat her neck, making sure the horse could feel both his feet against her belly. His method worked—and their friendship and journey began with a wobbly start downstream, first angling up the bluff, then skirting the eastern boundary of the town as they ventured toward West Port.

He shielded his eyes to gaze back at the smokestacks of the steamboat he had ridden the day before and saw the Christ Church steeple rising above the town. He took one last look before redirecting his horse and his attention to catch up to the man that he called Pa.

A well-traveled, rutted wagon road appeared in another quarter mile, the road they referred to in Lexington as the Santa Fe Trail. He guided his horse along the road as it abruptly made a long loop south to avoid a steep incline, watching warily for travelers who might question the business of a young boy traveling alone on such terrain.

Finally, and seemingly with a sense of purpose, the road turned westerly and Ben felt the hopefulness that marked the thousands of travelers who went before him.

Rolling hills similar to those found in Indiana spread to the horizon. The farms, however, were considerably different from the small homesteads like his Pa's. Vast fields rolled across the land, dotted with hay-laden wagons driven by Negro workers. The air carried their soft voices that lapsed occasionally into soulful melodies, and Ben was confident that this last day of March was a fine day, indeed.

However, his confidence quickly eroded as he emerged from the rolling hills with a powerful thirst and the realization that a small creek ahead wouldn't provide him water as long as he was atop a horse without a downed tree, stump, or log that would allow him to remount. At dusk, a drizzling rain began to fall, while the temperature and his previous good humor dropped right along with it. After crossing the creek, he wondered why he made such a decision to buy a horse that was so tall when his legs were so short, let alone to travel such a distance to find his Pa when he was so thirsty and tired.

As he rode, a light flickered in the distance, which seemed to come from a lane lined with pecan trees, which veered off the road. A lane with a light meant a house, and a house meant a dry place to sleep, a way to mount his horse, and maybe something to eat. He nudged the horse up the drive and came upon a house so large it looked like the courthouse back in Indiana. What kind of people lived in such a place with four round columns that rose upward to support a porch that came from the second story? How would a body live all over such a house when it only took a little space to set up your bed? And what were those little shanties in back of this big house? Who used these raggedy shacks when there was such a fine place to sleep? These questions filled Ben's head as he approached the house and slid off his horse, shakily adjusting his legs to the ground.

Not wanting to surprise anybody, he shouted out, "Hello, the house!"

The front door opened to reveal a light-skinned Negro man in a collared shirt who gave Ben a cursory glance before pointing to the side yard. "Come round the back of the house. Claree'll see you there."

Before Ben had time to thank him, the door slammed shut. Legs sore, britches wet from the rain, he hobbled to the back where another, smaller structure stood separate from the house. He ran his hand through his damp, dirty mop of hair and vowed to make a good impression on the cook, who must be important to have her own separate house for cooking. As he was thinking about his approach, a large, ebony-skinned woman with a shining face and red kerchief tied around her broad forehead opened the door. Folding her arms across an ample bosom dusted with flour, she glared at Ben. "You on de Trail?"

"Yes, ma'am . . . I'm making my way to West Port and. . . ." He was interrupted before the words came out of his mouth.

"How many wit you out dere? I'm done sick and tired of these hungry tramps showing up jest a starving and takin my cookin' when I got mo than I can handle with dis low-down family. . . ." She drifted off into thought and Ben spoke up quickly.

"Nobody ma'm, I'm on my own and needing a place for me and my horse to stay for the night." He hurriedly launched into his speech as her face grew more clouded.

"You 'spect me to believe dat? You just a boy."

"Yes'm. I'm alone and trying to catch up with my Pa and sure appreciate a little supper, and my horse would need a bite as well, and I'd be glad to pay a quarter for it." He was out of breath as he looked up at her, hoping she was listening.

Her face softened as she smiled reluctantly while looking at him and muttered, "I got me a boy . . . somewheres . . . come on up heah on de stoop and get out de rain." She disappeared into the kitchen, and by the time Ben tied up his horse, she was back with a plate of beans and ham hock and jar of buttermilk. "Now, how 'bout dat quarter?"

As he was about to thank her, she tested the quarter with her few remaining teeth, pointed to the barn, and turned to lumber back to the hot kitchen and the never-ending work that she called her life.

He scrambled around in the dark inside the barn, finding some hay in the loft and what felt like a leftover handful of corn in a feed-bag that was hanging on a stall. The horse was as grateful for supper as he had been. He took off his wet clothes, wrung them and the horse blanket out as best he could, and hung them on the side of the stall. His bag was wet, but the contents were still fairly dry. The change of clothes felt awfully good, and he fell asleep to the sound of his horse chewing on the kernels of corn.

He awoke to a milk pail clanging against the barn. The sky was already a pale grey—the kind of day that made you feel cold just to look outside—but at least it had stopped raining. He climbed back into the loft to get his horse another armful of hay, and was hoping to get lucky for himself as well. He had no trouble finding four hens on nests, and turned a sheepish gaze upward. "Forgive me for harvesting these eggs without asking or paying." He put them in his bag to eat later on the trail.

With some difficulty, he got his saddle lifted up on the side of the stall. He was able to get the bridle on his pony, threw the blanket on her back, and led her over to the side of the stall. By hooking one leg over the top rail in order to hold on, he put his saddle on the horse. He then climbed down and secured the cinch. His clothes weren't quite dry, but he stuffed them in the bag, resolving to dry them out later when he cooked his eggs.

He climbed up the side of the stall, tied his bag behind his saddle, and got seated himself. Leaning over the horse's neck, he unlatched the stall door and got his horse started back down the lane, hoping he wouldn't have to get mounted in a big hurry anytime soon. A filtered sun squinted over the distant tree line back toward Lexington as he regained the wagon road. He squirmed around in the saddle, trying to find a position that didn't hurt his still sore backside, but apparently, such a position was not to be had. There was no wind, but it was still cold enough to bite.

He began to realize the properties nearby were full of both white and Negro field hands. All were engaged in turning over the corn-stubbled fields with mule-drawn plows. Apparently planting time was close at hand. Most of the workers were lightly dressed for a chill morning, wearing only long shirts and trousers, and at least half appeared to be barefoot. Ben knew from experience that bare feet and corn stubble didn't mix very well.

He noticed the mules all had their heads cast down, as though there was no hope that the day would get any better, and as he passed by, he realized the field hands looked every bit as forlorn as the mules. Another Negro was sitting on a grey stallion in the middle of the activity. Ben was surprised that the man had a musket across his saddle. He couldn't help but wonder why the two races were working side by side, as though both were slaves.

The land began to roll again, and within another mile, Ben spotted a line of trees ahead that undoubtedly meant another creek to cross. Probably the previous day the creek had been little more than a trickle—what his pa used to call a jump-across creek—but the evening's rain had turned it into an obstacle. It was running muddy, so there was no way to tell how deep the water might be.

He was able to retrieve a dead branch hanging from a sycamore and decided to use it to test the depth of the stream. The pony stepped gingerly into the creek, with Ben holding the saddle horn with one hand and the stick with the other. It seemed like the water was only about a foot and a half deep. Ben leaned ahead to test the bottom again, but the stick broke suddenly and Ben hit the water so fast he barely had time to hold his breath.

He tried to stand up in the creek, but had trouble keeping his balance. The current pushed him about ten yards downstream before he could regain his feet and scramble up the far bank. Thankfully, his horse stood waiting on him. He spoke to the animal and got his hand on the reins, but, unfortunately, there was nothing in sight that would allow him to remount. There was no choice but to walk until he found a stump or a wood fence or some other aid to get him up on the horse. He was going to get cold pretty quickly.

He heard a splash behind him and turned to see another horse and rider enter the creek. The man had no problem in crossing and came up to Ben. "I saw you fall in the crick there. You ain't hurt are you?"

Ben looked at the man. He appeared to be about the same age as his pa and wore a slouch hat and a long brown coat. He had sandy blond hair and a mustache of the same color, as well as eyes that were positively green. Although it was hard to tell on horseback, he appeared to be fairly tall. His horse—a palomino—was well turned out, and it was obvious that someone had spent a lot of time taking good care of him. "No, I'm not hurt, but I can't get back on my horse."

"Why not?"

"I'm not tall enough to mount her without the help of a stump or something."

The man sidled up to Ben and lifted him by the back of his jacket until Ben could grab the saddle horn and slip a foot in a stirrup. "Thank you, sir. Uh, what's your name sir?"

"D. G. Harris is my name. How about yerself?"

Ben had a revelation. He'd wanted to do something like this for at least a year. Now he was in a position that nobody would ever know the difference. "My name is B. F. Windes." Just like that! He was a brand new person. In fact, he even felt different. He could swear he felt the earth give a little shiver of recognition beneath him. Just to think—nobody would know any better!

"Well, B. F., where are ye headed?"

"I'm headed to West Port to try and catch up with my pa before he leaves for California, Mr. Harris."

"My friends just call me D. G."

"Where are you headed, sir?"

"I'm goin' into Independence, hopin' to find some good taters. I'm so tired of turnips I don't know what to do. And I'd like to buy some dried apples too. My wife can make some fine apple pie if she gets the makin's."

"I'd sure appreciate it if I could ride along with you to Independence."

"Glad to have the company."

"I've got four fresh eggs in my kit. It wouldn't take but a few minutes to fry them up if you'd like to split them with me." His teeth had started to chatter, and he was shivering.

"That sounds a lot better'n the hardtack I got in my jacket. It don't appear that a train has been through here yet this year. If it had, there wouldn't be a sign of firewood anywhere close to the Trail. But there's some dead wood hangin' from that beech tree yonder. Mebbe we can get a fire goin'. Looks like you could use a warm-up."

B. F. slid off his horse when they reached the tree. "You sound like you're from Kentucky too. I just met a man in Lexington from there yesterday—a Mr. Chadwick."

"I know Chadwick. He'd sell you a three-legged mule and swear it was a racehorse! But shore, I'm from Caintuck too."

A fire was started. Ben stood as close as he could, and steam began to come off his wet clothing. He took off his shirt, as best he could with shaking hands, and put on the still damp shirt from his bag. It was only marginally better, but it would have to do. He wrung out his wet shirt and rigged it on a couple of forked sticks as close to the fire as he dared. He then retrieved the iron skillet from his bag, and in no time they were feasting on scrambled eggs. D. G. appeared to hesitate, then asked his question. "Do yore initials stand for anythin', or are you just named B. F.?"

"My pa told me that my momma wanted to name me after her favorite patriot, Mr. Benjamin Franklin. Her pa was partial to him, being from Philadelphia hisself. So my name is actually Benjamin Franklin Windes." B. F. looked at his new friend. "What about you, D. G.? Does that stand for anything?"

"I ain't told nobody my given name since I left Caintuck, includin' my wife. My ma fancied herself an educated woman. She come to Caintuck from Virginny, and she was always fond of usin' French words. So she named me Dieu Geuid . . . Dieu Geuid Harris." D. G. looked hard to see what kind of response his confession had gotten.

"She named you Do Good? That ain't French!"

"No, it's all in the way you spell it. My name is written DIEU GEUID. It's just pronounced Do Good."

"Well, D. G., you've sure got a fine name—the kind of name that people could remember if you ever decided to make use of it. By the way, I've got another question. This morning I passed several fields with both white men and Negroes turning over the soil. I hear Missouri is a slave state, so why was everybody doing the same work?"

"Them white folk were most likely indentured."

"I never heard that word before."

"If a white man gets hisself into debt, and he cain't pay it, then the county magistrate can sell his debt at an auction at the courthouse. Whoever pays the debt then owns the man until he's worked long enough to pay it off. Some of them big farmers would druther get an indentured man as a slave. The slave costs a whole lot more—maybe four hundred to six hundred dollars for a healthy young buck. Course, it seems like they're all tryin' to run off over to Illinois to get free. Anyways, them coloreds is a lot of trouble."

"How long does the white man have to work to pay off the debt?"

"Well, it depends on lots of things. Does the man have a skill that's sorely needed—like a blacksmith or a wheelwright? Is the man young and full of vinegar or all stove-up? Most of these indentured servants workin' in the fields is prob'ly worth only about eighty to one hundred dollars for a year's work. Course, it falls on the farmer to provide that servant with a shack and enough food to eat for the year, just like he does for a slave. I heard of some folks who get indentured for four or five years before they get free."

"Don't those folks ever run off?"

"Every now and then. But what usually happens is the farmer adds his expense of catchin' the servant to his debt. A feller that runs off and gets caught might be lookin at three or four more years added to his time. I reckon most feel like it ain't worth it."

D. G. pointed from the top of a rise. "You see the church steeple to the north along that line of trees? That yonder is Independence, and the Trail leads right into town. Most folks travelin' by wagon from Lexington generally get here toward the end of the second day. You can come into town with me if you like, or you could cut a little bit to the south, and then bear back to the north gradual like. You'll hit the Trail about a mile the other side of town. It ain't yet noon, and West Port is just about fifteen more miles. You can make it easy afore dark if you come into town and get somethin' to eat then light out for West Port and don't laze around."

B. F. considered for a minute. It's possible that the Lexington sheriff could have come all the way to Independence to find him, but that didn't make much sense. Moreover, he was hungry again. "I'll ride with you if you don't mind, but I'll need to move right along as soon as I get a meal."

The town appeared to be about twice the size of Lexington. On the way in, they passed at least fifty big wagons and a tent city that smelled suspiciously like an overflowing latrine then corrals filled with mostly oxen and mules. There was Weston's Wagon Factory and Repair—est. 1830, two general stores, Noland's Inn, three other non-descript hotels, and at least as many saloons. The entire town seemed to be geared toward the traveler. They approached the town square, which had a much smaller courthouse than had been in Lexington. Here in Independence, the courthouse was a plain, foursquare stone building, surrounded by a large lawn and enclosed by a four-rail, white wooden fence. B. F. realized he didn't even know what the Lexington sheriff looked like, so it was pointless to try and keep an eye peeled for trouble.

They stopped across from the courthouse to water their horses, and B. F. noticed there was a message that someone had cut into a walnut tree that proclaimed the place Rose's Spring. D. G. pointed across the street. "That tradin' post yonder once belonged to the son of the great man hissef, Dan'l Boone. The place was a sight more active until West Port opened up. Now West Port gets steamboat traffic to deliver goods at West Port Landing, there at the big bend of the Missouri. There's a little settlement there called the City of Kansas—ain't much of a city if you ask me. Anyways, travelers can save themselves about a day's journey if they get off a steamboat there insteada stoppin' just north of here at Blue Mills. But most folk believe it's best to avoid that wagon long as they can. So West Port sorta cut deep into the traffic here in Independence."

Near the square, Dieu Geuid turned his horse down an alley, behind one of the hotels, and dismounted at the back door. He tapped on the door and was soon hugged around the neck by a woman within perhaps a year or two of his age. B. F. was quickly aware that she was a woman most men would stare at. "Hello, Gertie. I want you to meet a friend of mine—B. F. Windes. B. F., this here is Gertie Rupe. Her pa was one of the first white men to settle this part of the country, and she claims she was the first baby born out here." He stuck his head inside the door and gave a long, happy inhalation, "And Gertie makes the finest biscuits in the whole state of Missouri."

B. F. slid off his horse. "Hello, ma'am. Nice to meet you."

She gave him the kind of smile that appeared to have at least fifty teeth in it. B. F. had noticed that when most folks met a kid, they sort of looked past you, but this Gertie—she looked right into you, as though she really cared about you. "D. G., would you and your friend like to try a couple of these hot biscuits with some of last year's muscodine jam?" She smiled yet again—right at B. F.

In a couple of minutes, two large, very hot biscuits were handed to B. F., along with a mug of coffee. "Ma'am, I never thought I'd find anybody that made better biscuits than my aunt, but those are the best I ever tasted."

"Be sure you don't tell your aunt that. Most women like to think they're the best at things like that."

D. G. had a beatific, jam-smeared smile on his face. "If there's anything finer in this world than Gertie's biscuits, I reckon the good Lord just kept it for hisself."

Gertie smiled at him. "Your flowery words don't turn my head one bit."

"Say, Gertie, B. F. is tryin' to get to West Port tonight, so he cain't dawdle none."

"You want to ride that direction with me, D. G.?"

"Naw." Dieu Geuid looked at Gertie and smiled. "I believe I'll stay right here for a spell. Gertie and I got some catchin' up to do." Gertie had her hand on the back of his arm. "You just go back to the square and keep to the right. You'll be outa town and headin' toward West Port afore you know it. You'd best hurry a bit to be sure ye don't get into West Port after dark. Keep an eye out for that pony of yorn. They's a few sharp fellers that'll be happy to relieve you of yore pony—and anythin' else you got if they get half a chance. I sure enjoyed ridin' with ya'll."

B. F. stood on the back step and got up on his horse. "Thanks for your kindness and your friendship, D. G. And Miss Gertie, thank you for those fine biscuits."

She handed him two more fat biscuits, each filled with a generous slice of ham. "Put these in your bag, son. You might get hungry before you get to West Port."

As he rode out of town, B. F. touched Gertie's biscuits in his kit, and he briefly wondered if he was destined to always carry a biscuit or two, just in case someone made him go to bed without any supper.

B. F. thought it must be around three o'clock in the afternoon when he caught up to a train of ten wagons and a small amount of livestock that had probably come out of Independence that morning. The wagons were involved in crossing a stream at the bottom of a wide, shallow valley. A bearded man sat on a mule on the other side of the creek, screaming at the top of his lungs at the people in the wagon that seemed to be mired dead in the middle of the water. "I told ye you'd regret bringin' that damned piano. I told ye to get out and walk yore wagon across. We ain't even got to the Territory, and you already stuck. Now we gonna have to pull ye out." Two men were trying to rig up another brace of oxen to assist the animals that were mired fast in mid-stream.

B. F. crossed above them, tipped his hat to the screamer, and kept going. There was really not a thing he could do to help. He wondered how many times they would get stuck like this before the people in the accompanying wagons decided to take matters into their own hands and get rid of the piano theirselves. There had to be quite a few creeks and streams to be crossed between here and California.

In a couple of miles he passed another small train of wagons, said his hellos, and kept riding. He began to feel exposed, as it seemed that every man he saw was armed with either a pistol or a musket. The carving knife and hatchet in his bag suddenly didn't seem to be sufficient. At the very least, he needed to get a scabbard for the knife so he could wear it in his belt, or maybe under his pant leg. It wouldn't do him much good hidden away in his bag. It was a hard thing, having a little bit of money, and having no one to count on except himself.

Eleven

An Honest Man

Westport, Missouri 1849

B. F. heard the town before he could smell it and smelled it before he could see it. At the top of a low hill, he saw a large meadow off to the left that seemed to be filled with at least five hundred oxen and mules, all bellowing and braying in a cacophony of sound. Two men on a wagon pitched hay off the back, while a third man drove a team of mules across the pasture, standing with his legs spread wide apart in the front of the wagon.

Beyond the livestock was a sea of tents and wagons of all descriptions, with hundreds of people milling about. He then passed Horning's Vineyard, surrounded by freshly white-washed stone walls, and just beyond was a frame house with a sign out front declaring Dr. Franklin Moret, Renowned Physician and Surgeon, while across the street was Vogel's Dram Shop, then Highsmith's Grocery, and a nameless tavern with a very drunk man sprawled half on and half off the board sidewalk out in front.

The wooden sidewalks on both sides of what turned out to be Main Street were full of merchandise of all description, thus rendering them fairly useless for walking. There were mountains of furs and huge brown robes or blankets stacked in front of stores and one entire alleyway seemed to be piled with nothing but bleached bones and great horned skulls that reached almost to the eaves of the buildings on either side. Given the size of the skeletons, he wondered if they could possibly be the remains of buffaloes.

There were brown-skinned men, with black hair and mustaches, all seeming to wear a variety of the brightest colored blankets and jackets he had ever seen. Several jingled when they walked due to small silver bells that were sewn into the hems of their pants and jackets. They spoke a language he had never heard before. He wondered who these men were and where had they come from? Were they from out in the Territory somewhere?

Two very different looking brown men turned right in front of him on the shaggiest, most ill-kempt ponies he had ever seen. Each had a solitary feather woven into a long hair braid hanging down the back of their shirts. B. F. gave a start of fright and involuntarily jerked backward on the reins. His horse was surprised by this action and hopped a couple of steps to the side before calming. But nobody else on the street seemed to be paying any attention to the men. He had not expected to see live savages in a town, assuming that they were somewhere out on the plains plotting attacks on wagon trains and innocent travelers. However, here they were, mostly talking amongst themselves but also engaged in what appeared to be trading with store owners. Several others had pack horses piled with skins, which they were apparently trying to sell or trade. Two more of them looked hard at him as he brushed by. He wondered if they were thinking about his scalp or his pony.

He passed by a two-story frame building on his right that had a wide staircase running outside of the building to the second floor. Two men with stars pinned on the outside of their jackets were standing on the second-floor landing. They seemed to be watching the hullabaloo below but with no expression whatsoever on their faces. The sign on the building stated West Port City Hall. Another man came out of the door. It was a large Negro, and B. F. was shocked to see that he was also wearing a star. A colored lawman! This was indeed a different kind of place. Even in St. Louis he had not seen so much activity in the streets, this much trafficking in goods, so many guns, and such a variety of wild-looking characters of all descriptions and backgrounds.

He came to a rough log bridge that covered a shallow, clear spring that ran off to the south. Waiting in line for his horse to get a drink, a man on a snow-white mule behind him said, "Where ye fer, Californy er Oregon?"

"I'm headed for California, and I'm looking for my pa. He probably got here a few days ago—you wouldn't know a man named Daniel Windes would you?"

The man was dressed in buckskins, had a bowie knife at least a foot and a half long stuffed into his belt, and wore a big revolver tied high on his right leg. He was extremely red-faced. It was hard to tell if he was just sun-burned or if that was his usual color. "Don't believe I know yore pa. Reckon it's alright to water yore horse here at Spring Branch, but if I was you, I wouldn't drink here myself. Bunch of people got sick off this here spring after they put a stable upstream on the next street, above Mistuh Purdom's house."

"Fact is, last summer they say about fifty people died of the cholera here in West Port. They're all buried about a half mile north of here. Don't know that it was this here spring—I was out on the Trail at the time—but some mornin's they's a downright brownish cast to that water. I either do my drinkin' up above that stable or at one of them grog shops. I don't want no water with shite in it."

B. F. grinned. "Thank you for the advice, sir. I'll be sure I do the same."

"Name's Delbert Coggins. Most call me Del. What's your name, boy?"

"Name's B. F. Windes, Mister Coggins."

"Not Mister—just Del. Say, you had that hoss long?"

"Only a few days. I got him over in Lexington when I got off a steamboat."

"A steamboat? Some of these days I swear I'm gonna take a ride on one of them, no matter how much racket they make. Seems like I never gone anywhere 'cept sittin' on my backside on old Bony here." He patted his mule. "Has anybody told you that yore hoss ain't likely to make it crossin' the Trail?"

"What do you mean? He seems healthy enough. And he's easy to ride."

"Once you get in the high country, hosses don't do too good. They get colicky on what grass there is, and there just ain't anythin' else to eat. Hosses gen'ly give out some wheres in that fourth month out. And if you expect mules to pull one of them big Conestogas, they give out too about the time ye start askin' them to climb the big mountains. Mules can make it if ye just ride them, but a purty good number of 'em cain't pull them wagons to Oregon. Your best bet is a couple o' braces of oxen—between three and five year old, and built sorta thickset."

"Sounds like you've been out there before," B. F. said.

"I been across and back four times. I seen maybe a dozen hosses make it, outa thirty or forty what started. Probably the ones that make it without no problem is Injun ponies. Them animals could get by with eatin' dirt and drinkin' mud. If I was you, I'd sell that hoss to some feller that lives here, or maybe somebody goin' to Santa Fe. Headin' down south don't seem to be near as hard on hosses. If you aim to ride, you're gonna need a mule."

"I sure hate to give up this pony, but I don't want him dying on me either. Do you suppose I can make a trade?"

"Shore. But you gonna need at least four or five dollars boot. Where you figure on settin' up camp? I'm east of here about a half mile, just on the far edge of Tent City. They's maybe ten of us out there. Plenty of room for you if ye like."

He couldn't hide the relief on his face. "Thanks, Del. It's been a long day, and I do need a place to sleep."

"Looks to be a clear night, so you oughta stay dry. We're just sleepin' on the ground. Ain't no cover out there to speak of, save folks sleepin' in their wagons."

The sun was far gone as they rode back along the Trail and out of the crowded town. Within five minutes, Del turned south toward a lone campfire and B. F. followed. He realized he knew nothing about this man, let alone his friends, but he also acknowledged that there were few options available that didn't involve having to trust people he didn't know. For the second time in two days he wished he and his horse could just become invisible while it was dark. And for at least the tenth time in the last month, he wished he was brave.

Del dismounted and walked his horse into the firelight. "Evenin' fellers. Say howdo to my friend B. F."

B. F. couldn't really make out faces in the dark, but all said their howdies. He tried not to reveal to them what a novice he was by limping when he got off his horse and walked the animal over to where Del led his mule. He hobbled the pony and began struggling with his saddle. He wasn't having much luck when a slightly built man grabbed the saddle and lifted it easily to the ground. "Thanks, Mister. I wasn't getting anywhere."

"Me name's Patrick Dowd. These uncivilized divils refer to me as Saint Patrick. Now mind you, I don't hold with makin' fun of the greatest saint in the history of Ireland. 'Tis Paddy I prefer meself."

"Thank you Paddy. My aunt married a man from Ireland back in Indiana—a Sean Finnerty. I don't suppose you'd know him?"

"Might he be a short, ugly man?"

"Why yes, he is. So you know him?"

"Never heard of him." He clapped his hands together and laughed out loud as he walked back to the fire. B. F. searched his bag and retrieved one of Gertie's biscuits. Could it have just been this morning when he met her? He ate it quickly before walking into the glow of the fire, as he had too little to share with the others, Five or six of them were saddling their mules. A voice in the dark said, "We're headin' in town to get a supper and some liquid fortification. Comin' with us, Saint Patrick?"

Paddy leaned toward the horsemen and gave an exaggerated sniff. "Might I suggest to ye, Nathan Allen, ye rude little Scot, that ye keep yer distance from that red-haired Minnie Quick over at the Bottom's Up Saloon. Ye know perfectly well that black-hearted card cheat is her beau—and he might catch a whiff of all that bay rum ye've drowned yerself in, let alone you tryin' to wiggle yer little trouser schnauzer at his lady friend."

"Now don't get yer knickers in a knot. There ain't no crime in smellin' good, insteada resemblin' horse sweat, like some people I know. Would you care to bet the farm on my chances with Miss Minnie?"

"I'll not even wager the outhouse on you gettin' through the evenin' without the undertaker fitting you for your own private pine box!" He nodded toward the five of them. "Just remember, if ye start something in that place, there'll be lots of hair and eyeballs scattered around the floor—probably belongin' to the bunch of you ne'er-do-wells."

"Well, ain't none of us gonna leave this world alive."

Paddy turned his head and winked in B. F.'s direction. "I suppose not, but I'd just as soon not leave it *tonight*."

B. F. slept with his head on his traveling bag, feet on his saddle, and his blanket pulled over him. As much as he would have liked to take them off, he kept his boots on all night—he just didn't know these men.

> *My story. On April 3 year of 1849*
>
> *I never expected to acquaint myself with the likes of such folk on this journey and will tell Pa of their ways when we meet. I do not recollect such learning in school as I have had on the trip to West Port. I dare not tell him all for he might send me back home where I would not find comfort. Except I do so miss Abbie's biscuits and gravy and find myself sorely hungry more often than not.*
>
> *As I travel these miles I have many hours to reflect upon my new life and have now taken a new name, B. F. Windes. The old Ben Windes is left behind forever and I feel different somehow—older—not just a boy anymore.*

He was surprised that morning to find that only Del and Paddy were there, and Del was still in his bed roll. Paddy was kneeling over the fire, but the other men were nowhere to be seen. Either the fun in town had lasted all night long, or Paddy's prediction had come true.

B. F. was hoping to be offered some of the bacon he could smell that was starting to come to life in a skillet. He realized he had not had a meal since he bought one from the Negro cook a couple of days before. "How are you this morning, Paddy?"

"It's always a good day when I wake up on the top side of the grass, lad." He couldn't help but notice the hungry look on the boy's face. "You got a cup?" Paddy asked.

"Yes sir, I do."

"Come drink some of this coffee just to be certain it's safe for Paddy Dowd's consumption." He poured into B. F.'s bowl.

The smell of the bacon was overpowering. B. F. couldn't stand it. "Paddy, I'd like to make you a trade. I'll trade you a sure enough hair cut for some of that bacon."

Paddy stroked the wild thatch of hair on his head. "I don't know as I need a haircut. I had one in Oregon just last September." He hesitated for a minute. "But you got yourself a deal. Just be careful with them nippers, as the ladies do like me hair."

Both of them were pleased with their agreement. B. F. received four thick slices of bacon and a second dose of coffee, while Paddy was having a hard time letting loose of the mirror, just making sure he had admired his new haircut from every conceivable angle. When Del woke up, he didn't recognize the Irishman until he spoke a few words in his lilting voice. It was only then that he would accept that the new face belonged to Paddy. Once Del realized their new friend had a real skill, he asked for a haircut as well.

B. F. obliged, but when Del offered to pay, he waved him off. "If you'll let me bunk with you for a few more nights, there's no charge."

Del had an idea. "If you're willin' to cut hair on some wild characters, you oughta ride over to the edge of Shawnee land about a mile west of town. Men comin' in from Santa Fe generally stop out yonder to spruce up a bit in the crick afore they get to town. They'd be wild as a buck Indian, but you could get mebbe fifty cents for a haircut."

"You said Shawnee Land." He tried to ask his question in a calm manner. "Are there likely to be Indians out there?"

"When you get to OK Crick, that's the western border of the United States. Everthin' the other side is the Injun Territory, and the Shawnee has the first of it. The law won't allow no white people to live west of OK Crick. Cain't be no towns or anythin' civilized out there except Army forts and trading posts. So when you hear West Port is a jumpin' off place, that's the cold truth. Course it ain't the Injuns ye hafta look out for around here."

Paddy helped B. F. with his horse. They shook hands all around, and B. F. headed to town to look for his pa. The proposal to cut hair appealed to him. He certainly needed extra money, but he hated the vulnerable way he felt when everybody knew he had money. He passed by the vineyard again and then rode into a pandemonium of incessant banging from blacksmith, farrier, wheelwright, and carpenter hammers on either side of the road as he entered the business center of West Port. Signs out front proclaimed Wagons Ready for the Trail, Oxen and Mules Shod, and Wagons Repaired.

B. F. heard a loud scream from a building next to a saloon. He looked at several people on the street, but they had either not heard the terrible sound or were just indifferent to it. But as he looked closer, there was an explanation printed on a sign in the window.

Joseph Halifax, Painless Dentist
Last Dental Surgeon twixt here and the Pacific Ocean
Don't go west without a good set of teeth
Looks and feels like the real thing
Guaranteed to please

Upon reaching Walnut Street, he was stopped by a line of bigger wagons coming up from the river at West Port Landing and then turning to the west on Main Street. It appeared to B. F. that there were no families in this train, but rather each wagon was only manned by what seemed to be a professional teamster. He gathered that this was a freight outfit engaged in moving supplies and gear to Santa Fe, as each wagon was uniformly outfitted and pulled by four pairs of big mules.

If a team hesitated, they were immediately rewarded with the crack of a braided whip over their backs. The teamsters had no sympathy for dawdling animals, as they only made money when freight was moving. There was no doubt these men were experienced in the ways of draft animals. Likewise, they all were ready for anything else that might come their way. All wore at least one pistol at their waist, and most had a rifle beside them on the seat. Moving along with them were five men on horseback. One was obviously the Trail Boss, as all gave deference to his commands. The others were likely scouts and hunters—always necessary for the safety and well being of the train. Forty wagons and maybe ninety guns—probably more fire power than a full cavalry troop.

As the train moved off to the west, his attention was drawn to loud conversation from a gathering group of men on the north side of the road between Cross and Water Streets. B. F. rode closer to see if he could spot his pa in the crowd. The discussion seemed to be focused on when they could depart on the Trail. As B. F. crowded nearer, he was surprised to see Del Coggins stand stiff-legged in the stirrups on his white mule in the front of the group and speak. "It's just the third of April. There ain't no good reason to leave afore April ten."

A skinny man that had the look of a storekeeper about him spoke up. "What makes you say that, Mister? The weather is mild. We want to be the first train out of here this spring." Plenty of others joined in with agreement.

"There's sure enough good reason to be one of the first trains. But if you start now, you'll be sittin' on the south bank of the Kaw River for at least a week, waitin' on low water after that rain two nights ago. Ain't no wagon master worth his pay gonna head to Oregon afore the tenth. That train what just left here is headed for Santa Fe. They need to leave early, because by July they cain't hardly find no water atall where they're goin.'"

The storekeeper again. "So what do you know about the Trail?"

"I been out and back four times on that there 'Great American Desert.' Three of them I was master. If you go now, you'll just sit out there and eat up yore vittles, waitin' on low water. Besides, the grass ain't started growin' good enough yet for yer animals to pasture. A good rule to go by is to wait 'til grass is four inches high afore ye head west."

Another man spoke up from the crowd. B. F. realized it was Paddy. "Ya sound like an experienced mon to me. I've been lookin' for a good mon for a week, and it's little success I've had. How much would ye be chargin' to lead a train, sir?"

"Pickin' a master is serious business. Ye need to be sure ye pick a good one."

The storekeeper again. "Some of us are bound for California, and others are going to Oregon. What happens when we split?"

"I'd lead a train to Oregon. Them that's headed to Californy can hire a guide at Fort Hall. That's where the trails go their separate ways."

"Are you a drunkard sir? We can't have no drunkard leading us."

"I take a drink—but I ain't no drunkard."

"How much do you charge?"

"The goin' rate is twenty dollars a wagon or ten dollars for a single man. I expect cash money the mornin' we leave. Every man, woman, and child needs a hunert pounds of flour, fifty pounds of bacon, five pounds of salt, twenty pounds of meal, ten pounds of coffee, and sugar if you got a taste for it. Don't figure on bummin' food off yer neighbor. Pay yer own way or stay right here. Fill yer water barrel outa the spring yonder, but fill it up above that new stable. Don't want nobody sick the first day out. Oh yeah, If yer wagon breaks down, the train don't wait for ye.

"Remember, the train I master leaves here at sunup, the mornin' of April ten. If ye don't like them rules, find another feller what's been across that desert and them mountains as much as I have."

Del stood taller in the stirrups and looked out across the crowd. "Who'll be goin' with me?"

The first man made a show of stepping forward—it was Paddy—"'Tis a lovely trip we'll be havin', I'll wager." He was quickly joined by three others, and within five minutes, almost the entire group was confirming their participation in his train. At one point, Del looked over in his direction. B. F. pointed at his chest and nodded his head. Del smiled. He was signed up for the Trail!

Remembering his conversation with Del at the spring, B. F. turned north up Water Street to see what kind of market there might be for his pony. He passed a blacksmith's forge that appeared to be devoted entirely to the wheelwright trade, as there were at least a hundred iron-rimmed wagon wheels stacked out front. Conveniently, a ready-made

customer, a wagon manufacturing operation, was situated immediately across the street.

Sure enough, there was a corral and stables behind the McCoy
Trading Post and passing directly down the hill below was the Spring
Branch. It was pretty easy to see why the water "had a brown tinge to
it" some mornings.

Tying his pony to the hitching rail, B. F. entered the store, noticing the place was packed with would-be travelers. There was a large,
hand-lettered sign occupying one wall, which he studied intently.

SUPPLY LIST FOR THE TRAIL

All Sold Here at McCoy's

Wagon	Canvas	Oxen or Mules
Ox-Yoke	Ox shoes	Axle Grease 10 pounds
Harness	Water Barrel	Tarpaulin
Scrub Board	Iron Pot	Iron Skillet
Dish Pan	Looking Glass	Knife/Fork
Canteens (2)	Stout Knife	Rifle
Gun Powder	Bullet Mold	Powder Horn
Lead 8 pounds	Boots or Brogans	Tin Dishes
Candle Mold	Tallow	Awl
Ball of Twine	Spare shirt / pants	Coat
Wide-Brim Hat	Blankets (2)	Rope—200 foot
Lanterns (2)	Axe	Saw
Hammer	Nails 20 pounds	Wood File
Whet Stone	Wood Chisel	Wood Plane
Draw Knife	Level	Curry Comb
Bullwhip	Coffee Pot	Coffee Grinder
Buckets (2)	Canning Jars (24)	Paper
Lead Pencils	Fish Hooks /Lines	Veterinary Liniment
Castor Oil	Sulfur	Whale Oil
Soap	Books	Alcohol (Medicinal)
Molasses	Saleratus	Rice
Vinegar	Tobacco	Pipe Bowls / Stems

Flour	125 pounds a man	Corn Meal	25 pounds a man
Taters	50 pounds a man	Beans	50 pounds a man
Bacon	50 pounds a man	Sugar	10 pounds a man
Lard	10 pounds a man	Coffee	10 pounds a man
Dried peaches	10 pounds a man	Salt	10 pounds a man
Dried apples	10 pounds a man		

MINERS	FARMERS	
Pans—2	Hoe	Corn Sheller
Pickaxe	Plough	Squash seed
Shovel	Rake	Beet seed
Buckets—4	Pitchfork	Carrot seed
Scale / Weights	Adze	Cabbage seed
Lanterns—4	Bridle / Traces	Turnip seed
Candle Holder—4		
Meal sieve, brass	Seed Corn	20 pounds/5 Acres
Candles—24	Potatoes	10 extra pounds
	Wheat, Red	50 pounds/5 Acres
	Beans, White	5 pounds
	Beans, Green	5 pounds
	Beans, Brown	5 pounds

How would he afford all that? And worse, how would he carry it? He waited until an old, grizzled storekeeper was free. "Sir, I'd like to sell my horse. He's well broke and easy-tempered. What kind of price can you give me?"

The man looked at B. F. over the top of his glasses. One lens was completely missing. He had a nasty looking, half-dollar sized sore on his forehead. "Where is this hoss?"

"She's tied out front—the black one."

He shoved the glasses back on his nose and looked out the door. "That's just a pony. Not interested."

"She might look young, but she's a stout horse."

"Not interested." He turned away.

"Sir, Just one more question. Have you seen a man named Daniel Windes?"

He didn't even turn around. "Never heard of him."

B. F. headed for the door. As he went out, a man in rough clothes tapped him on the shoulder. "How much might you want for that animal?"

"Twelve dollars for the horse. I'm keeping the saddle and bridle."

"That would be too much. I'd be lookin' for a horse for my daughter." He nodded toward a girl a bit taller than B. F., standing on the sidewalk. Her hair was so blond it was almost white.

She smiled at B. F. and he felt himself reddening. She had eyes that were two colors of blue—pale as a coneflower on the inside and indigo on the edges. But he had no idea why he had even noticed that. All he could get out was "Hello." He wondered why he couldn't talk normally. After all, it was just a girl.

The man cut in. "We'll be heading for Oregon, and Janie wants to ride all the way."

B. F. could see that the girl wanted the horse and knew he could make a deal here, but he had to stop himself. For some reason, he kept looking at the girl when he spoke. "Much as I need to sell my horse, I have to tell you the truth. Last night a man who's been over the Trail four times told me horses couldn't live through the trip. He says they can't seem to eat the grass in the mountains, and they don't make it. He told me to trade for a mule. That's why I came here today." He looked at the girl again, and she looked back.

"What might be your name, son?"

"B. F. Windes, sir."

"Name's George Fitzwater, and this would be my daughter, Jane. Until this very minute, an honest man I've not seen since we left Tennessee four months ago."

B. F. smiled, but he was not happy. "I guess I need to try and find someone who's headed back east, or maybe going to Santa Fe. This man said the grass was better on the south trail. Have you signed up for a train yet, Mr. Fitzwater?"

"Indeed—this very morning. It's Del Coggins we'll be going with on April 10."

B. F. smiled for sure. "Then we'll be traveling together. I'm going with Del too. Fact, he's the one who told me about my horse."

Mr. Fitzwater looked again at B. F. "Now that's lovely. I appreciate you being honest with me. But it's a favor I'd like to ask of ye. I saw you looking at that paper in there. I know it tells what a man needs to cross that desert out there. But I can't decipher some of the words. Might you recollect what it says?"

"I can remember most of it." B. F. recited a goodly part of the list. "Tell you the truth, I'm worried about how much it's gonna cost and doubt I could ever get it all on a mule."

Fitzwater whistled through his teeth. "'Tis many of those things we have already, but I didn't expect all of that." He turned to his daughter. "Janie, me lovely, a mule we won't be buying. I doubt we can pay for all that they figger we need."

She looked at her pa. "I know it pa. I don't need no mule. They're too mean anyway."

B. F. liked the fact that the girl could see the problem and didn't act foolish. What a difference between her and his stepsisters back in Indiana—they would already have been acting out. He also appreciated the basic honesty of the man. Then he had an idea—one that might solve several problems at once. "Mr. Fitzwater, you said you had lots of this gear already. Tell me, do you have a wash tub, a cooking pot, and some buckets?"

"Why, sure. My Mary would rather leave me behind as her wash tub. I might not look like I deserve it, but I do indeed have a quality wife!"

Twelve

Travel At Your Own Risk

West Port, Missouri 1849

B. F. explained his plan and told Mr. Fitzwater he'd meet him at the plank bridge over the public spring in a half hour. Then he went back in McCoy's and bought six bars of soap, two woolen blankets, and a piece of chalk for a dollar and seventy-seven cents.

They made a strange looking pair, leaving West Port on the Trail—the young boy on the pony, holding blankets and empty buckets, and the man walking alongside with a big wash tub and a cook pot. Within less than a mile they came upon OK Creek that flowed north to south through a narrow valley. Nailed to a tree on the other side of the stream was a sign.

> You Are Now Leaving the United States
> Travel At Your Own Risk

And the rutted wagon tracks—the Oregon, California, and Santa Fe Trails—collectively responsible for the greatest geographic displacement of people in history—climbed up and over the nondescript hill beyond, headed for who knows what.

They found a grassy spot near the water and while Mr. Fitzwater started a good fire, B. F. hauled water in the buckets, filled up the cook pot to heat the water, and retrieved two more bucketsful. He cut

the blankets into equal parts, then found a cast-off board and drew up
their own sign, facing toward anyone arriving from the west.

Haircut—50 cents Hot Bath with Soap—50 cents
West Port—Dead Ahead

Before the second cook pot started boiling, eight men came over
the hill—some on horses, the rest on mules. One of them was so tall
that he looked like his feet could almost touch the ground while he
was in the saddle. Mr. Fitzwater met them as they crossed the creek.
"Say there gents. Might you be interested in a good haircut and a
hot bath afore you arrive in West Port? Same thing will cost you
double in town."

"Been waitin' on this town for a thousand miles. I don't think I can
wait no longer."

"The grog shops and parlor houses won't be opening their doors
for another two hours. You might as well get all spruced up now."

The first of a parade of very scroungy looking men dismounted
and walked over. One with an eye patch spoke up. "Wilbur, get yer
hair cut whilst I have me a bath."

"Hell Josiah, I want the water fust."

But Josiah already had his boots off and was pulling down his
pants. "I'll be in this here tub afore you get one of them boots off."
True to his word, Josiah stepped in the tub, or at least almost did. He
howled and hopped backward. "Cool that water down some. Ya figger
on cookin' me fer supper?"

Mr. Fitzwater poured in a bucket of cool water then refilled the
bucket with hot water from the cook pot. The man called Josiah
slowly stuck his foot in and stirred the water around, motioned for
more hot, stirred again, and held up his hand. He then took his shirt
off, as well as the top half of an extremely grimy set of long under-
wear, and eased himself into the tub. Mr. Fitzwater handed him a bar
of soap, and the man worked himself over thoroughly then settled in
to soak as best he could, given that his legs were so long that his knees
stuck almost straight up in the air.

B. F. worked on his partner's hair for about twenty minutes until he pronounced the job done. After some complaining, Josiah got out of the tub, dried off with a half-blanket, and sat down in front of B. F. Wilbur wanted more hot water. In fact, it got so hot that his skin turned as pink as a rare steak, despite a significant, crusty covering of gray dust.

Two of their fellow travelers took the places of the first pair of men, but the others in their party were impatient for the town and went on in to West Port. Mr. Fitzwater stayed busy, running buckets back and forth to the creek, keeping the fire, and continually adjusting and readjusting the temperature. The blankets were hung on tree limbs to dry in between customers.

Before the second pair was finished, four men crossed the creek on bedraggled looking mules. Like other men B. F. had seen in the town the day before, these four had very dark complexions and almost shiny black hair. They all had on pantaloons with a slash cut in the cuff and a couple had the same kind of small silver-colored bells sewn along the legs that he had seen the evening before. The men studied what was going on for a few minutes, until finally one came over to Mr. Fitzwater. Through broken English and some sign language, they seemed to agree to the deal.

B. F. couldn't help but notice how much easier their hair was to cut. Although long, all four men had hair that was completely straight. He was able to finish each of them in less than fifteen minutes. When it came time to settle up, Mr. Fitzwater held up a silver dollar that one of the first customers had given them, and then four fingers, and pointed at each one of the men. He said, "Four dollars" very slowly and loudly.

One of the men said, "Cuánto dinero?" and pulled some strange coins from a purse.

Mr. Fitzwater looked at B. F. They traded shrugs. "No, no. Four dollars."

The men put their heads together, and one went to the saddlebags on his horse. Fleetingly, the thought went through B. F.'s mind that he was going after a gun. But the man turned around with nothing more threatening than a cloth bag, walked over and placed four small rocks in Mr. Fitzwater's hand that were each no bigger than a kernel of corn. He pointed to his new haircut and to those of his three friends, and said simply, "Gold."

B. F. and his partner looked at the rocks. Mr. Fitzwater held it up to the sunlight, as though the heavens would advise him. It certainly looked like gold. At least, it was gold-colored. Neither of them had ever seen real gold nuggets before. B. F. looked at the man and turned to Mr. Fitzwater, "I think we better take it—they're not trying to beat us." They said thank you and waved goodbye as six more customers came down the trail.

"Say there, we'll make yore deal. But you gonna have to dump out that wash tub them Mexicans was in and start fresh. We don't want to sit in no freeholey water."

It was almost dark when they got back to town. They had ten dollars and four rocks, which they hoped were worth at least four more dollars. The scale at the first store they could find ran their way, and they received seven dollars and eighty cents for their gold.

Mr. Fitzwater and his family were camped in the tent city just east of the vineyard, so they headed that way together. "B. F., come to my wagon for supper. We need to talk about this new business. Besides, my Mary will want to see you for herself."

Mary Fitzwater's dress was of faded gingham and fastened high around her neck. Her bonnet was grey with the ribbons dangling untied beside her face. And her apron was blue and white of a checkerboard pattern. She probably had hair as blond as her daughter's when she was a girl, but at thirty years old, it had now begun to darken with streaks of light brown. Her eyes, however, were as blue as a robin's egg. She was a tiny woman and couldn't possibly be much over four feet ten inches tall. There were too many lines on her face for her age. But when she laughed—and she laughed quite a bit—it sounded as though it was coming from someone twice her size, and the lines seemed to disappear.

She had put together a tasty dinner of potatoes, bacon, and gravy, with biscuits on the side. Mr. Fitzwater put one arm around Mary's waist and a hand on Jane's shoulder. "B. F., these are my favorite darlin's in all the world. And I'm thankful that they can serve a far better meal than me own mother ever could. For sure, the Irish excel in many things—doing the hardest labor that no one else wants to do, racing the finest horses for a wee profit, making lovely music to set a heart on fire, and enjoying a good toddy—but unfortunately, they are not even average when it comes to good food. Thank goodness for our appetite, Mary's mother was Flemish." He told them all about their day, the men they had dealt with, and the money they had made. Mary made a joke about their unfamiliarity with gold, calling her husband Mr. Astor.

But the king of the castle was their little boy Ethan. He was just as blond as his big sister but for some unknown reason had brown eyes. He was three years old, but talked like he was twelve, carrying on conversations with everybody in every campsite within sight. And when the little boy started talking, all three of his family members seemed to have a little glow in their eyes as they watched over him.

The Fitzwaters had come all the way from the little town of Cookeville, Tennessee. Selling their farm late the previous fall, they had put their belongings in a wagon and rode to the Tennessee River, where they loaded the wagon on a barge and floated down to the Ohio, then on to the Mississippi. They put ashore on the west bank of the big river at Cape Girardeau and spent most of the last two months traversing the state of Missouri.

Mr. Fitzwater had traded his mules and wagon for a Conestoga and two yoke of oxen in Independence, and after comparing schedules, B. F. decided they had been in the town not more than two days before he was. He also gathered that the funds from the barber and bath business were necessary if this little family was to get to Oregon. Over a final biscuit, they decided they had five more days to make money before having to get their supplies in order and be ready to leave on the tenth of the month. If everything went their way, they might have fifty dollars apiece to complete the outfitting shortages they had.

B. F. talked to them about another way to make a little money. He told about his aunt making mattresses out of canvas and hay, and asked whether Missus Fitzwater and Jane might want to use wagon canvas to sew mattresses, and stuff them with hay they could purchase at the stable? If they made six mattresses out of a wagon canvas and sold them for a dollar apiece, would it make sense?

Mary and Jane looked at one another. Could they make that much money just with a little sewing? Jane gestured toward the tent city behind them—just barely discernible in the distance—where there were at least a hundred campfires burning. "There's no shortage of customers here. And I know I'm sick of sleepin' on the ground. Maybe our neighbors are too."

Mary had been rummaging in their wagon and finally emerged with a creamy white root, which she placed in a pot of hot water to steep over the fire. "George, you best have a cup of 'sang tea this evenin'. Yer lookin' a bit peaked."

"I hate the taste of that stuff."

"Makes no never mind. Cain't have you gettin' sick."

B. F. turned to Jane. "What's 'sang tea?"

"It's some o' ma's ginseng root brewed up in a tea. She says I'm too young for it."

Satisfied that her husband was sipping on the bitter brew, Mary came over to B. F. and sat down cross-legged in front of him. "B. F., where do your people come from?"

"Indiana."

"No, I mean where did they come from before they came to America? You don't have no Scots-Irish blood do you?" She said it almost as an accusation.

"I don't know. My aunt always said they all came over from England."

She was obviously displeased with his answer but nonetheless nodded her head knowingly. "When were you born?"

It seemed an odd question, but he replied, "January, 1841."

"Exactly when in January?"

"The eighth."

She paused for a minute, apparently digesting the ramifications of his answer, before she got to the heart of the matter. "Have the people close to you suffered terrible sickness or death?"

What could this woman know about him? He lowered his eves, and replied in a low voice, "I guess some have."

"I thought so." She then stood up, looked hard at her husband, and walked back to their wagon without even saying goodnight.

Thirteen

Happy To Have You

West Port, Missouri 1849

Early the next morning, B. F. rode back to McCoy's and bought three pieces of canvas and two spools of stout thread. At the same time, Mr. Fitzwater found a wagon making a delivery of hay to the stockade and convinced the driver to make a stop at his campsite. As the two departed for another day at OK Creek, Mary and Jane had already started marking and cutting the canvas, with Ethan right in the middle of their work.

The day at the creek went pretty well. By four o'clock they had earned sixteen dollars, and with no arrivals in the last hour, had decided to extinguish the fire and start on their way back. No sooner had they made the decision, two men came riding over the hill on what appeared to be Indian ponies. They both rode well. In fact, it looked like they were almost glued to their saddles, and B. F. guessed they had been riding for a very long time. As they got closer, Mr. Fitzwater first thought they were Indians. B. F. was relieved to see that they were just tanned as cow leather.

The men pulled up at their fire. "That water hot?"

"Soon it will be when I add two buckets of hot."

The man that sat down in front of B. F. looked to be about half Indian in his clothing and his behavior. "Take care how ye cut this hair."

"Yessir." B. F. wet his hands and began to moisten the man's hair. The man flinched in pain. "Careful I said."

B. F. then noticed a ragged scar that began over the man's right ear, circled the back of his head, and ended almost above his left ear. It was roughly done and had bits of skin that were sort of hanging loose. "Oh, I'm sorry mister. What happened here?"

"Mescalero almost got my hair down south of Albuquerque along the Rio Grande. Hit me in the head with a rock. He was in the midst of takin' my scalp with his knife when Alvin shot him."

The man in the tub spoke up. "Charlie was 'bout as grey as you can get without bein' dead. I sewed him up with my darnin' needle. He was plumb crazy for a week or so, but he's back to bein' hissef now— only half crazy. You're the first one to give him a haircut since that Apache almost did."

"I'll be careful, mister. I'll cut it so nobody can see the scar."

When they settled up, the man called Alvin said, "We got no American coins. But mebbe what we got is better."

B. F. was hoping for another deal in gold. But what was placed in his palm were two pieces of silver coinage that he'd never seen before. They were a bit thicker than U.S. coins and had very rough emblems of some sort on the coins. "Them's Spanish silver—most calls 'em Pieces of Eight because ye can cut them into eight parts. Might be some of that old-timey stuff. We got them from a Mexican in Santa Fe."

Mr. Fitzwater picked one of the coins up and tried to make out the marks. B. F. wondered why he was so bent on deciphering the writing. The man couldn't even read English, let alone Spanish. "Thanks mister. I hope you're happy with those haircuts."

The one called Charlie looked at George Fitzwater and winked. "If we find a couple of them purty sportin' gals, we'd be downright overjoyed. Will you'ns guarantee these here haircuts will make that happen?" Both men laughed at the prospect.

They got back to the wagon before dark with eighteen dollars, as they'd gotten an even trade in dollars for the Spanish coins. As they unloaded, Jane came into camp with a big grin on her face. Her pa looked at first her and then his wife. "What luck did you have with the mattresses?"

"We sewed twelve of them mattresses but decided we didn't have no room for any more, so Janie been sellin' since about three o'clock. Whilst she went around with the mattresses, I sewed some more. I plumb forgot the time."

Jane piped in. "I sold nine, pa. It didn't take hardly any time. Once people laid down on them, they was quick to buy. Oh, and I raised the price to a dollar-fifty. That's all right with you ain't it?"

Two more days of the same routine and they met once more for supper. As B. F. watched the meal preparation, he couldn't help noticing that Mary used a knife to cut what appeared to be a cross on the top of her soda bread before she placed it in the Dutch oven. He turned to Jane. "Why did your ma cut that cross on the bread?"

"Well, if you asked Pa, he'd say it was to help the bread bake through and through. But Ma claims that she cuts that cross to let the fairies out."

Thinking it was a joke, B. F. started to laugh, but caught himself just in time when he looked at Jane's face. After the meal, they assessed their circumstances. They had taken in a total of ninety-six dollars between the four of them and only spent six dollars on canvas and hay. Plus there were twelve finished mattresses ready to sell in the morning.

Mary was thoughtful. "We got two more days before we leave here. My knees tell me it's fixin' to rain tomorrow. If it does, mebbe Jane and me oughta sell them mattresses quick. And you two take the wagon to buy supplies. B. F. you better make yer deal for that pony and find you a mule. And if my rheumatism is wrong, then we can make some more money tomorrow and do our shoppin' the next day."

B. F. figured thirty-four of those dollars belonged to him, based on his haircuts. He needed to buy supplies, but he also had to have somewhere to put them. He hoped his idea would appeal to them. "I'd like to buy something from you. I want one of those mattresses, and I want to buy enough space in your wagon for about one hundred fifty pounds of supplies. I can hunt, I can help look after Ethan, and I can help with chores. All I want besides that is about five dollars to trade for a mule. If you'll buy the supplies, then all the rest of the money is yours." He held his breath. There was no time now to start over if this didn't work.

They looked at one another and Mary Fitzwater spoke up. "I don't think we got enough room to. . . ."

Mr. Fitzwater quickly interrupted. "Now, Mary. B. F. here worked just as hard as we did for that money. If not for his sly ideas, its stuck right here in West Port we'd be instead of moving our family to Oregon. B. F., o'course you can have some wagon space. It's happy we are to have ye with us." B. F. tried not to notice that Mary's face didn't convey the same enthusiasm about the new arrangement as her husband.

But B. F. could only be grateful that he had found good people. He felt tears on his cheeks and turned away so they wouldn't see his reaction. He was so relieved he couldn't say anything but "Thank you." He remembered he still had four five-dollar gold pieces in his boots. He hoped he would have enough barbering money to buy what he needed, as he was pretty sure he'd need the remainder of his gold soon enough.

Fourteen

The Peace Medal

West Port, Missouri 1849

My story. On April 8 Year of 1849

*I shan't give up on finding my pa but the longer I'm here
in West Port without seeing him, the more I think he's gone a
different way to Calyfornia. Every day I have seen somebody
who was about the right size, or walked the right way, or carried
himself just so, and I always hurry to catch up to them to see if
I might be right. But I have had no luck at all. No one here has
ever heard of Daniel Windes.*

*For these last two days, I will look harder than ever. Unless
pa is traveling by ship, he should be here. No wagon trains have
left for Calyfornia yet this spring. But one thing keeps bothering
me that I try to push out of my mind. What if my pa was on
the steamboat that wrecked just ahead of the boat I was on?
As far as I can tell nobody knows a thing about that boat and
so far nobody has claimed to have been on it. I can't think like
that. I just know he is still alive but I surely can't figure where
he is.*

True to form, Mary's knees were on target, and the morning drizzle brought the pronouncement from Mister Fitzwater that it "'tis
a gorgeous, soft day." B. F. promised Mr. Fitzwater he'd meet him

at McCoy's to help load the wagon and headed out in the light rain toward a stock barn on the northeast corner of West Port.

He passed by a very large two-story house—perhaps the biggest one in town—and noticed it belonged to Colonel A.G. Boone. Could it be this was yet another offspring of the famous woodsman? He tied his horse outside Bernard's Livestock Sales and resolved to make a deal. He found William Bernard on his hands and knees behind the counter, pawing through a tangle of single-trees and harness on the bottom shelf.

The man was balding on top and had what was left of his hair tied behind his head in the old style. "What for ye boy?" He wore a set of false teeth that he could barely keep in his mouth and kept putting his hand to his lips to keep them from falling on the floor. B. F. wanted to ask if this was an example of the guaranteed dental work of Joseph Halifax, but kept that to himself.

"Have you seen a man by the name of Daniel Windes, sir?"

"The only Daniel I know is my slave. I don't believe he owns a surname."

"No, I was asking after my father." He changed subjects. "I have a fine horse outside I'd like to sell, sir."

Mr. Bernard slowly pulled himself to his feet. "There ain't much market for horses hereabouts. What's he look like?"

"He's there at your rail, sir. He looks real good when it's not raining."

He shook his head slowly. "It's a stretch to call that soggy animal a horse. He ain't close to two year old."

"I'm interested in trading him for a mule. The saddle and bridle goes with me."

"Son, I'd have to ask for ten dollars boot. That pony's gonna be hard to sell."

"I was figuring four dollars boot for a good mule. I can't go ten, sir."

"Then we can't deal." The old man went back to his inventory.

Dejected, B. F. rode back over to McCoy's. It didn't appear that Mr. Fitzwater was there yet with the wagon, so he went in the store and bought a knife scabbard then returned to the street to wait on his friend. There were two Indians sitting on their paint ponies, paying a lot of attention to his horse. The younger one had a travois rigged behind his own animal, which was loaded with hides. Not knowing exactly what they were up to, B. F. stood back by the door to keep an eye on them.

The older man had on leggings and a vest that were made of relatively new deerskin. The vest had white shells and blue beads sewn in a circular pattern on the front, and he had some sort of wavy lines and circles in white paint on his bare arms. His hair looked like it had been rubbed with grease, and around his neck he wore a large silver amulet. From a distance, B. F. couldn't be sure, but it looked like it bore the likeness of Thomas Jefferson on the front. Could it be this rough-looking character had one of the Peace Medals that he knew had been distributed to Indian chiefs across the west by Lewis and Clark? It was twice the size of a silver dollar and run through by a white bead necklace.

The Indian looked closer at his pony and put his hand on the bridle. The steel bit and connecting rings were quite a contrast with his own bridle, which was made completely of braided leather. B. F.'s pony was visibly nervous. Perhaps it was the close presence and scent of the strange horse, or maybe it was the unfamiliar appearance of the Indian. B. F. stepped forward, pointing at the horse, then himself, and said, "My horse." He patted the pony on the neck to quiet her.

The Indians spoke together in a short-syllabled tongue. The older one pointed at the horse and then at his hides. He held up ten fingers. B. F. realized they were trying to trade for his pony. He didn't know exactly what a buffalo hide was worth, but as many as were stacked around town on sidewalks and in sheds, even ten of them couldn't be worth too much. He shook his head no and said, "No."

The Indian held up his hand, indicating that he should wait. He took a sturdy knife from a leather scabbard on his belt, pointed at it, and again indicated ten hides. B. F. held his hand out to see the knife. He noticed a "U.S." stamped into the base of the blade. Somewhere in the past, this Indian had gotten hold of a U.S. Army issue knife. B. F. didn't want to think about how that might have happened. Again, he declined.

B. F. started to mount his horse, then stepped back a minute. He held up his hand for the man's attention. He stepped back and looked at the paint mare, then at the horse's teeth, felt her withers, and turned up her hooves. Of course, she was unshod, but her hooves seemed in good shape for all he could tell. He took the blanket and saddle off his pony, and set them on the sidewalk. First he pointed at the older man's horse and to himself. Then he pointed to his pony and to the Indian. Then he went for the deal. He was standing close enough now that he could clearly see that the medallion held the profile of Mr. Jefferson himself. He pointed at the Peace Medal and to his chest to finish the deal.

He couldn't tell whether the Indian was shocked or insulted or just acting. He shook his head violently to indicate no deal and put his hand protectively over the medal. B. F. guessed it had probably been in his tribe—maybe even with the man's own family—for forty-five years, since the Voyage of Discovery had gone up the Missouri River in 1804. For the rest of his life, he would tell how close he came to trading for a Peace Medal.

But B. F. realized there was a deal to be made here. He turned away and picked up the saddle to put it back on his pony. The Indian got off his horse and grabbed B. F.'s arm. In his other hand he held out his reins and his knife. B. F. acted as though he was wavering, then finally nodded his head. The younger Indian let out a whoop of excitement. Apparently his father had been negotiating for him.

Mr. Fitzwater was watching from his wagon across the street. He couldn't believe the boy had made a trade face to face with a wild Indian. He walked over and patted B. F. on the back. "You must be part Irishman. That might explain how you just out-traded that Indian! I'll get your saddle. Take that paint around to get shod. Then we can go see about all those supplies they say we've got to have."

They spent eighty-eight dollars and twenty cents on supplies. B. F. also used four and a half of his five dollars to shoe his horse and buy a new bridle, plus purchase six yards of blue and pink striped cotton material for Mary and Jane, some marbles for Ethan, and five thick sticks of licorice to share all around.

Their final day in West Port, Jane asked for one more piece of canvas. She was determined to sell more mattresses before the day was out, while Mary was to spend most of the day arranging everything in the wagon so that necessary supplies were easily accessible. This was not a simple task, given the inside of the wagon was ten feet long and only forty-two inches wide. She placed a wooden trunk in front, underneath the wide board—called a jockeybox—that would provide a place for Jane and her to sit for the next five months. She also made sure there was at least space to walk down the middle of the wagon, as this narrow aisleway would have to be Ethan's area to play while they were traveling.

B. F. and Mr. Fitzwater decided to spend the day at OK Creek. There wouldn't be much reason for people on the trail to get a fancy haircut or take a tub bath, so they knew their business was finished when they departed West Port. B. F. walked up to McCoy's to pick up his horse and Jane's canvas, while Mr. Fitzwater headed to their business location.

His new horse didn't care for the saddle or the cinch. She'd never had anything fastened around her belly before except for a woven rope, and for a little while she shook herself and kicked a bit. But B. F. waited her out, and finally rode back to the tent city to deliver the canvas then out to the creek without any incident.

One man had already had his bath and was waiting on a haircut, while another was in the tub when B. F. arrived. Both men had come from a place in west Texas, and had headed north to strike the Trail maybe two hundred miles east of Santa Fe. The one still in the tub was skin and bones. He had a terrible cough that he just couldn't stop once he got started, and when he finally did stop, he was gasping for breath. His skin seemed to have a pasty gray color to it. B. F. was relieved that the man lived through his bath and wondered if they shouldn't dump out the tub and start over as soon as they left. He knew he wouldn't want to sit in that water, as it might harbor some of the contagion that had rinsed off the man.

Both of the men were wearing necklaces made of unusual blue stones. They told how they had quite a few pieces of bracelets and amulets and necklaces made of the same kind of strange looking stones, saying they'd made a deal with some Indians for trade goods and decided to come to West Port to see what they could sell them for. But something in the way it was said made B. F. uneasy. He didn't know why, but he was sure they were being lied to. No telling what they'd really done to get that jewelry.

A group of six men crossed the creek about the time they were finished, and when the new arrivals didn't pass on by, the two men paid up, and mounted their animals. The short one glanced back around. "You boys out here ever' day?"

B. F. stepped on Mr. Fitzwater's foot and spoke up. "Yes. We're right here every day." The man nodded to his partner, and as they rode off, B. F. spoke quietly. "There's something wrong with those two. I bet they figure on coming back in a day or so and taking our money. But when they do, we'll be gone."

"I know what you mean. Those boys stole those jewels, I figure. It's downright fortunate we are that these fine gentlemen came along when they did."

In between customers, B. F. used his scissors on his horse. After trying unsuccessfully to work out the tangles and knots in her shaggy hair, he finally decided the simplest approach was to cut her mane very short, as it would grow out sooner or later. He was less able to do very much with the tail. He didn't trust the horse enough to get behind her, but was able to cut some of the long hair off the back of her legs. By the time another set of customers rode in, Mr. Fitzwater couldn't help but comment. "That little mare is beginning to look like another horse entirely. Of course, you might cut her hair off, but I doubt it's possible to cut the wild Injun out of her."

They finished late in the afternoon, well satisfied to have earned twelve dollars apiece. Both of them had a fee to pay in the morning to the wagon master, so they were relieved to have enough to take care of Del Coggins without dipping very deeply into the remainder of their money.

My story. On April 9 year of 1849
  Tomorrow we leave for Calyfornia. The Fitzwater wagon
  is packed to the canvas with gear and food. Good fortune has

smiled on me so far, as barbering has paid my way. The sunset tonight was red and orange and even purple. Del says it means good weather tomorrow. I must say I am excited!

I wish my pa was here to share it. I am pretty sure he is not here in West Port, so he must be traveling by ship. I reckon I will have to wait to find him when we get to Calyfornia. After supper, Mary tied a handful of pine needles and sage together in a little bundle. She made all of us stand at the back of the wagon while she lit the bundle afire. Then she waved the burning bundle back and forth and walked around all of us and the wagon. And I think she said, 'Spirit of the heaven, conjure it. Spirit of the earth, conjure it.' Jane said burning the bundle of pine and sage was called smudging and her ma was saying an old chant to pertect us from the evil eye on our journey. Reckon that really works?

They had paid their fee and now they sat, waiting on the train of fifty-four wagons to slowly unwind itself and head west. Many of the pioneers had painted their wagon boxes a grey-blue and the wheels bright red. Matched with the white canvas stretched over the frame, they looked almost patriotic.

B. F. laughed at some of the writing people had printed on their wagon canvases. He pointed and read them aloud for Mr. Fitzwater. Last Gasp. The 11th Commandment – Mind Your Own Business. 2000 Miles or Bust. Dreams of Gold. Oregon or Else. Prairie Boat. To the Willamette, Dammit.

B. F. was heartened to see Paddy Dowd riding by on a lop-eared mule. "Top of the morning to ye, B. F. I see you've changed animals. 'Tis a fine looking pony yer riding."

B. F. waved. "Did the ladies appreciate your haircut?"

Paddy couldn't resist the opportunity and reined in his mule. "They were lovely, they were!" He pulled off his slouch hat, stood in his stirrups, and bowed slightly in the saddle in the direction of Mary and Jane. "I see fortune has been kind to you also, lad."

Mary couldn't help but grin. "Cheeky Irishman!"

It was already half past seven. Del had told them to stay in the wagon track for a mile or so, then hold up and wait for everybody to catch up at the top of the hill beyond OK Creek. There was good new grass growing there, and their stock would be happy to stop. Mary was exasperated with what seemed to be no coordination whatsoever in getting the train moving. "If every mile takes this long, we'll still be on this trail next Christmas."

From his position standing beside his oxen, George looked back and half-smiled. "I expect you'd best grow some patience, Mary m'dear." He patted the rump of one of the animals. "I doubt these beasts understand the meaning of efficiency."

It was probably best that Mr. Fitzwater had his back turned when his wife raised an eyebrow and shot him a look.

B. F. hoped it would quickly get better as men and animals got used to one another, and sure enough, finally the wagon ahead of the Fitzwaters began to move. B. F. couldn't help but wonder if he should pinch himself. Was he really headed to California?

Fifteen

So Flat It Makes Your Head Hurt

Indian Territory 1849

As the last of the Coggins Train cleared the hill beyond West Port, B. F. looked back to see the first wagons of another train about a half mile back, and that train appeared to be every bit as big as their own. He wondered if they would be able to stay out front.

Del shouted to the group before they moved out again. "Look yonder at that train a comin'. We're the first out to Oregon this spring. The first train or two always has a good pick of firewood and a decent chance to find wild game. But in a week or so of reg'lar wagon traffic, the firewood is used up, and the game'll be long gone. So's if yer smart, you'll give it what for to stay out front."

Plenty of cries of, "Let's get goin." "Come on then." And despite the displeasure and resistance of mules and oxen, they moved forward again—still slowly, but not quite as tentatively as before. The first day's trip took them west by northwest with no obstacles to speak of, but any delay in the train's forward movement gave opportunity to the animals to taste the new grass sprouting along the trail.

All were grateful when they stopped around noon. A few folks started a fire long enough to heat up a coffee pot, but lunch for most was whatever happened to be left over from breakfast. B. F. hobbled his horse and let her graze near the wagon, but as soon as they finished a cold biscuit and maybe a piece of bacon, most people were ready to go again. They were definitely committed to staying ahead of the train just behind them. Shortly after mid-afternoon they trudged down a long hill, and could tell by the tree line that there was a fair-sized river ahead of them in a broad valley.

Rather than stop for the day when they reached the Kaw River, Coggins pushed on for another four miles, finally halting close to the south bank of the waterway. The train formed into a circle that was over a hundred and fifty feet in diameter, with the wagons pushed close together—the wagon tongue of one lying alongside the back wheels of the wagon in front.

The teams and other stock were turned loose inside the circle of wagons. The primary reason for the circle was not for a defensive posture against Indians but to keep the stock safe in an enclosed space. It would not take long for them to see the main disadvantage of this arrangement. The whole circle was loaded with fresh manure by morning, and required the casual stroller to be ever alert for their next step. Walking across the interior compound after dark frequently included a bootful of a fresh and unpleasant surprise.

Once supper fires were started, Coggins called the men together. "We'll be stayin' on the south side of the Kaw for about six more days, then we spend a day on the prairie, crossin' to the Vermillion. We'll water up again, then hit the dry prairie one more time and cross to the Big Blue. I'm tellin' this so's you'll know we won't spend more'n a day away from water for a long spell."

"They's plenty dangers out here. You'll see many a grave along this here Trail. Worse thing is the cholery. Next is crossin' these damned rivers. You best pay close attention when we're crossin'. Keep a sharp eye on yore young'uns. It's a awful thing for one of them wagons to roll over a young'un. Them big iron wheels just ain't forgivin'. They's vipers on this here Trail. Don't go playin with no snakes—they don't know yore playin'. And don't go gettin' kicked in the head by no mule neither. If it don't kill ye, you'll likely be stupid for the rest of yore days."

This was undoubtedly a speech Del felt obligated to give. He probably had no other occasion to speak so much at one time, and he certainly wasn't the kind of man who looked for opportunities to talk for the sake of talking.

A man from the back. "What about Indians?"

"I doubt you need to worry about injuns around here. Except that they'll steal anythin' you got. You can look for them to come inta camp. You might think they're just beggin', but it's somethin' to steal they're lookin' for. The ones you hafta worry about is them about eight weeks up the Trail. The Sioux an' Crow an' Pawnee—they's the ones that want yore animals *and* yore hair."

Spirits were high this first night out. Several men retrieved enough firewood from the tree line to set quite a blaze. People migrated to the big fire, and it took very little encouragement for a fiddler to begin to show off his skills. Another man came forward with a jew's harp, then a youngster proved that he could set fire to a banjo, then another fiddler. Mr. Fitzwater couldn't stand it and retrieved his old bagpipes from the bowels of the wagon. B. F. was surprised, as he didn't know the man had music in him. Quickly an area was cleared for dancing, and the orchestra was hard put to answer all the requests for favorite songs. As things died down a bit, B. F. was surprised yet again when Paddy walked over to the musicians and made a special request. They played a short, familiar refrain, and he shared his own gift with them as he began to sing John Newton's tune in a pure tenor voice.

> *Amazing grace, how sweet the sound*
> *That sav'd a wretch like me!*
> *I once was lost, but now am found,*
> *Was blind, but now I see.*

At this point, Mr. Fitzwater began to play his pipes.

> *'Twas grace that taught my heart to fear,*
> *And grace my fears reliev'd;*

How precious did that grace appear,
The hour I first believ'd!

Thro' many dangers, toils and snares,
I have already come;
'Tis grace has brought me safe thus far,
And grace will lead me home.

The Lord has promis'd good to me,
His word my hope secures;
He will my shield and portion be,
As long as life endures.

Yes, when this flesh and heart shall fail,
And mortal life shall cease;
I shall possess, within the veil,
A life of joy and peace.

The earth shall soon dissolve like snow,
The sun forbear to shine;
But God, who call'd me here below,
Will be forever mine.

When the song was over, it felt like the last note of the pipes kind of hung in the air, as though static electricity was lifting the hairs across the back of your neck. Everybody realized this was the ideal end to a long-anticipated day, and they found their ways back to their wagons with hardly a word spoken. With the bonfire subdued, the crystal clear, moonless night revealed uncountable stars above their heads from horizon to horizon. As B. F. made his pallet, he heard Jane in the wagon above him, "It's a good sign to start a trip with an Irish voice, ain't it Pa?"

"'Tis, Janie girl. 'Tis indeed."

The days became predictable. Up at daylight for breakfast, clean up and load, get the teams yoked, wait on the wagon ahead of you to move forward, travel until noon, break for lunch, keep going until about an hour and a half before dark, have supper, clean up, listen to stories and music, and sleep hard. Two men stood guard all night, rotating this responsibility with others every three hours.

The train progressed an average of twenty miles a day in good, flat country with the river just a short distance away. Their pace would soon slow considerably as they forded rivers and drove the animals up and down steep grades. All in all, a train would wind up averaging fifteen miles a day for the entire trip. The monotony of it all was hard to put aside. The driver spent the entire day staring at the backsides of their oxen, inhaling the dust of those ahead, and listening to the interminable squeaking of the wagon axles, the occasional beller of stock, and the constant verbal harangue of the teams by their masters.

Everything began to get very dirty—clothes, wagons, gear, everything. Most people put a curtain over the back opening of their wagon and tried to draw the canvas together in the front so that the driver only had an opening less than a foot wide to peer through.

B. F. alternated between riding his horse, driving the team, or just walking. The train's pace was so tedious that he had to force himself to walk slowly, as his normal walking speed was almost twice as fast as the progression of the train. Sometimes he put Ethan in front of him in the saddle. The little boy loved riding and talked almost continuously, if not to B. F. then to the pony. At least twice a day, Jane begged him to let her ride the horse. It had only taken her a short time to get very proficient in the saddle. Now sometimes B. F. would see her off in the distance, toward the head of the train with the horse at a canter and realize she was better at it than he was.

Other times, he, Jane, and Ethan would walk beside the wagon, with the little paint tied at the rear. Jane had started brushing the horse with her own hairbrush, and every evening the pony would stand still and rub her head on Jane's shoulder, begging for the brush.

The third evening out, B. F. decided to retrieve the book his aunt had given him and spend a little time with *The Three Musketeers*. He sat with his back to the fire and began the story. But within minutes, he was interrupted by three-year-old Ethan, who curled up beside him and asked what he was doing.

B. F. replied, "I'm reading this book."

"Me too."

"Can you read, Ethan?"

"Sure. You say the words out loud, and then I can say them inside my head."

Realizing he would apparently have an audience here in Indian Territory almost like the one he had back in Indiana with his cousin Sue, B. F. turned back to the beginning of the novel and began to read to Ethan. Before D'Artagnan met his first musketeer, B. F. was surprised to notice Jane and two other girls sitting right behind them, listening to him read.

The next evening, when D'Artagnan challenged his second musketeer, he and Ethan were accompanied by an audience of seven children and two women. And so it went on those evenings when he read to Ethan, he often had ten to fifteen others who just couldn't wait for the next chapter. Missus Broderick sat at the perimeter of the audience and would kindly help B. F. with a new word whenever it was necessary. But mostly she just sat and enjoyed the story.

When he eventually finished *The Three Musketeers*, Paddy loaned him a dog-eared copy of James Paulding's *The Lion of the West*, whose hero, Nimrod Wildfire, was modeled after the famous David Crockett. As the story progressed, there were more adults than children in his audience, and they hung on every word of the description of Wildfire's valiant deeds.

Later in the journey, Missus Broderick revealed that she had brought along the first fifteen articles of a serial by Francis Parkman, which had been published in 1847 and 1848 in Knickerbocker's Magazine, entitled "The Oregon Trail: Sketches of Prairie and Rocky Mountain Life." As the articles obviously matched much of what they were all seeing and experiencing, almost every member of the train listened to B. F.'s readings and sometimes could even compare what they heard with what they saw on previous days.

As they traveled across the countryside, there followed a great many penny novels in the evening, furnished by a number of travelers, such as *The Death Ship, Dead Man's Hollows,* and even *Hans of Iceland* by Mr. Victor Hugo. The result of these reading sessions was not only an entertained group of trekkers, but also a significant improvement in the reading and grammar skills of young B. F. Windes.

The sixth day out from West Port when they stopped for lunch, they could look across the Kaw River and see a much smaller creek entering from the north. Coggins rode back along the line of wagons. "This here's the crossin'. The Vermillion River is straight there. We'll be crossin' right above and stayin' on the west bank headed north for another day or so. We're lucky it ain't rained in a week, so the passage oughta go easy."

He shouted to the first wagon before it entered the river. "This here water is only two foot deep, but it might get in yore wagon. Be sure yore vittles is high and dry. Head them damned beasts at an angle upstream, and keep 'em movin. You let 'em stop, and them wheels'll sink in that sand and muck. You'll be diggin' for sure then."

The first wagons had a fairly easy time of it, but the last half of the train was following in the new ruts of the preceding wagons, and three of them needed help from other men to reach the other side. The crossing took four hours and they only traveled another couple of hours before stopping for the night.

Within minutes of getting campfires going, there was a shout. "Mr. Coggins—Off to the north—looks like wild Injuns comin' in."

Coggins walked out to the perimeter to view the rag-tag group. "Them's just Kaw squaws. Remember what I said about stealin'— them Kaws is good at it. Watch yore cook pots, and keep 'em out of yore wagons."

The four women were each wrapped in threadbare trade blankets and had apparently not seen a bar of soap in a very long time. Their hair appeared to have been oiled or greased some time in the relatively recent past, and they strolled into camp as though they were walking down the streets of St. Louis. They seemed to feel no embarrassment at walking up to several women and touching their clothing, then making some sort of remark among themselves—perhaps envious, maybe derogatory. The Indian women kept trying to maneuver in such a way as to look into the back of wagons, but people were wary and kept between the women and their provisions.

Missus McCreave was always the first to have her supper cooked, but this night her industrious habit would not serve her well. When she pulled the coals off her dutch oven, the Indian women were quick to hold their hands out in front of them for a hot biscuit. There was an awkward moment when Missus McCreave realized that there was no way out. She was going to have to give up her biscuits and fix another batch later for her family. They also looked to see if any more food was being prepared, but no other pots were on her fire. No thank you's were said. The women merely accepted the biscuits, turned on their heels, and left at the same methodical, unhurried pace as they had arrived.

It was unsettling. Mary Fitzwater had never hesitated to feed people that were needier than her family back in Tennessee, but this was different. She had enough food to get her family to Oregon. She didn't have enough to feed Indians—or anybody else—along the way. She resolved to refuse if she was put in a similar situation. The more she thought about it, the more she decided to speak out.

When they gathered around later that evening, she stood up. "I think we best not feed any more Indians. Once we start, those we fed'll tell the whole countryside. Before you know it, we'll be feedin' all of them, and we'll shortly find our ownselves outa vittles long before we see Oregon."

Coggins agreed. "The woman's right. You best say no before it gets outa hand. I seen a whole village foller a train for a week once. The people on the train felt sorry for 'em for a couple days, but by the end of the week, they was ready to shoot 'em all just to get rid of 'em." There was no objection from the travelers, but the proof of their will would likely be tested.

The next day began a bit warmer, and some hoped for fine weather. Mary Fitzwater's ague had a different forecast. "Rain's a comin' soon." Mr. Fitzwater had been witness to too many of her successful predictions to question.

His response was simple. "You and Janie use that tarp to get the stores wrapped tight in the wagon, B. F., and check the ropes on the canvas. Make sure they're snugged up."

As the train moved away from the river and the line of trees disappeared into the distance, B. F. was amazed at how bare and treeless the prairie was. It seemed to go on and on as far as he could see. The distance, and the sameness, almost hurt his brain. The day wore on like others before it, and they made good time on the rolling land until about five o'clock in the afternoon, when Coggins brought them to a halt. "Those clouds are gettin' blacker and comin' faster. We best stop here and get everthin' tied down. Get the wagons in close so the stock will stay put. Don't start cookin' 'til yer ready for a blow."

B. F. decided to hobble his pony while Jane gathered two good armloads of firewood and stashed it under the wagon.

Within minutes of them stopping for the night, the wind began to blow hard enough that the wagon canvas began to slap and pop under the strain. Rain came in fast and blowing sideways. The sound began to change as hail started popping against the wagons. Everybody headed for cover, and within a minute, the animals were bellowing and braying as the hail grew to the size of quarters. Mary pulled Ethan and Jane down on the wagon bed and lay on top of them, protecting them in case the hail penetrated the wagon canvas.

B. F. looked out from under the wagon, looking for his horse, but he was so low to the ground, he couldn't see her. All the stock had bunched up at the east side of the circle with their heads down and their backs to the wind.

Within another minute, it was over. The wind turned around from the north and it stopped raining. People gradually emerged from their wagons to find the ground completely covered with hail, some as big as hickory nuts with the hulls on. A few wagons had holes in the canvas, and several of the animals had visible cuts on their backs. The temperature suddenly seemed a good ten or fifteen degrees colder than it had been when they stopped for the day.

B. F. crawled out from under the Fitzwater wagon. He had held one of Jane's mattresses over his head during the storm and had only gotten hit on the lower legs a couple of times. Neither spot was bleeding, but he knew he'd have a couple of bruises in the morning. Jane came out of the wagon about the same time.

They found his horse wedged between two mules. The mare was still shaking when he got his hands on her. In the dim light, he didn't think there was any damage, but they stayed there for several minutes, talking to the horse and stroking her neck.

Coggins saw them and walked over. "Hail is hard on the stock. I seen it get big as a silver dollar once, and I hear it can get big as apples. If that happened, we'd all likely be bad hurt. We best call it a day."

Sixteen

You'll See The Elephant Soon Enough

Indian Territory 1849

Morning brought the challenge of crossing the Black Vermillion River. From the looks of the water, it would be the biggest hazard they had faced yet. Coggins stood in the middle of the wagons. "Empty yer water barrels on this side of the river. You'ns can fill 'em again once yer across. Those that're able oughta walk across. Get yer vittles high and dry."

The settlers couldn't help but see the group of small wooden crosses in the ground on the other side of the river, near the crossing point. One woman elbowed her husband, and he spoke up, "Mr. Coggins, shouldn't we wait 'til the river falls some?"

"This here river runs high purty near all spring. We might be waitin' 'til June for low water. Just do what yer told and you'll be all right."

Once the train started across, Mr. Fitzwater took Mary by the hand and waded the river with her. He returned for Ethan, carrying him in his arms, and then Jane. "What about you, B. F.?"

"I'll stay with my horse. We'll cross when you take the wagon through."

The water was lapping right at the bottom of the wagons as they crossed. The fifth wagon stopped square in the middle of the river. The man driving used his whip without let up but made no ground. Coggins was back in the water. "Lay that whip by Mr. Cooper. Them beasts won't pull no harder if they're in a strut. Yore wagon is settin' down in the water more than the others. What kinda load you carryin'?"

"How about rigging up another team to pull me out?"

Coggins looked in the back of his wagon. "Dammit, man. You got a cast iron cookstove in that wagon. You can either set there 'til the cows come home or you can throw the stove out. We ain't pullin' yore stove across this river."

Mrs. Cooper hollered to her husband from the bank. "Clyde Cooper, if you throw that stove in the water, you can forget about me cookin' a decent meal for you in Oregon."

Coggins spoke again. "Make up yer mind, man. You gonna see that elephant purty soon."

Mr. Cooper looked at his wife, then gave Coggins a pitiful look, but made no move toward the back of the wagon. Coggins threw Cooper a look of disgust and motioned toward the bank. "Next wagon, come on through on his upstream side."

The following wagons seemed to make good progress as they pulled around the stalled rig, but the wagon directly in front of George Fitzwater also seemed to ride low in the water. When it drew even with Mr. Cooper, it too stuck fast.

Coggins didn't even speak to the driver but went directly to the rear of the wagon. "Johnston, you got a settee in the back of yer wagon. Do you'ns think we're headed for a damned tea party? You two done blocked the whole crossin'. Either you lighten them loads or we'll do it for ye. And once we start, we might not stop with just the settee and the cookstove." He pointed to the wagons waiting to cross behind them.

Cooper climbed into the Johnston wagon, and between the two of them, they pitched the big settee into the water behind the wagon. They then had to get in the water and move it far enough downstream to keep from blocking the crossing.

Cooper then looked at his wife and threw up his hands. He and Johnston struggled with the iron cookstove but were unable to lift it over assorted gear in the back of the wagon. Mr. Fitzwater told B. F. to hold the reins to his oxen, and he waded in to help. Between the three of them, they pushed the three-hundred-pound, shiny black cookstove into the river. There were a few cheers from the people still waiting to cross, but the look on Miz Cooper's face promised long evenings of silence in the immediate future.

Mr. Cooper then returned to his wagon seat as both Johnston and Fitzwater pushed while his oxen pulled. The wagon began to move slowly forward and finally reached the far bank. Johnston's wagon followed suit.

Once the crossing was cleared, Mr. Fitzwater didn't hesitate. He took his team straight in, and across. B. F. went in directly behind him. His horse had to swim for a few feet in midstream, then felt the bottom again, and crossed with no problem. The remaining wagons crossed as well, but not before a determined man toward the rear pitched a large mahogany chiffarobe out of his wagon before entering the water. This was accompanied by an ear-splitting shriek and a hollered. "Yer a true ass, Gilead Bledsoe!"

Knowing they had another dry day waiting on them, Coggins held them on the west bank of the Black Vermillion. "Fill them barrels up again just above where we crossed. We got fifteen miles of dry road 'til we strike the Big Blue River tomorrow evenin', so we'll be stayin' here 'til mornin'. There's a passable fishin' hole about a hunnert yards up river. Be sure you take yer guns."

B. F. turned to Del. "What did you mean back there about seeing the elephant? Are there really elephants out here?"

Del laughed. "That's just an expression for the day when all these folks finally see just how hard it's gonna be to cross this whole country. It may not happen anytime soon—maybe not 'til we get in the mountains. But they'll all come to that point. They don't believe it when they hear about it. But one o' these days, everybody finds out that this here trip requires more than what a human being ought to be asked to do. They only believe it when the day comes that they see the elephant for themselves."

"Have you ever seen the elephant, Del?"

"Ever time I been across, and sometimes more than once."

The next morning brought tragedy. Missus Campbell found Del Coggins before breakfast to tell him. Normally a pretty, petite woman, today her eyes were swollen and her face was twisted with fear. Her husband Liam and her twelve-year-old son Robert, each had terrible diarrhea. They had both wakened with it about four o'clock. Now they were pale as a sheet, and both had been through a rigor that had made the entire wagon shake.

"Mr. Coggins, the water is just runnin' through them. They must have had twenty passages apiece, and it's only gettin' worse. Their skin is so dry it feels like clay. If you press on it, the skin won't snap back." She started weeping again and hurried back to her wagon. She couldn't stay away from them, they were too sick.

Del followed along behind her as she started back to her wagon. "Ma'am, we hafta keep movin'. Cover em with blankets in back of yore wagon. Make em drink water, and give em a thunder pot. And ma'am, yer gonna hafta hold yer wagon back and stay about a hunnert yards behind us. Could be the cholery. Bless ye ma'am."

"They're too sick to travel, Mr. Coggins." She unconsciously twisted a handkerchief in her hands. "Maybe it's just the flux. Please don't leave us here."

Del got no closer and retreated to his campfire. He sat there for a few minutes, mulling over his limited options. Directly, he and Paddy walked back to the Broderick wagon. Del hated to call for the woman. She had almost as many chin whiskers as he did, and he couldn't seem to stop staring at them when he spoke to her. It couldn't be helped. "Missus Broderick, we got a problem. Ye said ye was a midwife."

"Sure did, Mr. Coggins, you havin' a baby?" She grinned a brown-toothed smile at her joke, at least until she paid more attention to his face. "What is it?"

Del had not seen her smoking before, and it surprised him. He knew he was old fashioned about some things, as he just didn't like to see women smoke. She was working on a long stemmed corn cob pipe, stuffed with tobacco she had brought with her from North Carolina. "It could be the cholery. Mr. Campbell and his boy are real sick.

I ain't sure why the Missus don't have it too. You have any experience with cholery?"

"Well, Mister Coggins, good judgment generally comes from experience, but a lotta that comes from what you learn from bad judgment. I only know that cholera usually means the water is bad. We all filled our barrels at the same place. We ain't sick. You ain't sick. I think you need to go to every wagon and see if anybody else is sick."

Del nodded his head and he and Paddy started their rounds in opposite directions. Del was beginning to feel like they were safe until he reached the Connor wagon. He got no response to his call and stepped on a wagon spoke to peer into the front of the wagon. The smell of sickness was fierce. Missus Connor called out weakly, but her husband made no sound. He jumped backward off the wheel in fear. Had he breathed in any vapors that would infect him too? He breathed out so forcibly that he started coughing.

Paddy made it almost around his half of the circle without incident until he reached the wagon occupied by Mr. O'Rourke and his black slave, Rupert. If possible, the smell was worse here. The slave appeared to be lying in his own foulness and seemed to be dead. He banged on the wagon with a stick and called out for O'Rourke. There was no answer. It was only then that he noticed O'Rourke curled into a ball under the wagon beside his slave. They had died together.

After finishing their inquiry, Del went back to Missus Broderick. "It appears to be in two other wagons. Two or three are already dead. I been around the cholery several times. It always comes on fast and kills purty quick. I cain't figger why ain't more of us sick."

"We need to talk to Missus Campbell. You get all the wagons with no sickness pulled off from them that's infected. Tell them stay away from the wagons with sickness. And tell them don't drink no water."

Missus Broderick walked over to the Campbell wagon and called to her. Missus Campbell came out but was crying. "My Robbie is dead. He didn't last no time at all. His pa is still hanging on."

"Ma'am, I'm sure sorry about yore boy. They's two other wagons with the sickness. I need to ask if yer men had dealings last night with the Connors an' Mr. O'Rourke?"

"Yes, Mr. O'Rourke invited us to eat supper last night. His colored boy, Rupert, caught some perch and catfish. He said they had more than they could eat. Are they sick too?"

"Yes. What did you have to drink? And what did they eat or drink that you didn't?"

"Why, we all drank hot coffee. We ate the same thing." She thought for a minute. "Except for some potatoes—I offered to bring some boiled potatoes for the meal. But I didn't fix enough to go around. The men were all so hungry that I didn't have any. Are you saying I fed them poison taters?"

"Where did the water come from that you used?"

"Why, I used water from a bucket that Robbie brought me. The taters were too hot so I poured a little cool water on 'em after they were cooked. I think he got it down below the crossing where it was easy to climb down the bank."

"Boil some water in a pot and pour it in that bucket whilst it's still bubblin'. I think that water is what done it."

"Oh my God! I been giving my husband water from that bucket for his fever!" She hurried back to her wagon—crying again—with realization that her husband was lost too.

By the time the wagons were hitched and pulled away from the three that were quarantined, rumor was about to be replaced by panic. Del got them quieted, and Missus Broderick stood on the front of her wagon so she could be heard. "We got the cholera in three wagons. They all ate supper together last night. All are sick or dead except for Miz Campbell. She don't have no sign of the illness. The only thing she didn't do that the rest of them did was that she didn't use any water from the river down below our camp."

Del stepped in, "Did any of you'ns draw water fer yore barrels or canteens from below the camp? I told you to always use the water above camp."

Nobody said a word. "This ain't no time to hold back. If ye did, ye could git the cholery." Still no answer. "I'm gonna take that as a no. From now on, don't never draw your water below camp."

Mary Fitzwater, though diminutive in stature, spoke with a big voice. "My mam taught me a bit about doctorin'. She told me the best medicine for cholera is the juice of an onion. If you got onions, take a couple spoonfuls a day. Sometimes that works—at least afore you get real sick."

"We got no onions—would wild onions work?"

"It's bound to be better than no onions a'tall."

Missus Campbell walked over to the gathering, obviously in terrible grief. "My husband and my son are dead." She stood there with her head down, weeping. No one would come close enough to her to offer any real comfort.

Although a bulky woman, Missus Broderick quickly hopped down from her wagon and came to her. "Come with me, sweetie. We got work to do." They walked off. "You're gonna take off them clothes and burn 'em, then get in that river and scrub yourself good. We'll find some clothes you can wear."

Coggins took over again. "We need to save at least one of them wagons. It appears the O'Rourke wagon will be the one to use. The dead was under it, not in it. One of you men travelin' by yerself can drive it for Miz Campbell. I need volunteers to pull what ain't been touched by sickness and bile out of them other wagons. Then we'll put the dead in the two wagons and set 'em afire. We don't wanna bury that cholery. It might seep back in the river and get the next train. We'll use them spare two teams when we need extra pull. For sure, we'll need it soon enough."

Mary Fitzwater spoke up. "Mister Coggins, if nobody else wants it, I'd like to have the canvas off the wagons."

The sign they left behind read Cholery in River Down Below. It was painted on a board from one of the afflicted wagons and nailed to a cottonwood tree. Perhaps other lives in other trains could be saved.

Seventeen

The Turd Collector

Indian Territory 1849

My story. On April 30 year of 1849

We lost six travelers today to the cholera. Once they got sick they didn't last any time at all. The whole train is terrible quiet today. Just the other day I asked Del if we were all going to make it across. He just looked sad and told me there ain't nothin' certain in this life. We didn't bury them. Del said to burn the bodies. I guess we all know it could have been any of us lying back there.

Ever time we top a low hill, it seems that a body can see twenty miles in every direchun. And it all looks the same, no matter which way you turn. The grass is green as green can be, and waves all day in this wind that never seems to stop blowing.

The prairie grass was at least a foot high, and the stock ate greedily during every stop. Each wagon used their water barrel to provide fluids for their animals during the dry runs. It was early May, but the afternoon sun, shining right in their faces as they traveled to the west, forced them to pull their hat brims down low over their eyes. From the top of a rise, they could see thousands upon thousands of small brown spots on the prairie ahead. B. F. rode up close to Del. "What are all those brown splotches over there?"

"That's prairie firewood."

"Firewood?"

"Yep. Them's buffalo chips. Another four, five days we'll all be burnin' chips. Ain't no trees to speak of once that Little Blue River turns west."

"You mean we'll be using buffalo pies to cook with?"

"Won't be long you'll be glad to find 'em."

They struck the Big Blue River just after dusk. The morning light revealed that the river was too high and too fast to be crossed here. They kept to its eastern bank for two days until they finally reached a place where it was obvious that many wagons had gone before them. Del advised that they would cross the next morning.

The crossing went well enough, and the two extra brace of oxen came in handy in pulling heavier wagons across. Another twenty mile dry run the next day across to the Little Blue River, a crossing there while the river was still little more than a creek, then two days traveling northwesterly on the west bank of the river. True to Del's prediction, trees were few and far between, and what ones they saw were spindly.

The next morning, Del gave instructions on the finer points of buffalo pie selection. "Make sure they're dry. Believe it or not, the dry ones don't have much smell, and they kindle up purty quick. Gen'ly a good cookfire'll take twenty or so of them big chips. Ya'll won't see hardly no wood a'tall for the better part of six weeks. Might as well start pickin' up them pies, you'ns will be needin' em for supper."

The job of turd collector for the Fitzwater wagon fell to B. F. He longed for a small wagon or a wheelbarrow so he wouldn't have to make so many trips back and forth to the train. He could really only carry a maximum of four pies at a time, and usually would have to go fifty yards or more from the wagon track in order to find nice, dry ones. The families toward the front of the train always had first pick of the pies closest to the track.

After about ten trips with armloads of buffalo chips, B. F. remembered the way the Indians back in West Port had been hauling furs. The next morning, he spied a lone Osage orange tree along the river, and he and Mr. Fitzwater cut three limbs to build a travois. Mary volunteered a six-foot long piece of her extra canvas to accommodate the load. After that, B. F.'s collection job only required about thirty minutes a day. Mary constructed two canvas bags that hung on the outside of either side of the wagon when filled with buffalo chips. At least this separated the lovely load from her family's food and belongings.

It was B. F.'s goal to gather forty chips a day—enough for both supper and the next morning's breakfast. But he tried to keep about thirty extra in case of rain. It didn't take him long to figure out that trying to pick up wet buffalo pies was not his favorite job.

Nastier still were the mosquitoes that seemed to come out of nowhere after a rain shower. The only way to get clear of them even temporarily was to stand in the campfire smoke. So the choice seemed to be either get covered up by mosquitoes, or choke on turd smoke.

They had been moving west by northwest for several days, along the south bank of the Little Blue River. Wildflowers were blooming in huge clusters of white and yellows and literally every shade of red. They had actually feasted on strawberries for three nights in a row after B. F. and Jane, and even Ethan, found patches along the river. The berries were very small—half the size of the strawberries back in Indiana—but very tasty.

The Little Blue continued to get smaller and smaller as they approached its source, until finally one evening Del advised them that tomorrow would involve another long dry run up to the Platte. In fact, it was a distance of about twenty-five miles, so they should plan on one entire day and a piece of another away from any water source except what they could carry. The river was now little more than a trickle, so it required some real effort for everyone to top off their water barrels and canteens that evening.

By the time supper was completed, a fire, and perhaps a second were sighted way off on the prairie to the north and northeast. There was very little wind, which made it impossible to predict what direction the fire might take. Coggins spoke to the lookouts. "Ya'll keep a sharp eye on them fires. We ain't got no river to hide behind here. A fire could jump that little crick without no problem, and we'd have to fight."

About three o'clock, B. F. was awakened by what must have been thunder, but then he realized that it had to be close because he could hear it better when he put his ear on the ground. The odd thing was, it didn't stop and start, it just thundered more or less continuously. In fact, the ground was trembling beneath his straw mattress.

About the time he was well awake, he heard Del Coggins voice at the back of the wagon. "Hey George. You awake? There's a herd of buffalo passin' maybe a half mile north. We figure on shootin' four or five for the train. You game?"

"Let me get my boots."

B. F. was fully dressed, and waiting at the back of the wagon when Mr. Fitzwater came out. "Can I go with you?"

"I'll not say no, but I've never done this before. I hear those beasts are big as an ox. It might be dangerous."

"I'll stay right with you. I promise not to get in the way. But I've got to see those buffalo."

"I know what you mean. I have to see for myself. Come on then, but stay close."

Eight men were assembled at the north side of the camp. Coggins was speaking in a low voice. "Wind is in our favor. Only about a quarter moon. Prob'ly that prairie fire got em movin'. Some of them bulls can take a lot of lead before they go down. Anyhow, the cows is the best eatin'." He looked at B. F., winked, and took off at a fast walk.

By the time they walked a half-mile, the sound of the hooves and horns was tremendous. The group topped a slight rise and what they saw in the draw below was astounding. Thousands and thousands of buffalo spread out before them about three hundred yards away and extended to the horizon. Apparently, the beasts had finished their stampeding, and now various groups of them had begun to feed on the little bluestem grass, while others seemed to be slowly beginning to settle down.

"We cain't wait 'til they get quieted down. Reckon they're too busy to notice us. Each man get about twenty steps apart, then we're gonna stay low and go slow. Get to about fifty yards, pick yore target and shoot. No point in no signal. Cain't hear nothin' anyways."

B. F. and Mr. Fitzwater eased forward in the line for the better part of five minutes. They could barely see the outlines of the men on either side of them. B. F. figured they were close enough at least twice, and would swear later he could actually smell them before Mr. Fitzwater finally knelt down. The animals were all huge, but in the dark, it was difficult to tell a bull from a cow. B. F. was staring at what he thought was a good target. He jumped when Mr. Coggins fired. "Jesus, Mary, and Joseph! Don't know if I missed or what." He reloaded. "Here. It's your turn, son."

"I couldn't take your gun, I. . . ." B. F. started.

"Take a shot. You'll never learn any younger!" He handed B. F. the rifle. "I put in just a touch more powder."

The animals seemed to be milling around more. Possibly they were getting ready to run again. B. F. steadied the musket across one knee, slowly let his breath out and squeezed. The cow jumped forward, but maybe he had missed too. He started to reload when he saw her knees buckle and she went down. Mr. Fitzwater gave a shout and slapped him on the shoulder. B. F. finished reloading and handed the gun to Mr. Fitzwater. This time his cow went down almost instantly. They both stood up and hollered just about the time the herd bolted straight away from them to the north.

There were seven buffalo on the ground. They all moved back toward Del. "You'ns done real good. We're in for some fine eatin'. Paddy, you and B. F. go back and wake up the camp. Tell them to move the wagons up here. We'll start the butcherin' and skinnin'."

They had tasted very little meat beyond bacon and an occasional rabbit or prairie chicken since they left West Port. The hundred and forty trekkers made every effort to make up for the last month. By mid-morning, they had all eaten until they were absolutely glassy-eyed.

According to Del, the prime cuts were considered to be the tongue, the hump, and the liver, but most folks went after what they knew best—the tenderloin. Despite their efforts, the carcasses they left behind were still replete with good cuts of meat. They only had time to smoke and salt down a very small percentage of the remaining meat over a low, slow fire. When they finally pulled off toward the Platte, many an eye looked with a bit of shame on all the roasts they were leaving behind. "Next time we oughta only shoot three," remarked Mr. Fitzwater. "Never wasted so much meat in my life."

By the time they reached the Platte in the early afternoon of the following day, their oxen were in bad need of water. The contents of the water barrels had been exhausted that morning. They formed up their circle of wagons and then drove their teams into the river, not only for a long drink but simply to cool off. For mid-May, it had been an extremely hot two days.

After another fifty miles, the train stood opposite Fort Kearny, which was situated on the north bank of the Platte. The river was wide here, but for the most part, filled in with silt and sand bars. Del proclaimed it "too thick to drink and too thin to plow." Thankfully, the water was shallow, and they were able to cross with no distress.

Mr. Fitzwater sighted a group of ramshackle buildings. Most were constructed of sod and a couple of wood. They seemed to be built around a flat area that was devoid of all grass. He waved down a soldier on the side of the trail. The man's uniform had definitely seen better days. "Hello, friend, how far might it be to Fort Kearny?"

"Waal, if you'd jump down off that prairie boat, you'd be smack dab in the middle of the Fort Kearny Parade Ground."

"But where is the fort?"

"Ain't no real fort. Just them buildings yonder. Say, friend, you wouldn't have any whisky would ye? I'd pay a dollar for a bottle."

"So would I! Can't help you there."

As they passed along the dirty, unkempt road, Mary looked at her husband. "You mean this place is supposed to protect us from the Injuns? Why, the sodbusters we got on this wagon train are better men than them soldiers. I sure hope nobody told the Injuns what they're up against here."

Del called the train to a halt just as they passed the fort's buildings. "Kearny got supplies they're willin' to sell if you need anythin'. Miz Campbell, you'll be safe here if yer wantin' to go back. West Port is about three hundred sixty miles southeast. Anybody else wanta turn around? Its three hundred miles on to Fort Laramie. That's the next civilized place out here."

Missus Campbell spoke up. "I got nothing to go back to." She smiled at Paddy. "Mister Dowd has been a true gentleman to look after me. I reckon I'm going on to Oregon."

Paddy grinned at Del as he pushed his hat high on his forehead. "I'm guessing ye didn't know ye was in the company of a gentleman, did ye?"

Del shook his head at the thought. "Awright. We'll sit right here for an hour if anybody needs stores. This here fort has fair prices. If you'ns need anythin', get it now. From here on out, there ain't nothin' fair about what you hafta pay for goods."

Eighteen

He's Still Dead

Indian Territory 1849

Stopping that evening some ten miles beyond Fort Kearney, Del had a different conversation about Indians. "This here is Pawnee land. In about two weeks it'll be Cheyenne and then Sioux. I think you seen today that the cavalry ain't comin' to yer rescue. Them Pawnee is some serious hoss thiefs. And the Sioux might be even worse. We got to keep a sharp eye now. Hafta double the watch from two men to four of a night. Nobody strays away from the train night or day. Hunters go out in pairs."

Then began a series of days along the north bank of the Platte. The river bottom land was extremely flat, presenting virtually no obstacles to travel. The only variation was some eighteen days later when the South and North Platte Rivers joined as one.

They found buffalo two more times, and although they talked about not wasting meat, every man on the train wanted his chance to kill one of the beasts. So each time they left behind several thousand pounds of uneaten meat. And after the first attempts at skinning, they simply left the hides on the carcasses and harvested only the choicest cuts.

Unbeknownst to the train, the remains were not wasted, for no sooner had their wagon dust disappeared over the horizon, than Pawnee women seemed to appear from nowhere out of the ravines and low valleys. They quickly fell to work harvesting the meat and skinning the animals. But they did this with great disdain for their benefactors.

Every day the train continued to pass graves. Some appeared to have been dug up. One of the men asked Del if coyotes or wolves had dug them up. "Its most likely them two-legged wolves. If you stick a cross on a grave, that just marks the spot for the Injuns. They come along and dig 'em up for the clothes and the boots. Best thing you can do is not make the graves too easy to find."

Two evenings later, the train made camp within sight of two substantial landmarks along the trail. The Courthouse and Jail Rocks rose up out of the prairie in the distance on the opposite side of the river. Although they appeared to be close at hand, Coggins advised that they were still a good day's journey away.

Just after dusk, one of the lookouts spied a wildfire off to the north, and it seemed to be fairly close. Worse, although the wind was mild, it was blowing straight in their direction. Within a few minutes, another orange haze was spotted to the northwest.

Del asked Paddy and another man to get down to the river and check to see if there was a decent place to cross. Within a few minutes, they were back. "The bank is far too treacherous here, Del. Jeb went upstream and I meself went down. 'Tis no good crossing anywhere close, I'm sad to say."

Del hollered for a meeting. "That fire is comin' our way. We're gonna hafta fight it. It looks to be here in not more'n an hour or so. I need every man to take a hoe, pick, or shovel and get about twenty yards out front of the wagons and start clearin' prairie grass and sage brush at least twenty yards wide. Every woman start haulin' water from the river to the space in front of the wagons. Get every piece of spare canvas or rags you got and soak em in water. When that fire gets close, everybody grab wet rags an' get after the fire. Find a bandana or kerchief and tie it over yer mouth so you don't choke. We need at least four men that cain't work to stand guard. Now get movin'. Yer life is in danger!"

Before Mr. Fitzwater could pull a shovel out, B. F. already had a hoe in his hand, and they hurried together to the work detail. Junior Arbogast put his hand on B. F.'s shoulder. "Boy, you best help the women with the water. This here is a man's work."

Mr. Fitzwater spoke before B. F. could answer. "I reckon he's man enough."

Almost everybody flew to work. Two women herded the smaller children to one side of the wagon circle to get them out of the way and as far from the smoke as possible. Two other women seemed to retreat into the shadows by their wagons. They agreed that they had not been raised to engage in that kind of physical labor.

Missus Broderick spied them standing there with their arms folded and strode up to them. "Ladies, we're in a fight for our lives here. If I come back here an' see you'ns standin' around again, so help me Jesus, I'm fixin' to slap the stupid right out of you." She didn't wait for a response but trotted toward the river with her buckets.

"Can you believe that country woman talked like that to us?"

The other woman didn't answer directly but kept looking toward the river. "She'll be back here in just a minute. Maybe we better get busy."

There were eighty men struggling with clearing the prairie grass. The roots were deep, but they knew that their survival depended on what they would do over the next hour or so. Each man was separated from his neighbor by about twenty feet. The hoes and shovels were flying, but the cleared space grew very slowly.

The women and older children carried bucket after bucket from the river, up the steep embankment, across the wagon circle, and to where the men were working. Each of them was responsible for a ten-by-sixty-foot section from the point where the clearing started back toward the wagons.

The fire was close enough that the acrid smoke began to burn their eyes and throats. Most of them had donned their bandannas and kept them as wet as possible, but everybody was coughing. From time to time, one of the men would have to retreat behind the wagons to get a drink of water before they could continue working.

B. F. was to the right of Mr. Fitzwater, bent over at the waist, and slashing a hoe into the prairie grass. The smoke was blowing directly toward them, and the old shirt Mary had tied around his face was only marginally effective in keeping him from coughing constantly. In the worst way, he wanted to turn around and run. Run right past the wagons. Run all the way across the river, away from the smoke and the heat. Run!

But he looked at Mr. Fitzwater, resolutely bent over his shovel, then to Mr. Williams on his left side. Neither man wavered but just kept their head down while they worked. B. F. knew he couldn't stop until they did.

The cleared space was expanding, but was it enough to create a fire break? Del ordered the women to use the water in their water barrels to save the trip back and forth to the river. "And throw a few buckets on yore wagons to get em good'n wet."

He heard a shout from the east perimeter. "Injuns!" Followed by two muskets firing. At least ten painted Pawnee jumped through the wagon circle and ran toward the stock. Del fired his pistol almost point blank into one of them's chest. He heard the two rifles from the other side firing as the Indians grabbed at the animals to try and get them to stampede. B. F. saw what he would describe later as a blurred bucket, as Missus Broderick hit one of them in the back of the head with a wooden bucket full of water. The man went down like he'd been kicked by a mule. There was a snort from Missus Broderick. "Dadgum Injun made me bust my pipe stem!"

Del was fighting now hand to hand with a Pawnee wielding a steel hatchet. He remembered thinking, "Damned trade goods. He's gonna take my scalp with a trade good hatchet." Someone saved him by sinking a hoe in the top of the man's head. There was more shooting now—pistols. He saw one mule going through the circle, ridden by an Indian leaning low to keep from being a good target. But the quick assessment was that it appeared that was all they had lost.

One brave was surrounded by three men who had pistols in their hands. He tried to grab the Wingate girl, perhaps as a shield, but was shot dead before he could get her in front of him.

Del hollered. "They're comin' through us like a dose of salts through a widow woman! We need eight guards! Everybody else fight fire. Hurry!"

The roaring of the fire was so loud it made most communication impossible. Men retreated to the interior ring of where they had been clearing and kept at it, backing toward the wagons, throwing dirt behind them as fast as possible. The water kept coming until the barrels were dry. As the first flames began arriving at the cleared space, men used the wet canvas and rags to slap at the fire on the ground. It was all they could do to keep from choking. Their eyes were on fire with the smoke.

Del had to scream to be heard over the sound of the fire. He hollered repeatedly for everyone to get back. They started another bucket brigade to the river and back, throwing all the water on the wagons closest to the flames. Against all physical capacity, they kept going. Even the hardest man had to choke down his panic to keep from running. It seemed like hours, but within thirty minutes it was over. They had saved their wagons, their lives, and literally everything they owned.

B. F.'s hands were blistered from the hoe he had been using, and his eyes and throat felt like they were raw meat. Mr. Fitzwater's face was black with soot, and only his eyes were uncoated, giving him the appearance of a skinny raccoon. He put his hand on B. F.'s shoulder. "Let's you and me go see about our family."

Mary and Jane sported blisters as well—a result of hauling so many buckets that they had lost count. Both had witnessed Missus Broderick use her bucket on the Pawnee and were quick to tell B. F. and Mr. Fitzwater what had happened inside the wagon circle.

When they found Ethan, he was busy describing how he had chased the Injuns away. And according to an older girl, he had indeed thrown several rocks at them in the middle of the melee.

Mr. Fitzwater knelt down and pulled the little boy to him. It was hard to tell if his wet cheeks were from the smoke or gratitude that his family was safe. "That's my boy, Ethan. You sure showed 'em whose cow ate the cabbage!"

The night had taken its toll. Old man Flaherty had been killed by a Pawnee. He was one of the first guards to shoot, and had been felled by an arrow as he was trying to reload. William Jackson had died in the fire line. A couple of men had tried to talk him out of that kind of heavy work, but he wouldn't listen. The man who had been working next to him described what happened. "Old Will grabbed his chest, took no more'n two steps, and just fell dead. I pulled him off the line so's he wouldn't burn up, but it didn't do him no good. He's still dead."

One mule had been stolen, and a second one on the ground had been struck right in the ear by an errant bullet. There were six dead Pawnee. Del spoke to his charges. "You can betcha them prairie fires was set a'purpose by the Pawnee. The thievin' divils might try again. We cain't let our guard down."

My story. On June 12 year of 1849

I never seen so many brave men as I saw last night. The Pawnee set a prairie fire to keep us busy, then tried to steal our stock. The men from the train fought the fire right up to our wagons. The heat and the smoke were terrible bad. But not a single one of them run off. They just kept fighting. As for me, I tried not to let them see how scared I was.

Paddy rescued my pony when he hit a Pawnee on the top of his head with a shovel while he was trying to cut the hobble line. We lost two men and two mules in the fight.

Today we're passing some of the strangest rocks I ever saw. Del calls two of them the Courthouse and Jail Rocks. But off in the distance is one that is hard to describe. It looks to be a giant arrow shooting up from the plains. Del says it's the Chimney Rock. It seems just a couple of miles away, but he says there is two days of travel before we get there. I hope the trail comes close to it, as I intend to climb the Chimney as high as I can to see what I can see.

Nineteen

There Ain't No Good Choice

Indian Territory 1849

The train crossed easily to the south side of the North Platte. Over the last three weeks, they had gradually ascended to the high plains. The river was faster here but was not a difficult obstacle because it was already shallow in early June. Despite the relative ease of their crossing, there were four graves on the north bank, permanently testifying that even the Platte could be treacherous. Standing guard over the river was a discarded grandfather clock, which was leaning precariously against a hardy red cedar. The pendulum was missing. Whether taken by the owner or by a later visitor, that would remain unknown. But in that particular place, the rusted hands would always proclaim the time as a quarter past eleven.

The days were terrifically hot. One would think that the constant wind out of the west would make the heat a bit more bearable, but even the wind seemed to sear the skin. On this day, the wind was blowing straight into their faces, pushing all the dust from the wagons in front of them into their eyes, nose, mouth, ears, and even some locations you wouldn't expect to see dirt.

One afternoon, the iron rim on a dry, shrunken wagon wheel just rolled off the rim on the Fitzwater wagon. Del's advice was to remove the wooden wheel and roll it down to the river to soak so it would swell up enough to hold the rim.

Thankfully, it worked. So B. F. and Mr. Fitzwater walked along beside the wagon, keeping an eye on the other wheels, with their heads bent forward, kerchiefs over their faces, and axel grease smeared on their dry, split lips. "Son, if this wagon train is traveling only fifteen miles on a calm day, and this wind has got to be blowing at least thirty miles an hour, we might just get ourselves blowed all the way back to yesterday."

During the noontime break, Missus Broderick was approached by one of the unattached men. Most called him only by his nickname of "Polecat," which he had earned after a skunk sprayed him one evening when he walked into the brush to relieve himself. The poor man smelled like his name for three weeks. Finally, Mary Fitzwater had suggested he bathe in river mud, then spread a mixture of dried tomatoes and water all over his body, and leave it on for a full day before washing it off. Not only had Polecat been so grateful that he broke down and cried, but the whole train had been thankful as well.

Polecat's current problem had nothing to do with smell but rather with a terrible toothache. His lower jaw was swollen to at least twice normal size. He described his ailment. "This here tooth hurts so bad, I cain't chew no food at all. Fact, I can just barely sip water from a cup. Can you fix it, Missus Broderick?"

The problem was easy to locate, as the gum line around the faulty tooth was also swollen and inflamed. But just to be sure, Missus Broderick tapped each of the teeth on the left lower jaw with the butt end of a big metal spoon. When she struck on the second tooth from the rear, Polecat squalled like he'd been hit with a hot poker.

"You already sound like an old badger caught in a steel trap." She petitioned Del for six ounces of whisky, which she knew he kept for his own personal needs, then retrieved a stout pair of wire pliars from her husband's tools.

About thirty minutes after Polecat finished his medication, he was having significant difficulty walking and talking. "I'd really like s'more o' thet sour mash."

"Look here, Polecat—you're so drunk now you couldn't hit the ground with your hat."

He stumbled a bit before grabbing the wagon for support. "I beg to differ with you madam."

She sat him in a chair and had one of his friends hold his arms, while still another held his head still. "Polecat—you had plenty. Now let me see that tooth."

"It don't hurt near as bad now," he slurred, eyeing the pliars. "Mebbe I can just get by on soup. Fact is, I sorta have a fondness for soup."

"I'm gonna pull somethin' outa yore mouth with these pliars. If you don't be still, it might be that wiggly thing at the back of yore goozle."

Nobody would ever say that Missus Broderick was not a well-fleshed woman. In fact, it was difficult to consider that there was ever any reason for her to turn sideways—as she was just as broad one way as she was the other. The tooth was not the least bit anxious to come loose. But Missus Broderick was a mighty strong woman, and once she had hold of the tooth, she was determined to have it.

She began to gradually move the pliars in a back and forth motion, and Polecat tried to move his head in the same rhythm so she would exert minimal pressure on the tooth. But once his head began to sway with her, she reversed directions and went right when he went left. Polecat began to make a screeching sound that could only be described as a caterwaul—perhaps the strangeness of the sound had something to do with the pair of pliars that still remained jammed in his mouth.

Missus Broderick began to sweat—not just a dainty, womanly perspiration—but great rivulets of water ran down her forehead and dripped off her chin whiskers as she gripped and pulled and turned. She put a beefy knee against Polecat's scrawny chest to get better leverage while continuing to move the pliars back and forth. The men doing the holding were sweating as well, and perhaps not a small amount of their duress was due to the fact that Missus Broderick's dress had begun to ride up her substantial thigh within a few inches of their noses. It was the kind of sight that could haunt a man for years. As the hem of the dress continued its rise, both of the helpers closed their eyes tight at the prospect of coming nightmares.

When she saw the blood, Missus Broderick began to pull and rotate the pliars in earnest, knowing that the tooth was beginning to turn loose of the man. Finally, she felt the molar moving with her and began to slightly reduce the force of her efforts. She didn't want to yank it out so suddenly that she risked knocking half of his remaining teeth loose in the process. When it finally gave way, she raised the tooth high in the grip of the pliars for all to see. But Polecat could only slump forward in relief, as his holders gladly released their victim and quickly retreated to a safer place with far less exposure to things they wish they had not seen.

She wrapped a dried clove bud in a piece of wet muslin, packed the hole with the damp cloth, and instructed him to hold pressure on the area for a half hour. It was all Polecat could do to muster the strength to follow these simple instructions. In the following days, he would complain more about the knee-cap shaped bruise on his chest than his missing tooth. But sympathy was in short supply for anything less than terrible afflictions on the wagon train, and he was soon ignored.

Three days later they passed the massive Scotts Bluff. Because its base and the extensive rough ground extended all the way to the river, serving as an obstacle to wagon passage, it was necessary for the train to take a wide detour around the south side of the Bluff.

Two more days brought them to the Army's newest facility, Fort Laramie. The Laramie property had been purchased earlier in the year from a couple of traders. It had been the intention of the Army to then build a traditional, enclosed fort, but the realities of a lack of appropriate trees in the vicinity, money, and labor all contributed to what the travelers saw before them. Once again, they had to get used to the new definition of "fort" as Fort Laramie was no more than a series of buildings spread out across the prairie. There were no walls or impediments to siege whatsoever, except for the guns of the cavalrymen assigned there.

Two signs were nailed to a solitary post; one pointing easterly read West Port – 650 miles, while the one aimed in the opposite direction said Pacific Ocean – 900 miles. It had a rather sobering effect on the travelers.

The Fort's mission was to provide protection along a three-hundred-mile swath of the Oregon Trail, most particularly from the Cheyenne and the Sioux. The reality was that during the summer months it was not unusual to see six to ten wagon trains pass by the fort in a single day. So spread across their huge area of responsibility, it was very possible that there might be a hundred or more trains requiring their protection at any one time—an impossible task for five such installations, let alone Fort Laramie.

Unlike Fort Kearny, Laramie's soldiers appeared to be well disciplined and able men. Although there was little spit and polish, at least the men looked like soldiers. Also unlike Kearny, the supply store at Fort Laramie was only too happy to charge a huge mark-up to travelers. Sugar that was a nickel a pound in West Port, and no more than seven cents in Kearny, cost a dollar a pound in Laramie. Actually, most travelers were considering the ramifications of lightening their loads by the time they reached Laramie, so they had very little appetite for the expensive goods. As they continued to sight high peaks off in the distance, it was already beginning to sink in that the worst was yet to come in their journey. The elephant would arrive soon enough.

> *My story. On June 15 year of 1849*
>
> *Since we left Fort Laramie we are slowly climbing higher and as we look off to the west, it looks to be more of the same. This morning, Del told us we have come almost half way. He warned everybody to look at their stores and decide if there was anything we could do without. He said we had best throw it away here as the long uphill pull ahead is going to be hard on the oxen. He said if they dropped dead, we'd be walking the rest of the way.*
>
> *When the train pulled out today, the camp was littered with linen bags of flour and meal, and slabs of bacon. Folks who were saving heavy tin cans of peaches opened them and ate fruit for breakfast, lunch, and supper. Pan after pan of biscuits were made and carried in the wagons, instead of just throwing away*

the flour and lard. Most people walked trying to ease the load on their animals.

When I spied a perfectly good iron cookpot that someone had thrown away, I started to pick it up and put it in the wagon. But Del told me it was a leeverite. I said I thought it was a cookpot. He said a leeverite meant to leave 'er right there. Only Mary and Ethan are riding in the wagon now. I feel guilty for being able to ride my pony, so most of the time I walk too and just tie the horse to the back of the wagon.

They had been away from Fort Laramie for almost a week. This particular morning, B. F. and Jane were walking along, engaged in a conversation about the benefits of farming in Oregon versus setting up a business in the gold fields. Each of them thought the other completely unreasonable on the subject. Mr. Fitzwater was walking beside the oxen, every now and then giving them a slap on the rump to encourage them as they climbed a long hill. Mary was on the jockey box, and Ethan was playing in the back of the wagon.

B. F. looked to his right and saw that Ethan had apparently climbed out of the back of the wagon and was running to try and catch one of the green lizards that seemed to be everywhere along the trail. Ethan squealed with delight to be out of the confines of the wagon. When he did, his pa heard him and turned around to give him back to his mother. There were just too many things that could hurt a little boy while the train was moving.

Ethan decided he was not ready to be caught, and he dodged away from his pa. B. F. eased behind him in order to prevent his getaway. Suddenly, the little boy tripped on a rock and fell to his right, directly between the front and back wheels of the wagon. Both B. F. and George jumped for the little boy, but George got their first. He grabbed Ethan by the arm, pulling him backward. B. F. pushed the boy further away from the oncoming wheels, but saw that George's momentum had caused him to fall where Ethan had been. B. F. shouted, "Stop, Mary." and reached for George's outstretched hand. There was a brief second when he could see the dread on his friend's face. Too late, the wagon gave a lurch as the four foot in diameter, iron-rimmed back wheel rolled over both of his legs.

Mary jumped down and screamed when she saw him. The rear wheel had stopped atop his right leg, just above the knee. It took ten men to lift the wagon enough that George could be pulled out. He was white as he could possibly be and still be breathing. His pants were torn, and there was blood covering his right leg.

Del and Missus Broderick were summoned. After she knelt and looked closely at Mr. Fitzwater's injuries, she grabbed Del by the arm and walked away from the onlookers. Tears were running down her face. "I think his right leg is all crushed up, and the left one is broke. If we had a doctor, he'd probably take his right leg off and splint the other. I don't think he's got a prayer if his leg don't come off, and I don't know how to do that."

Del put his head down. There were now tears on his cheeks as well. It kind of surprised him, as he couldn't remember the last time he had been affected like that. He wiped his sleeve on his face and sniffed. "Don't let Miz Fitzwater see them tears."

They walked back together with their arms subconsciously inter-locked. Actually, they were holding each other up. Missus Broderick told Mary what she thought about the extent of George's injuries. Del cleared a frog from his throat. "Ma'am, I cain't tell you how bad I feel about this. George needs a doctor real bad. I don't know if there's one at Laramie, but its six days back. I don't believe he could stand the trip, as rough as this trail is. Besides, this here is Sioux country. You cain't travel alone. And the next chance for a doctor is Fort Hall. That's almost a month out. And the travel 'twixt here and there is lots worse than anything we seen yet."

Mary could not stop crying. "I don't know what to do. There ain't no good choice." Jane held her mother's hand, and Ethan stood between them, holding his mother's leg.

B. F. saw only one chance. "Miz Broderick, if you and your hus-band will stay here with the Fitzwaters, I'll ride back to Fort Laramie to get a doctor. Maybe there'll be a wagon train right behind us that will have a doctor. When I get back with the doctor, you folks can catch up with Del or join another train coming along. You're the only one on the train that can help Mr. Fitzwater until the doctor gets here. And if you stay, it won't just be one wagon and one gun if any Indians show up. I figure me and my pony can be back in four days."

She looked at her husband, who wouldn't look her in the eye. "I don't know if we can do that."

Del spoke up. "That's one dangerous idea, son."

"Yes sir, but a mule can't make time like my pony can. They can't go on, and they can't go back. It's the only way, if the Broderick's will stay."

Mr. Broderick shook his head to clear his mind. He couldn't believe he was doing this. "B. F., get on that pony and get goin' afore I change my mind. We'll be right here when you come back." He walked with B. F. to his pony and spoke quietly. "Son, I don't believe George'll last four days. If he dies, we'll leave you a sign and try to catch up to Coggins. Too many Injuns to stay out here any longer than we have to. And that goes double for you."

B. F. nodded and stepped around the wagon to where George Fitzwater lay. The pain was so bad that he was shaking and sweating. "Don't worry, sir. I'll be back."

George grabbed his hand, gritting his teeth so he could get the words out. "Be careful, son. I'm not worth your life."

Jane had stepped behind B. F., holding the pony's bridle. "I want to go with you."

"The pony can't handle two of us for such a long ride. Besides, you need to be right here with your ma and pa."

"I want to go. Maybe I can help if you get into trouble."

Before B. F. could respond, Mary put her arms around her daughter. "Your pa and I need you here, Janie." She looked at B. F. "Get goin, boy."

B. F. knew he couldn't ride the pony as fast as he wanted to. They both had to last for the next four days. Thank goodness the horse was well rested, as he had hardly been ridden at all over the last week, and the grass had been good. He had four days of biscuits and salted meat for himself and a small bag of corn for the horse, but he had not brought along a gun. If he found Indians—or worse, if they found him—one rifle wouldn't do any good anyway. It would just slow him down, and besides, the Brodericks and Fitzwaters might need all the firepower they could muster.

He rode steadily throughout the day, only stopping around nine o'clock when it was too dark to see. He and his horse slept in a thicket, away from the trail itself, and woke with the sunrise. B. F. guessed that he was traveling maybe five times faster than the train.

About mid-morning, he met another wagon train. He hollered at the man out front to assure him he was no threat. "Do you folks have a doctor on this train? A man is hurt real bad about three days up the trail."

"We ain't got no doctor. What happened to him?"

"Got run over by a wagon. Do you know if there's a doctor at Laramie?"

"Don't know." He shouted behind him, "Hey Smiley, is there a doctor at Laramie?"

"Was last year."

B. F. waved a thank you and rode on. In early afternoon, he passed another train with the same result. He began to have a sense of dread that he would find no doctor. How could he return to George Fitzwater with that news?

Inside of an hour he sighted a cavalry troop headed his way on the trail. The Sergeant in the lead pulled them up. "Where you bound for boy?"

"I'm headed for Laramie. Is there a doctor there? A man is hurt real bad up the trail."

"Waal, we sorta got a doctor. He come out from Kearny a couple months ago. But his second day in camp he got kicked in the head by a mule. He ain't been outa bed since. Lieutenant says he ain't got sense enough not to piss his pants."

B. F. looked at him. "Are you saying he can't doctor anybody?"

"That's what I'm sayin'. He don't even know his own name."

"Is another doctor on his way?"

"Probably not 'til next year. How far you goin, boy?"

"About a day-and-a-half ride."

"Say, this is bad territory. You cain't do that."

"My friend's waiting on me to bring a doctor. I gotta get back." B. F. turned his horse around.

"Corporal Daniels, take Private Swanson and go with this cussed boy."

B. F. again rode well into the twilight. Corporal Daniels was not happy with this long day as he pulled his horse alongside B. F. "We been ridin' all day. It's time to make camp."

"I got a long ride tomorrow too. Maybe you can make camp and catch up with me in the morning."

The Corporal reached out and grabbed his reins. "We're stoppin' here, I said."

"Alright. Guess I don't have much choice."

The Private pulled out his cook kit and began preparing to build a fire. B. F. looked at the Corporal. "It's probably not a good idea to have a fire. There'll be a good moon tonight. You can see that smoke from a long distance with no wind."

"Mind your own business, boy. We intend to eat a supper."

"Then if you don't mind, my horse and I will bed down away from your camp."

"Suit yoresef."

B. F. led his pony a good half mile west of the campfire and again bedded down in a thicket of honeysuckle well off the trail. His horse nuzzled him awake while it was still dark. The full moon was well past vertical on the horizon, allowing him to estimate it must be between two and three o'clock. He heard what sounded like a rifle shot, followed by a single shot of lesser caliber—probably a pistol—then five or six rifles, then silence.

He had left the saddle on his pony, simply loosening the cinch when he bedded down. His shaking hands made it difficult to tighten the cinch, but he scolded himself about not being a coward, removed the hobble, added the bridle, and got back in the saddle as quickly as he could. He guessed that if the Sioux had prevailed, they would spend some time at the campsite making sure they had taken everything of value, so he probably had at least a fifteen minute head start. Of course, if the cavalry had won, then he had plenty of time. There was enough moonlight that he had little problem finding the trail and staying on it.

By daybreak he felt safe enough to stop so both he and his horse could get a long drink from the river. Even so, he felt exposed when he dismounted and got down on his knees at the water's edge. He could almost feel someone sighting in on him as he knelt. He wasn't as thirsty as he thought.

It was a very long day. He finally rested around noon so that his horse could get some grass. He ate two biscuits and some buffalo jerky and rode on. Around four that afternoon, he overtook the wagon train that he had met after leaving the Fitzwaters. He shouted out to them that he was coming in.

The wagon master asked if he had news. "I'm pretty sure there was a fight between two soldiers and some Indians back about forty-five miles. I don't think they knew I was around, but I'm not positive of that. You'd best be sure your lookouts are sharp tonight. I think I've got about fifteen more miles to go. Got to get moving."

Both he and his pony were worn to a frazzle, but B. F. was committed to getting back as soon as possible. He felt a terrible weight in his chest that if he didn't get back tonight, he might not see Mr. Fitzwater alive again. He had no idea what they were going to do when he arrived, but he just knew he had to get there.

The sun had long since set, but there was enough moonlight for B. F. to believe that he had arrived at the place where he had left the wagon train three days earlier. He searched for a sign of the Fitzwater and Broderick wagons, but to no avail. Could it be that this was not the place after all? Then he saw the fresh pile of dirt and stones off to the side of the trail. His heart fell into the pit of his stomach.

He inspected the grave to see if the Broederick's had left anything to confirm that this place belonged to Mr. Fitzwater. He located a piece of wagon canvas stuffed under the largest rock, with an inscription that read, *Here lies George Fitzwater – the finest of men.* His friend was gone. Not only had he failed in his mission, but now it was too late to even tell him goodbye. He had wanted to say thank you for so many things, but now there would be no chance.

It was too dark to go further, and he had no familiarity with the trail beyond this point, so he led his horse back into the brush for another night and bedded down. Despite his fatigue, he sought out his mother, there beyond Orion's Belt, and spoke to her with an uncharacteristic anguished heart. For the first time since he left Indiana, he cried himself to sleep.

He was up and gone at daybreak and saw the two wagons ahead of him at mid-morning. He slowed his horse to a walk before he caught up to them, trying to think of something he could say to Mary and Jane. There was nothing. The emptiness returned to his chest.

> *My story. On June 26 year of 1849*
>
> *Mr. Fitzwater was run over by the wagon and it crushed his legs. I rode back to Fort Laramie to fetch a doctor, but couldn't get one. What I write next is awful bad. Mr. Fitzwater died around three in the afternoon yesterday, before I could get back to him. Missus Broderick says his right leg was swole to twice its normal size and turned as black as night. He had a fever that put him out of his head that last day, and he died right in her arms.*
>
> *Mary just sits on the wagon seat like a statue. I don't think she's crying but her face never changes. Little Ethan keeps asking about his pa, but his ma won't answer him. She just sits there. Jane can't hardly talk at all about it, and to tell the truth I can't either.*
>
> *Mister Broderick came and told me that before Mister Fitzwater got out of his head, he told him to tell me that he thought I was the finest boy he ever knew. I didn't know it, but he told him when I took off to Laramie that he knew he'd never see me again. I think this hurts as bad as anything I've ever felt.*

Mister Broderick put his hand on B. F.'s shoulder and nodded toward the Fitzwaters. "Son, they're really gonna need you now—but I know you can do it. Coggins said we might catch up at the Mormon Ferry.

He said it was about four days ahead, but that it'd take at least a day for them to cross. So it's possible that we can get there in time."

The river turned to the southwest for three days, and at about five o'clock in the afternoon, they reached what had to be the Mormon Ferry. Coggins' train was nowhere in sight. Mr. Broderick knocked on the door of a cabin at the side of the river. "We need passage across the river. We'd appreciate gettin' over to the north side this evening."

The man at the door had half a slice of cornbread in his hand, and when he spoke, it was easy to see that the rest of the piece was in his mouth. "We'll be down soon as we finish our dinner. Unhook your stock right at the river bank. Since it's after my suppertime, it'll cost ye two dollars and fifty cents a wagon."

The ferry consisted of two large, hollowed-out cottonwood canoes that were fastened together with cross bars and then covered with wooden planking. It was operated with oars, but there was a stout rope tied from a tree stump on one bank to a big pine tree on the other. A second rope was tied from the raft to an iron ring that encircled the main rope. A third rope was tied to the front of the ferry. As the contraption left the opposite bank, a team of four oxen and two men pulled the load across to the north bank.

The Broderick wagon with the Brodericks and Jane on board crossed on the first load, with their oxen swimming behind. The Fitzwater wagon, carrying Mary, Ethan, and B.F was on the second crossing; followed by B. F.'s pony and their stock. They decided to keep going for another hour before stopping for the night. Until they caught up with the Coggins' train, they resolved to travel at least an hour longer each day than the train normally did. They felt like they could gain some miles anyway with the lack of wasted time in getting the whole train moving after every stop.

The next day the trail turned back to the west, and again they were climbing. They noticed a peak to the southeast that still had snow on top. Jane announced that it was the twenty-ninth day of June. What manner of place was this that you could see snow in the summer?

The third day, they came to the confluence of the North Platte and the Sweetwater River near Muddy Gap, where the larger river ran straight to the south. The trail began heading up the Sweetwater River, and there was now a succession of snow-covered peaks in sight off to the north. The second day on the Sweetwater, they saw a broad open saddle with prairie grass and sagebrush. This was the famous South Pass, the pathway that straddled the Continental Divide in the Rocky Mountains, and at least a mile ahead of them, they spied what had to be the rear end of Coggins' train.

The Sweetwater began on the east flank of South Pass, and its water flowed eventually into the Mississippi River. On the west end of the pass rose Pacific Creek, which would flow into Big Sandy River and eventually find its way to the Pacific Ocean.

They finally caught the Coggins Train as they were making camp for the evening. Del came to see them straight-away, and listened intently while Missus Broderick told the story, including some of the details of B. F.'s ride that he had shared with them.

Del took off his hat and put his arms around Mary. He suddenly realized it had been a good eight or ten years since he had hugged a woman, and he took a quick step backward. "Beg pardon, ma'am. I was about to give ya'll up. Didn't know if you'ns went back to Laramie, or mebbe them Sioux found you. And B. F., I don't know what to figger about you!"

Over an evening campfire, they brought everybody up to date on their sad news. B. F. noticed that a couple of the single men were extremely attentive to Mary, offering to help out with anything she might need during the remainder of the trip. He had not noticed them being particularly nice before.

Twenty

The Devil Can't Be Far From This Place

Indian Territory 1849

The next morning, Del spoke to the travelers. "Today it's our Independence Day. We're gonna stop early this evenin' and do some celebratin'. How about a couple you men ridin' ahead to kill us a buffalo or some deer. Today oughta be celebrated in fine style."

About four o'clock that afternoon, the train came upon the hunters in a narrow valley, busily dressing a bear and the hind quarters of a cow elk. Their efforts were worthy of a rousing cheer from the train. One of the hunters had a request. "We kilt this bear up on that ridge while he was eatin' huckleberries with both hands. It sure would be tasty if we had us some huckleberry pie to go with these steaks."

Del spoke up. "We can send a dozen younguns to pick, but we got to have three or four men up there with muskets. Them bears won't take kindly to us stealin' their candy."

Fires were started, potatoes peeled, biscuits readied, and thick steaks provided to each wagon. Most of the women prepared a cobbler crust for their Dutch ovens in anticipation of huckleberries. They weren't disappointed. The children returned with full buckets and stained mouths.

The single men on the train were invited to the families' dinner tables, and they ate until they were almost stupefied. The huckleberry cobblers were pronounced as the best ever tasted. Of course, for most of them, they had never even seen huckleberries before.

One of the more studious men of the company, Rupert Osgood, stood up before the group. He had a large, purple birthmark on his forehead, so it was his habit to wear a hat on all occasions. Some said he wore the hat to bed so as not to distract Miz Osgood. But on this particular occasion he held his hat in his hands. "I think we should say somethin' about our Declaration of Independence."

He was encouraged, "Go ahead, Osgood."

He squared his shoulders and spoke out so all could hear him. "It was seventy-three years ago that our ancestors wrote a Declaration of Independence from King George. Since that time, we fought two wars with England and one with Mexico to protect our liberty, and that don't count all them wars with the savages and the pirates. There may be some in this company who fought for our United States. To them who did, we're grateful for what you done. And as to this journey, to use the phrase of a great man, Mr. Thomas Paine from my home state of Pennsylvania, there sure aren't any summer soldiers or sunshine patriots in this company. In the face of daily hardship, you're all showin' great faith and courage in this strange and untamed land. Of all the people I ever met, you are the best fitted to take our country to the Pacific Ocean."

There were cries of "Huzzah!" from the crowd.

In short order, musical instruments were retrieved from wagons. Songs were sung, and dancing begun. Both B. F. and Jane were completely mesmerized to watch Miz Culberson and Miz Carrollton dancing together. Their amazement had nothing to do with the fact that two women were dancing together. Not at all. But the two women were stout in the extreme. When they danced, they had various body parts and bulges that shook and rolled so that it was impossible not to watch.

Whether the two women were conscious of their effect on the settlers, it was hard to say, but they certainly let nothing stand in the way of their joy of the moment. When the music stopped, B. F. could swear all those bulges kept on shaking for a good minute even when the two women were no longer dancing. For B. F., the memory of all that wiggling flesh was something he would visualize every time he celebrated the Fourth of July for the rest of his life.

Del chose this moment to step in front of the musicians. He held up his hand. "This was a wonderful evenin'. Thank you to our hunters who provided for us, and to all them good cooks that turned out such a fine meal."

"I need to warn you about them bears. We gonna be in their territory for a couple of months. They's two kinds of bears—the black bear we ate tonight and the griz. A big griz might weigh seven or eight hunnert pounds. He has a front paw that's mebbe a foot long. And I seen em that was harder to kill than a big bull buffalo." He looked at them intently. "You don't wanna get nowhere near a griz."

"One thing you can do is make sure them bears know yore around. Some people sew those little silver bells on their clothes—like them Mexicans wear—so's the bears'll know where they is and they'll keep their distance. But if they do get close, people carry little bags of black pepper so they can throw the pepper in the bear's face."

"We all need to keep our eyes open for bear sign. For one thing, look out for bear scat. If ye see scat with berries and bits of fur in it, then it's purty sure they's a black bear close by." Del paused and made sure his audience was listening.

Miz Culberson asked the question they all were wondering. "How do you tell there's a griz around close?"

Del looked at them intently. "Griz scat has got little silver bells in it, and it smells like pepper."

They looked at Del. He was straight-faced. They looked at each other. Someone snickered. Miz Broderick started laughing. She looked at the blank faces of the settlers, and she whooped and hollered even harder. Del could stand it no longer and couldn't keep from laughing himself.

Realization hit his audience about the same time. "Aw, I knew he was carryin' us along the whole time."

B. F.'s eyes were shining, and he said it before he thought. "Your pa would have loved that story." Jane looked away, not bearing to answer. She choked out a goodnight and ran back to the wagon. B. F. could only shake his head at his stupidity.

The train continued a slow descent along first the Big Sandy, then the Muddy River. B. F. was excited to hear they would reach Fort Bridger by the end of the day. Everybody knew of the exploits and discoveries of the famous mountain man, Jim Bridger. He was credited with discovering the Great Salt Lake and exploring much of the west. In his younger days, he had been shot in the back with an arrow. According to the story, he carried the arrowhead for three years until it was finally removed by a frontier doctor, "cause it irritated me some."

He and his partner, Louis Vasquez, had established the Fort Bridger trading post in 1843, which was nestled in a mountainous area surrounded by the lands of the Shoshone Indians. From outer appearances, it seemed they had chosen their location well. The fort was located on perhaps a thousand acres of level, green pastures, had a great number of trees nearby, and was well watered. The fort itself was composed of a stockade about ten feet high, and inside was a well-supplied store with clothing, food, liquor, tobacco, and ammunition. Bridger's log home was also located within the stockade.

However, a closer look revealed that the stockade was little more than a line of poles that were bound together in some semblance of a line, and filled with daubs of mud. The three buildings were also crudely constructed and filthy inside. Arranged around the front of the fort were about twenty-five lodges that were occupied by the Indian wives and children of trappers that frequented the fort. The women attempted to trade their skins, clothing, and moccasins with wagon trains for food. Some travelers were only too happy to exchange excess food that they might have to throw away anyway for a pair of soft and supple elk hide moccasins to give their aching feet some relief.

B. F. was prepared to meet the famous frontiersman himself and looked forward to hearing his latest stories in great detail. Instead, upon entering the trading post he saw a middle-aged man sitting cross-legged in the corner with scraggly gray hair and wearing a filthy jacket. He was running his tongue over the surface of a broken front tooth. "What'll ye need boy?"

"Nothing, sir. I just wanted to see Jim Bridger."

The man curled his lip, sort of waved his hand over his head in a dismissive manner, then turned his attention once more to his whittling. When others who entered the post got much the same response, it became obvious that Bridger was only interested in making a favorable trade and did not spend any time recounting a single one of his famous adventures for the entertainment of his visitors.

In a very few years, Bridger would be gone from the fort. He and the Mormons would fight repeatedly about his sales of alcohol to the Indians before he finally sold them his fort and went back to the edge of civilization. There he would run a store in West Port, providing supplies and a constant stream of advice to travelers on the Santa Fe, Oregon, and California Trails well into his old age.

Within a day and a half, the train struck the Bear River, where they turned to the north, and came to a spot, which Del called Soda Springs—with good reason. The water from the spring foamed like bicarbonate of soda mixed with water, and even tasted like soda, only stronger. They did not bother to fill their water barrels with the foul-tasting brew. There were other springs in the area, some of them bubbling heated water, with steam rising up from the earth.

All of the children wanted to touch the hot water, if for no other reason than to say they had. About the time Ethan leaned over to stick his hand in the heated water, he was suddenly grabbed by the nap of his shirt and dragged backward by his mother. "Get away from there." She turned to all the children and shook her finger at them. "Get back from this here spot. Don't ye know what this place is? The divil and his hell cain't be far from this here place."

Just beyond they struck the Blackfoot River, which took them further north until they crossed the Snake River, and then headed west. The entire area was filled with various rivers, creeks, branches, and standing water that seemed to head in every conceivable direction, but eventually all flowed into the Snake. Cattails were everywhere in the slow moving waterways. The valley was surrounded by timber, which was only exceeded in number by mosquitoes. At dawn and dusk they were everywhere. The beasts and the travelers could get no relief. For every one that was swatted, another ten volunteers took its place in the obvious effort to drive animals and humans crazy.

Mary pulled some dried up flowers out of a cloth bag in her wagon, ground them up, and mixed in a little vinegar. "Ya'll pat this fleabane on your arms and faces. It'll keep most of them skeeters away."

Jane and Ethan were quick to protest. "Ma, that stuff smells terrible. Nobody'll want to come close to us when we're usin' this."

"Them skeeters feel the same way. That's why they'll leave ye be."

In the midst of this environment stood Fort Hall. Finally, this was indeed a true fort—a stockade eighty feet by eighty feet square, constructed of cottonwood trees that had been sunk in the earth, and extended some fifteen feet in the air. There were two square guard towers standing at diagonally opposite corners of the fort, while inside stood two well-built log structures—one a supply post and the other a barracks for the men assigned there.

Here the Snake formed a huge river valley, with massive mountains to the north and south. The stock had plenty of grass, but B. F. wondered if his pony was finding enough to eat to keep him going. He couldn't forget the warnings about the horses who couldn't withstand the rigors of the trip and the poor forage in the high plains and mountain valleys. It did give him hope that the Shoshone Indian ponies which they saw from time to time appeared to be in good shape. He hoped his horse was from the same stock.

Twenty-One

The Choice

Indian Territory 1849

My story. On July 29 year of 1849

We are heading up the Snake River getting closer and closer to the day when farmers headed for Oregon and miners headed for Calyfornia must go their separate ways. Mary has said nary word about what she intends to do. I don't know how they can make it without me, or how I can make it without them. How can a woman and two children start up a farm, build a cabin, plow their fields, harvest a crop, and stay safe by themselves? Let alone that they don't have any money.

For myself, I cannot figure how I can carry what I need without their wagon. How can I even protect any money that I earn in Calyfornia? If I don't find my pa, can I truly do it by myself?

He kept hoping Mary would bring up the subject, but she didn't. He couldn't figure what her silence meant. Did she assume that he would just stay with them? Was she waiting for him to start the conversation? Did she not care? The train moved on and the days wound down. Without saying anything at all, the decision would be made for them when the two groups separated.

He decided to talk to Jane one afternoon as they walked beside the wagon. "Has your ma said anything about going to California instead of Oregon?"

"No. She don't talk as much as she use to since pa died. How many weeks 'til the split?"

"Del says it'll be sometime tomorrow afternoon."

She looked at him quickly. "I didn't know that. I don't think ma knows neither."

"I guess I'm going to California. I was hoping you'd go that way too."

Jane looked away. "I think ma figured you'd go with us." She walked back to the wagon and climbed in the back.

When the full train circled up for the last time, Del spoke to them. "After lunch tomorrow, we'll strike the Raft River on the south bank. Them for Californy'll cross the Snake and head up the Raft. Them for Oregon will stay on the north bank. Both roads is hard, but the Californy Trail is worse. I hope you boys goin' to find all that gold is lucky. I been proud to lead all of you'ns. Startin' at the Raft, you'll be led by Louis Vasquez's boy, Roberto. He led one group to Californy last year, so he's a proven guide."

Paddy Dowd walked Miz Campbell back to her wagon. Although they weren't trying, B. F. and Mary could overhear most of the conversation. "Ma'am, I know ye've had a terrible loss on this journey. And I know I'm not the best-looking man you ever did see, but it was a good farmer I once was in County Clare. I know how to build a snug house. I seldom take a drink of whisky—except on special occasions of course. And I'll treat you good as can be, and take care of you good as any man. If you'd consider me for a husband, I'd like to go with you to Oregon."

B. F. couldn't hear what she said, but directly they walked back to the firelight together, and Miz Campbell had her hand on Paddy's arm. He envied them. He failed to notice that Mary's eyes were watering.

Some time later that evening, B. F. decided he just had to say something and walked over to the Fitzwater fire. "Ma'am, I guess you know I'm headed to California tomorrow. I still hope to find my pa there. I'm sure grateful for the way you treated me these last four months. And I'm so sorry about Mr. Fitzwater. I believe he was the finest man I ever met." He waited for her to lift her head back up. "I wish you all would come with me."

"You're the third man today that's asked me to go to California. Both Leon Quinn and Clyde Hancock asked me. But, B. F., I don't know nuthin' about gold minin'. To tell the truth, I don't know much about farmin' neither."

"I don't aim to mine for gold. A man I knew in Indiana said the only ones who made any real money in the gold fields were people who sold things to the miners. I figure on doing just what we did back in West Port. I can cut hair."

She stared at him with a look of disgust. "Well, me and Janie ain't about to sell no hot baths in California!"

"I didn't mean that. You and Jane can cook real fine. What if you opened a dining establishment near Sutter's Mill? All those miners have to eat. I bet they'd pay dearly for some of your biscuits."

That brought a hint of a smile. "Where would we get the fixin's for all that cookin'?"

"According to Roberto Vasquez, it comes by wagon from San Francisco." He pressed his case. "This way, you can take the money you earn after a couple of years in the gold fields and do whatever you want—buy a farm, open a store for women's clothes, live in town, live in the country—whatever you want."

"Let me talk to Janie."

The next morning, B. F. gave a questioning look to Missus Fitzwater, but she just said, "We ain't decided yet." She and Jane rode in the wagon all morning.

When they stopped at lunch, he got the same response. He began to think that she just didn't want to tell him the bad news. He knew exactly how she felt. He remembered how he had spent a day and a night struggling with how he could tell her the terrible news that no doctor would be coming from Fort Laramie to save her husband.

Around three o'clock a substantial stream cut into the Snake from the South. Del pulled the train up. "All fer Californy, here's yer gittin' off place." As the two groups began to pull apart, Del said his good-byes. He found B. F. quickly enough. "Son, I'd wagon train with you anywhere and anytime you say. I wouldn't trade you for any man in this outfit. It's real courage when yer skeered to death, but ye git on yer hoss anyway—an that's what you done back at Laramie for old man Fitzwater."

B. F. had seldom heard Del compliment anyone, so he instantly knew he was being sincere. He couldn't help the blush that came to his cheeks. "Thanks, Del. You're a true friend. We were all lucky to have you leading us. For a fact, you saved our lives more than once. Good luck to Oregon." They shook hands, the big, rough hand of the wagon master, and the hand of the boy, no more than half the size.

B. F. quickly sought out Paddy. "So it's a farmer you'll be?"

"How did you come to know that?"

"One of those fairies you're always talking about told me your secret."

"'Tis true. I aim to grow the fruit of the gods in that Willamette Valley."

"Fruit of the gods?"

"Aye. The best Irish potatoes Oregon ever saw. You're welcome to come too if you ever decide you miss following behind a plow."

They shook hands. "I'm for California. I still hold out hope to find my pa there."

As he turned back toward the Fitzwater wagon, he saw Mary carrying a gallon-sized stoneware crock. She grabbed Paddy by the sleeve and took him aside. "Mistuh Dowd, I have something precious here for you that I brought all the way from Tennessee. It was my intention to save it for my husband, but that's no longer possible. Mistuh Fitzwater thought a lot of you, and I'm sure he'd want you to have this." Paddy started to speak, but she held up her hand. "It's not my intention to cast doubts on you in any way—but I can't help but notice that the Widow Campbell is quite a bit younger than you are."

"Age is only in the mind, m'dear."

"Not necessarily, Mistuh Dowd. Age can find other locations aside from the mind. I have here a jug of the best Tennessee River bottomland blackstrap molasses, and it might be a godsend to ye one of these days."

"Why do you call it 'blackstrap'?"

"Blackstrap is the most powerful of all molasses. It's the third boiling of fine cane sugar syrup, and its chock full of what must be solid iron.

But here's what's real special about it. If you take a tablespoonful a day of blackstrap, it will provide a source of powerful vigor to your blood."

Paddy gave her a strange look. "Do you mean. . . ."

She nodded her head. "That's exactly what I mean, Mistuh Dowd. One of these days, your young wife may have expectations of you that are hard to meet. As long as you have this blackstrap, you will be ready, willing, and able."

Paddy doffed his hat and accepted the gift. "I sincerely hope those days are a long ways off, but thank you for your kindness—and maybe the Widow will thank you as well!"

For the life of him, B. F. couldn't figure out what they were talking about, but then he turned to the task he dreaded and began pulling gear from the back of the Fitzwater wagon and wrapping it in a blanket to affix it behind his saddle. The voice came from behind him. "What do you think you're doing?" He turned to see Mary standing there with Jane and Ethan beside her. "Put that right back where it came from. We got a river to cross, don't we? Janie, you and B. F. see if you can sell some of those farm tools to them sodbusters headed to Oregon."

He couldn't hide how relieved he was. He hugged Mary and slapped Ethan on the back, but when it came time to express his feelings to Jane, all either of them could do was stand about four feet apart and grin at one another.

It was obvious that Jane was the better salesperson. In fifteen minutes, she had lightened the wagon's load by 150 pounds and increased their pocket book by eleven dollars. She and B. F. unloaded the seed corn, red wheat, corn sheller, and plough, and watched as it was carefully placed in the back of the Zimmerman wagon.

Seven wagons and fifty souls could almost smell their fortune ahead as they waved farewell to the rest of the train, crossed the Snake and headed southwest, up the Raft River, then over Granite Pass and along Goose Creek, Little Goose Creek, and Rock Spring Creek. They then spent an entire day fording waterways in Thousand Springs Valley, then traveled along West Brush Creek to Willow Creek, and finally to the headwaters of the Humboldt River.

B. F. couldn't help but notice the frequent attentions of Leon Quinn and Clyde Hancock. At least once or twice a day they each stopped to tip their respective hats and ask if there was anything they could do to make Mary's trip more tolerable. Mr. Hancock had even started filling up their water barrel every evening. But both men were convinced that it had been their own gift of gab that had gotten Miz Fitzwater to come south, and who knows, maybe that was the case.

They followed the Humboldt for many days, passing through Carlin Canyon, where the river was high enough that the water was flooded across the wagon road in two places. They then had a steep climb through Emigrant Gap, then an even steeper descent into Emigrant Canyon where they rejoined the River.

There was discussion about taking the Truckee River Route or the Carson Trail. Roberto Vasquez had taken the Truckee Route on the way in, and the Carson Trail on the way out last year. Both routes required a terrible two-day trek across the Forty Mile Desert. But the Truckee Route required some thirty additional river crossings. By comparison, the Carson Trail would require pulling the wagons up an almost vertical, three-hundred-foot-high bluff—the Sierra Crest. They would accomplish the latter by using all seven teams to pull a single wagon up the obstacle. The wagons would be completely unloaded, and the gear carried by hand to the top of the bluff. When Vasquez mentioned that the Truckee Route had at least two hundred graves along the trail, they all voted for the Carson route.

They filled every container they had at the Humboldt Bar, and made sure their oxen were grazed well on the grass along the river. At daybreak, they headed south toward the Carson River. By mid-morning of the second day, their water barrels were empty, and they had to rely on what was left in their canteens for the remainder of the trek.

They were all suffering in the late August heat, with the temperature close to 100 degrees. But if they suffered, the oxen were in misery. They had received nothing to eat for the second day in a row. Not a drop of shade anywhere, and no water to drink. As he trudged along, B. F. began to feel as if he was being cooked in the fierce sun, and he suddenly remembered his conversation with Del. He had finally "seen the elephant" and began to seriously wonder if they could survive for the rest of the day.

At dusk that evening, the dark formation of a tree line formed in the distance. All prayed that it marked the river in front of them. The stock could undoubtedly smell the water, and despite their exhaustion, they quickened their step. As soon as they reached the river bank, the men unhitched the pitiful beasts and they trundled into the water to stand belly deep for at least an hour. When they finally exited, they spent the first half of the night eating the emerald green grass along the river.

> *My story. On September 5, year of 1849*
>
> *We must be high in the mountains as it was very cold last night. There was even ice on the river this morning, then hot as blue blazes during the day. We have seen a lot of trash along the road for much of our trip mostly around campsites, but along this river the whole trail looks like a garbage pit. There must be some real trouble ahead, because people threw out wagon parts, harness, trunks, tools, and furniture; and that doesn't even count the mule and ox bones.*
>
> *Last night it was already cold while Mary was finishing dinner, and she looked over at Jane and said, "This here is a hellish place—hot as the devil's outhouse durin' the day, and cold as an Eskimo's bare behind at night. I'll be glad to get shut of this place."*
>
> *I feel the same way. Sometimes I get the feeling that something real bad is just about to happen to us again. That something is just waiting for us to make a mistake around every crook in the trail.*

They then were faced with traversing the Sierra Crest. In looking up the side of the bluff from the river, it seemed like a foolhardy, let alone impossible task to move everything they had to that distant height. The first requirement was for the wagons to be positioned close to the base of the bluff. Then every person who was able unloaded wagons and began carrying the gear to the top. Once this was completed, twenty men ascended to the top of the bluff with the fourteen pairs of oxen. It was almost too steep for the beasts to climb without pulling anything at all. They then tied together two lengths of rope that would total at least five hundred feet apiece and dropped them down to the bottom of the bluff. They tied both ropes to a wagon axle and the other ends to the teams of oxen at the top of the bluff. In this way, every wagon was hauled up to the top, one vertical foot at a time, where they were finally reloaded with gear and supplies.

The teams were rested through the remainder of the day, and on the morrow all passed through Carson's Pass and then to the South Fork of the American River. Within two days, they began to see mining operations along the river. They shouted to the miners. "How far to Sutter's Mill, friend?"

The reply came back. "Takes about two days, less'n yore thirsty!"

When three men got sick that evening with terrible diarrhea, B. F. remembered what Del had said about not drinking downstream. He warned the Fitzwaters, and they resolved to find good water. B. F. rode higher up the mountain to fill their canteens with what appeared to be clean spring water.

By morning, three more men were sick, and the original three were dead and gone. Almost all the men without wagons slipped away from the small train and proceeded on downstream toward their destination. By early afternoon, the wagons were released from their obligation when the last of the six men died, including Mary's two potential suitors, Quinn and Hancock. They had crossed a continent, and the gold fields were down hill from where they fell. It just didn't seem right.

They descended out of the Sierra Madre Mountains into what could only be described as foothills. From that point downstream, there was a solid line of prospecting operations on both sides of the River. Some of the digs were right at the riverbank, others had shoveled trenches at least ten feet long into the hillside, and a few men were working in deep shafts starting some fifty feet up the hill.

One of the claims involved men working in a group over a sluice box. One man shoveled dirt, clay, and gravel into a wooden box, while another washed it down by means of redirecting at least a portion of the flow of the stream through the box. Other sites were using a larger trough with a sieve on the lower end. Underneath the sieve was a smaller box with ripples on it. Gold and finer gravel filtered through the sieve and got caught in the ripples. In this process, two men shoveled and a third washed down their quarry.

Panning for gold was actually referred to as "prospecting" In other words, the miner was checking the prospects of that particular area with a pan. If he found adequate evidence of gold in his pan, then he would stake his claim and pursue his prospects further by digging, or mining, into the embankment.

Claims were marked with painted stakes and all manner of signs, then defended with powder and lead and lives. Every man they saw wore a gun. Holes were dug everywhere—beside the road, along the creek, and up and down the hillsides. The location of the diggings seemed to be so uncoordinated that they must have been the result of a combination of greed and wild hunches or a group of very inebriated strategists.

Everything seemed to be wet because of all the operations involving large volumes of water. The road was so muddy, the assumption would logically be that a big storm had just passed through. The sides of the hills in every direction were spotted with dirty canvas tents strung under scraggly digger pines. The tents may have been white once upon a time, but that was long past. Their wagons approached a group of wooden buildings, which were gathered along the south bank of a creek. The sign on the road proclaimed the place Hangtown. It was September 12—five months and two days out of West Port.

Twenty-Two

The Miner's Rest

Hangtown, California 1849

B. F. considered the huge oak tree standing beside the town's main street. He couldn't help noticing there were remnants of at least three different hemp ropes strung around a large limb twelve feet above the ground. Perhaps this tree was the source of the town's name?

The few remaining wagons began to separate away with all the resulting tears of parting. But the urge to dig, to get hands in the dirt, was almost overpowering. They had been traveling across a whole country for this. This was no time to stand around and reminisce—it was time to get rich.

The strategy in the Fitzwater wagon was not so simple. They looked at their resources—cook pots and skillets, comb and scissors, and a quarter of their food staples left over from the journey. They still had a bit of money, but it would last no time at all in an economy where flour was a dollar a pound rather than the six cents they had paid in West Port.

Faced with splitting up and looking for a location for their business, Mary spoke up. "B. F., why don't you look for something close to where all those miners are walking up and down this main road? Me an Janie an Ethan'll ride down this way. We need somethin' out of the weather. And maybe you better find out where the competition is and if they can cook. We'll meet back here around five o'clock."

It was early afternoon when B. F. stopped at the El Dorado Hotel and Parlor House, where three tables were already playing cards. At least a couple of the men looked and sounded as though they were already under the sway of the bottle of whisky in front of them. He spoke to the old man at the desk. "Sir, do you have a room for rent?"

"We got a room with a bunk that you can share with another feller. One of you sleeps nights and one days. Comes with breakfast and supper. Be twelve dollars a day."

"How's the food?"

"Hardly anybody has died of it. But you need to get to the table early if you figure on getting anything to eat."

"Is there a barber around here?"

"There's one over at Bottle Hill, and I think over at Shingle Springs." He called to one of the tables. "Hey Irish, where is that barber cuts yer hair?"

One of the gamblers answered back but kept his eyes on the table in front of him. "Me former barber, Wilmot Klady, unexpectedly met his maker last week over to Shingle Springs due to a sudden case of lead poisoning. He and an agitated fellow from Australia got into an unfortunate disagreement over the accuracy of Wilmot's gold scale."

B. F. looked on down the street for other opportunities. When he entered the Placer Saloon, he was surprised to see at least fifteen men drinking. Most appeared to be dressed in rough clothing, but they all apparently had gold to spend. A sign on the wall said "Our finest champagne $16 a quart. Aged whisky $16 a pint."

"Boy, what're you doin' in here?" The voice came from a woman with absolutely red hair that was almost the same color as her rouged lips.

"Ma'am, I'm looking for a good meal at a good price."

"They serve one meal a day here in the evening. They only cook one thing—a big steak and the fixin's. It's sixteen dollars."

"Why is everything sixteen dollars in here?"

"Not everything is sixteen dollars. Some things cost more." She halfway smiled, but there didn't seem to be any joy in it. "Sixteen dollars is the price of an ounce of gold dust."

"Thank you, ma'am."

"Name's Eliza Bedwell, honey. Nice to meet you—and stay outa places like this. There's nothing good ever happens in here."

He turned at the east end of the main street when the line of buildings ran out, and headed back the other direction. Just west of the hanging tree was a supply store. Like the other places in town, it was a frame building that appeared to have been thrown together pretty quickly. None of the businesses had seen a coat of paint, and all were in various degrees of weathering. The supply store was a large building that had a lean-to storage room off to the side, and a rough sign that proclaimed it Yukon's Grocery and Supplies. Maybe it looked bigger than it actually was, because the only customer was an older fellow on crutches whose sole interest seemed to be sitting by the wood stove and chewing the fat.

B. F. looked at several prices in the store. A dozen eggs were six dollars, ten pounds of potatoes was twelve dollars, and a plain old roasting hen in a wooden cage was ten dollars. No wonder the place was so empty. How could anyone afford to live here? Was there really enough gold for men to pay these prices?

The man behind the counter wore a pistol strapped to his waist. He appeared to be around forty years old—plenty of grey hair beginning to show through the dark brown—and he seemed to cough too much. "What do you need, son?"

"Sir, we just came in on a wagon train this afternoon, and I can't help but notice these prices. Do the miners find enough gold to pay this much money for food?"

"Some of them are rich as Croesus. Most of them just find enough dust to make them keep digging. When they do find anything to speak of, they spend it in one of the saloons. Most live off corn mush and beans the rest of the time."

"Why are prices so high?"

"Everything has to come in by wagon from Yerba Buena. It takes five days just to get here. Since everything costs so much, there are bandits on the road, so the wagons all have a couple of guards too. I'm beginning to think I oughta be in the grog shop bizness. I did some mining myself 'til I got this here consumption. The doc said I had to get out from under the ground. Sold my share off and bought this doggone store."

"You don't know a man by the name of Daniel Windes do you?"

"Never heard of him. Friend of yours?"

"He's my pa. I hope to find him here. My name's B. F. Windes."

"Well, B. F., nice to meet you. I'm Jakob Benkov. Most folks around here just call me Yukon Jack. I come down here from Alaska last year. Got so I'm used to this weather, and I ain't intending to go back."

"Nice to meet you sir."

B. F. met the Fitzwaters back at the hanging tree. "What did you find?"

Mary had to smile. "Well, I got me two proposals of marriage this afternoon, and plenty offers to share a cabin with all kinds of miners. The craziest one was six fellers that musta been some kinda furriners. They all had real black hair and had it tied in a long pigtail down their backs. They had some strange lookin' eyes, like I never saw before. Only one could speak English, and he says they all wanted to marry me." She laughed for the first time in two months. "One big happy family. Durndest thing I ever heard."

Jane looked at her ma and shook her head before she spoke up. "We went down two streets, Cedar Ravine Road and Log Cabin Ravine, down to Oregon Ravine. Don't know why everthing is a Ravine here. Anyway, all we found was miners and shacks and holes in the ground. Ain't no business down that way. We're starting to think we'll have to work out of the wagon."

Mary looked at the expression on B. F.'s face. "You got a grin on yer face like the wave on a slop bucket. You found somethin' didn't you." It wasn't a question.

"It's possible. I didn't talk to the man yet. Let me tell you what I'm thinking."

The deal was a mixture of what they wanted and what they had to give up. It turned out that Yukon had no desire to go into the saloon business, nor did he want to sell out. What he wanted was to hang around his friends and be a witness to those rare days when some miner hit it big and the whole town celebrated. Plus he wanted more miners in his store. What B. F. and the Fitzwaters needed was a place out of the weather, space enough to work, and access to cheaper groceries. A compromise was reached and hands shook.

My story. On September 15 year of 1849

After five months on the trail, we are here in Hangtown, California. The town is nothing but saloons, hotels, gambling halls, and two stores and all of them are here to make sure the miners hand over their gold as fast as they can dig it up.

A man named Yukon Jack has let us put a diner and a barber chair in his store. For the last three days we've been moving his stock into a smaller area, turning his bedroom into a kitchen, and building me a barbershop in a lean-to on the side of the store. We took apart some of the shelves and turned them into tables and benches. Mary even ordered a cast iron stove from San Francisco. We open for business in the morning. I have seen no sign of my pa.

The five of them were proud of their work as they stood outside in the street and admired the new sign *Miner's Rest - Good Cooking - Supplies - Barber.*

They speculated it would be a while before they turned much of a profit, as Yukon had to spot them some tin plates, cups, and utensils, as well as his entire stock of eggs and ham. But within a week, Mary and Jane were serving three meals a day, B. F. was cutting some of the scroungiest heads of hair he had ever seen, and Yukon's store was never empty.

If they had been able to hire a driver and guards to make runs back and forth to the suppliers in San Francisco, they would have kept the wagon and oxen. But it didn't seem to make sense to just keep them out back and continually struggle to find feed for the stock. They stripped everything out of it and the Fitzwaters simply slept in the kitchen, while B. F. put a pallet down in his barbershop.

Because most miners rode mules or horses, or just walked into town, it was rare for wagons to go on the market in Hangtown, and those that did were commonly used for sleeping quarters. So within two hours of putting a sign out front to sell her covered wagon and double yoke of oxen, Mary had the ridiculous sum of thirty ounces of gold in her hands. Of course, that little transaction meant that now she had to stay—unless she wanted to spend half her gold on stagecoach transportation for her family to San Fran.

The next day, B. F. did something he hated to do—he put a similar sign up to sell his pony. He had quickly discovered he had to cut three heads of hair every day just to keep the horse fed and in a stable, and he had not ridden her a single time since they arrived. When Jane saw the sign, first it hurt her feelings, then it made her good and mad. "That little horse brung you all the way from Missouri, and now that she's earned a rest, you up and sell her. Did you ever figger that other people cared about the pony?"

"Jane, it doesn't make any sense to keep the horse. It costs five dollars a day just to feed and stable her. And she hasn't been ridden since we got here."

"I'm gonna ask ma to buy her."

"Jane, I'm asking a hundred and fifty dollars."

She stomped off in disgust. Later that afternoon he was paid nine ounces of gold for his pony by a miner who was buying her for the chaste and innocent Miss Lila Fontaine over at the Pot o' Gold Hotel.

B. F. had known that Mary was a talented cook, but his experience up to this point had been under the primitive kitchen resources of the Trail. When she had the luxury of a cookstove and a fireplace, the meals she produced made addicts out of her customers. It was hard to tell if the miners who came by every day were there because of the feeling it gave them to be around an attractive, unmarried, pleasant, and wholesome woman or because her biscuits were so good you would wake up dreaming about them.

The barbershop was improving. B. F. was able to put a bench around one wall to accommodate the two or three men who always seemed to be sitting around—whether talking or waiting their turn. He and Yukon built the floor around his barber chair six inches higher than the rest of the shop, so he wouldn't have to stand on his tiptoes all day.

He purchased a full-length mirror to go on the wall, and it served as a final primping point before miners went down to the Placer Saloon to talk to Miss Bedwell or Miss Monique Orleans. Haircuts, like everything else, were more expensive in Hangtown—two dollars for a haircut and a dollar for a trimmed beard.

Some of his customers tried hard to get themselves together before they came by, but others smelled like they had been sleeping with either a wet dog or a dead dog. He finally prevailed on Mary to help solve his problem, so she used a knife to mix gum of camphor and menthol crystals into a liquid. It was a mystifying thing to see her mix the two solids together and end up with a liquid. She finished off the concoction by mixing that into some lanolin. Thereafter, when a particularly noxious gentleman entered the barbershop, B. F. would take a bit of this ointment and dab it on his upper lip, right under his nose. It usually was effective, but unfortunately, a few customers had a stench that would even penetrate this layer of protection.

Yukon Jack generally spent as much time sitting at the long serving table as he did behind his store counter. It had become pretty obvious that he had packed on at least fifteen pounds in the short weeks since his business transformed. Part of the fiscal arrangement was that he was able to eat his meals for free. The problem was that his meals seemed to last about an hour and a half. If Mary pulled a hot cobbler off the fire, he was determined to have "just a taste" every time she did.

Per the observation of one of his friends, Eb Benson, "Yukon— you done swole up like a dog tick in less'n a month. It's harder to git you off the bench in this here café than it is to get a hot mule out of a cool barn!"

He also seemed to have a hard time staying away from the barbershop, particularly when it was obvious that a funny story was being told. Many times, Yukon simply left a customer standing at the counter at his end of the store so he could get close enough to hear the reason behind the laughter in the barbershop. For B. F.'s part, he learned enough in a month about gold mining, miner frustrations, and what really went on at the Pot o' Gold that he could have filled a good storybook.

He was also learning some very colorful phrases of expression. At least once a day, Mary stuck her head in the barbershop doorway to shake her finger at some miner that had gone too far with his language. B. F. got the idea that most of them were in love with her in some abstract way that he couldn't explain. It was almost like she was one of the few representations of something decent in that place, and they all seemed to realize it.

But you didn't have to travel very far, or wait very long, for something bad to happen in Hangtown. For the most part, the miners worked hard, struggled in terrible conditions, didn't eat regularly, stood in mud or icy water for hours at a time, slept in the clothes they worked in, drank whisky to excess, gambled away a week's work in fifteen minutes, and mostly lived for that perfect day when their pan would be filled with nuggets. There were plenty of people preying on the miners—gamblers, thieves, prostitutes, and so-called business men who charged outlandish prices for necessary goods.

The actual gold rush had been going on for well over a year by the time B. F. arrived in Hangtown. The initial discovery had occurred in January of 1848, but no easy way existed to get this information back to the eastern United States. In fact, there was no real validation of the gold strike until President Polk's State of the Union Address in December.

However, the ability to transport information on the Pacific coast was not nearly so restrictive. Vessels spread the word much more quickly to willing ears in China, the Phillippines, Hawaii, Mexico, Australia, and the west coast of South America. Even though it would always be referred to in American eyes as the Gold Rush of 1849, there were many thousands of people already there by the time the first wagon trains of 1849 arrived. B. F. was continually amazed at the wide assortment of nationalities, languages, and cultures to which he was exposed almost every single day in California.

Even so, the almost universal miner's greeting was, "How was yer pan today?" Everybody was focused on the gold. Once in a while, a story would circulate that got everybody in a big way, and it usually found a ready audience in the barbershop.

The gambler, Irish Dick, told a story that got everybody's hopes up. "There was a young fellow who came in the El Dorado this morning. He swore he saw a champagne bottle full of half inch nuggets that came from three shovelfuls of dirt along Cedar Ravine."

"Who was he, Irish?"

"Said he was from Illinois. He was red-headed—but he appeared to be reliable."

"I hear Hangtown Creek is still full of good dust. They's some of them Celestials brings in three or four pounds every week."

"Somebody'll be takin' that claim away from them noodle-eaters."

"If they do, they best be cocked and loaded. There's six of them Chinymen on that claim, and they're all packin' a gat."

As B. F. remembered later, he was half through with cutting Irish Dick's hair, when two gunshots sounded that seemed to come from right outside the store. Every customer ran out in the street, including the half-barbered Irish Dick. With no more business, B. F. and Yukon went out after them just in time to see a crowd of at least a hundred miners coming down the street toward the hanging tree. They were dragging three men, two of whom appeared to be Mexicans.

The three had allegedly robbed a man in his mine shaft down on Log Cabin Ravine but had failed to kill him outright, even though they stabbed him in the back. The victim had been able to pull himself up to ground level and quickly raised the alarm. His attackers were still in the neighborhood, thinking they had plenty of time to get away.

They didn't. The general agreement of the crowd was that, since they hadn't actually killed the miner, each man would receive forty lashes with a bullwhip and then take a ride out of town on a rail.

One by one, the thieves were tied to the trunk of the hanging tree and whipped. At the end of it, only one—the American—was still able to stand. As it turned out, he would have done well to have collapsed with his mouth shut, along with his pals. Instead, he raised himself up and hollered out to the crowd, "You poxed bastards! May yous roast in hell for dis."

At that point, a man standing toward the front says to his partner beside him, "I bet those are the boys who murdered that miner over on the Stanislaus River two weeks ago. They stabbed him with a knife too." He said this, not particularly in a loud manner, but in one of those voices that can always be heard in a noisy place.

The comment was quickly repeated in all parts of the crowd. "Them's the murderers from over on the Stanislaus." From there it was only a short step to, "Let's string 'em up." Three ropes were brought forward and thrown over the great oak's dominant limb.

The men were in such terrible shape from the beatings that they were too weak to defend themselves, or even protest what was happening. Confusion and terror were reflected in the Mexicans' eyes. They kept looking at their companion to explain what was happening. B. F. saw the answering hard glare of the American, and realized it was unlikely the Mexicans even understood what was being said about them. For days afterward, B. F. asked himself—had this really been justice?

The crowd, which had grown to over three hundred by this time, wasted little time in delivering their version of due process—decision by popular vote. The men were in such a state that they had to be dragged to their feet so the ropes could be tied around their necks. Unlike the usual fashion of putting them on horseback and then forcing the horse to run out from under them, thus instantly snapping their necks, no horses were used. After their hands were tied behind their backs, two strong men simply hoisted each of them up in the air and others tied off the ropes. The three men dangled there, side by side, choking and kicking for several minutes until, one by one, they gradually stopped all movement excepting the final emptying of their bladders. The second Mexican twitched for almost fifteen minutes before he too no longer moved.

B. F. and Yukon walked back in the store, but for a time, B. F. continued to look out the store window at the three lifeless bodies hanging from the tree. He was startled when Yukon put a hand on his shoulder. "Son, you got to realize them boys ain't hangin' there just because they sang too loud in church. They's a good reason behind it." It was over. Hangtown justice had been delivered.

My story. On April 7 year of 1850

Mary has been telling everybody that the name of Hangtown is not good for business. She's had a little company from the three women who started the Temperance Union, and just yesterday they hung a new sign up. We now live in the town of Placerville. I'm not sure, but I doubt putting up a new sign is going to change the way they hand out justice for a long time to come.

Every day new miners arrive from San Francisco. Lots of them are here just long enough to find out that mining is really hard work, and they end up leaving just as broke as they were when they got here. The doc says he figures that at least one in twelve men die before they're able to leave. He says most of them get sick because of the cold and dampness underground in their mines. But it looks to me like plenty of them don't get enough to eat. It's pretty common to see a man come in here and spend everything they dug up that day on a good meal. I guess they think tomorrow is going to be their day.

I've seen Mary stick a potato or a biscuit in many a miner's coat before they leave here because she knows they won't have anything to eat except corn mush until they find more gold. It's no wonder so many of them think she is some kind of angel of mercy.

We have been here 8 months now and I have seen no sign of my pa. When I talk to men from other mining camps I always ask after my pa, but nobody has seen him. He has had plenty of time to get here. I am starting to think he was truly on the steamboat that wrecked on the Missouri River. I do not want to give up hope, but it just does not make sense. I surely miss my pa. But without him, I can never go back to Indiana.

Twenty-Three

One Helluva Way To Go

Placerville, California 1850

Gold was getting harder to find. It had become a rare occurrence that gold nuggets appeared in stream beds. Now the miners almost exclusively had to dig—and some of their mines were quite extensive. Also, it was much more common for several miners to join forces as they used more sophisticated techniques than simple panning and sluicing. It seemed to make more sense to band together and take advantage of the additive effects of many hands and picks and shovels. Mining as a group also made it easier to defend your holdings against claim jumpers.

There was no land office or office of records. Miners simply found a place that was unoccupied, staked the place as their "claim," and began to look for gold. However, if it was generally perceived that you were no longer actively mining a spot, then your claim could be taken over, or "jumped" by someone else. If you were mining by yourself, particularly if others knew you were finding gold, it was not unheard of for your claim to be jumped if you simply went into town for the night. When you arrived back at your claim the next morning, and several men were there working it and telling you it was now theirs, you had few options.

These fragile understandings were not enforced by any lawman— for there were none. Only the miners themselves enforced the rules.

As often as not, these problems quickly escalated into a fight. However, it had also become fairly common for a group of miners to arbitrate a disagreement between two opposing viewpoints, and their decision was generally observed. It was also not unheard of for a similar group of miners to act almost as vigilantes to correct perceived injustices and punish obvious criminals and trouble makers.

Seldom did vigilantes stay on the right side of the law for very long. As gold became harder to find, groups of miners decided to drive away the "foreigners"—particularly the ones who seemed to possess the best claims. The attacks were the most brutal against the Chinese, the Mexicans, and the Indians. Some said that around ninety thousand people had come to California in 1849, but only around two-thirds of them were Americans. So there were plenty of targets around for jealous miners and vigilante "justice."

It was during 1850 that the new state of California passed a Foreign Miners' Tax. This required all non-Americans to pay a tax of twenty dollars per month for the privilege of mining for gold in the state. This effectively caused "furriners" who were not working a productive mine to leave the gold fields, or seek other employment.

It was said that the docks of San Francisco were filled with abandoned ships. As soon as they made port, crews jumped ship and made for the gold fields along with the passengers they had transported. Some people in San Francisco had started taking over the empty ships and turning them into businesses at dockside. Other ships were dismantled in order to quickly provide the milled lumber needed to build shops and hotels in the rapidly growing city. Before gold was discovered in early 1848, there were no more than a thousand people in Yerba Buena, but in 1850 there were more than twenty-five thousand residents in what had become San Francisco.

The city served not only as an arrival point for all miners traveling by sea, but it was a depot for supplies, equipment, furnishings, and food for at least thirty mining camps that had sprung up within forty miles of Placerville. The miners in the area were often moving from one creek to another as rumors popped up about the latest find. And sometimes those rumors were strategically spread in order to jump decent claims when miners decided the grass had to be greener up at Portuguese Flat or Weaverville or Mormon Springs than it was in their gradually ebbing but still-producing mine outside Placerville.

One afternoon, B. F. was cutting the hair of a miner by the name of Wilbur Wilcox. According to Mr. Wilcox, he had come into town to "spend some of my money. Me and Hoolihan struck a good vein, and while one of us is diggin', the other got to be spendin', otherwise we'll have too gol'durn much gold. So I volunteered to come spend some."

There were three other men sitting there, listening but envious of Wilbur's good fortune, and asking themselves that ageless question, "Why is it always the other fellow who has all the luck?"

B. F. noticed another man standing at the doorway. He was short but appeared to be powerfully built in the shoulders. He was very dark complexioned, but what was so striking about him was that his eyes seemed to be on fire with anger. "Hey, you Wilcox. You jump my claim!"

"Now, Sanchez, you left your claim and took off somewheres else."

"I walk up to Dutch Flat to see what going on, then come right back. I only gone a day."

"You picked up all your gear and left the area. Far as I'm concerned, you abandoned your diggings, and your claim was there for the taking."

"You send that Hoolihan around to tell about new strike at Dutch Flat. Try to make miners leave good claims."

"I don't have no control over the rumors around here."

Sanchez reached behind his back and pulled a knife out of his waistband that had a long, narrow blade. At this, Wilbur started grasping for his pistol, but the barber cloth was interfering with his draw. Sanchez realized that he was going for a pistol, and rushed at him. B. F. tried to jump back out of the way, but inadvertently nudged Wilbur's shoulder as the pistol went off. The room instantly filled with a cloud of acrid smoke from the cap and ball pistol.

Realizing his hat had been blown off his head, Sanchez hesitated briefly, reasonably assuming he had been killed at a distance of six feet. But as he quickly came to the conclusion that he had survived, he jumped on Wilbur and knocked him backward onto the floor.

Wilbur's arm movement was still restricted and he could not fend off the knife. With an overhead stabbing movement, Sanchez sank the knife at least three inches deep into the top of Wilcox's head, just about an inch above his hair line, and straight above his right eye.

The shock of this sudden assault had frozen the shop patrons in their seats, until they realized they had to act. The three of them finally sprang into action, pulling Sanchez off of Wilcox. The victim was left in a seated position on the floor with a ridiculous look on his face. The left side of his mouth seemed to have gone slack, and his left eyelid was hanging down as though he was in the middle of an overstated wink. On top of his head, about half the knife blade and the handle of the knife stuck straight up.

Yukon burst in the barbershop doorway at about the same time as Mary and Jane. Truth be told, Yukon was far more upset about missing the action than about the man who'd been stabbed in the head in his store. Jane cried out, "B. F., are you alright?"

A tentative hand rose from behind Wilcox. The man had fallen backward onto B. F. as he tried to get out of the way.

Yukon looked at Wilcox. "That's one helluva way to go right there."

With some help from Yukon, B. F. slowly pulled himself out from under the victim, and repositioned himself to kneel behind Wilcox. "I don't think he's gone anywhere yet—at least not so far. He's still squeezing my arm with his right hand."

"Jesus, Mary, an' Joseph!" Yukon looked sheepishly at Mary. "Sorry ma'am. I believe my tongue got in front of my eye teeth, and I couldn't see what I was sayin'." He turned to one of the men in the barbershop. "Go get Doc McDaniel. Unless he's already been at it, tell him to take a stiff drink before he comes. He's gonna need it today."

By the time the doc arrived, Wilcox was sitting in the barber chair as though he was ready to have his haircut completed. Mary was trying to give him a drink of water, but the liquid was only running down the left side of his chin. Although he had opened his mouth several times as though to speak, it appeared that the knife had struck him dumb, for no sound would come from him other than an indecipherable, piercing squeak.

Doc McDaniel had seen several traumatic injuries from knife encounters, but certainly nothing like this that had not resulted in immediate death. Although not having the benefit of university training, he had heard about injuries in usually fatal locations with arrows and swords. Perhaps it was in Wilcox's favor that the Doc was at that rare point during the day wherein he had imbibed enough to stop the trembles but not so much to exhibit poor judgment. "I heard some scientific discussion about people who had these kinds of injuries, where the weapon is still sticking out of them. My doctorial opinion is that we leave the knife right where it is. If we pull it out, chances are he'll meet his maker real quick. I'd say Wilcox needs to see one of those doctors that specialize in this kind of thing in San Francisco when he's able to travel."

As to the fate of Sanchez, although a small number of miners were sympathetic to his plea of self defense, the majority held that Wilcox only had a single shot pistol, and he had missed, so there was no longer any immediate threat to Sanchez when he stabbed him. They didn't bother with the small detail that Sanchez had no idea whether Wilox had a single shot or one of those new, six-shot revolvers underneath his barber cloth, and thus would have been in plenty of immediate danger after the first shot was fired. As Yukon Jack reported later, after they hung Sanchez in front of the store, "A couple of fellers is still arguing about the verdict. I don't know what the big deal is. After all, he was just a Mexican."

Until Wilcox could travel to San Francisco, Doc McDaniel rigged up an elaborate protection for him out of an old beaver hat. He stuffed it with cloth packing, and then created a fitted space in the packing for the knife to rest in. He then affixed the hat firmly to Wilcox's head with a piece of rawhide tied under his chin. The patient was ordered to sleep sitting upright and to wear the hat twenty-four hours a day, no matter what.

As might be expected for such an oddity, every miner in Placerville wanted to see for themselves that a knife could actually be stuck in a man's head and he could survive. Everywhere that Wilcox went, he was asked to remove his protective hat. For a few days he obliged this sick curiosity, as he was not able to speak and thus talk his way out of it. But on two occasions, he had to draw his pistol to prevent curious observers from grabbing the knife to see if it indeed was stuck in his head. From that point on, he stayed completely away from town.

A few days later, Patrick Hoolihan was in town with the bad news. His first day back in their mine shaft, Wilcox had bumped his protective hat on a wooden beam and instantly dropped dead as a wedge. Some said Hoolihan was not above thumping the protruding knife himself so he could take over sole ownership of the mine. No one would ever know the answer to that except Hoolihan. But within a week, he was back in town again.

Yukon had been in the Pot o' Gold when Hoolihan came in, and he repeated the conversation as he overheard it. "That Hoolihan was trying to sell his claim on the mine him and Wilcox had. He said he cain't stay there no more, that the place is haunted. Says every time he goes down in the mine, he hears that sound like Wilcox made—something like the sound a door makes that needs to be greased—a long squeaking sound. Says he figgered it was just his imagination 'til he saw Wilcox sitting on a bucket—still with that pig-sticker in his head, and him sitting there making that terrible noise. The man done had the bejesus scared out of him."

Mary, who usually said nothing about the shenanigans discussed in the store, could not contain herself on this particular subject. "Does the idjit think that somebody's gonna buy that mine with a ghost livin' down there?"

Yukon was only too happy to give her the latest news. "Irish Dick gave Hoolihan fifty dollars for the claim on the spot. Then he went up on Oregon Ravine and sold it to three Chinamen for three hunnert dollars."

Sadly for Irish Dick, his name came up again all too soon. Once more, Yukon served as their source of the news. "I was just up at the El Dorado Hotel watchin' a card game betwixt Irish Dick and two young miners. Dick was winnin' most every hand—took them fellers for every dollar they had. So the red-headed one throws his cards on the table and says to Dick, 'Ain't no way you can pull that king of hearts three times in four hands. Yer waxin' them cards mister.'"

"Dick got that mean look on him and kinda talked with his teeth all set. 'If you're calling me a cheat, I'll cut your damned heart out, ye ignorant hillbilly.'"

"Dick is the kind of feller who'd give you the shirt off his back—just afore he steals your coat! Everbody knows you don't mess with Dick when he gets riled, but this kid was either too new to know any better or dead set on bein' stupid, so he says to Dick, 'There's two of us, and one of you, and I'm sayin' yore a low-down cheat.'"

"Dick was always fast—he had his bowie knife in his hand before I could blink—and he jumped at the kid and stuck that big knife in his chest. The kid stared down at the knife with this ridiculous look on his face, and Dick says to the kid 'I'm going to cut you up like boarding house pie.' So he just yanked his knife out and stuck it in him again. This time he twisted it around before he pulled it out. A great gush of blood come out on the table, and the kid pitched over face first right in all that gore. Dick looked over at the kid's partner and he says, 'Now I believe those odds are even.'"

"The kid's so-called friend ran backward so fast he was hid behind the bar before Dick finally ran out of the hotel and off into the woods. They called in a bunch of miners to help look for him, and there wasn't no shortage of volunteers. Dick took a lotta dust off these miners the last couple years."

"Anyway, they found him holed up over at Coffee's Tavern, hiding in the Duchess's room whilst she was gettin' a horse for him. I just come by here for a quick bite to eat. They're gonna hold his trial in about fifteen minutes. I doubt you're gonna have any customers this evening. Everbody's gonna be at the trial."

When B. F.'s waiting customers heard the news, they decided their hair could wait another day and departed to join the crowd in front of the El Dorado Hotel. The news had spread from one end of town to the other by the time B. F. and Yukon arrived, and they had to settle for a spot across the street, and just barely in hearing distance.

Like previous judicial decisions meted out in the old Hangtown, there was little time spent on formalities in the new Placerville as well. The only question that seemed out of place was an inquiry of the accused. "Say Irish, what's your given name, anyhow?"

"Dick Crone," was the response, and the trial began in earnest. They heard testimony from six men who claimed to have been eye-witnesses to the murder in the El Dorado, and per Yukon's memory, a couple of them hadn't even been in the hotel at the time. They heard from two men who had examined the deck of cards. There was no wax on the king of hearts, but they did point out that the card had been marked by somebody.

They gave Dick Crone a chance to defend himself. Never let it be said they weren't fair-minded men. "Sure and 'twas self defense—two idjits against the one of me. It was no choice I had in the matter with the both of them armed and rarin' to have a go at me!"

"Do you have anything else to say in your defense, Irish?"

"My mam warned me when you wallow with pigs, you should expect to get dirty. For sure, she was correct today. I believe twas that fat Englishman, Samuel Johnson, who said 'the prospect of hanging indeed tends to concentrate the mind.' But no, self defense is all I have to offer. If the court is fair minded, you'll leave my precious neck alone."

A verdict was called for, and five hundred voices supplied it. A noose was provided, and Irish Dick Crone had skinned his last miner.

The hanging tree was used again the very next week to deliver justice to Junior Dyer for the most heinous crime ever committed in the town. The evidence was clear that Mr. Dyer had shot and killed the lovely Miss Monique Orleans in her room at the Pot o' Gold. It seems he had been wildly in love with Miss Orleans for the previous three weeks, and was distraught when he entered the establishment on the evening in question and was told she was already entertaining another gentleman. It was easy to understand that Mr. Dyer was smitten with her, for no miner would disagree with the fact that she was a woman whose many fine characteristics had been visible for all to appreciate.

It was also understandable that it might have been the honorable thing for Mr. Dyer to shoot her gentleman caller, but for him to also take the life of one of the few women in the town, not to mention one that had been willing to share so many tender moments with a majority of the members of the jury—well, that was unforgivable.

Some speculated that Miss Ilsa, the Swedish Princess, would be forced to work overtime, due to the sudden departure of Miss Orleans. And several men pointed out that she seemed to lose all enthusiasm for her job when she worked overtime.

For his evil deed, Junior Dyer was hung twice—once until he was almost dead and then a second time just to give him time to reflect on his terrible deed. They decided to bury Miss Orleans in the shade of a tall ponderosa pine, overlooking the gold fields on the edge of town. Two volunteers were found to dig her grave late that evening, and the task began just as the sun was setting. Thankfully, they were able to finish sometime after dark and just before a sudden downpour forced them to take cover.

Word of Dyer's cowardly deed traveled quickly, and Miss Orleans' funeral the next morning was widely attended, with at least three hundred genuine mourners. At the service, many a tear was seen to roll down the grizzled cheeks of the miners in attendance. The procession to the gravesite was somber, in keeping with the occasion. But as the heartbroken pallbearers set the coffin beside the grave for the final prayer of departure, all four men spied what the rain had revealed from the night before. The bottom and the sides of the grave almost danced in the sunlight, for they were covered in nuggets!

Two of the pallbearers forgot themselves completely and jumped into the grave to start stuffing shiny nuggets in their pockets. The other two started picking up gold from the mound of dirt piled beside the grave. As realization set in, within seconds men from the crowd were elbowing one another and grabbing for the shiny stuff. Two others staked the area on all four corners and proclaimed the site their claim. Quickly, others staked directly above, below, and on either side of the gravesite. The two who had staked the area that included the grave were forced to draw their pistols in order to stop the two pallbearers from stealing their gold down in the hole.

There had previously been no real digging this far away from the river, and recognition ran through the crowd that here was new ground to be worked. Other stakes went into the earth, while picks and shovels began to clink as they struck the dirt. Miss Orlean's final rest would just have to be relocated to a less lucrative location.

Mary and Jane lived in a world composed almost entirely of men. The few women in town were not the sort that Mary would allow Jane to talk to. It's true that there were a few women who came with their husbands to the gold fields, but they generally stayed away from town because they were treated as such oddities. Mary and Jane had been around long enough and were such a known entity that they really did not have many problems with the miners. Only rarely did they encounter a new man who didn't know who they were, and in those cases, they sometimes had short-term problems. Short-term, because invariably a group of miners who did know them would quickly step in and pull the new man aside for a quick education on how he was to act around the Fitzwaters.

Some of the women at the mines were treated poorly by their menfolk, being expected to live under extremely arduous conditions with little appreciation for their work and sacrifices. A story began to circulate around town that a woman over at Angels Camp had been mistreated by her husband for weeks on end, with that abuse only getting worse as the man's lack of knowledge in mining techniques became obvious to all, and this was illustrated in his continued poor luck in finding gold. But it seemed that the woman, Alma Fogg, had recently made her case to all the miners surrounding their campsite that she was the one in the family in possession of mining skills.

One afternoon, Mr. Fogg made quite a stir over having a terrible case of the green apple quick-step, so he told his wife he was head-ing into town, "to fetch a bottle of Doc McDaniel's Ox-Bile Extract to ease my bilious innards." When he dragged back into camp the next morning he was a bit out of sorts with the world, wore some rather incriminating red rouge on his shirt, and was very loud about demanding his breakfast.

Missus Fogg went about her task of preparing breakfast while he continued to berate her. His neighbors had heard this kind of behavior all too often from him in weeks past, and they were about ready to take the domestic matter into their own hands. After all, a woman was too rare a commodity in Angels Camp to be treated that way. And several miners were quick to point out that they were willing to overlook Miz Fogg's backside, which closely resembled that of a Percheron horse, if she would but consent to keep their bed warm on cold California nights.

But it seems that Missus Fogg resolved the issue herself when she presented the breakfast skillet to her husband. The cast iron pan did not contain his usual bacon and corn mush, but rather a huge hunk of gold, which she had discovered in their mine the evening before while he was in town for his "medication." The monster ingot weighed a full sixteen pounds. No sooner had Mr. Fogg begun to exclaim to his neighbors over his new found riches, holding it up for all to see, but what the little Missus dealt him a resounding blow to his head from the aforementioned skillet. She looked down at her unconscious spouse. "I sure hope that settles yore digestion, ye low down whoremonger!"

Twenty-Four

The Pickled Head Has Straight Hair

Placerville, California 1852

Their third year in California the population of Placerville reached just over 5,600 souls. And there were almost a hundred smaller gold rush towns up and down the Sierra Madre foot-hills. Men paid in gold more often than they used money. Everything was so expensive that it was unhandy to carry enough money around to pay for their purchases. Also, the bank charged ten percent just to weigh and assay their gold before turning it into cash. So gold was commonly the method of exchange.

This led to Mary and B. F. beginning to have a problem with gold. They didn't know what to do with it. Even after paying rent to Yukon, purchasing a second cast iron cookstove, improving the appearance of their businesses, and paying ridiculous prices for supplies, they were still accumulating a significant amount of gold. Mary often cleared fifty dollars a day in her restaurant, while B. F. himself was saving at least fifteen dollars a day.

Both of them had several bags of gold hanging beneath the floor-boards or in hiding places in the walls of the store. They did not completely trust either of the two banks that had sprung up in town. The banks had printed their own private bank notes, secured only by the individual bank, which they would then trade to miners for their gold. In the first few years of the gold rush, access to enough United States coin and currency to keep the gold towns in business was just not possible, given their great distance from a U.S. Mint. The alternative had been for local banks to print their own private paper notes.

The stories of bankers absconding with hundreds of thousands of dollars in gold from two new banks in nearby towns were often objects of discussion in Placerville. Although the two bankers in Placerville seemed like straight arrows, a significant number of people would not do business with them just as a matter of principle. Mary had accounts in both banks, in which she continued to put a small amount of money every week. But this was only to prevent people from assuming that she kept her gold on the premises, and these accounts represented only a small portion of her holdings.

With all of the shipping traffic coming through San Francisco, she began to see Spanish gold coins—doubloons—and most recently the new U.S. twenty dollar gold piece—the double eagle—among her customers. So she and B. F. began to hoard gold coins in their hiding places. And when she went to the local banks, she asked to trade gold dust for coins, "So I can pay them suppliers without having to do all that weighin' and hagglin'."

They were frequently reminded of just what a good idea it was to conceal their gold—and their wealth. The presence of great wealth held by others, and the greed of some men to find ways to relieve them of it, was a recipe for thievery, larceny, and murder.

One Saturday afternoon, B. F. was as busy as he had ever been in the barbershop, as miners were bent on putting their best foot forward to get the attention of a new arrival at the Pot o' Gold. Miss Cordelia Clapp had created quite a stir among the miners when she arrived in town less than a week earlier. The creator, in all his wisdom, had decided that Miss Clapp should be the recipient of unbelievable physical endowments. And her special gifts were packing the house at the Pot o' Gold.

Two Mexicans who he had never seen before entered the barbershop, and with a single look from the younger of the two, the miner who had patiently been waiting for over an hour, immediately vacated his chair. B. F. started to make a remark, but something about the Mexican made him think better of it. The man was very handsome, with black, extremely wavy hair that really did not need to be cut, a pencil-thin mustache and a square chin. His clothes were much nicer than what was commonly seen in Placerville, and included a beautiful red and brown serape thrown over his left shoulder.

The other man was a few years older, of smaller frame, with the nose of a hawk, eyebrows that looked like two fat caterpillars, and graying hair. Both men had a look about them that ensured they would not be interfered with.

"Señor, may I help you?"

The younger man seated himself in the chair. "A shave and a trim for the benefit of Señorita Clapp."

B. F. recognized that the man was handsome, but the ego behind the demeanor and the remark was hard to take. He complied with the request, and at the conclusion of the haircut, he was replaced in the chair by the older man—who really did need the assistance of a barber. As his second customer removed his kerchief, B. F. noticed that he only possessed a thumb and two fingers on his left hand, with a terrible looking scar replacing his absent little finger and ring finger.

B. F. noticed both men seemed to be interested in the amount of business going on in the store, as well as the location of the cash register. "I think you have a good bizness, sí?"

"Every now and then we are busy. I guess the miners are coming to town to see the new lady at the saloon."

"Ah, yes, Señorita Clapp! Maybe Señor Joaquin will want her all to himself!"

B. F. laughed, then realized the man was not joking, and changed the look on his face. He was uneasy with them in the store, and after the men departed, he told Yukon about it.

When Yukon heard about the three-fingered man, he gave a low whistle. "B. F., you just cut the hair of Joaquin Murrieta an' Three-Fingered Jack."

B. F. looked skyward, pressing his memory. "I heard of them." "I reckon you have. Murrieta and his brother come to Hangtown about three years ago. They had a mine up at Shingle Springs, but the other miners run them off and jumped their claim when they made a little strike. To get even, Murrieta and four other fellers—including Three-Fingered Jack—started robbin' an stealin' an murderin' all over the gold fields, callin' themselves The Five Joaquins. Wonder why they're here in town?"

"That three-fingered fella said Murrieta wanted Miss Clapp for himself."

"Oh, Lordy!" Yukon thought a minute. "I better go up to the Pot o' Gold and tell Roscoe." Yukon stayed gone for four hours. When he finally returned, he was subdued and not a little bit inebriated.

"I been up there at the Pot o' Gold, helping Roscoe watch out for Murrieta and Three-Fingers. We been sitting in the saloon all evening, waiting on them boys to show their faces. But when it was time for Miss Clapp to perform, she didn't come downstairs. The place was packed with miners wanting to see the woman—she's got herself several hunnert de-voted admirers, that's for sure."

"Roscoe finally went up to see about her, and she was gone. Looks like they took her right out the window. When Roscoe come back downstairs and told them miners that she wasn't there, I feared they was gonna hang him. One of them said he was lower than a snake's belly. But when he told them who he figgered had took Miss Clapp, those boys put together a posse on the spot. Must be over a hunnert of them out covering the whole country right now to bring poor Miss Cordelia back to us."

Mary shook her head and sniffed at the thought of referring to the painted hussy as "poor Miss Cordelia." Yukon continued. "Roscoe sent a telegram tonight to Governor Bigler hissef, telling him what a vile thing Murrieta done and asking for some troopers to stop them low down criminals from stealing away our innocent women folk."

Neither Murrieta nor Three-Fingered Jack was found, but even worse, there had been no sign of Miss Cordelia Clapp. Whether finally pushed to action because of Roscoe Dibb's letter, or because of their continued lawless acts, or more likely because of the presence of a $5,000 reward, the governor sent the "California Rangers" to the gold-fields, with the express assignment to arrest or kill the Five Joaquins.

This news was unhappily received by others of Mexican descent, as many of them regarded Murrieta as a Robin Hood figure. There was considerable discussion in Placerville about whether or not the Mexicans in the area were hiding the Five Joaquins.

In July, the rangers finally encountered the band, killing two of the Mexicans. There were some who doubted that the rangers had indeed succeeded. So in an inspirational moment, the rangers cut off the head of the one believed to be Murrieta and the incriminating hand of Three-Fingered Jack. The rangers placed the evidence in two large jars of brandy and began a traveling exhibition of sorts, showing the morbid proof throughout California to anyone willing to pay the admission price of a dollar.

They obtained the signatures of seventeen people—including one priest—who indicated that they knew the men, and that indeed the remains were those of Murrieta and his three-fingered compadre. Despite the claims of several others—including Murrieta's own sis-ter—that they had the wrong man in their jar, the rangers received the $5,000 reward.

> *My Story October 10, 1852*
>
> *Today Yukon and I went up to the El Dorado Saloon, where the California Rangers had set up a tent outside to show off what they claimed to be the remains of the outlaws, Joaquin Murrieta and Three-Fingered Jack. We waited in line for at least an hour, and finally stood before two large jars of brandy with the grey-skinned evidence floating there, right in front of our eyes.*
>
> *Yukon elbowed me and tried to whisper. "You seen him as close as anybody. Is that truly Murrieta?"*
>
> *"Well," I said, "I have to admit that people sure do look differ-ent after they've been dead for three months, even though they're pickled. It's hard to tell whether the head in the jar belongs to the same fellow who was sitting in my barber chair last spring.*

*After all, he was talking at the time. I do know that the man in
the barber chair had some of the waviest hair I ever saw. But
the pickled head has straight hair. Maybe the brandy has something to do with it, but to tell the truth, I don't think it's him."*

When B. F. made this observation to Yukon, one of the rangers was
standing directly behind them, and he roughly pushed both B. F.
and Yukon to the side. "Move on, you two." He raised his voice. "Let
everybody see for theirsefs what comes to outlaws at the hands of the
California Rangers."

Twenty-Five

The Tarantula Dance

Placerville, California 1853

It didn't seem possible that B. F. had been in the gold fields for four years. Mining operations in and around Placerville had changed significantly. There were very few small mining operations left. The true "prospectors" had moved on to other towns in California, chasing one strike after another. What remained were larger groups of miners, working in ever more complex mines.

In many locations along the streams, organized groups of miners built a large sluice alongside the waterway and diverted a significant portion of the flow of the river through the sluice so they could dig for gold in the now-exposed stream bottom. Others pumped a stream of water against the sides of the river bank to try and loosen gold from the clay, then used other sluice-boxes to capture the grit being washed from the embankments.

But the most sophisticated technique was to extract gold from rock. Rock suspected of containing gold was placed in a stamp mill or some other rock-crushing device powered by a steam engine. After the rock was crushed to the size of gravel, the miners ran water through the crushed mixture to extract the pieces that contained gold.

Placerville, at least for a time, became the third largest town in California, behind only San Francisco and Sacramento. Many merchants came to Placerville, all with their own scheme to extract gold directly from the miner rather than from the hills along the river. But the majority of them were unsuccessful. They were often under-funded or not ready for the hard living conditions. Also, they failed to appreciate the loyalty the miners had for those businesses which had been there with them during the hardest days.

The singular exception was the interest generated by new female employees at the saloons and gambling halls. Men who had gone to the Pot o' Gold every night for a year could easily be swayed to switch loyalties to the City of Cibola Grog House with nothing more com-pelling than the arrival of a new young lady.

In August of 1853, as the full, triple digit heat of summer bore down on the town, a black-haired lass arrived from San Francisco in a private coach that pulled right up to the door of the Pot o' Gold. Roscoe had finally recruited someone he claimed could adequately take the place of Cordelia Clapp, who unfortunately had still not been found.

The new entertainment was Miss Lola Montez. She parted her black hair right down the middle, wore large gold ear bobs and dresses that included a generous amount of fine Irish lace placed in the most aggravating places. Her second evening in town, not a sin-gle extra miner could find room to squeeze into the Pot o' Gold after seven o'clock.

She sang for them—sad songs of frustrated love. Those that couldn't get into the place stood out front just to hear her voice. But if they were outside, they missed something that defied description that night—a historical event even by Placerville standards—something that lit a roaring fire under every man in the grog house.

Another woman came up on stage with her, introduced as Miss Lotta Crabtree. Lotta was just possibly a stage name, as it was very descriptive of so much of Miss Crabtree. The audience figured they were about to hear a duet between the two ladies.

But nobody would say he was disappointed when only Lotta Crab-tree sang—particularly when Miss Montez came back on stage in a black, tight-fitting dress with long, tantalizing slits up the sides. She had on black stockings and long black gloves, and she began to dance.

Or rather, some of the witnesses might argue that it was not so much a dance as it was a dream come true that night. Slowly she began to move all four limbs in a mesmerizing fashion that soon found her on the floor, balanced ever so lightly on her fingers and toes, and swaying like some kind of wild animal, the likes of which had never been seen in the forests of California before. As the music increased in speed and volume, it was hard to keep up with just what were arms and what were legs.

It had suddenly become very warm in the place, as men around the room were pulling off their jackets, downing their drinks, fanning themselves, and still they were red-faced. Not only had they never seen a woman move like that before, but they never even imagined one could. The song came to a frenzied end, with Miss Montez still on her hands and feet but finally moving as rapidly, and with just as much vibrato as the singer's voice.

The place went wild with applause. Miss Montez gave them a couple of low bows, and then finally stood in front of them with her hands on her hips. "Boys, that's my Tarantula Dance. Maybe I'll do it again for you some day," she gave an exaggerated wink, "if you're real nice to me." First one and then many gold coins were tossed up on the stage as tribute. And they cheered until they were literally out of breath.

That night, his long history of regular attendance at the Pot o' Gold finally paid off, for Yukon Jack was seated at a table very close to where she performed, and as she ended her dance, he rose like a real gentleman and held his chair for her to sit down. As long as he didn't launch into a coughing fit, he was still a handsome man, and Miss Montez accepted his invitation.

In the few minutes she sat with him, he learned she had been engaged to a French prince, but before they could be married, he was killed by a pirate who also sought her hand. Then the pirate was beheaded on the island of Jamaica, and she faced a future all alone in the whole world. She decided to come to California to forget her sorrow. Not only did Yukon fall head over heels for the woman, but in the next few days he predictably provided her story to every man in town. At least she wouldn't have to repeat herself.

Within a week, Yukon had come to Mary with an offer to sell her the store. This, he explained, would give him more time to be with Miss Montez so that she wouldn't have to spend any evenings with some of the riff-raff at the Pot o' Gold. After all, Miss Montez had confided in him that he was very special to her, and it was her desire to give him her undivided attention, if only he could keep paying Roscoe for her time. He almost quivered when he assured Mary, "And she's a true daughter of the cross, too!"

To that description, Mary had to choke back the response that came to her lips. The price for the Miner's Rest was $7,500, and Mary asked for two days to consider his offer. She sat down after the evening meal with B. F. and Jane, thinking that sometimes she had to pinch herself when she reflected on how far they had come since arriving here. They had been almost penniless, and now she estimated she had somewhere around $5,000 in each of the banks, and at least $60,000 in gold coins and gold dust under the floorboards of the store. But the price of the store was not the point. Her daughter was the point.

At fourteen, Jane was a striking young woman. It had become impossible to disguise just how much this was so by simply pulling her hair back severely, binding her torso, and requiring that she wear shapeless smocks. The attention she now drew from the miners, both in the store and on the street, had gotten to the point that it was impossible to ignore. Jane needed to be in a more civilized environment. There was absolutely no culture in Placerville, despite what Yukon might say about the new, refined entertainment at the Pot o' Gold since the arrival of Miss Montez.

It had been Mary's intention to move her family to San Francisco in the very near future, but she had more or less set a goal of accumulating $100,000 in order to be sure they would have enough money to live in a fine home, associate with proper neighbors, and make sure her daughter was introduced to a better life. As she learned more about the cost of living in San Francisco, she was afraid her $70,000 would not be enough. Strange that just four years previously they were ready to start from scratch in Oregon with little more than a half-filled wagon and less than twenty-five dollars to their names.

Mary stamped her foot. "Yukon is bein' played for a durned fool. That floozy has got him as worked up as a lovesick rabbit. He wouldn't know a good woman if he saw her every single day! The man acts like the butter has done slipped off his flap jacks!"

But as B. F. listened to Mary describe Yukon's proposal and her concern about staying in Placerville, he was torn between making more money and finding a way to stay with this family—and Jane in particular. It was impossible for him not to hear many of the whispered comments and notice the lecherous looks directed toward Jane; and there were times when he had been afraid for her safety. For the life of him, he couldn't see a way ahead to make money, stay with the Fitzwaters, and still keep them safe. And yet, Mary felt strongly that they didn't have enough money yet to move to San Francisco.

Jane had a different perspective. "I think we oughta stay right here. I can't tell you how glad I am to be here instead of being on some old farm in Oregon. Can't say I appreciate peeling taters every morning, but at least there's people to talk to. These old men don't mean any harm. If I had my sooners, I'd sooner we buy this place."

Mary was not convinced. "Yukon don't sell near as much as he use to before all these big mining operations come in here. Why, he's still trying to sell prospecting pans, while the miners have moved on to sluices and baffles and water cannons. About the only things we're gaining is the store building and a good way to buy food outa San Fran. Besides, we'd still hafta hire a feller to run the store."

B. F. tried to frame the issue differently. "The most important thing to me is the three of you. You being happy and safe is what counts. But if you believe you don't have enough money yet to leave here, then the question is whether or not this deal makes sense. If you buy the store, then you stop paying one hundred fifty dollars rent every month. You'll start getting the fifty dollars rent from me for the barbershop. You can get rid of prospecting pans or anything else you don't want to sell. And you can hire whoever you want to work here. But if you don't buy it, Yukon'll sell it anyway—maybe to somebody that you might not even like, you'll keep paying rent, and there's no telling what they'll sell in here." He half-smiled at her. "Maybe even hard liquor!"

Mary snorted. "Over my dead body!"

B. F. laughed. "All I'm saying is that you have control if you own the place, but not if someone else does."

"Mr. Fitzwater used to say if it's worth thinkin' about, it's worth sleepin' on it. This here'll wait 'til morning."

B. F. felt pretty sure about the way her decision would go, and he decided this was reason enough for him to spend some of his gold. He'd been considering the purchase of a handgun for some time, but faced with the prospect that Yukon would no longer be in the store, he felt like now was the time for some extra fire power. As soon as Yukon arrived the next morning, he was there to greet him. "How much for that new pistol?" He knew perfectly well what the price was but was hoping Yukon would give him a better deal.

"With the holster, a box of lead, a pound of powder, and a hunnert of them percussion caps—eighty dollars. Who wants it?"

B. F. looked him in the eye with as mature a look as he could muster. "Me."

"Are you sure you're ready for a gat like this? This here is one terrible weapon. I seen a feller win a bet over at the Pot o' Gold by shooting one of these six times in the same amount of time it took for a wad of chewin' tobacco to hit the ground."

"Yukon, right now I've only got one shot from the old musket in the barbershop. That might not be enough whenever you're gone."

Yukon hung his head. "So ye know about that. I was hoping to talk to you separate. Gimme sixty dollars for the lot—and don't tell nobody what ye paid for it."

The 1851 Colt Navy revolver was a beautiful piece of work, with brass fittings, a brass trigger guard, and fine walnut grips. B. F. was careful to follow Yukon's directions regarding the amount of powder to use. He added the ball and patch to each chamber and tamped it down with the rod. Then he placed a percussion cap over the six chambers. He hoped he wouldn't have to use it, as he'd seen way too much blood in Placerville to think violent death was somehow romantic.

He tried wearing it on his waist for about ten minutes in the barbershop and realized it was too cumbersome. Even worse, the gun threatened to pull down his pants. His solution was to hang it on the back of his barber chair. That way he could get to it quickly, and any thief would probably not realize, just by looking, that he was armed.

Twenty-Six

I Figured I Kilt Ye

Placerville, California 1853

Mary hired Lester Purdy to run the general store portion of her establishment. Yukon had introduced him as a man who knew something about the business, having worked in a store in San Francisco. And he certainly seemed to know what he was doing. She caught him looking at her every few days and gradually came to realize that it didn't displease her.

He was taller than most men and sported a short beard. His hair was black but flecked with plenty of gray. He arrived at work on time and never left early. Although she couldn't be certain, she was fairly sure that he stayed away from the liquor and the ladies at the other end of town.

On three different occasions she had nicked silver dollars along the edge and then got Ethan to use them to buy something in the store right before closing time. The marked money was always still in the cash box when Lester left. Of course, that didn't prove anything, but all the same it gave her a level of comfort with the man. Very soon they had a good working relationship. She even heard herself laughing at some of his remarks, and realized she hadn't heard that sound for a long time.

My Story October 20, 1853
   Something is just not right about Lester Purdy. He acts nice
to Mary and Jane, but has no use for me and Ethan. Maybe I'm

comparing him to Mr. Fitzwater. I know that's not fair, but it's hard not to when you're accustomed to the genuine article.

This morning Lester came to work with a boy around sixteen. The son was almost as tall as his father and had a chin full of pimples, an adam's apple that seemed ready to pop out of his throat, and a flaming chock of red hair sticking up in the middle of his head.

Lester introduced him as his boy, Roger, but admitted that everybody called him Rooster. You couldn't help but hear the giggle from Ethan's direction, and Mary shot him a glare. I just wish she hadn't been looking in the wrong direction to catch sight of the purely evil look Rooster shot toward little Ethan.

"Roger, this here is Miz Fitzwater, and that there is her girl Janie and her boy Ethan. Yonder in the doorway is B. F."

Rooster spent too much time looking at Jane for it to go unnoticed. There was a split second of awkward silence before Mary said, "Good to meet ye, Roger. Are ye working somewhere around here?"

"No, I don't have no work yet. I was wonderin' if I could work here?"

Mary cringed at the thought of this boy gawking at her daughter all day. "No, we just don't have the business for another worker. But since they run off the Celestials and Mexicans and killed most of the Indians, the mining companies are always lookin' for help."

Lester broke in. "Thank you, ma'am. I'm sure he can find work."

That evening Mary took Jane and B. F. aside. "I seen an omen this morning. 'Twas well past sunrise, and I saw an owl perched outside the window. It was staring straight at me."

Jane drew in a sharp breath. "Are you sure, Ma?"

"Sure as can be. An owl looking in your house in the daylight is the lookout for the death angel. It's even worse than a black crow. I want you two to be real careful. Course, that owl mighta been looking for Yukon Jack. But you can't be too cautious. I don't want you goin' nowhere without a good pinch of salt in your pocket to protect you."

Over the next several weeks, it became more obvious to B. F. that Lester was pursuing Mary, and that Mary wasn't trying to run very fast.

It also was clear that Rooster had set his sights on Jane. The boy was in the store twice a day, and for no good reason that B. F. could see, other than making eyes at Jane. So far at least, she was paying him no mind.

Mary, on the other hand, was paying plenty of attention. The more she saw of the boy, the less she liked him. Her conversation with her daughter was straightforward. "Janie, ye got to get outa this place. Me and the boys'll stay here for another year, but you got to go to San Fran and start a new life. Go to school. Be around people your age. Go to some of them fancy places."

"Ma, please don't make me go. I don't wanna leave my family. I ain't scared here."

"That's one of the problems. You ain't scared of nothin'. You're just stubborn enough to deny that fat means greasy. That Rooster makes my backbone crawl. He's just plain wormy. You just as well get ready. You and me are headed to San Fran next week."

"What about the store?"

"These old men will have to miss our cooking for a week or so. Lester and B. F. can keep the rest going."

Friday afternoon was a lazy fall day. B. F. was busy cutting the hair of an Indian named Six Toes, but it was too early for the supper crowd. Mary heard a scream—then another. "That sounded like Ethan."

The sound was so unlike him that she ran out of the store and started up the hill behind the place. She met Ethan running at full tilt. He was crying, but in a panicked way. "I got snake bit!"

Mary caught him and picked him up. "Calm down son. What kind of snake was it?"

"I think there was two of them—both rattlers."

She was walking toward the store, hollering for B. F. "Where did they bite ye, son?" He pointed to his legs. She could see a clear imprint of fangs on his left calf and similar marks on his right ankle. "Where were ye when it happened?"

"I went up to my fort to play, and they were inside."

"B. F. take a shovel or hoe and go see what kinda snakes are in his fort. Be careful. He says they're vipers."

He felt Six Toes' hand on his shoulder. "I go too. I know snakes that rattle." B. F. was relieved. He hated snakes.

Once in the store, she sent Lester for Doc McDaniel, put Ethan on the table, and poured cold water over his legs. Then she began to suck on the bite marks, as they were already swelling. She tried to spit out everything in her mouth, but in a few minutes she felt herself getting dizzy. Despite this, she kept up the suction, and then she was sick to her stomach.

B. F. came back in. "They were Oregon Rattlers all right. One was as big around as my calf. And there's another thing. Six Toes says there was an empty flour sack in Ethan's fort. He thinks somebody brought the snakes in that sack and put it in there on purpose."

"How could anybody do that to a little boy?"

Lester came back in. "Doc says to bring the boy to his office so's he can cup him. I'll tote him over."

Mary looked at him with a helpless look. "I thought you was supposed to keep them still. I heard about that cupping. The Celestials believe in that. I just hope the doctor knows what he's about."

When they were gone, B. F. and Jane began to clean up and close the store. They had already started preparing the big supper meal, so there was plenty that needed to be done before they could go see about Ethan. Jane was crying as she worked, and B. F. felt like it himself. They worked together in the dining room until Jane finally walked over to B. F. and put her arms around him and sobbed. Neither of them said a word, but they knew they needed something from each other. They stood there like that—heads on each other's shoulder—for at least five minutes, neither saying a word, until Jane pulled away and went back to the kitchen.

B. F. heard the door open behind him, and without even looking up from his work, he said. "We're closed. There won't be any supper here tonight." The door opened again, and he kept up his work, assuming that the customer had left. Too late, he heard the sound of a step behind him, but before he could get turned around, there was a whooshing sound, and the club struck him in the back of the head. B. F. hit the wooden floor hard and didn't move.

He must be dreaming, because he heard someone scream his name. Then there was a voice. "Shut the hell up or I'll smack you again." Who was that? Then his name was screamed out again. It was Jane!

He heard the sickening sound of a fist striking a nose, and the screaming stopped. "Hurry up, pa. I been waitin' on this." It was Rooster's voice coming from the kitchen.

B. F. forced himself to be quiet. He pulled himself up to his knees and held his hands on the floor to keep his balance as the room slowed its spinning. He silently crept behind his barber chair, retrieved his pistol, pulled it out of the holster, and cocked it as quietly as he could. When he stepped to the doorway of the kitchen, he had to force himself not to look at the unconscious Jane. Rooster was kneeling over her, and Lester had his back to B. F.

"Get off her, you low-bred dog." Both of them twisted around toward his voice and saw the gun.

Rooster spoke again. "Must be losin' my touch. I figured I kilt ye."

"I said get off her." B. F. had most of his attention focused on Rooster, but he reacted quickly when he saw the knife in Lester's hand. Lester lunged at him and B. F. stepped sideways as he pulled the trigger on the big pistol. The man fell against the table and hit the floor like he'd been hit by a hammer.

B. F. was off balance enough that the concussion of the gun knocked him back into a chair. He cocked it again as Rooster jumped up and ran for the door. He pulled the trigger again and Rooster fell into the front door frame. He grabbed his side and got out the door before B. F. could recover himself to shoot again.

He looked at the spreading pool of blood under Lester. At least one of them was done. In looking at Jane, he was not sure she was in much better shape. There were big red whelps on her face where fists had struck her, the bridge of her nose was badly cut, and there was a nasty bite mark on her shoulder. She made no sign of responding when he tried to wake her. He did what he could do to get her decent and began to holler for help.

A voice from the front door. . . . "What's going on in there, B. F.?"

"Two men attacked Jane Fitzwater and may have killed her. Will you get Doc McDaniel?"

When the doc showed up, B. F. was holding a wet cloth on the back of Jane's neck. She had not stirred. "What happened here, son?"

"This man here, Lester Purdy, and his son Rooster were attacking Jane. One of them hit me on the head and must have knocked me out. When I woke up, Jane was screaming. I got my pistol and shot this one when he tried to jump me with his knife, and I shot at his son as he ran out the door. I think I hit him."

"There's blood on the door jamb, so I'd say you did."

"What about Ethan—is he going to be alright?"

"I left Miz Fitzwater with him. I'm afraid he's awful little to take two rattler bites. Both his legs are swollen at least two or three times normal. I've done everything I know to do." He looked like he was about to cry. "It's in the Lord's hands now."

B. F. told him about Six Toes finding the flour sack near the snakes. "I believe these two men were figuring to kill both Mary's kids." He pointed at the figure on the floor. "Lester there was trying to talk her into marrying him, so maybe that's how he was going to do away with any interference."

"What that Indian says he found won't do any good in court."

"Why is that?"

"Because California passed a law about three years ago that says no Indian or non-white can testify in court against a white man."

"What?"

"Look here son, I've got to get back to Ethan. This man is dead. I'll send the undertaker over to get him out of here. The girl is alive, but she's unconscious. I don't want to move her 'til she wakes up. Can you stay with her? Just send for me if she gets worse."

My story. On November 24, 1853

   The most terrible thing ever has happened. Lester Purdy and his boy attacked Ethan and Jane yesterday. Jane is alive, but beat up so bad that we can't wake her up.

That's not the worst of it. They put rattlesnakes in Ethan's fort. He got bit twice, and they buried him this afternoon. At least half the town showed up for his funeral. I stayed in the store with Jane, in case she woke up, but I watched the procession of miners following along behind Mary to the cemetery. His little casket didn't seem anywhere near big enough to hold all of his personality.

Lester is dead and gone to hell, and I'm the one who sent him there. I can't say I regret it, but I know I've committed one of the deadly sins. Rooster got away—but it wasn't because I didn't try to kill him too. I don't want to scare Mary, but I think he'll be back.

Over the next several days, B. F. and Mary took turns sitting with Jane. They tried to get liquid nourishment down her, but were just marginally successful. The store was still closed, and neither of them had any heart in being open and having to talk to people. Doc McDaniel came every afternoon to check on her, but he had no more idea about Jane's prognosis than they did.

Rooster's description had been circulated around Placerville and in surrounding towns, but that gave B. F. little reason to feel safe. Awkward as it may be, he had begun wearing his pistol twenty-four hours a day.

He had a terrible time sleeping and kept getting up all during the night to check on Jane. Anyway, if it hadn't been for his not being alert, this wouldn't have happened to her. He was determined that nothing bad would happen again.

Mary slept beside Jane in the kitchen, while B. F. alternated between his pallet in the barbershop and sitting in a chair at the doorway to the kitchen. The fifth night after the attack, it must have been around midnight when he thought he heard something outside. He lifted his head off the pallet in order to hear better, holding that pose for at least ten minutes and didn't hear another thing.

He was mentally and physically wrung out and finally put his head back down, but just before he drifted away, he heard a light popping sound. He argued with himself that it must be the fire in the wood stove in the kitchen, but just the same, got up and walked into the kitchen. The room was dark, save a glow of light through the chinks of the stove, but before he turned back to bed, he realized there was another glow coming from the window at the back of the store. He took a couple of steps toward the window and saw the fire.

"Mary! Jane! The store is on fire. Get up." Then he saw the outline of a grinning face looking in the window. The hair had been cut short, but he knew it was Rooster Purdy. He drew his pistol and fired where the face had been, then ran to the window to shoot again if necessary. There was no sign of anyone out in the darkness. Surely his imagination wasn't running away with him!

He and Mary dragged Jane's pallet to the front of the store and left her near the door, then ran back to fight the fire. B. F. knocked out the rest of the window to see what they were dealing with. Thankfully, they had two large pots of water in the kitchen, which were always there for cooking or dishwashing purposes. Each of them began to carry bucketfuls of water to the window and dump it on the fire. The pots were soon emptied, and they turned to using the contents of the slop jar.

B. F. then tried to run out into the street, but the knob on the front door seemed to be loose somehow, and he could not disengage the lock. Had Rooster somehow loosened the door knob so they were unable to escape? The door was sturdy enough that it resisted his stout kicks, and he ended up prying the door lock open with his Army knife before he could get outside. He shot his pistol into the air and hollered "Fire" several times as loud as he could, then raced across the road and down the embankment to the river, filling his two buckets. Once he was able to pour water directly on the fire at the back of the store, he could use the water more effectively and began to believe he was making some progress.

By the time he had run back around to fill his buckets again, five men had shown up with buckets and Mary was directing them. In five more minutes, the fire was out. Several of the mining camp towns had not been so fortunate in their experience with fires. The stores were generally built very close together, and they were always built of wood—a recipe for total destruction of some of the towns. Although a large area of the back of the store was heavily blackened, they had been very lucky.

As they continued to pour more water on the rear of the building to make sure the wood was saturated, B. F. told the other men about the face he thought he had seen at the window, and his gunshot. The general opinion was to wait until daybreak to see if they could find any sign of Rooster. Mr. Percy Night, the hardware store owner, put it very well for all of them. "Ain't none of us got the desire to walk through them woods at night looking for a damned lunatic."

When B. F. finally walked back in the store, he was bone-tired and filthy with smoke and soot. But his weariness melted away when he saw Mary sitting on the floor by her daughter, and Jane finally had her eyes open. He sat down beside her too and held her hand.

They sat there for a while, not really knowing what to say. Mary made some small talk about getting her up and getting all cleaned up and fixing her a meal, but Jane seemed to be paying no attention to her. She didn't make any attempt to respond when B. F. squeezed her hand, didn't show any feeling when her mother hugged her, didn't say a single word. The only response they got was when they were getting her into a chair, and Mary put her hand on her right side to support her. Only then did she cry out in pain when her mother touched her ribcage. When Mary unbuttoned Jane's shift, she saw the large bruised area that possibly meant a broken or cracked rib. Mary fed her a soft-boiled egg, but that was about all she was interested in.

With Rooster out there on the loose, B. F. couldn't allow himself to sleep. He pushed one of the long tables against the damaged front door and spent the rest of the night sitting in the kitchen, watching the broken back window. He must have been in a haze sometime before daybreak, because he jerked wide awake when he heard a strange sound out beyond the window. He couldn't identify what he had heard in his half-awake state, and finally put it down to the wind blowing in the pines.

In the morning, B. F. handed his pistol to Mary, made sure she knew how to use it, and went to get the doctor. While Doc made his examination, B. F. retrieved his pistol and walked back behind the store to see if he could see any sign of Rooster. There had been quite a bit of traffic in the area the previous night, and lots of water slopped everywhere, so he tried looking for evidence a bit up the side of the hill. After ten minutes of fruitless searching, he was ready to give up when he saw two drops of dried blood.

The trail was about seven hours old by that point, so it wasn't easy to follow, particularly in the rocky terrain, but he persisted. More blood. Another few yards and he found a place where Rooster had apparently stopped for a few minutes to collect himself—there was a small puddle of congealed blood behind a big pine tree.

Perhaps he had tried to stanch the blood by some method that had worked the wrong way, or perhaps his clothing had become saturated with it by that time. At any rate, the trail had become easier to follow. B. F. drew his gun and laid his thumb across the hammer. He was convinced the only way to stop this was to do it permanently.

He moved as silently as he could, knowing that nobody would continue to lose this much blood and keep going for very long.

He looked ahead about forty yards further up the hill and saw a rocky outcropping—certainly a good place to hide. He looked hard at the spot for at least ten minutes and finally saw something move. It was such an obscure movement that he couldn't tell what he'd seen. He had to move closer.

He maneuvered sideways until he put a large digger pine directly between himself and where he had seen the movement. Then when he reached the pine, he braced the big pistol against the right side of the tree and eased his head around ever so slowly in order to get a closer look. It moved again. But the outcropping looked almost impossible to reach, so he doubted that it was a human being lying up there. Maybe some kind of an animal—something big.

He took one more step and felt his foot give slightly. A rock rattled away down the hill. The big cougar lifted his head, and with no more than two quick, effortless bounds, was gone. He hadn't wanted to shoot, because he didn't want to warn Rooster that anyone was in the area. But to be honest, he couldn't have cocked the pistol fast enough to get off a shot.

He moved back to the blood trail and continued up the steep incline. He didn't have to go far. Apparently, he and the cougar had been looking for the same fellow. About all he could recognize was the short-cropped, red hair. The smell was terrible. B. F. leaned against a pine tree as he threw up. There was no way to tell if Rooster had been dead when the cat had found him, but B. F. fervently hoped he had still been alive. He spit on the carcass and walked back down the hill.

My story. On November 30, 1853

Rooster came back last night and tried to burn the store down with all of us inside. I shot him through the window and he got away up the side of the mountain. I don't know whether my shot killed him, or a panther did it for me. Makes no difference to me, but he's sure enough good and dead.

Jane is eating a little bit, dressing herself, washing her face, walking to and from the necessary, and sleeping on her pallet. But the rest of the time she just sits in a chair by the window. Mary and I talk to her as often as we think we should, and I've even tried reading to her to see if that might get her interested in something. But there is no acknowledgment of anything we say or do, and she has yet to speak a single word. It really hurts to see her like this.

Doc McDaniel recommended that Jane go to San Francisco to see a nerve and melancholy specialist. Mary has no idea if that kind of doctor can even be found in the city, but she's made arrangements to take Jane on the Tuesday stage.

Twenty-Seven

Get Away From Me
Once And For All

Placerville, California 1853

The last Monday in December, a storm blew in from the Pacific and it began to pour down. By mid-day, the wind had picked up from the west and the rain was slanted almost to the horizontal. Not a soul was moving outside.

B. F. used the situation to sit with Jane again. He pulled a chair close to hers so they were sitting side by side but facing in opposite directions. He sat there quietly for a few minutes, trying to tell if anything in her demeanor indicated she was uncomfortable. The steady hammer of the rain on the tin roof seemed to desensitize the situation somewhat.

He leaned his head close to hers, but did not touch her, keeping his hands resting on the tops of his thighs. "Jane. I am so sorry that I wasn't there for you when you needed me. The men who hurt you had knocked me out. What woke me up was hearing you call my name. You are the most important person in the world to me, and nothing can change that. Please talk to me."

He sat there. He didn't know which was louder—the rain on the roof or the blood pounding in his brain. He finally bowed his head and rubbed the place behind his left ear. His headache hadn't stopped throbbing since the night they were attacked. He suddenly realized

Jane had placed her hand on top of his right hand. He wanted to pull her close. But he sat still.

"Nothing is the same no more." He could barely hear her. "I ain't the same as I was. Then I was brim full of life and joy. Now it seems like all that is dead. I remember I used to dream about what was gonna come next in my life, and how I looked forward to seeing what would happen. But now I can't seem to remember *how* to dream, even though I sit here all day trying. Now everything is so . . . empty."

And then, "And where is Ethan? Did they hurt him too?"

B. F. couldn't—wouldn't—lie to her. But he knew how fragile things were. "Let's get your ma in here to talk about Ethan." He felt her hand go slack on his. "Mary, would you come in here please." Mary left her place at the front door where she had been watching the storm. "Mary, Jane has asked about Ethan."

Mary looked at B. F. with the slow realization that her daughter had started talking. He read her look and nodded. She drew her daughter to her and held her tightly. "Janie, I got some terrible news to tell ye. The men who hurt you was the ones that put rattlesnakes in Ethan's little fort. He got bit and took awful sick. We lost him that next morning. He's gone to be with your pa now." She began to weep. "I know they're together in heaven and watching down on us."

Jane was shivering. "What about those men?"

Her mother wrapped a quilt around her shoulders. "They won't bother nobody, not never, ever again. You're safe now, Janie."

It poured all the remainder of the day and all night and continued into the next day. The roads were impassable during bad weather, as the stage had to cross three significant streams on the trip down to San Francisco. The normally shallow Hangtown Creek across the road from the store had overflowed its bank on their side and was close to reaching the road itself. If it rained much more even the town might flood. Many of the mines were already flooded, and most of the miners were trying to exist in miserable conditions, huddled under leaking tentage or makeshift shelters.

Mary decided the only Christian thing to do was to feed them. The meals wouldn't be fancy, because she had not been open for business in over a week and had not replenished her supplies. But she could certainly put bacon and biscuits on the table.

She and B. F. served over a hundred men for breakfast and almost three hundred for supper. They ran completely out of food before five o'clock, and she wouldn't accept payment from anybody. Jane worked with them but stayed back in the kitchen. They made no attempt to push her.

It finally stopped raining, but the temperature had quickly become much colder. As she and B. F. were cleaning up for the day, Mary suddenly realized that Jane was no longer in the kitchen. They looked through the store for her, but with no success. They ran outside about ten minutes before sundown, hollering for her. B. F. asked every miner he encountered if they had seen Jane.

Finally, one pointed toward the footbridge that crossed the swollen stream. "I seen her down by the bridge just a minute ago."

B. F. trotted toward the bridge, calling her name. Then he saw her, and his heart stopped. Blind fear seized him and he began to run as hard as he could. She was out on the footbridge, and the bridge was being battered by the roiling water underneath. The structure was normally at least eight feet above the creek, but the rain of the last two days had the water blasting underneath no more than a few inches below the walkway.

Mary had also seen what was happening, and was now running herself. Both of them were screaming her name, trying to be heard above the roar of the water. Jane had maneuvered to almost the middle of the footbridge. Even her slight weight on the bridge pushed the walkway into the rushing water. It appeared that she momentarily struggled to keep her balance, but let loose of the handrail on the right hand side and looked down at the water. B. F. was almost to the bridge. "Jane. Hold tight, Jane. I'll be right there."

She turned and looked straight at him, seemed to shake her head once, her left hand came off the rail, and she fell forward into the brown, foaming water.

It was impossible. No one could survive in that water. B. F. now began to run back downstream, hoping to see her head bob up to the surface. If he could just see where she was, he might save her. He ran for over a mile, scrambling over rocks and fallen timber, shouting her name. He knew the creek would soon empty into the South Fork of the American River, and if anything, it would be far worse than the usually mild Hangtown Creek. He had seen no sign of her whatsoever, but with the sun disappearing behind the foothills to the west, it was getting difficult for him to distinguish objects in the water. He kept thinking—praying—that every dark thing in the water would be her, but there was a great deal of flotsam churning along in the current, and nothing looked like Jane.

Panicked, he called to her again and again. He should have jumped in with her at the bridge. Maybe he could have found her in the water. He cried out into the dark, now realizing that he could no longer see anything in the river, save the white, frothing water. He had known for a long time that he was in love with her, and he had no idea how he could keep having a life without her in it. He wondered if she had even known how he felt. He should have told her. Maybe that would have changed everything.

He was almost hyperventilating as he trudged up the road, clutching his arms across his chest. How could this be? All he could think was, for the second time, he had failed to save her when she needed him. When Mary saw him on the road, she knew any hope was lost. From somewhere, a cry came from deep inside her and she fell to the ground.

B. F. and two men picked her up and carried her back to the store. B. F. suddenly realized what a frail woman she was. It had been hard to see anything but her strength and toughness, and you just didn't think about her being such a small person. However, her strength had all been for the benefit of her family—and now she had no call for it.

She quickly roused with wet compresses on her forehead and the back of her neck. B. F. thanked the men for their help, and when they had gone he moved to hug Mary. But before he could do so, she turned her back on him. He didn't know what to do. She walked into her kitchen and curled up in a ball on Jane's pallet. It was one of the straw tick mattresses the two of them had sewn together so long ago in West Port. B. F. stood there, feeling completely helpless for the better part of a half hour, then finally retreated to his own pallet.

As soon as he was by himself, the tears came—first in rolling drops that stung his eyes, and later in sobs that involuntarily shook his body. He cried until the tears wouldn't come any more. Mercifully, he must have gone to sleep sometime during the night.

When he awoke sometime before daybreak, he lay there in a confused state for a time, believing that he must have had a terrible dream. He jumped up and dashed into the kitchen, sure that he would see Jane there on her pallet. Instead, he saw Mary sitting there, rocking back and forth with her arms around her knees. It wasn't a dream.

B. F. started a small fire in the cookstove and put a coffeepot on. Then he found a tin can of peaches in the store and opened it for them. "Mary, you have to eat something." She sat at the table and dabbed at the pickled peach without any interest, although B. F. knew they were usually her favorite treat. He brought her a mug of coffee with a good spoonful of honey.

After she sipped a bit, she cleared her throat. "B. F., I was scared of what bad luck ye might bring upon my family when you come on a full moon back in West Port. You was even born under a bad sign. But I pushed aside my fears when I saw how you got on with Mister Fitzwater and my Janie. I'll blame myself for that poor judgment for the rest of my life. I shoulda listened to what my Granny Leary taught me about the moon and strangers.

"I lost my husband because you didn't bring no doctor. Then I listened to you and brought my family to this here wicked place, and my Janie and Ethan are both dead. You even kilt the man that was trying to spark with me. I want to sell this here store and never come back. Every place I look I see Janie and Ethan lookin' back at me. I fear they's a demon livin' inside of you. Maybe you can't help it, but it's still there. I want you to take what's yours, and get away from me once and for all."

My story. On December 30, 1853

Everything left that was good in my life came to an end yesterday. Jane fell into the Hangtown Creek after a big storm, and was swept away in a flood right in front of me. I never saw her again.

This morning, Mary told me that all the bad things that had happened to her family—the deaths of Mr. Fitzwater, and Ethan, and now Jane—were my fault. It's bad enough that they're all gone, but I didn't ever figure she'd blame me for it. I guess she's felt this way for a long time—all the way back to West Port—and it finally came out this morning.

She told me she never wanted to see me again—that I had a demon inside me. I wonder if that could be true? She once asked if the people closest to me met with a bad end. When you put all these things together—maybe she's right.

Mary is in such a state, the chance of her leaving Placerville with all her gold, and getting both it and herself to San Francisco in one piece is not very good unless I can figure out a way to help her. I owe her that. She's the nearest thing I've had to a mother since I left Indiana.

He sat her down and told her his plan. She didn't object. He spent three hundred dollars on two buckboard wagons and two horses. Next he tore out a five foot wide section of the south wall on his barbershop lean-to and pushed one of the wagons inside and out of sight for "improvements." After measuring the wagon bed, he found a bolt of heavy cloth in the store, and cut a section four feet wide and eight feet long, which completely covered the existing wagon bed. Then he removed flooring from the barbershop and cut them into exact, four-foot sections. He pushed the freshly-cut ends of the boards into the dirt so there was no visible evidence that would reveal his recent carpentry work.

He retrieved every hidden bag of gold coins and gold dust with "BFW" written on the side. He then placed the coins evenly over the cloth. There were eight hundred ninety Double Eagles, twelve Eagles, and ninety-nine Spanish Doubloons. The coins completely covered an area about 3½ x 4½ feet. He also put fifteen of the seventeen bags of gold dust he had on the cloth, each of them holding some twenty-four ounces apiece. Five Double Eagles, all of the Eagles, and two bags of gold he placed in his pockets or his kit bag.

Next he poured the contents of two bags of rice on top of the coins to ensure they were well cushioned and would not be clinking together. He followed this with another layer of cloth, and then covered the entire bed with the just-cut four-foot boards. He then used a wide board to make a tailgate of sorts, which would conceal the fact that there were two layers of boards in the back of the wagon. Rather than use shiny, new nails, he used only nails from a rusted keg. The final step was to go out in back where he had tied the two horses and retrieve a mixture of hay, dirt, and manure, which he spread haphazardly in the bed of the wagon.

He stepped back to review his work. There was no indication that the wagon was any different than every other wagon on the roadways, and certainly no evidence that it held the equivalent of over $23,000.

The next day he switched out the wagons and repeated the process to carry Mary's wealth. She had miscalculated her holdings. By the time her coins and gold dust were loaded, gold reached from side to side and front to back. At least a hundred and fifty coins were double-stacked. B. F. estimated she had over $90,000 in the back of the wagon.

Including the money she had in the banks, she already had her $100,000. She could have moved to San Fran three months ago, and none of this would have ever happened. Both Ethan and Jane would be alive. B. F. figured that news was just too cruel. He decided not to tell her.

The wagon was so heavy that he couldn't push it out of the lean-to. He had to harness a horse just to pull it back in the yard behind the store. She had observed the whole process, but had done nothing to assist other than retrieve her bags of gold from their assorted hiding places. "Where's my spare gold?"

"It's still in the bank. It'll look mighty suspicious if you don't withdraw that money before you leave town. I'm going to completely tear down this lean-to, and block off the wall of the store with some of the boards. Once I'm done with that tomorrow, you need to try and sell this store. Even with what's left, it ought to bring four or five thousand dollars. Maybe even Yukon will want the place back."

"I hope the fool ain't already spent all his money on that Lola Montez."

"Even if he doesn't want the place, maybe you could hire him to ride you down to San Fran in this wagon. He's about the only honest man I met here. You might even hire him to take that wagon apart once you get there so you can get your money in two or three of those big banks."

"Maybe. He's probably up at the Pot o' Gold peeling grapes for the woman. That hussy went to seed a long time ago, and Yukon ain't got sense enough to see it."

Something in the way her mouth was set caught B. F.'s attention. All of a sudden he realized she was jealous! Why in the world had she not made her feelings plain long before this? He shook his head. "Just remember, if you do meet up with any bandits, give them the gold you'll be getting from the bank. Everybody in town will know you withdrew it within a half hour anyway, so as far as the bandits are concerned, they'll think they will have taken everything."

Mary paused for a minute to consider. "I reckon that's right."

By noon, he had finished his work on the side of the store. The freshly cut end pieces from the floorboards he had used to build the second-level beds of the wagons were shoved in the big cookstove and burned. He didn't want anybody—even Yukon—to suspect what he had done.

When Mary went to the banks, and then to find Yukon, B. F. loaded his wagon with his wall mirror, his barber equipment, four chairs, a piece of waterproof canvas, and the simple gear he had brought with him from Indiana. He retrieved his old cloth travel bag, his gun, and a collection of his clothes and put them in the wagon. He then packed a variety of groceries from the store's shelves, did a quick calculation, and left three Single Eagles on the kitchen table to pay for the food.

He started for the front door, turned back around, and picked up Jane's quilt. He held it close to his face and took in a deep breath. There was a part of her still there. He took it with him.

He decided not to wait on Mary's return. First of all, he couldn't think of anything to say, knowing now how she felt about him. Secondly, he suspected that whatever might be said would not really help either one of them. And he'd done all he could do for her anyway, under the circumstances. He stood in the doorway of the store and looked back one last time. He'd spent over four years here. He always knew he'd be leaving—but never figured it would be by himself.

Twenty-Eight

We're The Ones Who Call Ourselves Civilized

Columbia, California 1854

B. F. stashed the two bags of gold dust in the back of the wagon under two shovelfuls of manure and mud, but kept a single small bag of gold coins in his travel bag that he could give up in case he was robbed. He then placed Jane's quilt on the wagon seat, hid his pistol underneath, and sat on it.

He turned his wagon, not toward San Francisco, but to the south out of Placerville toward the town of Columbia. Gold had first been discovered there in 1850, but unlike many other locations, it had not quickly played out. He had heard reports of large nuggets being found near Columbia over the last few months, and knew that hundreds of miners had moved their operations down there as a result.

As a thirteen-year-old boy, perhaps he didn't fit the usual description of someone traveling with a lot of money or gold, or maybe he was just headed in the wrong direction to pique the interest of any potential thieves. Probably they were operating between Placerville and San Francisco. At any rate, he made the fifty-mile trip to Columbia by afternoon of the second day without even as much as a suspicious look along the trail.

The weather was damp and cold, although not quite so sharp as in Placerville. His new destination was at a lower altitude, and he saw no snow on the mountaintops to the east of the town. But what was all too familiar was the wretched appearance of the town, the mines, and the miners, as well as the absence of the milk of human kindness.

He stopped at Will Dugger's General Store, hoping for a repeat of his last arrangement, but the store was small and packed from floor to ceiling. He saw no opportunity there, but he did speak to the proprietor. "I'm new in town. Is there a barber hereabouts?"

"I think there's one up to Cosumnes River." Mr. Dugger scratched the top of his bald head, having long since reconciled with only the thinning gray hair over his ears. "I ain't had enough hair to worry about it for about five years. You don't look like you need one yourself neither."

"Well, I'm a barber myself. I was wondering if there was much competition hereabouts. Any idea if any stores in town have some extra space for a barber?"

Dugger thought for a minute. "Not really . . . leastwise unless Doc Butterfield would give up the space in his office that belonged to the dentist."

"What happened to the dentist?"

"Why, Doc run him off. The dentist was fond of that laudanum. Sometimes a feller with a toothache would have to wait a half a day for the dentist to sleep it off. About a month ago, the dentist was so befuddled from laudanum, he pulled four teeth on a man before he got the one that was causing his toothache. When Doc heard about it, he chased that tooth cobbler around the office with them big pliars, hollering at him the whole time. You'd thought the dentist was gonna get all his own teeth pulled—maybe would have if Doc had caught him. Anyways, the dentist departed our city that same day."

Doctor Ezra Butterfield was a short, barrel-chested man of about fifty. To B. F., he seemed to be a quiet, reserved fellow who must have been mightily provoked to run after the dentist with a pair of dental pliars. He had a short, gray beard, a head full of hair, and two extremely bushy eyebrows that greeted each other above the middle of his nose.

He'd had a medical practice in Philadelphia until 1850, when he'd talked his wife into going on a grand adventure to California. They had traveled by ship to Panama and then across the isthmus by donkey. His wife, Ruth, had died on the beach of the Pacific Ocean, apparently from some kind of tropical fever Doc had never seen before. He had decided to follow through on his trip, even though there was nothing grand left in it. After a bit of inquiry in San Francisco, he had come to Columbia because there was no doctor in the area. Also, he said he hated birthing babies, and figured there would be very few of them born in a mining camp.

> *My story. On January 3, 1854*
>
> *I arrived in Columbia on windy, cold day, and in no time made arrangements to set up my barbering operation in the home of Doctor Ezra Butterfield. This man appears to be a completely different kind of doctor than Doc McDaniel back in Placerville. He's a very educated man, with an actual medical degree up on the wall from back in Philadelphia.*
>
> *Doctor Butterfield is giving me free room and board, and he won't even charge me rent for my barbershop. But he says there are conditions in our agreement. If he has to perform surgery, I am to be his assistant. If he's called out in the evening with a patient, I'm expected to drive his buggy. If he has to sit up all night at a sick bed, I have to do my share of the sitting. It doesn't sound so bad.*

Doc had neglected to mention all of the "conditions" of their arrangement—that he would also expect B. F. to help him in preparing medicines, cleaning up after his surgeries, applying bandages of all kinds, and harvesting herbs and medicinals from his own botanical garden.

Within three months, B. F. had helped set several fractures, used alcohol to extract heart medicine from the digitalis leaf, rolled thousands of pills, used a suppository mold, made up hundreds of powder papers, mixed up a number of creams, ointments, and suspensions, gave various mixtures of belladonna leaf or goldenseal root to settle the bellies of hundreds of men with the "hell-roarin trots," and administered more calomel concoctions for constipated miners than he cared to remember. He feared his barber operation was generally regarded by Doc Butterworth as a totally unimportant part of his day.

In order to prevent the theft of his wagon, B. F. removed the rear wheels and kept them propped behind the door in the barbershop. It made him uneasy to think that there was over $24,000 sitting behind the building in his wagon bed, but there was no good solution to his problem. He certainly wasn't about to disassemble the wagon and put his gold into the First Columbia Bank. The only two men he had seen working in the bank appeared to be the kind that had a spare ace of hearts hidden in their sleeves. In fact, both of them spent a significant amount of time—and money—engaged in games of chance. He had no desire to find out the hard way that they were betting with his gold.

B. F. was beginning to show signs of the man he would become. He was neither tall nor short, but already had shoulders that were as wide as those on some men. He had begun shaving a few months previously, and had the kind of facial hair that promised to dull a razor in the not too distant future. Like his pa, he made it a point to stand as straight as he could. He might not be tall, but the impression people were left with was that he was someone who looked taller than others his age. Although he had been subjected to all the twangs—both harsh and soft—of every dialect in America over the last five years, most would say he had no accent that would identify him as being from neither here nor there.

He was particularly appreciative of the books owned by Doc Butterworth—both professional and otherwise—and had begun to work his way through the library. He had lost much of his humor. Perhaps some of that could be laid at the door of what he had faced the last several months in Placerville. It wasn't that he was depressed, but more like a piece of him—the one related to joy—was missing.

Many an enthusiastic and energetic young man came to the gold fields—most believing they were just one shovelful of clay away from striking it rich. Only a few, like B. F., believed that the most predictable way to wealth was to plod on every day, gradually—but consistently—accumulating their pot of gold.

One afternoon while B. F. was finishing a haircut, Doc Butterfield stepped in his doorway. "B. F., come in my office. You need to see something."

That could mean he would be gone for five minutes or five hours. There were two men waiting for a haircut. "If you'll excuse me, I'll be back in just a few minutes." He hoped that was true.

In Doc's examining room sat an Indian woman accompanied by three children. They appeared to be from about two to ten or eleven years old, and were sitting at her feet. Doc was talking to her. "Missus Mondoc, you're sure it's only been two days since you and your children came into contact with the two men?"

"I sure. You number three doctor I ask for help. The others say no help. I hear from miners that doctor can stop smallpox."

Doc's jaw tightened, but he held himself in check. How could any doctor refuse to help this family? "I can help you." He noticed B. F. and explained. "This woman, Missus Mondoc, is from the Siskiyou Tribe up north of here. Last week, her husband got sick in the gold fields, and his brother brought him home for treatment, but by the time he arrived, the husband was dead. The brother became so sick on his trip that he tied himself to his horse. By the time the brother arrived, he had to be carried from his horse. He had a high fever and was covered with weeping pustules."

B. F.'s eyes shot toward the woman, then to Doc Butterfield. "Then, you're saying. . . ."

"Yes. It sounds like both he and his brother had smallpox. Missus Mondoc traveled two days with her children because she had heard a doctor could prevent the smallpox."

"But, I thought. . . ."

Doc held up his hand. "Smallpox can't be cured once you have it. The only thing you can do is hope you survive. But it can be prevented if we act quickly. From what Missus Mondoc says, we have enough time. I want you to see how this is done."

Doc retrieved two glass plates, one on top of the other. He separated the two and put no more than eight or ten drops of water in the center of the glass. "On this glass plate is a dried specimen which I took from the last person I vaccinated about a month ago. For us doctors out here in these wild places, we have to keep our own smallpox source going. I scraped some of the pus from that man's vaccination a week after he was treated. Then that pus was dried between these two glass plates, and that's what I'll use on Missus Mondoc and her children. The water reactivates the dried smallpox."

He turned to the woman. "Missus Mondoc, you understand that you have to come back here in seven days so I can use your vaccination for the next person?"

The woman had a determined look on her face. "I unnerstand."

B. F. interrupted. "How long does that dried up smallpox last?"

"I think about two months is the maximum. I tried some after almost three months, and the man I gave it to didn't get any vaccination sores. If you don't get the sores, then it probably didn't work. So I have to vaccinate somebody at least every two months to keep it viable."

Doc pulled out three small white instruments that he called ivory points. They looked like very fine, curved pieces of ivory that were about an inch long, pointed at one end, and hollow. He used one of them to thoroughly mix the dried exudate on the glass plate with the water he had added. Again he turned to the woman. "I'm going to vaccinate you in three places, one on each arm and one on the back of your calf. To do that, I'm going to make two small cuts with a knife on each spot, then I'll rub in the vaccine, and put on a bandage. Do you understand?"

The woman nodded.

Again Doc turned to B. F. "In England, they vaccinate in five spots, but in Philadelphia they say three places are enough." He pulled up her sleeve. "Watch these two cuts. They don't need to be deep—just enough to draw blood." He picked up the ivory point that he had used to mix the smallpox mixture. "Then I rub this ivory point into the blood and on the cut. That transfers enough of the vaccine to the site. Next I put a wire guard over the spot and wrap a bandage around her arm."

"Why the wire guard?"

"The places seem to heal better if they get air circulation, but if you don't cover them, people start scratching the vaccination with their fingernails, and then get it in their eyes or nose or mouth. If they do that, they can end up with terrible sores. Some have even lost their eyesight after getting sores in their eyes."

He finished the other two spots on the woman, then turned to the eldest child. "Why has this child got black stain streaked on her face?"

Missus Mondoc turned her eyes down. "To keep men from stealing her."

Doc said no more and completed his task on down to the youngest. "Now, Missus Mondoc, you must come back in seven days. You should not bathe these places on the children, or even get them wet. Leave the bandages right where they are. If one of the children breaks out in a rash outside the three spots where I put the vaccine, you bring them back right away. And don't go back to your village. It takes several days for this vaccine to work and for them to be safe."

The woman pulled out a small bag that was tied inside her dress and handed him a nugget almost as big as his thumbnail. He had not really expected to be paid, but recognized the woman deserved her pride. "Thank you, Missus Mondoc."

He cleaned up his ivory points and his scalpel with water, put the glass plates back together, and then thoroughly washed his hands. "If you handle smallpox, you have to make sure you don't leave any on you. If I rubbed my own eye or mouth or nose before washing up, I could end up in trouble myself—or I could accidently pass it on to the next patient I see here in the office. One more thing before you go, B. F. Have you been vaccinated?"

B. F. pulled up both sleeves to show the raised scars. "Yes, sir—when I was little. My aunt almost died of smallpox, so she made sure I was vaccinated."

"That's good. If we had it show up here, plenty of these men would get it. Particularly the ones who didn't come from back east, where most doctors recommend it."

Later that evening, Doc spoke again about the Indian woman. "There's lots of these tribes that have been wiped out by smallpox and measles. They claim that in 1847 there were one hundred seventy thousand Indians in California. Now there are less than a hundred thousand."

"The story I keep hearing is that it was really a couple of Indians that first found gold at Sutter's Mill. By the summer of 1848 there were about four thousand Indians and no more than two thousand whites panning on the American River. But as more people arrived, the Indians got pushed out. There's hardly any mining now. Between disease, slavery, prostitution, and just plain murder; we're wiping them out and taking their country away from them." Doc continued. "Do you know why that Indian girl's face was stained black and she had her hair hidden under a cloth?"

"Not really."

"The miners steal these young girls and either keep them for theirselves as slaves or sell them as prostitutes. I hear that in some of these mining camps away from town, quite a few miners have young Indian girls hidden in their mines. And even if one of these so-called law officers wanted to do something about it, the Indian can't testify in court against a white man. So Missus Mondoc was trying to hide her daughter's looks when she came into these mining towns looking for help."

Doc went on. "Hell of a note. To find help, she had to ride at least seventy miles, went to three doctors before she found someone that didn't turn her away, and had to risk losing her daughter to slavery. And we're the ones that call ourselves civilized."

> *My story. On July 6, 1854*
>
> *It seems like my days are full and most nights are too. It's seldom that someone doesn't knock on the door at some unholy time of night. Doc is educated—with a diploma and everything—but he is no miracle worker. Men still die with great regularity around Columbia. The ways they die are not so much different here than they were in Placerville, but here it seems worse, because I know about every one of them.*
>
> *The acts of violence are the most interesting, but the majority of men die from things you can't see—cholera, typhoid,*

pneumonia, consumption, and just plain starvation. Given that almost every miner works in underground operations; cave-ins, flooded mines, and freezing to death are responsible for their share of deaths as well.

Because these men are underground for at least twelve hours a day, they exist in a place where the air is so clogged with dust and grit that you can easily see it suspended in the air in the light of a coal oil lamp. I know—I've seen it myself when we've had to go down in a mine to see a miner that was too sick to get out. Doc says this same dust mixes with the moisture in their lungs, and they clog up with this sludge-like mess. Most of them start having breathing problems that could eventually kill them, or at least leave them in such a state that they can't carry on a normal life. He says they'll spend the rest of their days struggling to move enough air through their lungs to keep them alive.

They've all heard of various miracle cures for their breathing problems, and they badger the Doc for one of these quack remedies all the time. He tells them there is no cure except to get out of the mines to keep from getting worse. Only a few men listen.

Because his time was so divided between working with Doc Butterfield and his own barbershop, B. F. did not make anywhere near as much money as he had in Placerville, but he didn't complain very much. Unlike almost every other man in the gold fields, he had a warm, dry place to sleep, relative safety, an opportunity to learn new things most days, and a chance to actually help somebody every now and then. Still, he did miss putting away five double eagles a week. Now he was lucky if he averaged two.

Twenty-Nine

The One-Legged
Easter Boy

Columbia, California 1856

It was not an odd occurrence to hear gunshots on a fairly regular basis in Columbia. Usually it just meant that someone had a bit too much to drink and he was firing a pistol for attention or celebration. But from time to time, the shooting meant Doc Butterfield had to be summoned.

Late one afternoon, B. F. heard at least three gunshots in rapid succession from somewhere close by, and within five minutes, two men carried a young fellow into the office. "Where's the doc? Wilbur Easter's boy been shot."

B. F. hollered for Doc Butterfield and directed the men back to his office with their cargo. "What happened?"

"This boy and his pa got into an argument with Max Sturdivant. Something about a claim jump. Max shot both of them before Wilbur shot him in front of the hotel. That was the last thing Old Man Easter did, as he breathed his last not five seconds later."

About that time, Doc bustled into the exam room and took a look at his patient. "What's your name son?"

The boy was white as rice and sort of gulping for air. "Norman Easter. Am I gonna die?"

"Are you shot anyplace besides your knee?"

"I don't think so."

"Then you're probably gonna make it." He turned to the men. "Put him up here on the table so I can see what we've got."

"How old are you, son?"

"Fifteen."

Doc looked at B. F. "He's about the same age as you, isn't he?"

There was another slamming of the front door and another shout. "Need the doc out here. Got a man shot!"

Doc shrugged and shook his head resignedly. "I guess that's the other one." He looked at the men. "Hold on to this boy and keep him still so I can check on the one out front." Patient number two was in fact Max Sturdivant, who had been shot in the face. His shirt was covered with blood when Doc got to him, but it didn't seem to prevent him from trying to break away from the men who escorted him. He wasn't really speaking in words that could be understood, as the bullet seemed to have struck him in the upper lip, smashed through two teeth in the front of his mouth, two more on the left hand side, and exited through his left cheek.

Doc spoke to one of the escorts, who appeared to be a deputy. "I've got another patient on the table who needs immediate attention." He stuck a small towel in Sturdivant's mouth. "Hold this towel real still so the blood will clot. I'll be back to work on this one in a few minutes." He retreated quickly to the exam room, followed by what were indecipherable but undoubtedly strong epithets from Sturdivant.

Doc turned to B.F when he came back in. "Another one waiting on us. Put a pan of water on the stove to heat, and fetch me a cup of whisky and two opium pills."

Doc used a pair of scissors to cut away his pantleg, poked and proded the knee, and faced young Norman. "Take these two pills and swallow down this whisky."

"I ain't a drinkin' man, Doc."

Doc gave him an exasperated look. "Son, it's for the pain and the shock. Drink it down." He looked more closely at the boy's mascerated knee, then back to B. F. "Now the chloroform and a cloth, a couple of scalpels, a tourniquet, a suturing needle with catgut thread," he paused to point toward a glass case. "That bottle of carbolic acid, and the capital saw there . . . better give me a new blade too. Now pour some of that hot water over the scalpels, the needle, and the saw blade."

Norman was watching the proceedings with wide eyes. "What you gonna do, Doc?"

"Son, that bullet destroyed your knee, and it looks like it got the top of the two bones in your lower leg. I can patch you up, and you'll likely be dead of the fever in less than a week. Or I can take your leg off at the knee, and you'll probably live. You got a good chance of making it if I do. You appear to be a strong fellow. The wound is fresh, and it's not full of dirt and filth."

"Can't you just take my knee bone?"

"Your knee cap is blown to bits, and all those pieces of shredded bone are spread all through your leg. The tops of your tibia and fibula are shot away as well. If you want to live, you really don't have a choice."

"I don't know how I can get along without no leg, Doc. I cain't work no mine with one leg, particularly since I ain't got no pa now." The boy struggled unsuccessfully to sit up.

Doc turned away, took the rubber stopper out of the chloroform bottle, sloshed some on the cloth, and nodded at B. F., who stepped beside the boy and grasped his hands together over his stomach. Doc Butterfield then placed the chloroform cloth over young Easter's mouth and nose, and held it fast. B. F. held on while the patient twisted to get loose from his grip, and wondered what the boy was going to think when he woke up and realized they'd done the deed no matter what his objections had been.

Within fifteen seconds, the boy stopped struggling and B. F. was able to release him. Nonetheless, he tied a sheet tightly around his upper arms and chest to keep him from thrashing about when the surgery started. Doc left the cloth in place on the boy's face and tied a tourniquet just above his knee to restrict the flow of blood. He waited another three minutes until the chloroform had the boy fully in its grip, then turned to B. F. "Hold that leg steady. I aim to save all of the thigh bone if I can. It'll be a lot easier for him to wear a wooden prosthesis if I can leave the femur undamaged."

Doc used the scalpel to slice through the flesh, muscle, and tendons, leaving enough skin to make a proper skin flap. He reached up and removed the chloroform cloth for about thirty seconds. "If you leave it on there for very long, they might not wake up." He then used the capital saw to cut through a bit of cartilage in the knee joint itself, and employed tweezers to pick away the detritus caused by the bullet. Then he used the scalpel again to trim the tissue at the back of the joint. B. F. jumped when the separated leg fell unceremoniously to the floor.

Doc then quickly used the suturing needle to close off the arteries and veins that he could see, probed as much as he dared for any remaining bits of bone in the tissue, removed the tourniquet, and finding no bleeders, diluted the carbolic acid with five parts of water and poured it into the wound as an antiseptic.

B. F. watched the suturing. "Is that really cat guts?"

"I understand they make it out of sheep or goat intestine. When you have a wound like this, if you use silk, you end up with a problem, because the body can't absorb it. So this stump would be festered up in a couple of days. But the catgut usually gets broken down by the body and eventually just disappears, so he shouldn't have as much trouble with it. Wish I'd had it ten years ago!"

Again, he removed the chloroform cloth for half a minute, dusted the wound with morphine powder, sewed a skin flap over his work, and took the chloroform away for good. B. F. bound the stump with strips of cloth, and realized only fifteen minutes had passed since they began work on the one-legged Easter boy, as he would undoubtedly now be known.

He then went into the front room to assist with Sturdivant. Although there would be no drastic limb removal, it was obvious there would be significant pain involved while Doc was working on him, hence the pre-operative preparations were almost identical.

Doc used pliars to remove the remains of the four shattered teeth, then sewed up the gums and front lip, as well as the inside and outside of the cheek. The only real change in procedure was to use Tincture of Iodine as an antiseptic rather than carbolic acid, as the latter was much too toxic when used internally.

In less than an hour, both patients were stirring awake. Predictably, each of them awoke with a terrific headache and retching to beat the band. It was all B. F. could do to keep the two of them cleaned up. Sturdivant's top lip and mouth was so swollen that his angry tirades still could not be interpreted specifically, although his generic meaning seemed to be pretty clear to everybody in the house.

Sturdivant was laid out on a pallet in the front room and handcuffed to a bench. The deputy sat in the room as well, trying his best to stay awake as the hours wore on. B. F. was up every hour during the night, checking on both patients, with instructions to call the doc if young Easter's leg started bleeding again, or if Sturdivant had so much swelling that he was having trouble breathing.

About three o'clock, B. F. was awakened by a shout. He ran in the front room to find the deputy sprawled unconscious on the floor by Sturdivant's pallet with a huge knot on his forehead. As he started for the exam room to see about Easter, he heard Sturdivant's harsh voice in the room.

It was still affected by his recent injury, but B. F. could make out, "you and yore pappy."

This was followed by "Mister, I don't know nuthin' about yore claim. We didn't come within fifty feet of yore diggings."

"Hell you say."

"You kilt my pa and took my leg. What more you want?" The pistol shot sounded like a cannon had gone off in the small room.

"Don't want no more damned Easters—that's what I want!"

B. F. realized too late that his own pistol was stuck behind his barber chair. He headed in that direction about the time Sturdivant came striding out of the exam room. B. F. scrambled into the next room for cover as Sturdivant fired an errant round in his direction. By the time he had his hand on his own pistol, Sturdivant had run outside into the street. B. F. ran to the front door to give chase when Doc stepped in front of him and put his weight against the closed door.

"Don't go after that man, B. F. He's crazy enough to shoot you down. The law will catch him soon enough."

"But. . . ."

"Let's see to our patient." It was quickly apparent to both of them that the bullet hole in the one-legged Easter boy's chest could not be fixed. The boy looked at them both in the doorway with a pleading look on his face, tried to speak, and was gone.

Doc walked slowly to the boy's bedside, closed his eyelids, and picked up the pair of crutches leaning against the wall that would not be needed now. "Why do these things happen?" The question seemed to hang there in the room, unanswered, for a long time.

> *My story. On December 10, 1856*
>
> *How can it be that so much medical skill is spent on a patient, yet something happens that always seems to be unknown. People up and die from a simple cut, a boil on their neck, a case of measles, a drink of bad water, breathing bad vapors. One miner even died within about ten minutes of getting stung by a single bumblebee! Why is death so finicky? Why does it happen to some and not others? Why doesn't Doc ever seem to know the answer? Why does someone innocent die for no good reason, and some low-life manage to survive? Shoot—not just survive, but prosper!*
>
> *Doc has been talking to me about what I want to do in life, and it didn't take long to figure out he wants me to go be a doctor. He told me some of his friends want to start a college in San Francisco to train doctors, but he figures right now it's only talk, and it might be years before that ever happens. So then he asked what I would think about going back east to college. He keeps telling me his old school is the best in the country.*
>
> *He says the Philadelphia Medical College offers a two year program. You have classes for an entire year, then they repeat them all the second year just to be sure you don't miss anything. After that, you see patients for a whole month with one of the doctors at the school before you graduate. He says he wants to write some of his friends at the school.*

Thirty

The Blue Baby

Columbia, California 1858

It was not something B. F. had ever really considered, particularly since he had attended school for a grand total of four months in his entire life. However, he had come to realize that being a barber was not what he intended to do from now on either. But he always struggled when one of Doc's patients died—particularly when they were young and it was unexpected. Could he really deal with that if failing to save someone was all of a sudden his responsibility?

He told Doc only that he would think about it. But with the decision yet to be made, it bothered him enough that it intruded on his thoughts almost every single day. It didn't help that Doc continued to bring up the subject on a regular basis.

He was sitting in his barber chair one afternoon, once again considering what he was going to tell Doc Butterfield, when he was interrupted by a commotion out on the street, and a woman hollering for the doctor. He hurried to the door, meeting a woman who had her arm around a very scared, and very pregnant young girl. The older woman looked accusingly at B. F. "You ain't the doctor. I need the doctor!"

"He should be back any minute. What seems to be the problem?"

She looked at B. F. as though he was the village idiot. "My daughter's having a baby! What's it look like to you?"

"Let's get her back here on the bed." He noticed there was blood on her clothing, as well as a bloody fluid on the floor beneath her feet, and he hurried to put a rubber cover on the bed before the girl laid down.

Thankfully, Doc Butterfield returned as he was getting the girl and her mother settled in. "Doc, ye got to do something. We thought we was gonna do this at home, but they's somethin' wrong." The room was punctured by the girl's screaming as she endured a contraction. "I made her drink some ground ivy tea about three months ago when she first started showin'. I heard that would bring on her flow. When that didn't work, I steeped some wild nettle and mixed it with the ground ivy, but it still didn't have no effect. How come that didn't work?"

"It works only if you give it in the first two or three months after a girl gets pregnant. I've never seen it work when a girl is so far along. Is this her first baby?"

The woman gave Doc a mean look. "What the hell ye think! Of course, it's her first! She ain't but fourteen. Ain't got no husband. Ain't got no business havin' no baby."

"Who is the father?"

"She won't tell me. I'd cut his damned heart out if I knew."

B. F. considered this response. Perhaps that outcome is the reason the girl neglected to share that bit of information!

Doc washed his hands and quickly examined the girl. The baby seemed to be sideways. He had no desire to have the mother in the room while he tried to save the girl's life. He turned to B. F. "Take this lady out to the front room so she can be comfortable, and you come back to help."

This was new territory for B. F. He had been in Columbia four years, and this was the first time he had dealt with childbirth. There were few women in town, save the ladies of the evening in the three saloons. But except for the red-headed whore—Queenie had been her name—it seemed that they never had babies, at least as far as he knew. The way Doc described the use of wild nettle and ground ivy tea, he wondered if that had anything to do with it. He remembered both of those items growing in the herb garden, and for just a second, he wondered just exactly what Doc was using them for.

When he got back in the room, Doc started throwing orders his way. "Put a stack of towels here on the foot of the bed. . . . Heat a pan of water. . . . Look in the back of that cabinet and see if you can find some large forceps—big ones. . . . Sponge off the girl's face and neck. . . . Sponge me off too. . . . Thread some silk in a suturing needle. . . . We won't need to use that new catgut—these stitches will just be on the cord. . . . Get me another towel—wet. . . . Stand beside this girl and help hold her knees back over her chest. . . ."

The girl's screaming drowned out any further understandable conversation between the two of them for a half minute.

Doc was examining her again and talking under his breath. "Got to get this baby turned around and get it out." He had his hand inside her, struggling. When he withdrew his hand, he was able to pull the baby's hand, then arm, and then shoulder out as well. Relieving that congestion, he then began to work from the other side, trying to get the head to crown. The room was unusually tight with August heat, and Doc was sweating like B. F. had never seen before. He was turning this way and that, trying to maneuver in any way possible to relieve the girl. Finally, the top of the head was visible, and in another agonizing ten minutes the baby was out.

B. F. was positioned so that he could see the baby when Doc Butterfield retrieved it, and he was instantly aware that the umbilical cord had twice encircled the baby's neck. Although this was his first exposure to a delivery, he knew that couldn't be right. Doc was working to untangle the cord, but the baby was a bluish-purple color and had made no effort to gasp or cry.

Doc quickly tied off the umbilical cord and cut it, then turned his back on B. F. and the girl. B. F. slowly let the girl's knees down, patted her shoulder, and stepped to the side to see what Doc was doing.

What he saw was difficult to absorb. If anything, the baby was more purplish than before. Doc was holding the little boy in his left arm and had cupped his right hand over the child's mouth and was pinching its nostrils closed.

B. F. started to react and grab Doc's hand to pull it away but froze when Doc turned his face toward him, tears running down his face. B. F. turned away, not wanting to watch.

In a couple of minutes, Doc Butterfield laid the infant on the table and turned to the young girl. He held her hand and spoke very quietly. "Your baby was born dead. The umbilical cord was tangled around his neck, and he could not get any air. There was nothing I could do."

The girl was so exhausted she could barely muster anything more than a weak cry. Her eyes were pleading, and she spoke in a whisper. "That baby was my Pa's. I know'd no good could come of such an evil deed. Pa said it was really my fault—because I looked too much like Ma when she was a girl." B. F. thought about the mean-spirited woman in the front room, and had a hard time even considering that she might have once looked anything like the heart-broken, sweet girl in front of them.

She looked at the closed door. Her voice was so weak B. F. had to lean over her. "Please don't tell Ma. I'm a'feared she'd be blaming me for it."

B. F. patted her shoulder. "Don't you worry about that."

"I knew something bad would happen. I knew I didn't deserve no sweet little baby."

"It's not your fault."

"Ye don't understand." She cried for a minute or so, then spoke again. "After the first few times, I started thinking my pa loved me better." She stopped, closed her eyes, and took a deep breath before she could continue.

"Where is your pa?"

"When he found out I was having a baby, he went off to some place in Canada, chasin' another gold strike. I expect he'll be back soon enough."

Doc came over to her. "What's your name, child?"

"Suelean Jastro."

"Suelean, will you promise to come tell me if your pa tries to do this again?"

She looked away. "I cain't say. I ain't got no other place to go."

"You come tell me, and we'll figure something out." She wouldn't look at him again.

At the end of the next day, when the girl and her mother were gone, and the barbershop had finally emptied, Doc sought out B. F. "So you'll understand what happened yesterday—that little boy was what they call a 'blue baby.' It's what happens when the baby can't get any air—usually when the cord is in a knot or wound around the neck like it was. If the baby goes without air long enough, it dies. But sometimes they live—and believe it or not, that can be worse than dying. If their brain doesn't get enough air, they usually turn into a half-wit, or something even worse."

"As purple as that baby was, it would've had terrible problems if it had lived. What I did was to make sure that didn't happen. Those blue babies only come along every great once in a while—but just often enough for me to hate delivering babies. I'm sure sorry you had to see that."

B. F. kept his head lowered so his eyes wouldn't give him away. "I understand, Doc."

But he continued to dream about the little blue baby boy for months. By the summer of 1859, his barbering business was much reduced due to miners gradually leaving the area around Columbia and heading to new strikes in British Columbia—places like Wild Horse Creek, Fort Colville, the Silkmeen, the Bridge River fields, and Cayoosh Canyon. B. F. realized he had to move on, and he began to think about where he might go. Although they had never had a final discussion on the matter, Doc had sensed that he didn't want to talk about going away to medical school, so the subject was no longer mentioned.

It was just as well. B. F.'s heart wasn't in it anymore. He didn't blame Doc Butterfield for his disenchantment. In fact, he couldn't have come up with a solid reason why he no longer had any desire to go—but it seemed like almost as many people didn't get any better as those that did. Lots of men died under his care, yet Doc really had no idea why in many cases. It's not that he thought Doc was incompetent—after all, he was highly educated—but rather that so much was unknown, even to doctors. If that was what doctoring was about, he didn't want sole responsibility for so much pain and suffering.

B. F. put his wagon back together, retrieved the gold he had earned in Columbia from the flooring of the barbershop, and hid it under the back section of his old wagon bed. When he told Doc Butterfield what he was about to do, the Doc was first argumentative, then angry, then hurt. He tried to appeal to B. F. to "do the right thing," but the town of Columbia was collapsing about them as miner after miner departed for greener pastures.

Thirty-One

Miss Grace Bodfish

San Francisco 1860

When he arrived in San Francisco, B. F. dismantled his wagon safe and deposited $11,000 in each of three banks. One of them stood right beside the new United States Mint and another was directly across the street. All three that he selected were constructed of substantial limestone or brick. He figured the more reliable the structure, surely the more reliable the bank would be.

B. F. couldn't help but wonder if he would see Mary Fitzwater in the city. It had been almost six years since they went their separate ways in Placerville, but it was altogether possible that she was still in San Francisco. He asked the head teller about her at each of the three banks, but no one had any information at all.

He had no idea what he might say to her, even if he did see her, but their relationship was one of those unresolved issues that had frequently entered his thoughts these past years. So he decided to place an advertisement in the only newspaper in the city, the *Daily Alta California,* every day for a week, asking that Mary Fitzwater contact him at her earliest convenience at his residence at Hillman's Temperance House on Davis Street.

He spent the week in torment, struggling with what he could say to her.

At the end of the week, he had to face the obvious conclusion that she was either no longer in the city or she had no desire to see him. All he had managed to do with his efforts was refresh painful memories and keep himself awake at night.

B. F. decided to continue barbering in the city while he thought about his future without much enthusiasm. The town was awash in potential customers, even though much of the mad dash to California's gold fields was over. By 1860, the city had established itself as the center of commerce on the Pacific Coast of the United States.

Many gambling houses had disappeared from San Francisco, and the city fathers were actively engaged in an attempt to establish a new, improved reputation. The Jenny Lind Theater near Portsmouth Square was no more, having been sold and turned into San Francisco's City Hall. Even the El Dorado Saloon on the Plaza had been recently converted to the Hall of Records, while retail stores and churches were also springing up in the immediate area.

Even the infamous sign at Clay and Kearney streets that read "This Road is Impassable. Not Even Jackassable" was no longer necessary. The mud and manure-filled streets had been replaced by fine plank roadways, and there was considerable discussion about even covering the downtown area streets with paved bricks.

There were sixty hotels in the city now, with most trying to give the impression that they embraced a less wild and woolly environment. At least some of this refinement was because of the presence of Miss Emma and Miss Grace Bodfish, the young and attractive leaders of the Ladies Protection and Relief Society.

It was a rare male indeed who was not impressed by the Misses Bodfish. They had come to San Francisco from Boston to be with their father, Cyrus Bodfish, a local land baron, after the death of their mother in 1859. When they became aware of the raucous and wild nature of their new home, Emma, at eighteen, and Grace, just two years older, had thrown themselves into the effort to bring some measure of culture to the city. Men who had an appetite for a wilder lifestyle found it almost impossible to argue their case when faced with the combined beauty, wit, and refinement of the Bodfish sisters.

Almost every single man and no small number of happily married men in the city were smitten.

However, the sisters were seen about town in the evenings with a number of young men who, some would say, were not exactly paragons of virtue. In fact, their escorts were generally those who had been commonly seen at gaming tables or in saloons and bawdy houses. When asked about their choice of gentlemen friends, the sisters explained that they considered it their duty to bring sinners into the fold. As Emma explained, "These boys are all a challenge to Sissy and me. It's no fun at all to be around gentlemen who don't possess great weaknesses for temptation. After all, if these rowdies were just goody-goody boys, we'd be bored to death. But as it is, each one of them is a project worthy of our skills to reform them into fine, upstanding citizens."

In due time, Miss Grace Bodfish came to the attention of B. F., who was aware of the sisters' daytime work to bring culture to the city. He reasoned that they might have interests in common—beyond the fact that she was a very attractive young woman—so he found himself escorting her to Tom Maguire's Opera House on Washington Street one evening, followed by dinner at the View of the Bay restaurant on Market Street.

He told her that he admired the efforts of Grace and her sister to improve the city. He was surprised by her questions about his thirst for strong drink, gambling, and loose women, but felt he had surely passed some sort of test when he told her he approved of neither gambling nor debauchery, and only drank on rare occasions. However, he suspected that somehow he had erred in his conversation, as she almost immediately became cool and disinterested in what he had to say.

In fact, the evening would undoubtedly have ended very quickly had he not mentioned his previous life in Hangtown. Grace quickly reacted to this, asking if he had ever witnessed a killing "in the old days." He replied that it was fairly common in the early days of the gold rush, and impossible to avoid.

He noticed that her sky-blue eyes, for the first time that evening, had a burning light in them. "What about you, Mister Windes, have you ever. . . ." She paused to consider that she had never asked the question of an escort before, and shivered slightly. "Have you ever killed anyone?"

"I don't talk about those days."

She visibly licked her lips. "But you must, Mister Windes, you must. It's good for the soul."

"For the good of my soul, I've spent the last six years trying to forget those days, Miss Bodfish."

She put her hand on his arm and gave him a reassuring smile. "You can confide in me, Mister Windes. You can trust me to keep your secrets." He realized he'd been staring at the candles on their table a bit too long, and shifted in his chair. He became conscious of her hand lightly rubbing the back of his own. "Every man needs to get these things off his chest, Mister Windes."

"Maybe someday I'll do that, Miss Bodfish."

She found a way to remove her hand without being too obvious. "I've had a lovely evening."

> *Journal Entry—July 10, 1860*
>
> *I must be one of several thousand residents of this city who live in a hotel. Lots of people are waiting on homes to be built in the neighborhoods like Happy Valley, Pleasant Valley, and Spring Valley that all seem to be located away from the center of the city. It's like they want to get as far away from the city as they can, and still live in the city.*
>
> *Mr. Cyrus Bodfish is a land speculator, and he, along with quite a few cronies, keep advertising in the newspaper about selling lots out away from town. Sometimes those building lots change hands four or five times in the course of a year. I thought about getting in on these deals, but I can't see a good reason why a property of eighty feet in width, standing out on the sand hills towards Washwoman's Lake, and a good buggy ride from town, could be worth a hundred dollars in January and two thousand dollars now in July. It's tempting, but surely everybody is going*

to soon see the folly in this, and prices will drop just as rapidly as they've risen.

I guess I miss working in a gold rush town—the wild characters, the constant barrage of stories, the excitement of a new strike, and the friendships you see when men have to keep on surviving in rough circumstances—that just can't be found in this newly respectable San Francisco. I have no call to complain. I make a passable living, but I've just got no real enthusiasm to be here.

As B. F. neared twenty years old, he had grown to five feet, ten inches in height. Some would say he was a bit stocky, in that he weighed almost 180 pounds, but he was well proportioned. He wore a short, black beard and was generally well turned out in his dress. Most of those who knew him would describe him as a merchant of limited means—friendly enough—but mostly quiet and reserved. He had acquaintances that were customers and fellow store owners but no real friends. In his own mind, he felt as though he was waiting on something to happen—to him, and to the country.

The newspapers were full of threats from the southern states regarding the impending inauguration of Abraham Lincoln. They would revolt, secede, start a revolution, walk out of the Congress, start an alliance with France or England—take your pick. Some laughed about these possibilities. However, B. F. believed there was substance behind the talk. He had heard men say these same things for several years now, and he had come to the conclusion that all it would take would be one state—one spark—to start a real fight.

For almost twelve years he had listened to men talk about states' rights, slavery, secession, slave states, free states, revolution, and every conceivable point in between. He'd heard men who he liked and respected on both sides of each issue. And as time pressed on, he felt that one side was right some of the time, while the other was right some of the time, and then there were several complex problems that neither northerner or southerner could satisfactorily explain and resolve, as far as he was concerned.

The news from the east seemed to get more threatening as the inauguration approached, and he became convinced that there would be war. He had seen enough men killed over the last twelve years to recognize that he had no desire to kill—or be killed—for either side, particularly when the "enemy" was just another American boy who happened to have been born on the other side of the Mason–Dixon Line.

His solution came in discussion with one of his regular customers. Nicholas Helms had been a ship's captain during the early years of the gold rush, ferrying passengers from New Orleans, around the tip of South America, and north to San Francisco. He had made six round trips from 1849 through 1854, then sold his ship in order to purchase a hotel in the city. Although the man was difficult to read, B. F. put his age at around sixty; but he had such a full, grey beard that the most telltale signs of age were hidden from view.

Captain Helms, as he liked to be called, believed the coming war would be won by the side that controlled the sea. The northern states obviously had more ships, as well as the shipyards in which to build more. The southern states could only succeed if they were able to convince a European seapower like England or France to come to their aide. Failing that, their only hope would be to pay privately owned ships to supply them. And if they were truly lucky, the South would be successful at pursuing both strategies.

"If it was ten years ago, I'd make another fortune on this war. The southern states got mighty little manufacturing capacity, and they're gonna need everything shipped to them. I'd bring in everything under the sun, and they'd pay dear for it. A ship would have to be fast. I'd set up a base somewhere in the Caribbean so I could get what they needed from Europe, then sneak it into a southern port. Ah, it sounds exciting just talking about it."

Although he didn't say so, B. F. had to agree. It was as though his sole purpose in life had become to simply go to and from work every day. His existence in San Francisco held no appeal for him, and he certainly had no ties to keep him there. A strategy to get involved in shipping could mean he would not be part of either side's army. And compared to his current situation of fifty cents a haircut, there might be some real money to be made.

He used the occasion to write two letters—one to Abbie Finnerty and one to his Cousin Sue. He told them where he'd been, a little bit of what he had done, that he had never been able to find his pa, and that he was leaving San Francisco, headed for South America. He took the two letters to the Pony Express office on Market Street, which had begun transcontinental mail service in April of 1860, and paid five dollars apiece to post them to Jeffersonville, Indiana.

Over the entire history of the California Gold Rush, few men left the gold fields with $35,000 in hand, let alone anyone earning that money between the ages of eight and twenty, but B. F. Windes was an altogether unusual man.

Thirty-Two

The Chagres River

Panama 1861

Even counting his two days of seasickness, the steamship voyage from San Francisco to Panama was a fine way to travel. B. F. reflected on the fifteen miles a day pace of a team of oxen, and the average of 150 miles per day on the ship. No breathing dust all day. No carrying buffalo turds. No clouds of mosquitoes. No endless diet of bacon. No rivers to cross. Instead, he was able to eat in the dining room and sleep on a mattress—of sorts.

The twelfth day out of San Francisco, they made landfall at Panama City, Panama. The place was a hubbub of activity due to the Panama Railroad. After completion of the line in 1855, at least 60 percent of American commerce back and forth from east to west traveled through Panama City. That the urgency of heading west was far greater than that to head east was reflected in the price of a railroad ticket. The price from Colón to Panama City on the west coast was twenty-five dollars for first class and ten dollars for second class, but heading east from Panama City to Colón was fifteen dollars and seven dollars respectively.

Journal Entry—January 10, 1861
I remember well Doc Butterfield's warnings about the strange tropical diseases here in Panama, and frankly I have no desire

to spend any more time than absolutely necessary in this country. After leaving the ship, I went straightaway to the train station and purchased a ticket for an early afternoon departure.

I write this as the train pulls out of the station, and I can't keep from staring at the sights. Commerce is everywhere, and every conceivable mode of transport, in addition to the train, is being used in the city—steamships, barges, canoes, sailboats of all types, carts, wagons, pack mules, drey wagons, hand carts, even balancing fantastic loads on one's head—all are here in endless sizes and descriptions.

Out of the city the train began a long, slow climb to the highest point in the journey—the 300 foot high cordillera separating the Pacific and Atlantic drainage systems. As we reached the peak of the elevation, it wasn't hard to compare the difference between this paltry nubbin of a hill, and the Continental Divide I traveled across via wagon train. I caught myself laughing out loud at the comparison.

A light-skinned Negro man with mild features—undoubtedly a mulatto, he realized—sat down beside B. F. "You are thinking it is not much of a railroad, yes?"

"Well, not exactly, but not too far off."

"My name is Galileo Baldonero. My brother worked on this railroad for a while."

"I'm B. F. Windes. So tell me about this railroad. What was your brother's job here?"

"He buried the dead."

"Was that a full time job?"

"Señor, it was a full time job for four men."

"How many people died?"

"Some say there is a dead man for every railroad tie between Colón and Panama City. But that is nonsense. There are seventy-four thousand ties over the forty-seven miles of the Panama Railroad. Probably a better figure is between twelve thousand and fifteen thousand dead. But the true number, Señor, will never be known."

"What does your brother do, now that the road is finished?"

Galileo pointed out the window. "See there at the edge of the rail bed. He lies underneath one of those crosses."

B. F. flushed. "I'm sorry. I didn't mean to pry. . . ."

"The Americans started work on the railroad in 1850. They said it could be built for one million dollars, and it would take no more than six months—after all, it was only forty-seven miles long. But it took five years and over seven million dollars."

"Why did it take so long?"

"They underestimated the jungle and the swampland. The engineers recommended starting the railroad at San Lorenzo. There was at least twenty-five miles of dry land running inland from there. But several wealthy families wanted top dollar for their land near San Lorenzo, so the brilliant railroad men moved about ten miles further south to what is now Colón, and started their road. From Colón, the land was cheap, but very little of it was dry enough on which to build their road. All they found in their path was mangrove thickets, snakes, mosquitoes, alligators, endless rain, and sickness.

"Everything they needed besides dirt and railroad ties had to be shipped from the United States. The people who lived here in Panama were not accustomed to such physical labor. So they brought in Irish and Chinese workers, even slaves from the American south. None were able to work here. They all died in terrible numbers.

"In the years before the railroad reached dry land, they had no way to bury the bodies. Many were left to rot, or be eaten by the alligators and panthers. But the company found ways to make money, even on the dead. They began putting bodies in large barrels and pickling them to be sold to medical schools and hospitals around the world. Thankfully, when my brother died that business was over, and he was buried on dry land.

"Finally the company came to the conclusion that Negroes from the West Indies were the ideal workers for the railroad. They had lived their lives in the heat of the tropics. They had been exposed many times to the same kinds of diseases that awaited them in Panama, and they must have developed some sort of resistance. When over a thousand of them were brought in, the work finally began to make real progress."

"But I thought the railroad was built by Americans?"

"It was planned by American engineers, paid for with American dollars, and the project was led by an American—that much is true. But few American laborers stayed alive long enough to see it reach beyond a few miles from Colón, let alone to see it finished. There is a poem you should hear that explains this land far better than I, called *Beyond the Chagres.*"

Galileo began to recite a James Stanley Gilbert poem from memory:

Beyond the Chagres River are paths that lead to death
To the fever's deadly breezes, to malaria's poisonous breath!
Beyond the tropic foliage, where the alligator waits,
Are the mansions of the devil, his original estates.
Beyond the Chagres River are paths fore'er unknown,
With a spider 'neath each pebble, a scorpion 'neath each stone.
'Tis here the boa-constrictor, his fatal banquet holds,
And to his slimy bosom, his hapless guest enfolds!
Beyond the Chagres River lurks the cougar in his lair,
And ten hundred thousand dangers hide in the noxious air.
Behind the trembling leaflets, beneath the fallen reeds,
Are ever-present perils of a million different breeds!
Beyond the Chagres River tis said—the story's old—
Are paths that lead to mountains of purest virgin gold!
But 'tis my firm conviction, whatever tales they tell,
That beyond the Chagres River, all paths lead straight to hell!

"I see what you mean. That poem makes it all very real. Tell me about yourself, Galileo. You seem to be a very educated man."

"Ah, there is little to tell. I was born in the Cape Verde Islands. My father was a Portuguese trader and my mother was his housekeeper. They never married, but they lived together for almost twenty years until she died. I went to school in Lisbon until I was twelve and then in London until I was sixteen. I had to leave school when my father died and came here to be near my brother. I was able to see him only twice before he died. The second time he was already very sick. I tried to get him to leave the swamps, but he would not hear me.

For the last six years I have worked for a shipping company in Panama City. But I tire of hearing only English and Spanish. I need to speak the tongue of my father. It is hard to explain."

He paused for a moment in his own thoughts. "And what of you, Señor? Where are you from?"

"Compared to you, I have not been very many places. I lived in Indiana with my father and stepmother, and ran away from home and went to California by wagon train. But I wasn't a gold miner, I was just a barber. For eleven years, I worked in two mining towns in California and for a while in San Francisco. Now I'm on my way to South America."

"Wait a minute. You worked in mining towns for eleven years? How old were you when you left home?"

"Eight."

"Eight? Señor, we shall have dinner when we arrive in Colón. I must hear this story."

The train ride was no faster than a trotting horse, requiring five hours to travel the forty-seven and a half miles, as it was unlikely that the track bed, built over so much muck and mire, could have withstood the strain of a fast train. Over the course of the trip, the train passed across three hundred bridges and culverts from Pacific to Atlantic.

The city of Colón was built on Manzanillo Island and functioned as the base of operations for the railroad. Activity in Colón was every bit as busy as that in Panama City, except that the chief activity here was unloading ships from the American east coast, and then loading those supplies and passengers on the train. On the Pacific side, most passenger and freight traffic were outbound rather than inbound.

Their dinner that evening occurred in the seaside villa of a female friend of Galileo. There were numerous smokepots positioned around the house, and the windows, although opened to take advantage of the ocean breezes, were covered with a fine netting that successfully prevented thousands of insistent mosquitoes from intruding on their meal. As the evening passed by, it became obvious that the dark-eyed woman who lived there, Señorita Maria de la Casada, was far more than just a friend to Galileo.

As they enjoyed a delicious caramelized pudding, the Señorita decided to explore this young American. "So what do you plan to do in South America, Señor B. F.? Do you have friends there?"

"I don't know a soul there. But from all indications there is about to be a war in the United States, and I believe there is money to be made in the shipping of goods."

"Forgive me for saying this," Galileo interjected, "but you have no contacts and you do not speak any of the languages?"

"This is true. But I've learned a bit about buying and selling—particularly when there are shipping problems. The more difficult it is to ship goods, the more you can charge."

Maria looked at him. "What do you mean?"

"When I lived in Indiana, flour was easy to get, and it was two cents a pound. When I reached the beginning of the Indian Territory, flour had to arrive there by steamboat, and it was fifteen cents a pound. When I finally got to California, flour had to come by ship all the way around South America, and it was a dollar a pound. The flour was the same in California as it was in Indiana. The only difference was the shipping.

If there is war, then the southern states will be desperate to sell their tobacco and cotton—probably at a reduced price—and England, France, and all of Europe will want to buy it—possibly at an inflated price—because the supply will be much diminished. Whoever is able to ship it from one to the other can make a lot of money."

Galileo's arm encircled Maria's narrow waist when he spoke. "I happen to know men engaged in the shipping business in New Orleans, Galveston, Mobile, and New York in America; São Luís and Rio de Janeiro in Brazil; São tomé Island in the Cape Verdes; Havana, Cuba; Lisbon in Portugal; Cadiz in Spain; and Portsmouth or Plymouth in England. I speak three languages. I know many ship captains." He nodded toward Maria. "Do you seek partners, Señor?"

They were awake until almost sunrise but had the framework of a plan. B. F. would act as their representative to the southern states, and he would travel immediately to the southern ports of Brownsville, Sabine Pass, Mobile, and Pensacola to make appropriate contacts with sales agents. Galileo and Maria would travel to São Luís in Brazil to find a vessel and a ship's captain. Gali, as he asked to be called, would also make arrangements to transfer goods to a shipping company in Brazil which owned ocean-going ships.

They theorized that they would need a rather small vessel, a sloop perhaps, with three masts, but one that could move in as little as six feet of water while loaded with as much as three hundred bales of cotton. The ship would also be powered by a steam engine in case greater speed was required. Such a ship could move into shallow draft ports and rivers that might not draw the attention of warships. Their sloop would then race across the Gulf of Mexico, skirt the northern coastline of South America, and transfer its load to a larger ship in São Luís or a closer port.

Their plan was to buy cotton at the lowest price in America and sell it at significant profit in a safe port in Brazil. The middleman would then ship across the Atlantic under a Portuguese flag to Portugal, Spain, or England, where a ready buyer could be found—again at a profit. Their assumption was that the price of cotton in America would drop like a stone because of the war, while in Europe it would be sky high because of the decreased availability, yet continued demand from English and French mills.

B. F. was in a hotel lobby in Mobile, talking to Winston Palmer, a local cotton merchant, on April 14, when a man rushed in. "They done it, boys. They done took Fort Sumter yesterday from the Yankees. I reckon old Abraham will be wonderin' what hit him!"

Mr. Palmer spoke up. "What about Virginia? Any news that they've decided to come with us?"

"Nothing in this telegraph, but I bet they'll be coming now."

B. F. spoke quietly to Mr. Palmer, a man possessing an exuberant, reddish-brown beard and eyebrows that must have been at least an inch thick. "It appears that we will indeed do business, sir. I will make contact with you in this place in exactly three weeks, despite the American warship that we encountered just west of Mobile, near Dauphin Island. Please be prepared to act at that time. For our part, we will deliver fifty thousand pounds of sugar, and I won't forget your case of the best dark rum to be found in the Caribbean."

Five days later, B. F. was making similar arrangements in Pensacola Bay when another telegram was read in public. President Lincoln had declared a naval blockade of the states engaged in insurrection, effective April 19. In his announcement, he gave all foreign ships fifteen days to get out of southern ports. All ships found in southern ports after that date would be stopped, boarded by the American Navy, and "sent to the nearest convenient port, for such proceedings against her and her cargo as prize."

This plan was the brainchild of General Winfield Scott, who referred to his idea as the Anaconda Plan. In reality, the Anaconda initially had no teeth, as the Navy only had three ships dedicated to the blockade of a coastline that reached from the Chesapeake Bay, which separated Virgina and Maryland, to the Florida Keys on the Atlantic, and from there to the Texas border with Mexico in the Gulf. However, by December 1861, there would be 160 Navy ships designated to the blockade, and by December 1864, there would be a total of four hundred seventy Union ships so deployed.

The telegram carried one more bit of news. Virginia had seceded on April 17. If you pull enough teeth, eventually you can no longer chew—or so the South hoped.

Thirty-Three

We've Just Risked Our Lives This Night

The Gulf of Mexico 1861

The *Rei de la Amazon* (the Amazon King) was a fast, three-masted sloop of 210 feet that could be powered by either steam or wind—or both. It appeared to ride low in the water, although with an empty hold it only required a draft of four feet in which to maneuver. Even with a full load, they were promised the vessel would need no more than five feet of water—perfect for their purposes. The ship was mastered by Captain Pedro Pesca and manned by a crew of twelve capable sailors. The *Rei* proudly flew the flag of Portugal.

Although Gali and B. F. had debated the wisdom of carrying guns, B. F.'s argument that they may have to outmaneuver pirates, let alone the Yankee Navy, carried the day, and the ship had kept its six twelve-pounders on board. However, under maritime law, the ship's crew would be regarded as pirates and would face the death penalty if they were captured after firing on an American warship. With that sentence in mind, there was little appetite among the blockade-runners to engage in a gun fight with the Union Navy.

From the viewpoint of the common sailor onboard a U.S. Navy ship, there was plenty of motivation to take over a blockade running ship without sinking her. It was common practice in the American

Navy to sell all of the contraband on board a captured vessel, and split the proceeds among the crew of the victorious ship. Even with a sailor's small percentage of the money, it was not uncommon for the lowest paid men on a Navy ship to receive $2,000 after the successful capture of a loaded blockade-runner.

The cedar sides of the ship had been painted a light gray color by the crew, with the aim of camouflaging the vessel so that it might blend in with mist and seawater. Although the *Rei* had originally been constructed with a crew quarters and six small staterooms, the ship had been renovated to maximize the amount of cargo it could carry. Hence, only two staterooms remained.

The crew slept in hammocks below the main deck that were strung three high, so that each of the twelve men had a sleeping space six feet long and three feet wide, with only six or eight inches separating his face from the bottom of the bunk above him. After visiting the crew's quarters once, Gali said he had no idea that anything could smell so bad. Obviously, the crew agreed with that analysis, as they took every advantage of moderate weather to move their blankets up to the rear deck to sleep as far away as possible from the foul air of the hold.

When given a couple of hours of relatively calm water, Gomez the cook, could produce a fairly decent meal of enchiladas stuffed with egg, cheese, bacon, tomato, onion, and various chili peppers. Of course, Gomez could really only cook the one thing, whether for breakfast or supper, with the only dietary variation being the addition or subtraction of an ingredient or two from time to time.

The crew was composed of a mixture of nationalities found in the Caribbean, but no matter their language of preference, all were required to speak Portugese. Captain Pesca reasoned that he wanted no misunderstanding or delay when he barked out his orders.

B. F. had insisted on being on board for the maiden voyage, and on the evening of May 5, the ship lay about five miles to the west of the entrance to Mobile Bay. In the hold were fifty thousand pounds of Cuban sugar, and snuggled safely in the midst of that cargo was a case of fine dark rum.

Just after 10:30, Captain Pesca guided the ship into the estuary, and then entered the bay. B. F. had already entered the city via rowboat and was sitting in the Palace Hotel with Palmer. He had embellished the truth somewhat, telling Palmer that they had paid a spotter to signal them when the Navy warship had moved off to the east. In reality, they had seen no sign of the ship, but the price of cotton was dependent on the perceptions of the seller and the buyer, that shipping was a very dangerous business.

A bale of cotton weighed approximately five hundred ten pounds but was squeezed into almost a cubical shape by a cotton press to reduce its required storage space. Gali had told B. F. that the cotton price in London in December had been thirty-two cents a pound. That figure would indicate that a bale of cotton would bring $163 on the docks in Europe's seaports.

They could agree on thirty cents a pound for the sugar, but argued about the price of two hundred fifty bales of cotton. Because of the danger to shipping in the Gulf, Gali had told B. F. that he should pay no more than seventy dollars a bale in Mobile. After all, they would have to sell the cotton to a dealer in Brazil who would then have to ship to Europe, and still be able to make a profit.

Palmer wanted eighty dollars, B. F. offered sixty-five dollars and they could make no headway. "Sir, I believe we have just risked our lives, our ship, our cargo—and your case of rum—for nothing tonight. I believe we will have to seek another buyer. Perhaps a few more months of the blockade and we can come to terms on your cotton." He stood up, very conscious that he had no one to guard his back in what was now a foreign country. He lightly rested the heel of his hand on the butt of his Colt and stepped backward toward the door.

"Hold on, suh." Palmer spread his hands. "Perhaps we can find a middle ground in our, uh, discussion."

"That depends, sir. What do you propose?"

"Seventy-five dollars a bale, suh."

B. F. sensed an advantage. "I can't pay you a nickel over seventy. But if you don't agree, I must depart. For we must be loaded and out to sea before daybreak."

The bushy eyebrows seemed to fuse together with Palmer's frown of resignation.

"Agreed."

"Let's hurry, shall we Mr. Palmer?"

It was difficult to unload fifty thousand pounds of sugar and load over sixty tons of cotton in a hold only seven feet high and twelve feet wide at its widest point. But the dockworkers and seamen worked quickly. B. F. was relieved to see a seaman standing by each of the three cannons that were on the dockside of the vessel. He didn't know if Palmer noticed or not, but he wanted no surprises when everybody seemed to be preoccupied in moving freight.

With less than an hour to go before dawn, B. F. handed Palmer his case of rum and one hundred twenty-five double eagles to make up the deficit in the trade. "Just to be sure we understand one another . . . all our business will be in gold or silver. There will be no banknotes or paper script—from either side."

Mr. Palmer stuck his hand in the bag, reveling in the feel of the gold. "Agreed, suh. Can I offer you a drink of this rum?"

"Thank you, sir—perhaps another time. The sun is on its way."

The *Rei* rounded the barrier island and headed into the gulf while it was still dark. As a precaution, they were running only under wind power, with no lanterns lit. Captain Pesca called to him. "Señor Windes, there's a light off to the east and it appears to be heading our way. Looks like the sparks and fire off the top of a smokestack if I was to guess. I intend to stay fast to the coastline and run west with all the sail we can muster. Perhaps before dawn we can hide ourselves beyond Dauphin Island."

The kind of coal burned by a steamship was extremely crucial if a blockade-runner was to survive. Soft coal was less pure and commonly gave off an obvious visual display of sparks and dark smoke. By contrast, hard coal was much cleaner burning, and the smokestack generally produced smoke that was almost white in color, and thus was more difficult to identify at a distance.

Unfortunately, coal that was readily available in the southern states of Virginia, Tennessee, and North Carolina was only of the soft variety.

Captain Pesca insisted on obtaining hard coal from the Granadine Confederation in Soledad, Colombia. It was his preference to reserve the majority of this fuel for use while he was near the southern coastline, in circumstances where he was trying to avoid detection by Union gunboats. Much of the rest of the time, he relied on the wind to power his vessel.

On May 12, the *Rei* dropped anchor in São Luís. Gali had already sold the cotton for ninety-five dollars per bale. They had cleared $10,000 on the sugar and $6,250 on the cotton. After paying for dockage and wharf fees in São Luís, paying their captain and crew, and giving each member of the crew an extra double eagle to ensure they would be ready to sail again on their vessel; they netted over $12,000 on the trip.

Over the next five months, they ran six similar shipments—all to Brownsville, Sabine Pass, Mobile, and Pensacola. After the last trip, they resolved not to go back to Mobile. They had run into three Navy vessels in the waters around Mobile and counted themselves lucky to have escaped without being sighted. The Navy vessels were generally side-wheel steamships and could commonly outrun most blockade-runners when their prey was heavily loaded with freight. Likewise, the *Rei* would have been outgunned in a fight, as they had good intelligence that the Navy ships were well armed with much heavier cannon.

Thirty-Four

You Aren't Worth Ten Cents In Ransom, Sir

The Gulf of Mexico 1861

The Confederacy had appointed Colonel Abraham Myers as their first Quartermaster General. Almost everything purchased by the southern states would go through the hands of Myers or his forty-eight employees and agents. In the not too distant future, his would become an almost impossible mission.

In August of 1861, Myers had contracted with Mr. Gazaway Bugg Lamar of Augusta, Georgia to provide one million pairs of shoes, eight hundred thousand yards of gray wool, five hundred thousand flannel shirts, and five hundred thousand pairs of socks. It was Mr. Lamar's intention to ship these items into southern ports utilizing European suppliers, but the blockade had already been very effective in preventing large-scale movement of these articles to support rebel troops.

Even wool became scarce in the winter of 1861–1862, and many of the southern mills went silent. Not only was the blockade working, but many sheep farmers in the Appalachian Mountains were not particularly sympathetic to the southern cause and resisted selling their wool to Colonel Myers except as a customer of last resort. Worse, there was no manufacturing capability in the south to mass-produce wool socks. The only alternatives seemed to be to purchase manufactured socks from Europe or knit them in the Confederacy individually, by hand.

Journal Entry—November 25, 1861

Gali and I know that we need to move quickly to take advantage of a new market opportunity with the Confederates. We sailed the Rei *up the coast of Mexico to Tampico, where Gali left the ship. He is to purchase 200,000 yards of Mexican wool yarn, contract with an entire village to turn the wool into socks, and also hire twenty men and wagons to transport what we hope are finished goods overland. The wagons will cross northeastern Mexico, travel 450 miles to Reynosa, which is directly across the Rio Grande from Edingburg, Texas, where we will sell to Col. Myers' agent based in San Antonio.*

Captain Pesca and I then sailed the Rei *to Havana, where I purchased 25,000 British Blucher shoes for a half dollar a pair from a fellow ship owner who had gotten cold feet about trying to penetrate the Union blockade, and was trying to cut his losses. The shoes are sturdy, consisting of waxed uppers and well sewn, hobnailed soles.*

Unfortunately for the marching Rebel soldier, I fear he will soon find that the sole of these shoes will gradually wear down and the hobnails slowly begin to protrude through the innersoles of his shoes, thus making walking a painful experience. Perhaps they will file down the nails sticking through the soles. But after wearing these Bluchers for a few months, whenever the opportunity presents itself, I'm guessing they will enthusiastically steal more desirable boots from their enemy.

Before departing Havana, I made another purchase from a British blockade runner, which I kept out of sight in my cabin. In five days, we were back in Tampico. Because of the size of our investment, both Gali and I have decided to travel by wagon with our cargo of 25,000 pairs of shoes and 50,000 pairs of stockings. We asked for, and quickly obtained, four volunteers from the ship's crew to go along with us for security. By now, the sailors have learned there is monetary reward to be had for extra work.

Captain Pesca would delay his departure by seven days, then sail up the coast of Mexico, slip south of Brazos Island, enter the Rio Grande, and wait on B. F. and Gali above Brownsville where the river made an abrupt turn to the north. They would meet on the Mexican side of the river, but if Pesca decided it was too risky because of blockade activity around Brownsville, he would return to Tampico. And for their part, if Pesca and the *Rei* were not there when Gali and B. F. arrived, they would return to Tampico via wagon.

Before the wagon train departed, B. F. made a point of showing Gali and the four sailors what he had purchased in Havana—six Henry rifles and an accompanying five thousand rounds of forty-four caliber ammunition. The Henry had been created in 1860 and was the latest in the industry's efforts to build a repeating rifle. For the first time, this rifle used a self-contained metallic cartridge—no extra percussion caps, no extra powder, and no lead ball. A good shooter could fire fifteen rounds in not much more than twelve seconds.

Unfortunately, the rifle had three weaknesses. It was awkward to load, requiring that the cartridges be loaded down a metallic tube running underneath the barrel. The rifle had no wooden forestock, so the shooter had to hold the front of the rifle by the loading tube and the barrel.

If more than a half dozen shots were fired in rapid succession, the barrel became extremely hot and could not be held at all if the fifteen rounds were fired rapidly. To complicate this problem, the brass loading tube was an excellent conductor of heat from the barrel, hence it was difficult to reload the weapon if it had been fired rapidly.

And finally, it was almost impossible to carry enough cartridges to keep a man supplied with ammunition during a battle that lasted for any length of time. In fact, many Army officers did not want their men to have repeating rifles because they ran out of ammo too quickly, and developed a tendency to be careless in their aim, compared to their counterparts who were forced to take a single, but careful shot before having to reload.

B. F. had learned about the problem with the over-heated barrel the hard way in Cuba, so he explained the situation to Gali and the sailors. "The point is, we want everybody to know we've got Henry rifles to defend ourselves. We're going to fire these guns before we leave town. Use a thick cloth to hold the barrel and don't let on like there's a problem. If the six of us shoot off about ten or twelve rounds apiece in a few seconds, word will spread, and nobody will have much enthusiasm for bothering us on this trip."

They made a big show of their "practice" in front of the wagon teamsters and several men from the village. When they fired their rifles, it gave the impression of an impenetrable enfilade from an entire company of men. Not only did the barrels get hot, but the shooters were almost entirely obscured by black smoke. B. F. realized they wouldn't even be able to see what they were shooting at within seconds of a fight beginning. But from the exclamations of the Mexican villagers when they finished firing, he was more than satisfied with the demonstration's results.

A journey that would have required twenty days with oxen only took five days with horses. No matter, B. F. had forgotten how miserable travel by wagon could be. Thankfully, other than the monotony of the trip, there were no bandits. At least, there were none who had an appetite for doing battle with Henry rifles.

When they arrived in Reynosa, they sent a horseman to San Antonio to alert Col. Myers' man, Lt. George Feathers, that they had goods to sell and that he should bring wagons and gold or silver if he wished to buy their boots and socks. Gali suggested they keep the goods on the Mexican side of the river until they saw the money.

In four days, Lt. Feathers sent word that he had arrived directly across the river in Edingburg. B. F. and Gali sent two men across to reconnoiter Feathers' forces, and they reported back that he had no more than twenty soldiers with his wagons. Hence, they decided to not divide their forces, but to sit tight and invite the Lieutenant to their camp. As the river was shallow in January, it was not necessary to utilize the Edingburg Ferry, and he came across with an escort of four horsemen.

B. F. was surprised that the man was almost fifty years old, figuring that a Lieutenant would be close to his own age. He came to the point. "I understand Myers is trying to buy boots and socks but has had no luck. We have twenty-five thousand pairs of good British Bluchers and fifty thousand pairs of wool socks. The lot is eighty-five thousand dollars in gold."

"Ya'll wouldn't be tryin to pull that wool over my eyes would ya'll? I make it about fifty thousand dollars for yore goods."

"That might have been the price before the war but not now. As you very well know, every port is under blockade, and it's only getting worse. There's not a place to make these socks in the whole south, even if you had the wool. And your boss is trying to buy a million pairs of boots. Are you ready for him to hear you turned down twenty-five thousand?"

Feathers pointed to Gali. "Why don't ya'll come on over to the Texas side of this river? I dasn't say that boy there'll find hissef standin' in a field of cotton with a hoe in his hand afore morning."

"Lieutenant, you're addressing my partner. I'd suggest you find your manners real quick."

"Are you and yore 'partner'," He spat the word out, "ready to stand up to my company across the river?"

B. F. pulled his Henry from behind the wagon seat, and Gali and the four sailors followed suit. "Are you and those single-shots ready to stand up to our fifteen shot repeaters? Now let's talk sense. Eighty-five thousand dollars—in gold. You just lost your chance to bargain!"

"I have the full authority of Colonel Myers to pay you in the currency of the Confederate States of America."

"We don't deal in paper. Send one of your men—say that sergeant there—back to San Antonio or down to Brownsville to fetch the gold. You and these other three will be our guests until he returns."

"Are you holding agents of the Confederacy for ransom?"

Gali spoke up. "Señor, I have an idea you personally aren't worth ten cents in ransom to anyone in your entire Army. But until this deal is done, you're going to remain right here in the line of fire between us and your men across the river."

It wasn't a quick resolution. Toward the end of the third day, B. F. was ready to turn his men around and head back to the south. But finally came a shout that wagons were coming across the river. The young sergeant had done well. There hadn't been anywhere close to that much gold in south Texas. But he had $30,000 in gold coins and $55,000 in silver on two of the wagons. They made their trade, with Henrys at the ready.

The lieutenant couldn't resist one more comment. "Don't be stupid enough to try this again."

"On the contrary Lieutenant, we've given you a unique opportunity to be *unstupid* today. We can bring lots of goods through here. It may be one of the few places left that's not blockaded. But two things must happen. You've got to change your attitude, and you need to get enough gold in here for us to trade with you. We can make you look good to your Colonel Myers, but we're only going to trade for gold or silver. These wagons can't carry enough cotton—or your scrip—to pay off."

Feathers pointed once more at Gali with a sneer. "I ain't tradin' with the likes of him."

B. F. looked at him with an empty smile. "That will be your loss."

As the soldiers turned to the north and began heading back across the river, B. F. and Gali and their wagons turned toward the south. B. F. was thoughtful. "Perhaps we don't need to take our chances again with Lieutenant Feathers. He's just foolish enough to try and get even with us the next time we want to do business."

Gali replied. "He's the kind of man whose stupidity made this war possible. I would be glad never to see him again."

Thirty-Five

Brave Men

The Rio Grande River 1861

They had earned $10,000 more than expected, as they had anticipated having to negotiate their price, but Feathers' rudeness had gone in their favor. They gave every wagon driver an extra twenty dollars before they headed back to Tampico. B. F., Gali, the four sailors, and two wagons loaded with gold and silver doubled back to the meeting point to look downstream for Captain Pesca and the *Rei*.

B. F. knew they were late, and he knew it was unlikely that Pesca would still be waiting for them, but he had no desire to retrace the trip overland—particularly carrying over 3,500 pounds of silver and gold. They traveled through the night, finding a dry ravine along the river to hide out during the day, then continued their journey the second evening, and arrived at the big bend in the river at two o'clock in the morning.

There was no way to look for Captain Pesca and the *Rei* at night, so again they found concealment and a place to rest. At daybreak, B. F. left Gali and the four sailors with the gold and went ship hunting.

By nine o'clock, he had seen no sign of the *Rei* and was about to return to Gali when he noticed a steep, vertical bank on the river with cypress trees that grew right along the river's edge. The sheer embankment was about one hundred feet high and afforded no path down to the water. He decided to walk upstream about a quarter of a mile, swim out in the river about thirty yards, and float by the embankment via a piece of driftwood.

The boat was almost invisible—but it was there.

He called out to Pesca and began swimming in the vessel's direction. He had taken no more than three strokes when he noticed the rail of the ship was suddenly lined with muskets. He quickly gulped a breath of air and dived beneath the muddy surface, angling toward the downstream end of the ship. Just as his lungs were about to burst, he touched the solid wood planking of the *Rei*'s hull.

B. F. stayed in the water and eased around to the back of the sloop. Using a tree on the bank, he pulled himself aboard, then lay there behind a furled sail, catching his breath and trying to listen to what was going on. The conversation was all in Portuguese, and he didn't speak enough of the language to figure out what was being said.

He maneuvered a bit closer and saw Captain Pesca using a spyglass on the surface of the river. B. F. thought, *Do I not trust this man? I've been in tough spots with him before and could always depend on him.* He stood up. "Looking for someone, Captain?"

He'd heard the expression 'white as a sheet,' but had never seen it illustrated so well as Captain Pesca did. "Was that you in the river, Señor B. F.? How did you get on the ship?"

B. F. grinned. "That was me, alright. I'm just glad nobody shot at me."

"Until you started swimming, we thought you were a log. You just took ten years from my life, Señor."

B. F. laughed. "How about your crew moving the ship about two hundred yards downstream right at dark. We'll meet you where that point of land reaches out into the river."

B. F. slipped back over the side, walked through the trees to a point where he could regain the river bluff, found Gali and the sailors, and told them when and where to reconnect with the *Rei*. "Tell Captain Pesca to stop for me at the dock with the big red lanterns in Brownsville, straight across from the docks at Matamoros. I'm going into Brownsville to find Joe Hudspeth. He's the Confederate agent I dealt with before. If we're lucky, he'll have cotton to sell, and we can make money on both ends of this trip."

Joe Hudspeth had a room on the second floor above Solomon Brown's Law Office in Brownsville. He had been a bookkeeper in Vicksburg before the war and was very capable in the way he handled his government's business. A slightly built man, he had thinning grey hair and wire rimmed spectacles. But when he spoke, his voice was extremely deep and resonating. If you closed your eyes, you'd never guess that the bass voice originated with the small man in front of you.

Hudspeth made no pretense in trying to give the impression he was somehow more important than he appeared. It was easy to like the man, and B. F. felt comfortable enough that he could be completely honest in relating their experience with Feathers.

"I don't have any authority over Feathers, Mistuh Windes. I suppose I could report this to Colonel Myers, but I hate to do business that way. At the same time, we need to keep trade lanes open. Maybe there's a way around Feathers."

"I'd rather do business with you, if possible. But the blockade has gotten much worse in the last few months."

"I'm painfully aware of that. We're lucky to see one ship get through every two weeks now on the Texas coast. You've got a good route to come overland from Tampico, but coming straight into Brownsville might be too chancy. What if we set up a rendezvous about fifteen miles above town on the Rio Grande? That'll keep us east of Feathers."

They agreed to a delivery in thirty days of similar size, and a price of two dollars per pair of boots and fifty cents per pair of wool socks. B. F. took the precaution of reminding him, "We only deal in gold or silver—no paper."

"I understand. It'll take some time to get that."

"Perhaps I can help with that problem. Do you have any cotton for sale, Mr. Hudspeth?"

"I got three warehouses full, but no way of getting it out until we can get a ship in here."

"If you'll take fifty-five dollars in silver a bale, I'll take my chances on getting three hundred bales past the blockade."

"When do you want it?"

B. F. turned to look at the Seth Thomas mantel clock on the cabinet. "In one hour and five minutes."

The two of them were standing on the Red Lantern Dock at nine o'clock that evening when the *Rei* slid out of the dark and lightly bumped the dock footings. The sloop didn't even come to a stop as B. F. and Mr. Hudspeth stepped on board.

Hudspeth had located five men who needed work, and assisted by Captain Pesca's crew, the cotton and $16,500 in silver changed hands before eleven o'clock.

There was a first quarter moon, but with the partial cloud cover, it provided very little illumination. Probably a good thing, in that they had a long run down the river, then a quick move to the south before running into the Gulf. It was unlikely a union gunboat would be in the river at night, as their heavily armed ships generally required a bit more draft than the sloops, so they probably would not risk the river except during daylight. But it was very possible that they would be sitting out in the gulf, at the mouth of the Rio Grande.

The moon was already gone, but there was just enough starlight interspersed between the clouds to reflect off the ocean's surface. Sure enough, a union steamer was there. It was almost impossible to see until Captain Pesca pointed it out, just barely visible on the dark night and sitting less than a mile off shore, beyond Brazos Island. They furled the sails of the *Rei* and released her anchor before they were so close to the mouth of the river that they might be spotted by the steamer.

Captain Pesca pulled Gali and B. F. aside. "Señors, we have limited options. The wind does not favor a fast run to the south. If they see us, we will not escape. They outgun us perhaps three or four to one, and they probably have twenty-four pounders against our twelves."

"What do you recommend, Captain?" Gali spoke up.

"I see three choices. We can move back upstream and hide as best we can before dawn. If we are fortunate, they will not come up the river, but if they do, they may see us and we will be forced to fight a losing battle. Another choice is to put two men ashore on the north shore of Brazos Island, and have them set up a diversion on the beach at least a half mile above the mouth of the river—perhaps a large fire. That may keep their attention long enough that we can escape. It is very risky."

"What else is there?"

"We lower a lifeboat into the water here, loaded with your treasure. The two of you go with the boat and two of my men. You will need to buy two wagons and horses and head back overland to Tampico. We will hide as best we can on the river, and wait for a better wind on another night. But if they find us, we will lose the *Rei* and your cotton."

B. F. put his hand on the captain's arm and whispered, "This is my fault, Captain. I didn't want to go back overland, so I asked you to bring the boat here to pick us up. I am sorry to have put us all in this position."

"I hate to lose this ship." Pesca glanced at the sky back up the river. "The clouds are getting thicker off to the west, but it will be good daylight in no more than three hours. We must make our move now."

Gali looked at B. F. "I vote for a diversion. That sounds like the best chance for the *Rei*."

B. F. gave an inquiring look at Pesca. "Can it work?"

"Let's give our two men a bag of black powder. They should start the fire with whale oil poured on a pile of driftwood up against some trees. The driftwood must be piled high. They will hang the bag of black powder about eight or ten feet up in the trees so that it will ignite when the fire is blazing high. The brightness of the fire and the explosion might make them think the fire is coming from a ship close to the shoreline."

B. F. turned to Gali. "Find two volunteers and give both men a hundred dollars in gold, with a hundred more waiting on them when they return to Tampico—if it works."

Gali answered by speaking to Pesca. "Tell the rest of your men that they can leave if they wish. They need only go over the side and swim to shore to get away, but this will be their only chance to get away."

Pesca spoke briefly to his sailors, then turned back to B. F. and Gali. "They choose to stay, Señors."

The moon had disappeared. All eyes stared into the blackness to where the men had swum off to the north, beyond the mouth of the river. Two sailors stood by the anchor chain, and six more were ready to raise the sails. It was taking too long. Perhaps the volunteers had dropped the whale oil. Maybe there was no driftwood. Had the powder gotten wet in the oiled sealskin bag? Had the men not reached their destination?

B. F. thought he saw a flicker of light, then there seemed to be nothing—was he simply imagining things? Then all of them saw it almost at once. Even at over a mile and a half, the fire was easily visible. In fact, it looked like they had set three or four fires at once along a fifty-foot wide area.

Pesca spoke to his men. "Let's move. We have no room for delay." As soon as the anchor was hauled up so that it was visible at the water line, but made no loud noise, Pesca spoke again. "Unfurl the sails. We head for the mouth of the river."

The *Rei* was nearing the spot where the Rio Grande emptied into the Gulf when one of the crew spoke to Gali, and he relayed the information to B. F. "See the sparks on the horizon. That is probably the smokestack on the Yankee gunboat, beginning to build up steam. I hope they are getting underway in order to see about the fire, and not because they have seen us."

They had just begun a turn to starboard to run south along the Mexican coastline when they heard a loud popping behind them. The fire had apparently reached the gunpowder, and it had blown into the trees above the fire. Now the fire appeared to be every bit as large as a ship. Could it have fooled them? The Union steamer was no longer visible. Perhaps the fire was so bright now that the sparks from the ship could not be seen. Then again, it could be headed their way, but in deeper water.

Pesca spoke to his crew. "Fire up the boiler. We will use both the steam engine and this cursed wind. I hope they will not see the sparks from our ship because the fire is so bright. Load the cannons on the port side. We may have little time to react." The sailors quickly fed coal into the furnace, then prepared the three small cannons for firing.

There was no doubt in anyone's mind they would be pitifully out-gunned if they had to face the gunboat. B. F. and Gali stood at the stern, staring behind them for an indication they were being pursued. Within twenty minutes, the only sign of the fire off to the north was an orange glow on the horizon, and try as they might, neither could see anything resembling a ship behind them. But it was not until day-break that they could look behind, as well as out to the east, and con-firm that there was no sign of a pursuing steamer.

Gali shouted something to the sailors, and they responded in kind. Relief washed over all of them, with pats on the back, great cheering, and much laughter. He put his hand on B. F.'s shoulder. "My friend, we have seen brave men here tonight."

Thirty-Six

Them Boys Is Awful Hungry

Gulf of Mexico 1862

Journal Entry—April 10, 1862

On my third trip into Brownsville, I again found Joe Huds-peth in Brown's Law Office, but he had company. He introduced me to a Captain George Todd and his scout, John McCorkle, from the Third Texas Cavalry. I admit, I'm not fond of too many people knowing about my business. I'll take no chance with sub-terfuge. Captain Todd was there for two reasons—to pick up the delivery and take it north to his troops, and also to see if we can deliver further north of here.

Captain Todd and his scout seem to lack what I would describe as an expected level of military decorum. Perhaps they have had a hard time of it. Todd is a wiry, scruffy looking man of no more than thirty years old. McCorkle kept his mouth shut the entire time, so I don't really have an impression of him except that he almost reminded me of a watch spring that was wound too tightly, and appeared to be on the verge of breaking loose as we sat there.

Captain Todd made a convincing case that a delivery on the Rio Grande is too far from his troops, who are fighting eight

*hundred miles north in Arkansas and Missouri. He called the
northern troops "Yankee Doodles," and talked about how they
were probably going to have to start fighting them up and down
the Mississippi River before long, as a sizable Yankee force
departed Cairo, Illinois in February, headed south along the
river.*

B. F. was not thrilled at the prospect of seeing more of the Union
Navy. "I've been into Sabine Pass twice, but that was several months
ago. I hear it's bottled up pretty tight."

"There's a ship every now and then that gets in. But we have a safer
spot around Galveston. There's three ways to get in the Bay—the San
Luis Pass south of Galveston Island, the main entry into the bay just
north of Galveston City, and at Gilchrist Point north of Bolivar Pen-
insula. That Navy blockade cain't stop up the whole thing."

"What kind of success are the blockade runners having?"

"They ain't many tried getting into the Bay. Most try to unload
right at Galveston City. Seems like that's where the Navy spends all
their time. If ya'll could get into the Bay instead of landin' here, it'd
save us a good six days travel time."

"Where do I find you and when?"

"They's a place called Smith's Point on the northeast side of the
Bay. We'll be there six weeks from tonight. Soon as we take this here
load back to the boys."

"What kind of supplies do you need?"

"Lead, powder, and nitroglycerin. Say, them boys is awful hungry. I believe we done kilt every deer in Missouri, and what squirrels
there is left are mighty lonesome. What about coffee, bacon, flour,
and some dried apples? Fact, if we cain't eat, we cain't fight. Can ya'll
bring in some vittles?"

"I don't have a good supply for ammunition. But how does fifty
thousand pounds of bacon, fifty thousand pounds of flour, five thousand pounds of apples, and twenty thousand pounds of coffee sound?"

Both Todd and McCorkle had grins as wide as their faces. "That'd
be mighty fine."

"One more thing, gentlemen, we don't take scrip. It'll need to be gold, silver, cotton, or tobacco. Understood?"

––––––––––––––––––

There was no sign of any opposing ship as the *Rei* glided into the narrow channel of San Luis Pass, overtaking Galveston Island on the starboard, then turning to the northeast up the West Bay. With a southerly wind, in less than an hour they emerged into the huge Galveston Bay, and continued north by northeast until they reached Smith Point at four o'clock in the morning. Captain Pesca found some cover on the north bank of the Point, virtually out of sight from the main body of water. Gali had chosen to stay in Mexico, saying he felt too vulnerable inside Confederate territory. Lieutenant Feathers' threat had preyed on him for weeks now, and he had no desire to risk his freedom in Texas.

At daybreak, B. F. went ashore with a large ham, a bag of flour, and some coffee to look for Todd and McCorkle. Thankfully, they and their wagons were there—concealed back in the saw grass and appearing to be well loaded.

After spending an hour feeding the grateful wagon crews, B. F. gave an accounting of his load. His price was $45,000. Their wagons held three hundred bales of cotton. At the current blockade price of fifty-five dollars a bale, Todd would need $28,500 to settle the bill. But the desire to negotiate had begun to ebb with the smell of the brewing coffee, and dissipated entirely with the taste of the country ham and biscuits. Captain Todd agreed to the price.

As they waited in the oppressive heat of the day, Todd pulled reflectively at his thin black beard:

"Mistuh Windes, we've had ourselves a bad spring. The Yanks purty well run us outa Missouri and Arkansas. In March, our boys done a hard three days march through the mountains from Fayetteville up to Pea Ridge, Arkansas. The weather was miserable. Lots of the boys is barefoot. They say you could track Gen'l Price's Army by the bloody footprints in the snow. We sure needed considerable more of them boots you brung in. Anyway, we outrun our supplies and had to leave the field after a two-day fight. Now our boys are with Price in Mississip', tryin' to help Gen'l Beauregard.

"Then they was a terrible battle in Tennessee two months ago—place the Yanks called Pittsburg Landing. We call it Shiloh. They say it was the bloodiest battle yet—over twenty-three thousand kilt, wounded, or took prisoner on both sides. Gen'l Johnston was killed there, and Beauregard took over. But this mean-fightin' son of a gun name of Gen'l Ulysses Grant of the Army of the Tennessee won the day. Last I heard, Beauregard was trying to get shut of the Yanks in north Mississippi.

"But what is gonna make it hard on us Texicans is that the Yanks is fast takin' over the Mississip'. This winter the Union Navy come down the Ohio to the Mississip' and right away took New Madrid. Course it ain't what most would call a Navy. There's ironclad steam-ships and rams that was built for river fighting. Even the Yanks call it the Brown Water Navy—cause it cain't make it out in big water. But within a month they captured a fort on Island Ten along with a garri-son of seven thousand troops. Last month they took Plum Run Bend on the River. Then not but two weeks ago they took Memphis. That battle didn't last much more'n an hour. They sunk seven Reb ships outa eight on the water."

B. F. spoke up. "What does that leave in Conferate hands on the Mississippi?"

"Just Vicksburg. And last I heard, that Brown Water Navy was headed south. I'd speculate they's headed for Vicksburg. So everything you run in here has got to then get across the Mississip' to do our boys any good."

At sundown, they transferred the foodstuffs from ship to wagons, and the cotton and silver from wagons to ship. Both of them had a long ride ahead. B. F. shook hands with Todd. "Good luck to you, Captain. Shall we make it here exactly two months from tonight?"

"Sounds about right. We got a long road ahead. If ye can find lead and powder, we need it bad. If ye cain't, we still need to keep our army fed." He turned to his teamsters. "Boys, git to yer critters."

By eleven o'clock, Todd and his wagons were headed to the north-east, toward Louisiana, and the *Rei* was speeding to the southwest across the Bay. They found the Pass empty again and turned back to the south. However, rather than hugging the coastline, Captain Pesca ordered them to sail fifty to one hundred miles out in the gulf in order to avoid any Navy gunships patrolling along the southern coast of Texas.

Over the next year, the *Rei* made three more successful runs into Galveston Bay, and B. F. continued to deal directly with Todd and McCorkle. The situation along the Mississippi was deteriorating as General Grant had begun moving his army toward Vicksburg in October of 1862. Captain Todd continued to maintain that he was able to get supplies across the river to the Third Texas Cavalry, and even said they had successfully transported food into the embattled city itself.

Vicksburg represented the last commanding position on the Mississippi, standing on bluffs some 250 feet above the river. Due to the extreme height of the bluffs, the Union Navy, under Captain David Farragut, was unable to elevate their guns sufficiently to fire into the city. So their responsibility was to simply prevent any enemy traffic on the river. The real fight was left to the armies.

On July 4, 1863, the commanding officer in the city, Major General John Pemberton, surrendered his command of over twenty nine thousand men to Grant. His troops and the civilian population were starving, having received no shipments of food for almost two months. Speculators inside the city had held warehouses full of food, but continued to wait on further price increases, and had not acknowledged that they had any food available. With the surrender of Pemberton, their warehouses were ransacked by the people, and many of the "businessmen" were forced to deny any knowledge or ownership of the contents of the warehouses. Major General Joe Johnston was able to escape with his thirty thousand troops and the Army of Mississippi intact, marching hard to the east toward Jackson.

On July 4, Grant telegraphed to President Lincoln, "Vicksburg is ours. The Mississippi is open all the way to the Gulf." General Pemberton was afterward commonly referred to as the most cowardly man in the South. A particularly inflammatory point was that he had chosen the most special of days to the Union—Independence Day—for the surrender. The city of Vicksburg would refuse to celebrate the Fourth of July for another eighty-one years.

Thirty-Seven

I Draw The Line At Weapons

Gulf of Mexico 1864

Journal Entry—February 10, 1864

This is our fifth trip into Galveston Bay, exchanging food for cotton and silver. There's certainly good profit in the run when we mix in the cotton, but this morning, Captain Todd was not the man who met me. To be sure, McCorkle was there as usual, but he was accompanied by a man I'd never seen before, a Major William Anderson.

Anderson is a large man, at least five or six inches taller than me, and well over fifty pounds heavier. The man wore a pair of holstered pistols, and another big Colt stuck in his waistband behind a large silver belt buckle. Several times during our meeting, I caught Anderson staring at me with the palest blue eyes I've ever seen. That look of his made me feel like I was a cornered rabbit and he was a wolf! He has an absolutely wild head of hair that is more than matched by his unruly black beard. There was no way to have a polite conversation with him. He is the kind of man that has very little to say in the way of niceties, seeming to be only interested in all things related to the fighting.

McCorkle explained Todd's absence. "Captain Todd been made Colonel Lane's Aide, and lit out with the army to Meridian, Mississippi. He says to keep them supplies a coming. Joe Hudspeth already left Brownsville, headed for South Carolina."

Anderson spoke up: "Mistuh Windes, I understand you been a good friend of the South. Probably done as much good for our cause as any brigade commander. We're much obliged for the food supplies, but our boys is desperate for arms. We come up against a troop of Sherman's cavalry that was using repeating rifles. Our boys couldn't stand up to them weapons. We took a couple off dead Yanks, and the rifles were stamped with the name of Spencer. They fire a cartridge like a Henry.

"Sherman and Grant are burning our cotton wherever they find it—in warehouses or even standing in the fields. What silver we got left we're stealing off of Yank paymasters. So from now on, we can only use that silver to buy what we got to have to keep fighting—Spencers and cartridges. If ye can deliver them, we'll be ready to buy all ye can get."

B. F. had been dreading the day when this would be the supply order. So far he had been able to look himself in the mirror and believe he was not engaged in trading true war materiel. Up to this point, it had strictly been clothes and food—no weapons, no ammunition, and no nitroglycerin. He realized he didn't even know how he felt about it—let alone how Gali might react.

Anderson was sizing him up, trying to gauge his reaction. "Mistuh Windes, unless you're ready to try your luck with the blockade around Mobile, we're all you got. If you're as loyal as I hear, I expect you'll find them guns in Cuba or the Virgin Islands."

B. F. made up his mind. "Let me suggest that you be in Galveston City the third week of April. My ship will put me ashore on the island, and I'll meet you at the Belle of the Bay Hotel. We'll make arrangements for the trade at that time. I'll be trying to bring in fifteen hundred rifles and three hundred thousand cartridges."

"Make it five hundred thousand rounds."

"I'll try."

The big man stood up, looked at B. F., and replied in a voice without any trace of emotion. "Do that."

B. F. found Gali in their small warehouse in Tampico. "Hello, my friend. Another good trip. After expenses, we're bringing in another twenty thousand dollars in silver and three hundred bales of cotton. By the way, what would you think of holding on to the cotton for a few months?"

"But why would we do that?"

"The buyer told me the Mississippi River is now completely controlled by the Union, and that they are burning cotton storehouses as well as cotton in the fields. It could be that the price is going to go up again in England and France once this new shortage takes hold."

"Well, I think we have just enough space to hold your new shipment. That will mean we are storing six hundred bales. At today's price, that is ninety thousand dollars. I would be happy to hold out for another ten or fifteen thousand dollars."

"Gali, we need to talk about something else. Our friend, Captain Todd, is now with the Rebel Army in Mississippi. The new buyer, a man named Anderson, says they will not be able to find more cotton for payment. He says they'll use silver, but that they will only buy weapons and ammunition from now on. I know you've been against that until now. How do you feel about this?"

"B. F., I just cannot be a party to selling weapons to them. I have a hard time selling them anything. After all, this is an Army that would not think twice about putting me in the chains of a slave. I have spent the last three years justifying to myself the boots and socks and food, but I must draw the line at weapons."

"We could look for another buyer and another landing site, but according to what I'm hearing, the Union blockade is pretty heavy from New Orleans to Florida. I understand the average survival of a blockade runner to the east is only about three trips. We've been extremely lucky—perhaps because we have a fast ship and a fine crew, but more likely because we have used lightly blockaded ports."

Gali shrugged. "This is not worth losing our ship and our crew. We have plenty of money. Why do we not stop?"

B. F. frowned. "Including these six hundred bales, we have just over two hundred twenty thousand dollars. I had hoped to walk away with at least one hundred fifty thousand dollars as my share."

"You are too greedy, my friend. We could sell the *Rei* for twenty thousand dollars and we would each have over one hundred twenty thousand dollars. That would make you a very wealthy man."

B. F. pondered this thought. The appeal of the money to be made in one big run was hard to shake off. He looked at Gali. This was hard to do. "Would you be willing to sell me your half of the *Rei*?"

Gali looked at his friend for a long moment, and then shrugged resignedly. "If you must do this, then I want no part of it. We will divide our funds. I will pay you today's price for the cotton, and you pay me today's price for the ship."

B. F. extended his hand. "You have been a true friend, Gali. I hope you hold no bad feelings for me."

"No, Señor. You have made me a rich man. With this money, Maria and I can be married, and finally her family can say nothing."

The *Rei* arrived in Kingston, Jamaica on April 2, and B. F. set about looking for a source of Spencer repeating rifles. The capitol city was full of European sea captains who were either trying to buy or attempting to sell. He took special pains to keep his plans to himself. Captain Pesca had inquired about their cargo, but he had only said he was looking for special goods. He had no desire to have the story circulating around the docks that his ship would be carrying guns when they departed.

After a week of no luck in finding repeating rifles, he began to think he had made a mistake. He decided to pull Pesca into his confidence to take advantage of his broader group of contacts, but made sure Pesca was advised to keep quiet around the crew.

Two days later, Pesca found their cargo through a Dutch sea captain, who he introduced to B. F. at their hotel, *The Britisher*. B. F. was very careful to ensure his purchase was everything it should be. The last thing he wanted to do was deliver defective rifles or ammunition to Major Anderson. He had no doubts that the brooding man would be swift in dealing with anyone who he perceived was cheating him.

The Spencers were packed in wooden cases, twelve to a crate. He purchased a hundred twenty-five cases—1,500 rifles—for $20 per rifle, and 500,000 rounds of ammunition for $5,000. Before actually taking delivery, he randomly opened five separate cases and retrieved a rifle from each, then pulled random cartridges from ten boxes, loaded each weapon, and fired a full seven rounds from each.

The Spencer was a seven shot repeater that was loaded through the back end of the stock. In order to fire the gun, the shooter operated a lever under the trigger to load a cartridge into the chamber, then cocked the hammer and fired. This was repeated each time the gun was fired. After shooting the first two rifles, B. F. easily became proficient enough that he could fire off all seven rounds in each of the last three carbines in just over fifteen seconds. The weapon was a bit lighter and shorter than the Henry rifles he had purchased before, and thankfully, unlike the Henry it possessed a wooden forestock, which made rapid firing much more comfortable for the shooter, as there was no direct contact with a heated barrel.

Still concerned that he was getting exactly what he paid for, he opened ten more cases of rifles to make the hair on the back of his neck lay down. He stood on the deck of the *Rei* and counted every case of rifles and cartridges that was loaded aboard. He couldn't help but notice that the serial numbers of the Spencers ran sequentially from 24,001 to 25,500. He wondered if the first 24,000 rifles had already found their way into Union hands, as he had heard that the Union generals had resisted purchasing Spencers because they were again convinced that soldiers would waste too much ammunition.

What a message to send to troops—that they might shoot too many rounds at a penny apiece in trying to defend their lives. Only after President Lincoln shot one of the weapons himself in the back-yard of the White House in the summer of 1863 did he countermand his generals, and the Union began buying the rifles.

Finally satisfied, B. F. paid Captain Roos $35,000 in silver, told the man in front of Pesca that they were headed for Mobile, and did not take his eye off the hold until they were out of Kingston Harbor and sailing to the west. He calculated the worth of his load in Texas at $70,000. Perhaps after this run it really would be a good time to quit.

He sought out Pesca. "Steer a course for Galveston, Captain."

Pesca gave him a strange look. "I thought you said we were headed to Mobile?"

"That was for Captain Roos' benefit in case his tongue begins to wag."

Late in the evening of April 18, Captain Pesca once again guided the *Rei* through the shallow San Luis Pass and turned his ship to starboard to slide along the west coast of Galveston Island. Some five miles to the southwest of Galveston City, at about four o'clock in the morning, Pesca ordered the anchor down, a small boat to be lowered, and B. F. was rowed ashore.

He stood on the beach for a few minutes, watching the rowboat being hauled back onboard the *Rei*. The anchor was winched up, and the sails filled enough to push the ship off on a northwest tack. Standing there by himself, with at least a five-mile walk in the dark ahead of him, and who knew what kind of roadway to guide him, he suddenly felt vulnerable. Instinctively, his hand rested on his pistol.

The road was little more than a path, and certainly did not consistently run in a straight line toward the city. It was dawn when he began to notice the horse path had turned into a wagon road, and within another half hour he entered the outskirts of Galveston.

When he asked the clerk at the Belle of the Bay Hotel what time breakfast was served, he was told that meals were only served to residents of the hotel.

"How much is a room?"

"Three dollars a night."

B. F. slapped the silver dollars on the counter. "Now then, what time is breakfast?"

"At six thirty, sir. Just a few more minutes."

"Do you have guests by the name of Anderson and McCorkle?"

"Yes sir. We're proud to have the famous Major Anderson and his aide at the Belle."

B. F. looked up at the clerk, and started to ask about his use of the adjective, but noticed Anderson coming down the stairs at that very moment. He walked over to greet him.

"Beginning to worry about you Mistuh Windes. I trust you're here with the goods we discussed."

"Fought headwinds most of the way across the Gulf, Major. Yes, I have your order as you requested. Shall we wait on McCorkle before we have breakfast?"

"He won't be dining with us this morning. He's out at Smith Point, waiting on your ship."

They sat on the veranda facing the bay. Anderson spoke again. "Your friend Todd has got himself a field promotion to lieutenant Colonel. He's now on his way to Atlanta with Ross' Brigade in the Army of Mississip. Those boys will see some hard fighting."

"Maybe the shipment I brought in will do them some good."

Anderson looked at him with expressionless eyes. "Yes, suh— maybe it will."

B. F. heard a rumbling sound out to the west. "Is that thunder I hear? I didn't notice a storm coming in."

After two more booming sounds in the distance, Anderson squinted out across the bay. "There ain't no clouds a'tall. Sorta sounds like cannon to me."

There were three lesser sounds in rapid order. B. F. felt like he was in need of more air. "You're familiar with this, Major. That sounded like the report of three lighter cannons."

Again the larger booming sounded. Anderson looked at B. F. "Them sounds like twenty-four pounders to me. Is your ship in that direction?"

B. F. nodded his head. "That's where they were headed. With this slight wind they might not have reached cover before daylight. Is there a Union gunboat out in the bay?"

"Hadn't heard of it."

"I need to find a boat. You want to come with me?"

"We'd best give it a few hours. If there is a gunboat out yonder, they might just wonder what we're doing out there. Might just fire on us too."

"I need to see about my ship."

"If a gunboat found them, they ain't nothing you can do nohow." Anderson looked at his pocket watch. "Let's give it about four hours. I got no desire to face a twenty-four pounder with just a brace of pistols."

They spent all afternoon searching the bay on a small steamer. The first place they looked in earnest was the west side of Smith Point. B. F. could see no indication that the ship had been there. No evidence of a ship's remains floating on the water. Nothing.

When they made landfall at Smith Point, McCorkle met B. F. on the beach. "Did you see any sign of my ship this morning?"

"No, suh. We was wonderin' when you would show up."

"Did you hear cannons out on the bay about six hours ago?"

"Yes, suh. I believe I did."

"Did you see any sign of a ship?"

"The shootin' was too far away. We did see some smoke—probably off a smoke stack—but no ship." McCorkle glanced from B. F. to Anderson. "Did you bring the rifles, Mistuh Windes?"

B. F. looked out across the empty bay. "They're on my ship—unless some Yankee gunboat found them this morning."

The small steamer traveled to the west, then turned and began a zigzag return back to Galveston. They put a man in the rigging with instruction to shout out at the indication of a sail, or debris in the water. All afternoon there was no sound from the rigging.

Finally, just before sundown the sailor called out. "Small boat in the water, about three hundred yards at eleven o'clock."

It was not the *Rei*'s. Or at least, not the *Rei*'s B. F. was looking for. Rather, it was the rowboat that had taken him to the beach the night before. It simply had *Rei*'s "II" lettered on its bow, and was riding low in the water due to what appeared to be a cannonball hole right at the water line. There was no other sign of anyone or anything.

Anderson looked at the boat. "This come off your ship?"

"I'm afraid so."

"Appears they sunk your ship with all aboard."

B. F. didn't want to think about it. *Captain Pesca! The crew he had sailed with all over the Gulf and the Caribbean. The Rei. The seventy thousand dollar cargo!* He called to the sailor on the mast. "Keep looking until it's too dark to see. Maybe there's somebody out there."

There wasn't. They made it back to the docks at Galveston well after dark. Anderson spoke up before they returned to the hotel. "We still need them rifles, Mistuh Windes."

"I just lost a fortune today. I have no ship. I have no crew. I can't help you." He couldn't even think about doing this again.

"Sometimes you get, and sometimes you get got, Mistuh Windes." Anderson didn't say another word, just stepped down on the dock and walked off.

B. F. spent another day on the bay, looking for any additional sign of the sloop and its crew, but to no avail. He couldn't even find anyone on the docks who had seen a battle. Everything just vanished without a trace.

Thirty-Eight

Will You Stand Up
With Me?

Gulf of Mexico 1864

He found Gali and Maria in São Luís, preparing for their wedding. When he told them what had happened, they sympathized with his loss, but when they realized their friend, Captain Pesca, was also gone, neither of them could keep from weeping. Pesca had worked for them faithfully for three years and had been in danger many times because of their work. Gali and B. F. had witnessed his bravery firsthand several times over. It was very painful to think about.

> *Journal Entry—May 15, 1864*
> *It's been over fifteen years since I left home, so last night I wrote letters to Cousin Sue and Aunt Abbie. With no ship, it looks like I'm going to be in one place for a while, so at least I can give them a return address in São Luís. I don't put much stock in the letters ever getting from Brazil to Indiana in the middle of a war. But I do know of a Portuguese ship headed to Cuba, and the Captain promised this morning to hand off the letters to any Union Navy vessel he found in port. I guess miracles do happen once in a while.*

In early November, B. F. saw a newspaper that had been printed in New Orleans in October. Hungry for any news of the war, he began to read the paper from front to back, not missing a single detail. But he spent almost his entire morning reading and re-reading an article on the second page that was accompanied by a photograph of an obviously very dead man who had been propped up in a chair to have his picture taken.

The header was in a bold typeface **Bloody Bill Anderson Killed in Missouri**. The story described the murderous killing sprees of Bloody Bill that had gone on primarily in Missouri, Kansas and Arkansas, first in cahoots with William Quantrill, and most recently with his own gang of some one hundred guerillas.

According to the article, neither Quantrill nor Anderson had ever been officers in the Confederate Army, although both often claimed to have been, or at least conferred military rank on themselves. Moreover, they and their gang had never even served side by side with true Confederate troops in any pitched battle of the war. Their activities were always completely independent of Southern forces, and furthermore made no attempt to observe any recognized standards of warfare.

The story described Anderson and Quantrill's raid on Lawrence, Kansas in August of 1863, when they had killed every male resident of the city they could find. That was old news to B. F., for everyone had heard that story. However, there were also more recent events in the article that were every bit as heinous.

In Olathe, Kansas, Anderson and his men were heard to brag that they had been shooting down Kansas settlers "like so many hogs." And in September, Anderson and his gang had ambushed 150 Union cavalrymen outside Centralia, Missouri. All the cavalrymen were found shot through the head, scalped, bayoneted several times, and many had their ears and noses "and other parts" cut off.

The Union Army had decided it was time to get even, tracked down his gang, and set up an ambush of their own on October 26 near the little town of Orick, Missouri. Anderson was finally killed while making a wild, solitary charge past the Union positions—in his own signature style—with reins held in his teeth and pistols blazing from both hands, when a bullet struck him in the forehead. They then leaned him upright in a chair for the enclosed picture. But in their own eye-for-an-eye message, they cut off his head and stuck it on a telegraph pole so every passerby would see what came to bushwhackers.

But what kept B. F. going back to the article time after time was the picture. He was almost in shock to acknowledge to himself that the man in the paper—Bloody Bill Anderson—was none other than the sullen man he knew only as Major William Anderson in Galveston. Was it possible that he had been providing goods to bushwhackers—even to the likes of men like Quantrill and Bloody Bill? Were Todd and McCorkle connected to the Third Texas Cavalry, or had that been a lie as well? At what time over the last three years had he stopped dealing with true representatives of the Confederacy, and started dealing with bushwhackers? At that point forward, could he have simply been running the blockade for the benefit of common criminals—even murderers?

He could not—would not—tell Gali what he suspected to be true. He couldn't share this evil burden with Gali, or with anyone. The bad judgment had been his alone. The realization tore at his sense of right and wrong, at the way he felt about himself as an honorable person. How could this be? He was naturally embarrassed that he had been hoodwinked, but worse, ashamed of just about everything he had done for the past four years. With one last sickening look, he put the newspaper into the small fireplace in his room and watched it disappear into the flames.

In February, he miraculously received a letter from Waynesville, Missouri. He opened it and read the signature first. It was from his Cousin Sue, who he had not seen or heard from in almost sixteen years.

Mr. Finnerty had moved them to Waynesville some ten years previously. They had sold the two small farms in Indiana and were able to buy a much larger place in Missouri. The next sentences were painful to read.

Momma died last April, and she continued to wish to her grave that her wandering nephew would come back home. We got two letters from you about four years ago that were sent to us by one of our old neighbors back in Jeffersonville. I guess it's a miracle that we got them at all. But you didn't give us a return address. We wanted so badly to write to you Ben, particularly when Momma took to her bed, but could not. After she died, Mr. Finnerty gradually just wasted away, and one day last July he fell off a windmill in the pasture and broke his neck. But I think it was grief that killed him.

You mentioned that you had never been able to find your pa in California. You must not have known that he never got there. He actually came back home only two or three days after you left. Mr. Finnerty went over to talk to him, and told him you had left to go to California to catch up with him. He figured your pa would head out to try and find you and bring you back home, but apparently his wife convinced him not to. He ended up taking a job working on a steamboat between Louisville and New Orleans, and the last I knew, he was still coming home to Jeffersonville every other week. Of course, that was long before the war.

Sue was now alone, but apparently not for long. She had met a man—Matt Durham—who had come to Waynesville to purchase Mr. Finnerty's two quarter horses after he died. Good horses were almost non-existent in Missouri at this point in the war, as most had been "appropriated" by the Union Army, the Missouri Militia, the Rebels, or the bushwhackers. For the two armies, appropriated meant "what used to be yours now belongs to the government, and I'm gonna give you a piece of paper that we both know is probably worthless." But for the Militia and the bushwhackers, it simply meant "or else."

Sue and Matt had continued to write to one another for several months, and now they were to be married in August in some place called Keetsville, Missouri. Apparently, Matt's father was a magistrate in the county, and they were well thought of. She went on in her letter.

I have no family in this world except you. Would you consider coming to my wedding and standing up with me? They say this war will be over soon, and if that's true, I hope you'll come.

Matt says to tell you there's plenty of good land on the prairie around Keetsville—lots of grazing, and good, clear spring water everywhere. The war has been hard on folks down there, and good land can be had for fifteen dollars an acre. The town is about halfway between Springfield, Missouri and Fayetteville, Arkansas on the Wire Road. If you can come, the wedding is on August 3rd, and will be at Matt's father's home. His place is right on the Wire Road, about a quarter mile to the north of the Keetsville stage stop.

I do hope you can come. Oh, and there's a girl I want you to meet— my best friend, Crocia Rayl.

Love, Sue

B. F. read the letter through twice more. Somehow it was hard to think of Sue as anything beyond the three-year-old little girl he had last seen in Indiana. Now she was ready to get married—and wanted him to be there with her. For the first time in months, he had something to look forward to. He decided if the war ended in time, he would go.

He talked to Gali, asking if he would like to go along.

"B. F., I think there is no place for a man who looks like me in your country after the war. I think it may be twenty years before a man with Negro blood is accepted as an equal in the United States."

"I hope you're wrong, Gali, but I do understand your feelings. I just want you to know, I never had a better friend."

"Ah, then now would be a good time for me to tell you something. Do you remember a Portuguese ship captain by the name of Gomes de Carmona?"

"Sure. We did a lot of business with him."

"Yes, and that is why I must take this seriously. Captain Carmona says he is positive he saw Captain Pesca in Freeport just two weeks ago."

"What? But that's. . . ."

"Impossible? Yes, but Captain Carmona says he saw Pesca—or his twin brother—in The Britisher Hotel in Freeport. He says he believes Pesca did not see him."

"That's the same hotel he and I stayed in on my last trip. All of us shed a lot of tears over that man. And now he is not only alive, but it appears he is also a back-stabber and a thief."

After four years, Gali could read his friend very well. "B. F., I did not tell you this to have you try to go after Captain Pesca. You are but one man, and he may have an entire crew at his disposal. Also, in a British port, if you kill him they will put you in prison and throw away the key. You must not even think of such a thing."

"I lost seventy thousand dollars in goods and a twenty thousand dollar ship—all because of Captain Pesca. What authorities do I report that to? I don't know who he betrayed me to, or even what country he betrayed me to. Nobody is going to do anything about it, unless I do."

"I wish I had not told you."

B.F.'s second reason to visit Freeport, besides finding Pesca, was to convert his holdings into something he could travel with. In São Luís he obtained a letter of credit valued in one of the few world currencies that remained dependably stable—the British pound sterling—which was directly pegged to the value of silver. He carried his letter for fifty-three thousand pounds sterling, along with $1,000 in gold British sovereigns. When he arrived in the Bahamas, he deposited the letter of credit in a Bank of Britain and had a letter of credit reissued on the British bank. He had much greater confidence in his ability to convert a British document into cash when he finally arrived back in the United States.

His first act in preparing for his arrival was to shave his beard. Certainly Pesca had never seen him without a beard, in fact he had not seen himself without hair on his face for at least six years. Perhaps he wouldn't pass a close inspection, but he doubted that he would be identified at a distance. He began to very cautiously make inquiries at the Britisher as well as other hotels that catered to a customer with real money to spend. And very early in the mornings, he also visited the docks, looking for his ship.

For three weeks, he accomplished not much more than sprinkling money around to pay for information. He began to suspect that Pesca was long gone. It was in this environment that a bundle of newspapers from Washington were delivered in Freeport. At least one of the papers was dated April 10, 1865 and had three-inch headlines **Lee Surrenders to Grant**. The story was penned from a place called Appomattox, Virginia, and went on to opine that the war would surely soon be over, after upward of six hundred thousand deaths and one million casualties.

As the paper was read around the hotel drawing room, B. F. watched the other men sitting at the tables. He noticed only a single man in the room was cheered by the news. He could imagine that the others were suddenly wondering what in the world they were going to do with a ship load of munitions or Confederate clothing for sale. Others were undoubtedly dealing with the realization that the hundreds of thousands of dollars of Confederate scrip they were holding may now be completely and utterly worthless. The twenty or so other men in the room would immediately be seeking any available market for their shipments, and probably their ships as well. He realized he might very well have been in exactly the same situation if he still had owned a ship.

B. F. was briefly tempted to make a rock-bottom offer on a ship but had enough sense to reflect. After all, the market was now gone. Most in the south would be drowning in poverty; their currency worthless; their cities, businesses, and farms in ruins; and a returning army of tens of thousands of men who had no money, no employment, and no prospects. Their only common possession would be a memory seared with visions they would never be able to forget.

He also realized that if Pesca was not already in Freeport—and he had begun to doubt that he was—then given the war news, there would be little reason for him to sail there. His quest for revenge was going to be frustrated as a result of the end of the war. However, the end of the conflict was definitely in sight, as he couldn't imagine that the other Confederate commanders would continue to fight much longer now that the Army of Northern Virginia was done. Apparently, he would now have an opportunity to go to a wedding.

Thirty-Nine

The Worst Hole In All The Country

The Mississippi River 1865

Journal Entry—July 15, 1865

I'm surprised to see that the Port of New Orleans is almost deserted, particularly when compared to Freeport, Havana, and São Luís. The harbor pilot came on board about an hour ago to guide us in a zig-zag path around the tops of at least a half-dozen ships' masts that are visible just above the water line in the harbor. Apparently all of them were early victims of the Yankee blockade. I can't help but wonder how many more are just out of sight underwater, but close enough to the surface to rip the bottom out of this packet steamer I'm riding on.

There appears to be very little commerce being carried out on the docks, and this is also surprising, given that New Orleans has been in Union hands for most of the war. I wonder how long it will take before this city returns to its former prominence? Today it looks like that may be a long time off. Only a small number of Yankee troops are visible from the waterfront. Perhaps the majority are already being relieved, and headed toward family and home.

He had made friends with the ship captain early in their journey, especially after the man learned B. F. had been on steamboats sixteen years earlier on the Ohio, Mississippi, and Missouri. So B. F. was standing in the pilot house with Captain José Belardo, with the harbor pilot at the wheel. The height of the pilot house allowed them a view over the top of the embankment along the river. On the left was a large area of statues, standing stones, and crypts. "What is this called, Captain? It appears to be a cemetery of some kind."

"It is called the City of the Dead. The bodies are buried above the ground in those stone crypts. It is impossible to dig more than a foot or two without striking water in much of New Orleans. In fact, only the slave levee prevents the river from flooding the whole area.

"The City of the Dead is very old. The oldest stone there is dated 1787—just after your American Revolution. There are others that look even older, but there is no date."

B. F. couldn't help but wonder how many untold stories there were in the hundred acres of the City of the Dead.

After conferring with an agent on the dock about the most appropriate way to travel to southwestern Missouri, B. F. booked passage on a river steamer bound for St. Louis. Most conversation on board dealt with the long, gradual ending of the war. Robert E. Lee had begun the process in early April, followed by the surrender of General Joe Johnston to General Sherman in North Carolina later that month. Then General Richard Taylor, the son of Zachary Taylor, surrendered in Alabama in May, and then General Edmund Smith of the Confederate Department of the Trans-Mississippi Army in June.

In answer to B. F.'s earlier question, there were four hundred recently mustered-out troops on the boat with him. Although some fifty of them had injuries that were disabling, spirits were high on the steamer, and B. F. did not have the luxury of a full night's sleep during his entire week on board. The troops on board passed the time by singing and telling stories. The few Confederate troops seemed to never tire of singing a favorite ditty, which was apparently named after the boiled peanuts they had been forced to rely on as their only source of food for weeks on end. They called it *Goober Peas.*

Sitting by the roadside on a summer's day
Chatting with my mess mates, passing time away
Lying in the shadows, underneath the trees,
Goodness, how delicious, eating goober peas.
When a horse-man passes, the soldiers have a rule
To cry out their loudest, "Mister, where's yer mule?"
But another custom, enchanting-er than these
Is wearing out your grinders, eating goober peas.
Just before the battle, the General hears a row,
He says, the Yanks are coming, I hear their rifles now.
He turns around in wonder, and what d'ya think he sees?
The Georgia Militia, eating goober peas.
I think my song has lasted almost long enough
The subject is interesting, but the rhyme is sorta rough.
I wish the war was over, so free from rags and fleas,
We'd kiss our wives and sweethearts, and gobble goober peas.

B. F. disembarked in Cape Girardeau, Missouri and sought out a stagecoach company to carry him westward. If New Orleans had been damaged, this little town was a sad place indeed. Other than the single steamship, there didn't appear to be anything going on at all. Small groups of men stood on street corners, almost all in the classic grayish-brown uniform of the Confederate soldier used toward the end of the war. Their uniforms were generically described as "butternut," but in many troops, no two uniforms were exactly the same color. The dyeing process involved boiling a large number of butternut or walnut husks in a pot and then soaking clothing in that mixture which was to be converted into uniform wear. Not only did no single pot of boiling dye have an equivalent amount of husks in the mixture, but different materials accepted the dye in different ways.

Hence, the men who stared hard at B. F. in his well-tailored clothing, as he walked from the dock to the stagecoach stop, were all the same but still with a discernible difference. As he approached the stop, a coach pulled up from the west. Among the dusty passengers who disembarked was a Union lieutenant about his age, so B. F. struck up a conversation to see if he could get some information about his destination. "Lieutenant, where have you come from?"

"About a hunnert miles the other side of polite society. God-forsaken place called Cassville, Missouri."

"Whereabouts is Cassville?"

"You take this stage to Springfield, and then transfer to the Fayetteville-bound stage down the Wire Road."

"You ever hear of a place called Keetsville?"

The soldier raised the brim of his hat and squinted at him. "There ain't no way a man that looks and sounds like you lives in Keetsville."

"I don't live there, but I'm headed there for a wedding."

"Take some friendly advice, friend. Don't go!"

"Why do you say that?"

"I was quartered in Cassville for the last three years. Just under five hundred of us the last year or so. That Keetsville was about nine miles to the southwest. The whole area was full o' them Scots-Irish. I guarantee you the first thing those people did when they come to that country, was build their cabins and a little church, set up their stills and raise a barn to play their devilish music. It's no wonder the whole county was infested with Rebs and Bushwhackers. Even the women was Secesh!"

B. F. was puzzled at that. "Secesh?"

"Sorry. We just used it as a short term for all these Secessionists. Anyways, sit down here and I'll tell you a story about Keetsville. That stage ain't heading back to Springfield for another hour or so." They both sat on the edge of the plank sidewalk, their boots dangling in the dust of the street.

"General Schofield took Cassville in the fall of 1862 and put up his officers in the courthouse. They dug a good trench all around it and turned it into a decent enough fort. The General busted out portholes in the walls of the second floor and put eight cannon up there. Nobody budged us outa that courthouse for the rest of the war.

"Most of the Brigade was bivouacked on a high hill just to the west of the courthouse, and they pretty much controlled four valleys from there. A rag-tag bunch of Rebs held northern Arkansas, and Cassville was the southern point of the Union Army in southwestern Missouri. So Keetsville was a sorta no-man's-land in between. There was skirmishes round about almost every day for two years. And those that was foolish enough to be Union sympathizers was terrorized or kilt by either their neighbors or the bushwhackers. So we was surrounded by Rebs.

"We had a purty good battle down at Keetsville when we first come into the area, and my Colonel, Clark Wright, spoke true when he said that the citizens of Keetsville all knew about the coming Reb attack, gave intelligence to the enemy, and kept all knowledge of it from us. That afternoon, all the ladies quietly left town one by one, and by the time of the attack, all was out safe and sound. That alone showed every last citizen in the place was a part of the plan. The Colonel was tryin' to figure what to do with the town and the people. He said Keetsville was the worst hole in all this country! Colonel Wright and all that come after him tried to turn those folks, but between them bushwhackers and the rest of the citizens, I don't think we made no progress."

"Lieutenant, thanks for the history, and good luck on your travel home. Looks like my stage is ready to go."

The lieutenant looked at him with what appeared to be pity. "You best be real careful where you're headed. You look way too much like a Yankee for it to be healthy for you down there. Just remember I fulfilled my Christian duty and tried to talk you out of it."

The Eureka Stage Line took the old Indian Trace from Cape Girardeau to Rolla for an all-day run, then hit the Wire Road and headed to the southwest, passing through Waynesville. It was the last week of July, so B. F. knew that Sue would already have left the town and traveled to Keetsville to prepare for the wedding. By mid-morning of the third day, they reached Springfield, where he switched to another stage and continued on until almost dark, stopping in Cassville for the night.

There were no real quarters for travelers in town, as the Barry Hotel had been burned to the ground during the war, so the stage passengers stayed in the home of a Mr. S.K. Burton, who served as the county postmaster. B. F. inquired of the driver why they had not continued on to Keetsville, since there was no hotel in Cassville. The driver replied, "We been held up twict in the last month just south of Keetsville, so if it's just the same to you, I druther make that trip in daylight."

After an early breakfast of eggs and biscuits at the Burton table, the coach departed for Fayetteville and all points south. There was very little activity in Cassville at that time of the morning, although B. F. couldn't be sure that there was ever very much going on. At least half of the stores in town were partially burned or about ready to fall down.

Two miles out of town, the driver paused for his team to get a good drink from an artesian spring bubbling out of a rock cliff. "This here's McMurtry Spring. Best water in this part of the country. Spring runs all year long, no matter how dry everything else is."

"There's a feller, Wilbert Ledgerwood, lives about a half a mile west of here that's got a wet weather spring on his place, and it runs across the stage road. Every time it rained, he'd be out there on the road with a team of mules, charging anybody who got their wagon stuck to pull them out. That warn't too bad, 'til folks caught Wilbert hauling water from McMurtry Spring down to his place to dump on the road so's it'd stay muddy. That way people would keep on getting stuck, even when it was dry weather. Couple of his neighbors is kinda high-strung. They told Wilbert if he done it again, they wuz gonna turn him into a steer."

The further they rode from Cassville, the more he noted burned out farms or barns. The war had obviously been hard here. It seemed within a few miles that they had arrived on a flat prairie—certainly not anything to compare with the broad expanses of Kansas and Nebraska—but a flat plain of land that was at least four miles wide and perhaps ten to twelve miles in length. A number of the fields appeared to be in good shape, but cattle were absent. He noted other spring branches along the way and remembered what Sue had written to him about the land.

He took particular note of some property just before they arrived in Keetsville. It ran off to the west for a good half mile and was bordered on the south side by a running spring. Although there was a farmhouse, the yard was grown up and it did not appear to be occupied. He resolved to find out more about it.

Forty

They Cooked The Skin Off His Feet

Keetsville, Missouri 1865

The stage stop was only that—a stop. The Eureka Stage Line would run another forty miles or so before they exchanged teams in Arkansas and continued their journey to Fayetteville, then on to Fort Smith. B. F. dismounted the stage and got directions to the home of John Durham, which was just a couple of hundred yards back up the road.

As he walked up to the door of the large farmhouse, he began to feel very awkward. It was the first day of August, two days before the wedding, and he was totally unknown to these people. He paused at the bottom step, thinking that there must be a better way of introducing himself than to simply show up with a traveling bag in hand. The prospect of walking back to the stage stop wasn't appealing in the heat of the day, but perhaps they could direct him to someplace in town to stay.

About the time he finally decided to turn around and walk back out the gate, the door opened behind him and a woman's voice called out, "Can I help you?"

With some embarrassment, he turned around. There was a woman of about forty standing there in a blue house dress. But looking over her shoulder was one of the prettiest women he had ever seen, a tall, slender, curly black-haired and blue-eyed version of his cousin Sue. "Is that really you, Ben Windes?"

He couldn't help grinning at the joy of seeing his cousin. "I'm sorry for just showing up without letting you know I was in town."

The older woman came down the steps and slipped her hand through his arm. "Shush. I'm Minnie Durham. This girl has been talking about you ever since she got here. Come on in the house and tell us about your trip. How on earth do you get here from Brazil? Isn't that the other side of the world?"

They sat him in the parlor and the older woman disappeared into the back of the house. B. F. wanted to sit and talk to Sue for about a month, hearing everything about her life. But that conversation didn't get started before Missus Durham reappeared, carrying a tray of lemonade, with yet another pretty, tall girl.

B. F. stood up, looked first at Sue, then at the newcomer, then at his hostess. "How many pretty women have you got in this house, anyway?" They laughed at his red face, and it got redder.

"Ben, this is my best friend, Crocia Rayl from Waynesville. She's come all the way here with me for the wedding."

B. F. noticed that she was almost as tall as he was. He couldn't remember seeing a girl that could look him straight in the eyes like that. "Hello, Miss Rayl."

"Mister Windes, all I've heard about was you as a young boy. You hardly fit the image I had. Not too many eight year olds have a beard."

He grinned. "I'm sorry to disappoint you."

She peered closer at him, then glanced at her friend. "Why, Sue, I don't believe his eyes are nearly as black as you said!"

Matthew, Sue's husband-to-be, had matching red hair and a red beard. B. F. couldn't help noticing that his head and his hands seemed to be way too big for his body. He walked with a decided limp as a lasting reminder that half of his right buttock had been shot away at the Battle of Pea Ridge two years previously. That he survived at all was due to his captain sending him home in the back of a two-wheeled ambulance wagon.

It had been a trick to stay off the Wire Road, avoid the Yankee patrols, and travel the long way around via the little settlement of Semmesbury. Matthew had spent the trip face down and buttocks in the air, but would never forget the four hours of rutted track, switchbacks, and deep valleys that stood between Pea Ridge and the loving care of his mother.

Matthew and his father farmed 160 acres east of their home, and his father, John, had been a local magistrate before the war. The Yankees hadn't put much store in his judicial impartiality, so since 1862 he had spent all his time farming—or at least trying to farm. Their property ran toward the south and behind the stage stop. About twenty acres of their land was in corn, twenty in sorghum, twenty in hay, and the rest in fenced pasture, but right in the middle of the sorghum they had created a huge, two acre vegetable garden. The placement of the garden was important, as they wanted to keep it completely out of sight of foraging Union troops.

Matthew took B. F. out to see it that afternoon. "We stuck it out here to be close to this spring. When we lay this pipe into the spring, the whole garden is trenched out so we can irrigate the two acres in less'n two hours. If it hadn't been for this garden, we would have starved to death several times."

"Do the Yankees pay people when they take their crops or livestock?"

"Depends on their mood. Sometimes they hand folks a voucher for their goods, but you have to take it to St. Louis to get any money. Most times, they just take what they want. Lots of folks been killed around here if they object about anything. Some are just called outa their house in the middle of the night and shot dead."

"Has that been reported?"

"Not really anybody to report it to. We make it about forty-two civilian men and boys from this part of the county murdered in cold blood since I come home in sixty-two. The Yankees even used bloodhounds to hunt down our friends and neighbors who hid out in the hills—not bad people, just too scared to stay in their homes."

"Isn't all that over now that the war is done?"

"There's still a company of Billy Yanks in Cassville. We don't know how long they'll be here, but they're still getting even with folks every chance they get. Most of the culprits aren't regular army—they're part of the Missouri State Militia. Even so, the army doesn't really make any attempt to keep them under control."

B. F. had seen people married before. Every now and then one of the miners in the gold fields found a woman who agreed to put up with him, and quite a crowd would gather in hopes that the groom would spring for drinks for all two or three hundred of the close friends he didn't realize he had. But he had never actually been a part of a wedding, let alone a proper wedding. It was a good thing that Minnie Durham was around to direct them, because he had no notion whatsoever as to what was expected.

Just before the ceremony, when he came downstairs in the suit he had purchased in Freeport, he realized that he had gone too far, as neither of the Durham men were wearing anything other than what looked like their very plain Sunday meeting suits. Had it not been for Crocia taking his arm and telling him what a beautiful suit he was wearing, he would have gone back upstairs and changed clothes to something less expensive.

The wedding was only marred by one incident. As the guests began to arrive, a squad of Yankee cavalry cantered down the Wire Road and came to a halt, positioning themselves directly across the road from the Durham home and making it a point to closely observe every man that arrived. They made no move to interfere with anyone, but certainly made theirselves unwelcome.

B. F. sought out Matthew and asked what was going on. "They likely figure somebody will show up that they're looking for. They must be desperate for something to do—coming to a man's wedding and standing out there on the road in the heat of the afternoon."

Just as the ceremony started, B. F. noticed a tall man emerge from the cane field and stride across the pasture behind the house. Before B. F. had escorted Sue to the waiting pastor and bridegroom, the man had arrived in the backyard and was standing close to John and Minnie Durham. It was obvious that he was well known among the guests, as almost every man at the gathering came over to shake his hand. But immediately after the vows were said and refreshments served, he walked back the same way he had come, taking special care to never come within sight of the troops out on the road.

When B. F. had the chance, he asked Matthew about the odd visitor. "Oh, that was Shorty Johnson, an old friend of the family. He was in my regiment. You mighta noticed, he don't care much for Yankees."

"Would he be the one those troops are looking for across the road?"

Matthew replied, "Could be a whole list of men they might be out for. But they've been trying to get hold of Shorty for a long time. About a year ago, Shorty and some boys were suspected of stealing Yankee supplies. Captain Mitchell got all hot about it and sent some troopers out to get information. They caught his younger brother, Ephraim, out on the road at night. Supposedly he had a round of Army cheese with him, and they figured he'd been connected to Shorty some way or another.

"They took him into Cassville to see Captain Mitchell, who musta decided it'd be easy to get a boy of thirteen to talk. They took him to their no-count prison at what used to be Crout's Carding Mill there in town, and built up a fire in the fireplace. Then two of Lincoln's finest held Ephraim down close to the fire. They cooked the skin right off the bottom of his feet, trying to get him to tell where Shorty was. Ephraim says his feet were sizzling like bacon in the skillet before they stopped. Fact is, his feet were burned so bad he ain't walked without a crutch since. They transferred Mitchell outa here right after that. Just as well, Shorty woulda killed him, then they sure enough woulda hunted Shorty down."

B. F. spent a good amount of time during and after the wedding watching Crocia Rayl. He had discovered to his surprise that she was two years younger than Sue, as she looked and acted considerably older than seventeen years old. Her father ran a mercantile store in Waynesville, where she had lived her entire life. B. F. had no idea how she and Sue accomplished the feat, but for the ceremony each of them had created huge curls in their hair almost as big as a fist. He couldn't decide whether Sue's coal black hair was more attractive than the reddish contrasts in Crocia's auburn do, but there was no doubt they were the two prettiest girls he had ever seen.

Later in the evening, he was finally able to corral her attention and have a conversation. He couldn't be sure if she was flirting with him or laughing at him, for it seemed that she had a clever reply to everything he had to say. It was only when he struck upon the subject of her returning to Waynesville that she became serious. "Now that the wedding is over, everybody is going to want to get back to normal. The last thing a new married couple needs to do is entertain company."

B. F. realized she was not just talking about herself. "I think that goes for me, too. Would you think I was being rude to suggest that I ride back to Waynesville with you?"

She quickly put her hand over her face. "My parents would be suspicious of your motives, Mister Windes."

"My motives, as you put it, are to get to know you better and to provide an escort, Miss Rayl. I saw some fairly rough characters on the stage coming out here. Surely my motives are better than theirs might be."

"When Sue and I came out here on the stage two weeks ago we traveled much of the way with seven men that were not exactly model citizens, so I know what you mean."

"Would you feel better about it if I got a phaeton carriage and we rode by ourselves?"

"My Mama would have a hissy fit if I was to ride in a carriage for three days with a man I hardly know."

He looked her in the eye. "I've been a lot of places, and nobody—man or woman—has ever had a reason not to trust me."

It was her turn to feel a flush on her cheeks. "I'm sorry. I didn't mean to imply that. It's just that my Mama would never approve."

"All right. Then we'll ride back on the stage. But we both know how unpleasant it is to sit on those three narrow seats; squeezed every which way by seven other people; listening to their conversations, and snoring, and other impolite sounds; not to mention only stopping twice a day."

She looked straight at him and gave him an innocent look. "I know how uncomfortable it is. You don't have to go with me. I'll be just fine."

B. F. boarded the stage the next morning with Crocia, heading back in the direction they had both come from. The bulb thermometer at the stage stop was well on its way to ninety degrees as they got under way. Thankfully there were only two other passengers during the first part of their journey.

Their riding partners, the Rasmussens, had traveled from Fort Smith to Fayetteville, where they caught the stage the previous day. The couple had run a small store on the western border of Arkansas, and had just discovered they were almost penniless. Ironically, Mr. Rasmussen said they were millionaires eight times over. The problem was that their millions were all in Confederate scrip. Apparently, most of their business had been with Confederate forces in Arkansas, Texas, and the Indian Territory. They had faithfully clung to the belief that the South would survive as a separate nation, and their "fortune" would be preserved. But when General Stand Watie handed over his sword and his Indian troops on June 23, becoming the final Confederate general to surrender, it was inevitable that the South was no more—and the Rasmussens were ruined.

After their introductory conversation, the Rasmussens withdrew into their own privacy on the front seat, leaving B. F. and Crocia to talk without interruption with one another in the back.

As they drew closer to Waynesville toward the end of the following day, both of them seemed to be aware that not only their trip was coming to an end, but that neither of them had made any overture to suggest that they should find a way to continue their relationship. Over the last twenty miles of the trip, it seemed to Crocia that B. F. was withdrawing from their conversation.

In B. F.'s defense, he was desperately trying to think of a casual way to infer that he was interested enough in her that he didn't want things to come to an abrupt end in Waynesville. But he had received no sign from her that this was even on her mind. Did the woman not know that her home was no more than two hours down the road? It was exasperating.

Forty-One

What Did You Do In The War?

Waynesville, Missouri 1865

W hen they arrived about four o'clock in the afternoon, B. F. made a point of asking the station agent in front of Crocia when the next stage would come through for Springfield.

"Twelve-forty tomorrow. Be on time. It don't stop but for ten minutes."

"Is there a hotel close by?"

"One block north—Mad Anthony Wayne's Hotel." The agent shrugged. "Waynesville, ye know."

"Thank you, sir." B. F. started in that direction, but Crocia pulled his arm.

"Let's go see my Papa at his store before he leaves for home. Our house is a pretty good walk if we miss a ride."

Like his daughter, Luther Rayl was tall, but that was about the extent of the resemblance. He had a long, wispy beard that was shot full of grey, and bad scarring on his cheeks, nose, and forehead from what had probably been a severe case of acne. B. F. wondered if the beard was an attempt to cover up what he could of his face. When he saw his daughter enter the store, Mr. Rayl's craggy old face lit up with a big grin. "About time you came home. Your ma said just this morning that she expected you in a day or so." He motioned toward the back of the store. "I saved a ton of bookwork for you."

About that time, he realized the man who had entered the store was actually with his daughter. He gave B. F. a wary look, obviously sizing him up. "Papa, this is Sue's cousin, B. F. Windes. He was nice enough to escort me back home."

"Thank you, Mistuh Windes. That stage ain't always the most hospitable way to travel."

"Glad to do it, sir." This was uncomfortable. "I'm gonna walk up the street and get a room at the hotel. I hope to see you before I go back, Miss Rayl."

"Don't be silly. You go get your hotel room and Papa and I will be by to pick you up for supper in about forty-five minutes. Mama will want to meet you, too." Her father gave her an inquisitive look, and she gave him one right back that made it clear he shouldn't make any comment on the matter.

B. F. walked to the hotel, suddenly seeing the situation from an entirely different perspective. He had seen the look in Mr. Rayl's eyes, and he couldn't exactly blame him. Here he was almost seven years older than Crocia. He was completely unknown to the family, and what little information they might have had about him was how he had run away from home when he was eight years old—not much of a recommendation!

He had to acknowledge that he was attracted to Crocia—really the first girl he had been seriously interested in since he lost Jane. He wished he had more time to think about how he should conduct himself this evening, but all he had time for was to quickly trim his beard, wash the road grit from his face, and brush his clothes as best he could. He was still in the midst of his puzzlement when the buckboard arrived at the hotel.

Elizabeth Rayl was even prettier than her daughter. She was also tall, though not quite so much as Crocia. Her brown hair was still unmarked by any gray, and from what B. F. could tell, there was little indication in her appearance that she was anything other than Crocia's older sister. It would be very easy to guess that she was still in her late twenties.

B. F. decided that there was a bit more than seven years difference in the ages of Mister and Missus Rayl. That could be favorable to him, but then again, it might run counter to their plans for their own daughter, depending on what they thought about the appropriateness of their own union.

He resolved to give them no immediate reason to suspect he was interested at this time in sparking their daughter. Although he would not divulge anything specific related to his financial status, he intended to make sure they understood that he was an industrious man, and it shouldn't be difficult to deduce that he would become a good provider. There was certainly nothing wrong in at least laying down a little food for thought.

B. F. had no desire to talk about the war or politics, but it soon became apparent he wouldn't have that option. For Mr. Rayl, that was the only thing worth talking about. His sons, Robert and William, had both been killed near Springfield, at the Battle of Wilson's Creek. They were from his first marriage, Elizabeth explained, and the boys had lived with them until they enlisted in the Confederate Army.

"The war hardly had a chance to get started good—it was August in '61. My boys were there in the thick of it, shot right beside Colonel Weightman on the hill where they took five cannon from the Yanks. The youngest boy, William, wasn't kilt outright. He was shot in the thigh. But they didn't get him to the surgeon for two days. By the time they took his leg, the fever already had him, and he was gone before I even knew he was hurt. It was the blackest day of my life when Junior Yarbrough came home and told me they was both gone." Mister Rayl stared off in the distance for a few minutes, swallowing repeatedly, composing himself. "Sorry, I ain't talked about it in a long time."

"I'm sorry for your loss, sir."

Rayl turned back around to look B. F. in the eye. "Where were you in the war, Mistuh Windes?"

There it was. It was pointless to say anything other than the truth, although he realized this man would see little value in his service, compared to that of his sons.

"Brazil, Mexico, Texas, Louisiana, Alabama, Cuba, Bahamas."

"What kinda outfit was that?" The man squinted. "You in the Navy?"

"No sir. I spent the whole war trying to get supplies through the Navy's blockade."

"Did it work?"

"Usually. Sometimes by wagon train through Mexico to Texas, but most of the time by ship."

"They say them blockade runners is what made everything cost so dang much."

"Most blockade runners only made a couple of trips before they got commandeered or sunk by the Union Navy. What made things cost so much was losing that many crews and ships and shipments. I lost my own ship toward the end of the war."

"What happened?"

"It looks like the ship captain stole my ship and the cargo and sold it to somebody who paid him more money."

"Did you catch up to him?"

"I tried 'til the war ended. It's a big ocean. I gave up."

Crocia spoke up. "Mister Windes, why do you always wear that gun now that the war is over?"

B. F. glanced over his shoulder at his Navy Colt hanging on the hall tree by the front door. "I've carried a gun since I was about ten years old. Ever since then, there always seemed to be people that wanted to take what I had, or hurt the people I cared about. I don't plan on letting anyone ever do that again without giving a good account."

Mr. Rayl nodded his head. "I been thinking about wearing one myself. The country is full of desperate people these days." He looked sideways at B. F. "You ever come across any desperate people, Mr. Windes?"

He looked at the man and his wife—they were both paying full attention. "Sir, I left home when I was eight because my stepmother abused me. I became a barber and earned enough money to travel to California on a wagon train. Along the way, I saw people die almost every week from disease or accidents. When I got to the gold fields, I kept on barbering. Even worked for a doctor for several years.

"Lots more people died from disease, gunfights, and just plain starved to death.

I've seen people stabbed, shot, hanged, and drowned—some of them were close to me."

He hung his head for a second and composed himself. "And lots more besides that. When the war began, I started running the blockade. I've worked hard my whole life, whether I had to deal with desperate people or not. People who have known me will tell you I hold up my end."

He looked from Mister Rayl to his wife—at least there was nothing in their expressions that made him feel unworthy. Then he chanced a quick glance at Crocia. Her eyes were shining, and she was smiling at him with a look that seemed to be—what? Pride? Or maybe just relief. At least he hoped it was something like that. He really didn't want to go into some of the darker things that had happened.

The conversation at dinner was thankfully in a different direction—all about the mercantile store, the weather, and the prospect of another tough winter because so few crops had been planted that spring. It seemed as though they had heard enough of his background and were only too glad to move to more polite topics.

B. F. told them he would be leaving on the Eureka Stage the next morning, as he was interested in a piece of land he had seen near Keetsville, and he was ready to get to work building a home and a business. He spoke to the Rayls, but he looked at Crocia when he said, "You have an exceptional daughter. She conducts herself like a real lady at all times. I know you must be very proud of her." He turned back to face Elizabeth Rayl. "Thank you for your hospitality this evening."

Just after noon he was at the stage stop, bag in hand. The dread he felt for the monotony of the coming two-day trip clung to him like the humidity on the August afternoon. He was reflecting on the evening events, trying to figure out whether he had acted appropriately, but with the sudden arrival of Crocia Rayl at the station, those doubts were even less resolved than before. Somehow, she was prettier today than yesterday.

"I was thinking you would at least come over to say goodbye, Mister Windes."

"Why, I thought we'd all said goodbye last evening."

"I meant that you might come over to say goodbye to *me*."

The stage pulled into the stop and the station master trotted a fresh team out of the barn lot and began to unhitch the four spent horses. B. F. turned away from the noise and the sudden audience of the disembarking passengers. "I thought you might be busy at your father's store, and I didn't want to be a nuisance. Besides, I think he's suspicious of my motives."

"And just for clarification, what are your motives, Mister Windes?"

"I hope to see you again one day. I meant what I said last evening. In fact, I always mean what I say. Your parents have an exceptional daughter."

"In case you haven't noticed, they're not here right now."

Whatever his strategy had been wasn't really working in the face of her straightforward talk. "Miss Rayl, I'm very interested in continuing this friendship. May I ask if you have the same interest? And . . . may I call you Crocia?"

The driver's call from behind them was interruptive. "Board!"

The questions sort of hung there as they walked toward the open stage door. He threw his bag up to the driver on the roof of the stage and looked inside. Wonderful! The only empty space was on the back-less bench seat in the middle. It promised to be a very long trip. Nothing seemed to be working very well. He stood in the doorway and turned toward her, still with a questioning look on his face.

The driver repeated himself, "Board."

They were out of time and she knew it. "I'll write to you, B. F. Windes."

Forty-Two

Sundry Illegal And Unchristian Acts

Keetsville, Missouri 1865

By the time the stage reached Springfield, B. F. was as miserable as he could ever remember. Rather than endure another eighty miles in similar circumstances, he decided it was time to buy a horse. Sitting in a saddle couldn't possibly be as bad as bouncing around on the hard, wooden middle seat of a stagecoach for another long day.

He also took advantage of the opportunity to deposit his British Letter of Credit in the Missouri State Bank and the Bank of Greene County in Springfield. He didn't remember seeing a bank in Cassville, but even if there was one, he had no desire to have the local citizens know anything about his financial status. He had no faith in the ability of people to keep their mouths shut.

When he arrived at the Battlefield Livery Stable, he tried to remember all the instructions he had received back in Lexington, Missouri on evaluating horseflesh. Fortunately, he came away with a butternut stallion and good saddle for twenty dollars. Times were exceedingly hard, and the power in a negotiation belonged to the man with cash money.

The next afternoon he rode into Cassville and found an attorney, by the name of Joseph Cravens, who occupied an office across the main road from the courthouse. Cravens had a nose that turned down at the end, sort of like a hawk's beak. His ears were almost half as long as his entire head, with large, flapping lower earlobes. And his chin had a big dimple right in the center of it that was so deep, B. F. wondered if the man had trouble keeping it clean. Despite the preference of the day, Cravens was one of the few men in town who did not have a beard, or even a mustache. Perhaps he was proud of his distinctive features and didn't want to obscure the view in any manner.

B. F. described the property he had noticed just north of Keetsville and asked Cravens for his assistance. They walked over to the courthouse together, and in less than fifteen minutes, held what appeared to be the Deed of Trust for the eighty acres in question. But there was an adjacent farm of eighty acres also for sale, which B. F. had not noticed, probably because it abutted the first farm on the west side of the property furthest from the road.

Taxes had not been paid on either property in the last three years. Of course, in 1865 in southwestern Missouri, overdue taxes was the norm rather than the exception, but the unpaid taxes and the fact that the place was unoccupied, were good indications that the land might be for sale. Cravens said he knew the current landowner for both properties, a Widow Mongomery, whose husband had been killed early in the war in Texas, and he would talk to her.

In the meantime, B. F. wrote down information on some survey markers and rode out to look closer at two other plots of land in the area. The property bordering the road included a house, but it appeared to have been deserted for some time. He was able to open the front door, but the only recent occupants seemed to be yellow jackets, field mice, and a few thousand spiders. It looked as though the fireplace and chimney were in decent shape, the wooden floor was sturdy in most spots, and apparently, the roof didn't leak very much.

But there was no pump in the house and no dry sink. And once he was inside, he realized how many places the sunlight showed right through the cracks and gaps in the walls of the house. He remembered some of the living quarters of the California gold miners and reflected that this was a regular palace by comparison. He did some quick guessing and estimated that he could make the place livable for less than five hundred dollars.

There were four outbuildings—one divided into a tool shed and a chicken house, another used as a stable and hayloft, a root cellar, and finally a two-hole privy. Every time he saw a two-holer, he had to ask himself why in the world anybody would construct a two-hole outhouse. Did someone actually make it a practice to sit there, side-by-side with their family member—perhaps having a conversation about high society—while each completed their daily functions?

The spring not only bordered the front property but ran along the southern boundary of the second eighty-acre plot as well. Despite it being mid-August, the spring was running at a decent clip. That certainly added value to both places.

He spent the remainder of the afternoon riding around the area, with the purpose of identifying other properties that might be for sale. Not that he was really interested in anything else, but he thought it a wise strategy to be able to go back to Lawyer Cravens and make him think that he wasn't entirely sold on the Montgomery land.

He noticed that almost every home on the south side of Keetsville was either significantly damaged or burned out, with many farms only represented by a standing chimney. It was rare that land was occupied out there, as the property destruction had been particularly bad the closer to Arkansas you got. He decided being on the north side of the town made the most sense. At least a majority of those farms had people living there.

The next morning, he told Cravens he was having a hard time making up his mind between three properties, giving him the locations of two other plots west of town.

Cravens hated doing this kind of work. "I thought you were just interested in Missus Montgomery's farms. I'll need to do some search work on the other two."

"Did she decide how much she's asking for that land?"

"Twenty-five an acre for the front property and twenty for the back. That's a fine price."

B. F. looked at him and shrugged. "Could be, but that sounds like more money than the asking price on land just north of here. I'd be interested in finding out about these other two places though. I have to believe there's a better deal out there. But if that's not the case, I looked at some good land at a better price about thirty miles back up the Wire Road just this side of the McDowell community. I may have to head back up there. Anyway, I'm staying over at the Postmaster's house for another day or so if you find out something."

B. F. was confident that his conversation would be repeated verbatim to the Widow Montgomery, perhaps with some lawyerly embellishments to ensure the deal went through in a very few minutes. He doubted that Cravens had too many irons in the fire and probably was very interested in earning a fee for a change.

Before lunchtime, Cravens had come to see him; and well before supper, he owned a hundred and sixty acres of well-watered prairie land and a cabin for eighteen dollars an acre.

He was honest enough with himself to admit he had no desire to be a farmer, but the land was simply too good a bargain to let it pass. Over the next few weeks, he resolved to find someone to farm the property, but his next objective was to find a business that he might purchase. In riding back to Keetsville the next morning, he decided to spend the day in what was left of the town to find out what businesses were there, and what was not.

B. F. stopped by the Durham home before he went into town to let them know that Crocia had been delivered home safe and sound. But when Minnie asked him to come in and visit for a spell, he decided he was wasting a valuable source of information. After he told her and Sue about the trip back to Waynesville, he decided to just barge ahead.

"Missus Durham, I need your advice on something. I'm interested in starting a business—possibly here in Keetsville—and I wonder if you'd tell me what kind of store the town needs. That is, what kinds of goods do you need that you can't get in Keetsville?"

Sue interrupted. "That would be wonderful to have my only kin so close by."

"Well, that's what I was thinking too. Other than you and the people I met here, I really don't know a soul in the whole country. Or if I do, I wouldn't know where to find them."

Minnie responded to his question. "So many stores got burned-out or run-down during the war, there's a lot of things we need that we can't get here. It seems like every two weeks John and I have to go into Cassville. There's a general store downtown, but they've only got the basic necessities."

"Can you tell me some of the things you've had to buy in Cassville lately?"

"Right now I need some canning jars and lids to put up some rhubarb preserves. I can't find a spool of thread here in town—let alone a decent bolt of calico. We all have to go to Cassville for clothes and shoes. I need lye for some soap I want to make. Sue needs curtains in their bedroom. That sorry grocer never has a decent vegetable in his store. We buy all our garden seeds in Cassville, even seed potatoes. I'd love to have a good feather pillow. And I broke the handle off my only decent cook pot. Matt complained that he had to go to Cassville to buy ammunition, and he was afraid the Yankees would figure he was a bushwhacker."

"Maybe I should have asked what you can buy here." B. F. laughed.

"If you need farm tools, you're in luck. There's all kinds of live-stock supplies. You can get a horse shod in three places. There's basic groceries, but when I wanted some white sugar to bake Sue's wedding cake last week, Mister Brown's General Store couldn't help me. So we ended up with that apple cake instead of the angel food we wanted. You can get a tooth pulled at the barbershop. And we got a doctor—or at least we got a man who says he's a doctor—but he only gives out camphorated opium and Hinkle's pills. So all he knows how to do is make you go or make you stop. And thank the good Lord—the nerves of half the men in town are safe, because Peevey's Dram Shop made it through the war without a mark on it. In fact, both sides were downright careful not to damage that particular business. So you can see, we've got all the modern conveniences."

B. F. assured her the information was very helpful, and made his way down to the business district of town. Of course, the "business district" consisted of not more than nine stores in operation. At least a half-dozen buildings had been burned to the ground, four or five more were severely damaged or just deserted, and numerous bullet holes were visible in every building on the street. There were two cannon balls—probably from a six pounder—buried in the trunk of an old red oak beside the livery stable.

He could tell very little about the condition of the empty buildings by trying to peer in the windows, so he visited J.M. McClure (Esquire—in case you didn't think he was the real thing), who seemed to be the only attorney in Keetsville. It wasn't necessary to search courthouse records for any of the buildings in town. Mr. McClure had been one of the town's earliest residents, and he not only knew the owner of every store, but probably more history about each of them than they would have cared to acknowledge.

B. F. asked about a building along the main thoroughfare with a long frontage. Apparently, it had once possessed two large windows in front, but they were busted out and boarded up. The front of the store looked like it once had a long front porch on it, but the posts supporting the roof were in various stages of decline, imparting a sad droop to the face of the place.

The building had previously housed a seed and feed store, which belonged to Norwood Barefoot. Or at least it had until he was killed in a stagecoach holdup about six months earlier. His widow, Esther Barefoot, had inherited the property, but, Mr. McClure confided, she was no longer welcome in the town. "Norwood was at least twenty years older than his wife, and he stayed on the road a lot after the war started. I don't know that any of us knew what he was doing—some said he was a spy. But anyhow, the seed and feed business really didn't do well a'tall with him gone so much. Esther had lots of time on her hands, and you know what they say about idleness and the devil.

"Anyway, there were several Yankees that spent a lot of time in the store, and the story got out that Esther was, well, indulging in *collaboration horizontale* with what appeared to be an enthusiastic percentage of the soldiers quartered in Cassville, so as to keep herself in whisky. But her spreading the joy around was going on long before Norwood got himself killed. Some even say she was providing information to the Yankees about some of the people here in town. Two or three of the local men finally told her to get outa town or they were gonna shave her head bald. Now that Norwood is dead and buried, I'm supposed to sell the place for her—but she's long gone to St. Louis."

It seemed that the building had not been opened in months, as the appearance inside was not much different from the spiders and wasps he found in the house he had bought the day before. There was not a whit of evidence in the place that it had ever contained seed and feed supplies except for the remaining odor of moldy grain. Save a half dozen shelves, a counter, and a wood stove, the place was entirely empty.

B. F. walked around the bare walls, trying to determine just how much work would have to be done on the place. There were three big damp spots on the floor that made it pretty obvious the roof leaked, and so many cracks and knot holes in the walls that he stopped counting at fifty. But the rafters and beams looked to be in good shape. The building was unbelievably hot inside—undoubtedly the result of an August afternoon, a tin roof, and no circulation. He figured it would probably be a good idea to add three or four tall windows at the front and back of the store in order to get the air moving.

He turned to McClure. "I'm not sure this is going to do. No circulation, broken windows, leaky roof, holes in the walls, rotting posts out front, a dirt floor, and the nearest well is down at the end of the street. I saw some stores in Cassville that are in a lot better shape. And at least they've got more people coming to town."

"What would you be willing to pay for this building?"

"Not very much. There's too much money to be spent before I could start any business."

"Mr. Windes, I have authority to make you a good deal on this property."

"I don't want to offend you, sir."

"Please. How much?"

"Not a dime over four hundred dollars."

"I was hoping you'd say a thousand."

B. F. laughed. "Only if it was ready to move in and start a business. I'm going on back to Cassville. If you change your mind today, ride over and let me know. But I intend to look at two buildings there this afternoon." He held out his hand. "Thanks for your trouble. Good luck selling this place." He walked out the door and untied his horse from the hitching post.

McClure stood in the open doorway and watched him grab the saddle horn, then put his left foot in the stirrup and swing up into the saddle. It was too much for him to see his only prospect leave town. "Mr. Windes, come back over to my office."

Later that same afternoon, B. F. stopped again at the Durham's home, but this time to talk to father and son. When he told them what he had done, they clapped him on the back and welcomed him to the town. He appreciated their enthusiasm, but he had come for advice. "Anybody around here much of a carpenter? That store is in need of a lot of repairs."

"There's a sawmill down at Roller's Ridge—seven miles south of here on the Wire Road. I hear they're starting to cut logs again. Sounds like you're gonna need quite a bit of lumber. One of Mr. Trollinger's boys, William, is a good carpenter, and he hangs around the sawmill. Ain't much building going on around here, so you can probably get him."

"Didn't somebody get killed from Roller's Ridge recently? Seems like I heard something about it at the wedding."

"You're probably talking about Joel Mitchell. He was an old Baptist preacher from Roller's Ridge, and before the war he owned five or six slaves. A couple of his young bucks run off when they heard about the war, and Reverend Mitchell went after them. They say he caught them both before they could get to Kansas—although one story is that he didn't catch up to them until they were well inside the city limits of Pittsburg, where they probably figured they were safe. Anyway, he brought them back to his farm, all beat up and hog-tied in the back of a wagon. He punished them boys in front of the other slaves— whipped them so bad they both died.

Knowing the Reverend, I doubt he meant that to happen, but he had a tendency to let his temper run. Anyhow, one of the other slaves took off when the Union troops come through, and apparently she told what she saw."

"So they got the Reverend charged with 'sundry illegal and unchristian acts,' whatever that means, exactly. But when the Yankees went to take him into Cassville for trial, the Reverend had run off. That was about three years ago, and we ain't seen or heard of him in all that time.

Finally, about a month ago, he came into Keetsville and surrendered to five Yankee troopers. I reckon he got some real bad advice from somebody. They musta thought bygones would be bygones when the war was over."

"Anyhow, a hollering, screaming mob assembled in no time and demanded that the Yankees turn the Reverend loose. There was a lot of pushing and shoving. The blue bellies were outnumbered about ten to one, and they finally decided to let him go."

"What started out as a mob turned into just a bunch of his former church members. They were celebrating their reverend getting turned loose—he was praying with all his might, and they were in the midst of a bunch of 'amens,' when all of a sudden, a rifle shot rang out and the reverend fell over dead with a bullet that went in one ear and right out the other. We figure one of the troopers done the deed. It happened in broad daylight, betwixt Peevey's and Brown's store, but nobody saw a blessed thing. Those in the congregation all said they had their eyes closed on account of Reverend Miller being in the midst of praying and all. So we don't even have a suspect."

Forty-Three

The Faux Pas

Waynesville, Missouri 1865

B. F. spent two days with William Trollinger, talking about his plans for his business. William was black-headed except for a strip of completely white hair that ran from his forehead to the middle of his crown. He had high cheek bones and rough features, with skin almost the color you'd expect on a Mexican. Some said he had a grandpa who was pure-blood Cherokee. The ring finger and little finger of his left hand were completely missing. "The sawmill got 'em both when I was just twelve years old. If you look around this mill, most of these fellers is missin' some part or another 'cause of that saw."

It appeared that William would be able to build everything B. F. had in mind for the store, but he would need a considerable amount of glass to put together the windows and three showcases. As an example of the many shortcomings of goods in Keetsville, there was no glass available. In fact, there was none in Cassville either—except for plenty of the broken kind—so B. F. had to order glass panels from Springfield. He had serious misgivings that such fragile objects would ever survive a trip along the Wire Road. He involuntarily rubbed his lower back just in thinking about his personal experience on the stage—but there was no other option.

About noon, Matt Durham stopped by the store to tell B. F. there was a letter for him at the house. He apologized for forgetting to bring it with him, but to be sure and stop by.

He didn't say who it was from, and B. F. didn't want to give the impression that he was desperate for that information, so he didn't ask. Hoping it was from Crocia, he spent the rest of the afternoon alternating between being excited and feeling apprehensive. There was plenty of work to do, but he just couldn't get very enthused about it.

Finally, at five o'clock he could stand it no longer and rode over to the Durham house. Sue met him at the door with the small letter in her hand. "Crocia stuck this letter inside a letter to me—probably so her folks wouldn't see that she was writing you."

"Thank you, Cousin." He tipped his hat and turned to go.

"Aren't you going to open it?"

"Sure. I'll wait 'til I get back to the store. I've been sleeping there the last few nights."

"B. F., you get in here and open that letter. Don't you think I want to know what she has to say?"

"To tell you the truth, I'm afraid of what she might have to say. I'd rather open it by myself." This time he made a successful retreat, but not without Sue giving him a withering look as he walked out to his horse.

He forced himself to wait until he made a small fire in his wood-stove, then retreated to the open front door where there was plenty of light and carefully opened the letter.

> *Dear Mr. Windes,*
>
> *I enjoyed meeting you at Sue's wedding, and appreciate you escorting me back to Waynesville. I remember with pleasure some of the things we talked about on our journey. Mama and Papa also seemed pleased to make your acquantaince.*
>
> *You appear to be all the things dear Sue said you were, except she failed to mention a certain streak of stubbornness. Perhaps you will find your way back to Waynesville one of these days.*
>
> > *Sincerely,*
> > *Crocia Rayl*

Journal Entry—August 24, 1865

I just received a letter from Crocia, and after reading it three times, I have to wonder if the woman could possibly have said anything more confusing? What in the world am I to think is on her mind?

The only thing I can figure is write a letter myself—but to Luther Rayl instead of his daughter. I'll let him know I've bought a store building in Keetsville and that I'd like to turn it into a mercantile and general store. I'll ask him if he'll sit down with me in Waynesville and give me some business advice.

Bad as I'd like to, I'll not write a note to Crocia, and sneak it into a letter posted from Sue. I don't want the Rayls to think I'm doing something behind their backs. But I suspect that Crocia won't appreciate being left out of all this either. Maybe If I just tell Sue that I'm going to Waynesville, she'll end up writing to Crocia about it.

When the actual work began on the store, Trollinger brought a young carpenter with him by the name of Archibald Roller. Given his last name, the boy must have had something to do with the family for whom Roller's Ridge was named, but no explanation was given. Apparently, the boy was making a great effort to grow a mustache, but its current status was closer to a naked caterpillar stuck on his upper lip. At least ten times a day, B. F. noticed him smoothing the hair on his lip as though he was encouraging it to grow faster. Young Roller didn't seem to have very much experience, but he was certainly a willing worker. The first part of the job was back-breaking labor, in that it was necessary to remove four inches of the packed dirt floor before they put in the framing for the plank floor. Practically every shovelful of dirt was moved by young Roller. And as he toiled with pick and shovel, Trollinger began to put up the interior walls.

The glass arrived as baggage on the Eureka Stage Line from Springfield. B. F. fully expected wooden boxes full of glass shards, but was surprised to find how well each piece was packed in sawdust and old newsprint. Trollinger then transformed each pair of glass panels into windows two feet wide and five feet tall, which could be opened in order to provide air circulation. Four of them were mounted at the rear of the store and four at the front. When the interior walls were completed, with trim work added, no gaps whatsoever were visible around the windows.

By the time this work was finished, the floor framing could begin, and with both men working, it proceeded rapidly. B. F. paid Trollinger two-thirds of the money they had agreed on for the entire job, and repeated his instructions for the remainder of the work, as well as let him know that he would be back in eight days and they would settle then.

After two less than desirable experiences on the Eureka Stage, B. F. opted for his horse on the trip back to Waynesville. He knew how saddle sore he was going to be, but even with that it couldn't be as miserable as the stage. Also, it gave him the flexibility to spend some time in Springfield.

His first stop was at a hardware store to purchase a pistol for Mister Rayl. After the war, stores were awash in rifles and sidearms, as returning soldiers on both sides sold their guns to raise much-needed cash. He found a high quality Colt 1862 pocket revolver, with walnut grips and an octagonal barrel, plus a holster for twelve dollars. It was referred to as a pocket pistol simply because the barrel was only five and one-half inches long and could conceivably be kept in one's pocket. An etching on the side of the gun portrayed two men engaged in a stagecoach holdup. He hoped Mr. Rayl wouldn't take offense at that.

His stop at a mercantile store was not so straightforward. He had no doubt that Mister Rayl would appreciate the pistol, but he had not a clue as to what his wife and daughter might like. After wandering around the store for a good half-hour, he decided on a large, silver-plated serving tray for Missus Rayl, and a silver and ivory dressing table set for Crocia. The tray was too large to fit in one of his saddle-bags, so he ended up tying it across the back of the saddle, where it inconveniently reminded him of its presence in the small of his back at every rough spot on the road for the rest of his journey.

He arrived in Waynesville at almost dark and once again checked in at the Mad Anthony Hotel. Not sleeping well at all, he spent much of the night playing over in his mind what he intended to say to the Rayls the next morning. Finally, he got up about five o'clock and stood at his window, looking out on the street, but not really seeing anything, save the imagined conversation that would take place in a few hours.

He put on a clean shirt and collar, ate a decent breakfast, and walked over to the Rayl store in a light rain. At least this was one piece of luck—he wasn't stuck out on the road in the weather. Luther Rayl was the only one in the store at that early hour, and thankfully he seemed friendly enough. He had received B. F.'s letter and appeared glad to be asked for his advice. The lack of customers allowed them an opportunity to at least begin a dialogue about what to sell, where to buy supplies and goods, how to display items, what to offer only via a catalogue, and how to determine a fair price.

When a couple of ladies came in, Mister Rayl turned his attention to them, and B. F. began wandering around the store to look at stock. He had written two pages of notes on his tablet when the front door opened again and he looked up. As it happened, he was standing in front of shelving that positioned him directly between the door and the back office, so he was literally the first thing she saw as she stepped through the doorway. She had a parasol in her hand and was trying to get the rain shaken off when they made eye contact. He dropped his pencil and she lost her grip on the umbrella.

B. F. quickly stepped over and retrieved her parasol from the floor.

"Why, Mister Windes, you gave me a start. What brings you back to Waynesville?"

"A couple of things. Your father is helping me get squared away with a store I've bought down in Keetsville."

"What's the other thing?"

"What?"

"The other thing. You said you were here for a couple of things."

He looked at her for a good fifteen seconds. She could feel her cheeks warming up, and realized she must be blushing. He glanced toward the two women and Mister Rayl and saw that all three of them had fallen silent and were looking at them. He turned back to face

Crocia and gave her a little sheepish grin. "I can't remember right this minute."

She also finally noticed their audience, quickly clutched her umbrella, and stepped past him, heading toward the safety of the office. "It's nice to see you again, Mister Windes."

He spent the balance of the day talking to Luther Rayl, interspersed by periods when he was occupied by customers, leaving B. F. to roam the store and write in his expanding tablet. About three o'clock, he noticed Crocia and her father having a conversation in the office, and he wondered if he came up in the discussion. This was apparently correct, as Mister Rayl invited him to supper when he emerged from the office.

Crocia went home shortly after that, and B. F. used this opportunity to give her father the Colt pistol. Luther's beat-up face came alive when he realized the pistol was a gift in appreciation of the information he was sharing. He had never shot one of the percussion cap weapons before and was delighted to now have one of his own. The two men closed the store together, with the promise that the next day would be spent talking about record keeping to complete their discussion.

B. F. retrieved the other gifts from his hotel room and his horse from the livery stable before making his way to the Rayl home. Crocia met him at the door and he couldn't help noticing that she had changed her dress since coming home from the store. He told her she looked nice, but he was particularly attracted to the smells coming from the kitchen. He believed he could identify the vapors from a heavenly mix of fried chicken and freshly baked sourdough bread.

The end of the meal brought something he had never even heard of—sweet potato pie. How in the world one could turn such a tasteless tuber into a wonderful pie like that, he could not imagine. Much as he wanted second and third helpings, he restrained himself in front of his hostess, but he could not contain his praise for Missus Rayl's pie.

"Oh, that was Crocia's pie. She makes them better than I can."

He looked at her with a whole new level of appreciation. "It is truly fine pie." And for the second time that day he saw her cheeks turn color.

He used this opportunity to present the women with their gifts and thanked each of them for a wonderful dinner. Crocia inspected the mirror, brush, and comb, and pronounced them beautiful, then looked at her reflection. "Do you think me vain, Mister Windes?"

He was surprised, then embarrassed. "Why, no. I never thought about it!"

"I just wondered if that was why you picked out a mirror for me."

"Of course not. I picked it because I thought you would like it. If you don't, I'll find something else."

"No." She smiled. "I love it."

Elizabeth Rayl spoke up. "Thank you very much for the beautiful tray." She put her hand on his arm. "I promise to use it when you come again." She looked at her daughter with a half-smile.

The next day, B. F. and Luther began with the intention of spending a majority of their time talking about keeping the books, but got side tracked into things like holding accounts for customers, catalog ordering, changing merchandise from time to time, and traveling to St. Louis to find out what the latest merchandise looked like.

Rayl also made suggestions about what kinds of goods should be displayed in full view rather than stacked on shelves, and B. F. asked his opinion about something he had seen in San Francisco. Stores there had a habit of displaying special items in the front windows of the store in order to get people to stop and come in and look. Rayl remarked he had seen the same thing in a store in St. Louis, but he had shelving stacked too close to his windows to make it practical. B. F. talked about how his store was to be laid out, and they agreed it might be worth a try to fill the windows with new, appealing merchandise.

They then began to put together an initial order for goods and supplies, primarily from a company in St. Louis, but also more basic supplies from one in Springfield. B. F. would post the St. Louis order the next day at the stage stop, and hand-carry the other one to Springfield on his way back to Keetsville. That would give him a chance to compare merchandise before ordering.

Toward the end of the afternoon, it became evident that they had talked through just about everything they could think of, so B. F. took the opportunity to ask the question he had practiced in his hotel room. "Mister Rayl, I really appreciate all the time you've spent with me. I hope I can remember half of what you've said."

Rayl interrupted, nodding toward his lap. "From the size of that tablet, you won't forget a thing."

"Maybe you don't know me very well, but I'm the kind of person that believes in straight talk, and I have no regard for sneaky activity. I want to write to your daughter, and I'd appreciate your permission."

Rayl's face was completely without expression. "What does Crocia think about that?"

"I really don't know. I hope she'll be for it, but I haven't asked her yet."

"How old are you, B. F.?"

"Twenty-four, sir. But I figure Crocia wouldn't get on too well with someone her own age. She's already a strong-minded woman, and that doesn't bother me one whit. Unless I'm mistaken, you married a strong-minded woman yourself—and neither one of you seems to be worse for it."

Luther had to smile at this, remembering some of his own early days in dealing with Elizabeth. "So you noticed that, huh?"

"Yes sir. I believe I did."

"As long as your letters are all right with Crocia, Lizbeth and I won't have no problem with it."

B. F. stuck out his hand. "Thank you, sir."

"Oh, before I forget. You're expected for supper tonight. Probably won't get no sweet tater pie, but it might be passable."

Supper was ham, white beans, and cornbread—plain food—but superb. Toward the end of the meal, Luther turned to his daughter. "Crocia, have we got any buttermilk?"

As realization hit Crocia, she appealed to her mother. "Mama, don't let him do it."

Elizabeth just shook her head from side to side. "Honey, you know your Papa by now, and you know I can't do a thing with him."

Crocia resignedly left the table and came back with a glass of buttermilk. She set it down in front of her father and arched an eyebrow at him. "Aren't you the one who always told me to mind my manners in front of company?"

Luther calmly accepted the buttermilk, crumbled a wedge of cornbread into the glass, and began eating the mixture with a spoon. "Crocia, B. F. ain't really company. After all, he says he wants to start writing to you."

B. F.'s eyes almost rolled back in his head. Crocia gave him a look that couldn't be interpreted, and Mister Rayl realized he had spoken out of turn. "Uh, have you had a chance to talk about that yet, B. F.?"

"No, sir—not 'til right this minute." There was no other way now. He turned to Crocia. "I asked your pa if I could write to you this afternoon—and I asked him first because I didn't want to go behind your folks' backs. I was going to ask you this evening."

Elizabeth looked at her husband. "You really should mind your manners, Luther." Then she couldn't hold back any longer and started laughing. Then her husband started chuckling with her.

He looked at his daughter. "I'm sorry, honey. I believe that's what you call one of them faux pas!"

Elizabeth was still giggling. "You sure you want to get involved with this family, B. F.?"

He peeked across the table at her daughter, who looked like she was still deciding whether to choke them all. "I guess that depends on Crocia, ma'am."

Elizabeth then turned to her daughter. "Come on, Crocia. Let's try some of that cherry cobbler you put together."

Crocia stood up and looked at her pa and B. F. "There might not be enough to go around for these two."

B. F. found himself scraping the bottom of his bowl to get every last morsel of the cobbler. He looked over and saw that Crocia was watching him. "I didn't think your pie could be beat, but I believe that cobbler was the absolute best."

Elizabeth stood up and put her hand on Luther's shoulder. "Come help me in the kitchen."

"But I wanted . . ." Luther looked at her raised eyebrow, "Oh, yes, ma'am."

When they were alone at the table, B. F. began. "That wasn't exactly how I had planned to ask you if we might write each other."

"I know that. It's just that I was surprised to hear it from Papa."

B. F. put his forearms on the table and interlaced his fingers. "Well?"

Crocia stood up, pulled her chair beside his, and put her hand over his. "You'd better write me, B. F. Windes. I don't like not hearing from you."

He smiled and folded her hand into his. They stood up and faced one another. Once again, he was surprised to note her height and her ability to stand flat-footed and look him straight in the eye. "With the store opening soon, it's not likely that I can come back to Waynesville anytime in the next few months. But I bet Sue would like to have you and your mother come to visit in Keetsville. I want to show you the store. And I forgot to tell you that I bought a farm on the edge of town with a small house on it. The house will take quite a bit of work, but I need somebody to tell me exactly what should be done. Do you know anybody that might be willing to give me some advice?"

She pulled his hand behind her back and stepped to within inches of his face. "I might know somebody."

He touched his forehead to hers and stood there like that for a full minute. "I'm going to miss you."

Forty-Four

The Raffle

Keetsville, Missouri 1865

Journal Entry—September 24, 1865

I can't believe it, but the store is finished! Supplies have been trickling in from St. Louis and Springfield over the last couple of weeks, and there was enough merchandise to actually open for business. The first day I had a grand total of two customers—Sue and Minnie Durham—and they didn't buy anything. However, they did give me plenty of "gentle" hints to change this or that in the store.

At the end of the first week, I have taken in a total of six dollars and eighty cents in cash, plus two dozen eggs and ten pounds of potatoes in trade. If I think too hard about the money I've spent in the last month—$400 to buy the store, $750 to renovate, and $1,100 to purchase merchandise—I wonder if it wouldn't have been better to go back to being a barber. But a haircut in Keetsville is only ten cents—at least before the barber took off to St. Louis. That's a far cry from the price I charged in California.

He knew people in the area had little money, but he hoped it wasn't as bad as his first week made it appear. There was also a doubt about whether anybody even knew he was open for business. With no newspaper in town, it would be necessary to do something himself to let people know his new store was ready and waiting on them to stop by.

B. F. spent his free time the next week lettering paper hand-bills on his counter:

Open for Business
Windes Mercantile & Supply
Main Street, Keetsville
Everything for the Family

On Saturday evening, he rode down to Rollers Ridge to a pie supper and put one of his hand-bills on the seat of every wagon sitting outside the church. Then on Sunday afternoon, he went house-to-house in Keetsville and up and down the Wire Road, handing out his advertisement. Between the pie supper and his Sunday afternoon venture, he calculated that he had given out about eighty hand-bills.

On Monday morning, he was not a little curious to see what kind of result his work would produce in the store. His business tripled to just over twenty-two dollars, three dozen eggs, and a roasting hen during the second week. But that still left a lot of dead time—time that he usually spent worrying about his business or thinking about Crocia.

They had traded one letter apiece, and it was his turn to write again. But she had asked about his store, and he hated to admit it wasn't going the way he had planned. So he'd put off the letter for almost a week now, hoping the store would give him something positive to say about his investment and his newly adopted home.

At least once a day he would lock his door and visit the other store owners in the town. It only provided marginal comfort to know that the lack of business wasn't confined to the Windes Mercantile. None of the stores had very much traffic. In talking to the others, it was evident that business had significantly declined in the three years that the Union Army had been in virtual control of the area. Two of the men postulated that quite a few families tried to stay away from town for fear of being harassed, or worse, by the Army. They hoped their stores might come back to life when the troops disappeared.

B. F. prayed they were right, but he doubted that this by itself would bring about the change they needed. He had an idea, but it would require the endorsement of almost all of the store owners to make it practical. He invited the other nine men to his store one afternoon "to sample some new root beer and hear an idea."

Squire Cave, Joseph Peevey, A.J. Stewart, John Burton, John Cureton, James Andrews, and D.O. George showed up, while McClure and Brown stayed away. "When I was in California, we had trouble getting anybody to come into town when the winter settled in; so the businesses came up with a scheme that I think would help here. But it won't work unless all of us agree to do it." They looked from one to the other.

B. F. explained, "I know I'm new here, and you men know the people a lot better than I do. But we've got to get them coming back to Keetsville. Right now, people are still going to Cassville and Rollers Ridge to get their goods. Give me a minute to explain.

"We start holding a lottery in downtown Keetsville every Saturday at noon. The only way people can get a lottery ticket is to spend money in one of our stores. We give them half a ticket every time they spend a dollar, and on Saturday we put the other halves of all those tickets in a big bowl, and hold a drawing of all the tickets that we gave away during the week. First prize is five dollars, and second prize is two dollars."

"Five dollars? That's a lot of money, friend."

"If each of us puts in a dollar a week, that will pay for the prize money with a dollar left over to print lottery tickets. If it works here the way it did in California, your stores will take in at least ten extra dollars a week—maybe even twenty. And on Saturday, Main Street will be full of people, because they have to be at the drawing to claim the prize."

"How're folks gonna hear about this idea?"

"We put up signs here in town and out on the Wire Road. We put out hand-bills at churches and anywhere there's a group of people. If you'll agree to try it for four weeks, I think you'll be convinced. But if it's not working by then, we'll stop."

Peevey was the first to speak up. "Sounds like a durn good idea to me. I'm in."

"Peevey figures to sell more likker. That's why he's for it."

B. F. spoke again. "That's just the point. All of us will benefit if we bring another hundred people to town every week. Think how that will help if just twenty of them stop in your business."

"Who'll hold the money? Would that be you, Windes?"

"No, Mr. Burton, not me. You men know each other. You decide."

They bought five hundred tickets from a printer in Cassville. The first week they handed out just over one hundred tickets, and by ten o'clock on Saturday the town was full of would-be winners. There were horses and wagons tied to every available hitch on Main Street.

Squire Cave emerged from his saddle and bridle store at ten minutes before noon with an iron pot, and proceeded to make his rounds to collect the torn half-tickets from the seven other shop keepers. The Windes Mercantile had the most elevated frontage on Main Street, thus Cave stood there so he could be seen, and called for the youngest person and the oldest person in the crowd to come forward. In the loudest voice he could muster, he announced the strategy to the assembly. "All right, folks. Missus Moore here will pick the winner of the two dollar prize, and General Brixey will pick the five dollar winner."

Missus Wilma Moore had lived in the community since the early 1850s, and was considered an old settler. She stuck her hand in the pot and stirred it around a bit, then produced a ticket along with a completely toothless grin to celebrate her new celebrity status. Cave called out the number. "It's one, zero, two, five." There was a shriek of joy and a skinny young woman pushed forward, carrying a youngster in one arm and brandishing her ticket stub in the other.

Despite his name, General Brixey was only three years old, and shy enough that he had to be pushed up on the porch. A Confederate General and his staff had commandeered the Widow Brixey's home for about three weeks during the early days of the war. And some nine months later, when she was casting about to name her newborn son, she realized she never knew the General's first name. So her baby boy was named after his father in the only way she knew how.

As General Brixey stood on the steps of the Windes Mercantile, he looked like he was going to panic and run back to his ma, but the crowd gave him a good clapping and he did his job. Cave called out. "The big winner is one, zero, four, two."

One of the most predictable drunks in the entire county hollered out, "Reckon I got the winner." He worked his way to the porch amidst half-hearted clapping, received his five dollars, and was immediately swept away by two cronies of similar persuasion who were intent on helping him spend his entire prize at Peevey's Dram Shop.

Cave did not lose this final opportunity. "Just remember folks, anything you buy betwixt now and next Saturday at noon gets you a ticket." His appeal worked on a few people, and they moved on to the stores, but many others were disappointed. The mood had left them, and they headed to their horses.

During the next week, two things happened that would solidify the place of the Saturday Raffle in the town for the next ninety years. On Tuesday, the remaining Union troops stationed in Cassville were released from service and quickly departed the county, thus removing the appearance of a threat to citizens who had previously stayed away from town for one reason or another.

And on Saturday morning, as people were beginning to fill Keetsville for the second drawing, two men from Gateway, Arkansas pulled out their fiddles and provided what you might call an outdoor concert. They were talented players, and after a rousing "Turkey in the Straw," the youngest one placed his frayed slouch hat on the ground, and called out to the crowd, "We'll play about anything ye wanta hear. Cost you'ns two pennies for us to play it."

Then a third man pulled out a harmonica, spoke to the two fiddlers—presumably about money—and joined them in playing "Tenting on the Old Campground" and "Dixie's Land." Someone hollered out from the crowd. "Cain't none of you fellers sing? We wanta hear "When Johnny Comes Marching Home Again."

The harmonica player turned once again to his fellow musicians, then stuck his instrument in his pocket, and sang while the fiddlers played the song in the traditional, fast-paced way they had all heard so many times before.

> *When Johnny comes Marching home again*
> *Hurrah! Hurrah!*
> *We'll give him a hearty welcome then*
> *Hurrah! Hurrah!*
> *The men will cheer and the boys will shout*
> *The ladies they will all turn out*
> *And we'll all feel gay when Johnny comes marching home.*
> *The old church bell will peal with joy*
> *Hurrah! Hurrah!*
> *To welcome home our darling boy,*
> *Hurrah! Hurrah!*
> *The village lads and lassies say*
> *With roses they will strew the way*
> *And we'll all feel gay when Johnny comes marching home.*
> *Get ready for the jubilee,*
> *Hurrah! Hurrah!*
> *We'll give the hero three times three,*
> *Hurrah! Hurrah!*
> *The laurel wreath is ready now*
> *To place upon his loyal brow*
> *And we'll all feel gay when Johnny comes marching home*

But then something happened to their song that they didn't think was possible. The fiddlers stopped their play, and the singer continued in a cappella with the last verse. But he changed to a much slower pace, and allowed his tenor voice to linger and caress and mourn every word.

> *Let love and friendship on that day,*
> *Hurrah! Hurrah!*
> *Their choicest pleasures then display,*
> *Hurrah! Hurrah!*

And let each one perform some part,
To fill with joy the warrior's heart,
And we'll all feel gay when Johnny comes marching home.

The crowd was transfixed. Never had they heard their song performed like that. The entire crowd hesitated as one, lost in the memories of so many friends and loved ones who they knew would never come marching home again.

The next week the Keetsville store owners needed 340 tickets to take care of business. B. F. was gratified to know that sixty-eight of those tickets had come from sales at his own store. From then on, you couldn't have forced them to give up the raffle.

He had written Crocia about ten days earlier, telling her about his idea and hoping that it was going to work. So it felt good to send her a new report on what appeared to be their success. He commented that the only downside was that he had very little time during the day to do those mundane things like keeping the store clean, the merchandise straightened up, and supply orders written. But, he reflected, better to be busy than to stand around all day, wondering if his business was going to survive. He failed to mention in his letter that he now had less time to moon around over her.

Forty-Five

I'll Be Taking What's Mine

Keetsville, Missouri 1865

There was also a negative side to the Army pulling out, although it was unlikely anyone in Keetsville would acknowledge there had been anything redeeming about their presence. The fact that troops had been quartered nine miles away and that they had patrolled the Keetsville area at least twice a week, had a dampening effect on the activities of local guerilla bands of bushwhackers as well as any visits from Kansas Jayhawkers.

Neither of these two groups had gone out of business at the conclusion of the war. Not only did each of them continue to make raids across the Missouri-Kansas border in repetition of their main function during the war, but they also maintained their other activities.

Both groups envisioned themselves as organizations that somehow upheld their loyalties to either the Union or the Confederacy. So the bushwhackers didn't necessarily need to travel over to Kansas to fulfil this role. They continued to target people on the Missouri side of the border who they decided had Yankee sympathies.

The word "jayhawk" was used as both noun and verb. To jayhawk was to steal goods and livestock from those of the Secessionist mindset, whereas a Jayhawker was simply one who engaged in jayhawking.

Like the bushwhackers, Jayhawkers did not strictly respect indistinct geographical delineations such as state borders. They were happy to attack their Missouri neighbors, but also quite content to distribute their brand of getting even among any Kansas residents who appeared to lean toward the rebel cause.

Many citizens in southwestern Missouri, southeastern Kansas, and northwestern Arkansas were robbed, maimed, tortured, burned out, or murdered by these guerilla bands. And as time passed, it became suspiciously evident that some of the crimes could not be explained in terms of whether the victims were pro-north or south, but rather their punishment might simply be meted out to get even for some long-standing personal grudge, past disagreement, or perceived insult.

However, the law-breaking activities of the bushwhackers related to stage holdups, bank robberies, and terrorizing businesses was of paramount concern to store owners like B. F. More and more, these actions had nothing to do with what side you had been on but were simply the criminal acts of guerillas. And with the absence of the Army in southwestern Missouri, the gangs' lawlessness would be emboldened.

B. F. talked to the lawyer, McClure, about his concerns. "I keep hearing about these bushwhackers around here, and to tell you the truth, I'm afraid they might decide that Keetsville would be an easy target. The nearest sheriff is in Cassville, and since our town is showing signs of life, they may think we've got something worth taking."

"You could be right. There's three groups of them around these parts—one close to the Arkansas line that's led by Calvin Dunaway. Even when he was a little kid, that Cal was always wild as a Kickapoo.

There's another gang just east of here in that rough country close to Roaring River—they say their leader is Tuck Smith. Then there's another bunch around Golden, Missouri. Course, they all might be one place today and fifty miles away tomorrow. It's not like any of them have a permanent mailing address."

"When I was in Springfield last month, I heard about folks up in Saline County forming the 'Honest Men's League.' Have you heard about that?"

"Can't say I have."

"Well, they formed this group to protect the county's property and lives from guerilla lawlessness because they couldn't get the local sheriff to do anything about it. My problem is that this League sounds like a bunch of vigilantes. They're operating outside the law too."

"Probably betwixt a rock and that hard place. They just decided something had to be done if they were gonna have a chance at living."

"What would you say the chances are of putting together a group like that here in Keetsville?"

"Probably not good. Lots of these men got friends or family that run with the bushwhackers. They aren't about to go chasing after 'em. Besides, some of these guerillas are unpredictable customers. For instance, that Tuck Smith I mentioned—last year he busted in on a wedding over at Branson. He and his boys ran the bride and groom and all their guests into the woods, shooting away at them. Didn't hit anybody except the damned preacher!

But then the guerillas ate the victuals and the cake, drank what whisky there was, and stole all the gifts. In fact, they started to make off with the bride herself, but when they saw how homely she was, they brought her back to the groom with their condolences. I wonder how that girl felt to know she was too ugly to steal? Anyway, there wasn't no reason for any of it except plain meanness."

"Thanks for the advice, but I sure don't feel good about there being no law whatsoever except in Cassville." The next week, B. F. ordered a 450-pound safe from St. Louis. They might get some of his money, but they wouldn't get very much.

Business was certainly improving. People were coming into Keetsville to buy their supplies from up to twelve miles away. In fact, some said they were actually pulling business away from Cassville because of the raffle.

The first Saturday in December promised to be their best drawing yet. Friday evening, they counted 430 ticket stubs and hoped for another 80 before the noon raffle the next day. B. F.'s new safe was installed in his office, and he had taken the extra precaution of attaching a heavy chain to the safe and then embedding the other end of the chain in concrete. There was no bank in Keetsville, and he was only able to get into Cassville once a month, so the rest of the time his store's growing deposit was kept in the safe.

Like the previous Saturday mornings, there was no shortage of entertainment in town. Along with the two fiddlers from Arkansas and the singing harmonica player had come yet another man who played a guitar and could sing any song anyone ever heard of.

About ten minutes before noon, the business owners came over to the Windes' store and added their tickets from that morning's sales to the pot. Squire Cave called to the crowd for quiet and once again asked for the oldest and youngest to step forward.

But before the drawing could proceed, a shot was fired in the air and five men stepped into the gap. All were holding pistols in their hands, each of them had tied a handkerchief over their face, and all were wearing various combinations of butternut-stained pants and shirts. There were a few screams as people realized what was happening, and the crowd quickly backed away from the bandits.

At that moment, a burly man with a large mustache that hung down below his lower lip pushed his big sorrel horse through the crowd and up to where Squire Cave stood. He wore no mask, as though it made no difference to him what people knew or thought.

B. F. heard several whispers in the crowd. "It's old Tuck hisself" and "That's Tuck Smith." So this was the guerilla leader! B. F. immediately thought how easy it would be to wipe out this gang right then, if only he could have counted on three or four others to help. But he realized there would be a slaughter of people if he pulled his gun and only was able to shoot a couple of them.

Tuck hollered out to the crowd. "I come for two things this morning. If you don't give us no guff, we'll just take them two things and be gone." He paused for a minute, saw no sign of resistance, and continued. "Cave, I got the winning number for that raffle. Hand over that prize money."

Squire Cave looked helplessly around, but finding no alternative in the crowd, did as he was told. Tuck hollered out again. "The second thing I come for is here someplace." He stood up in his stirrups and looked over the crowd, then grinned and clicked his horse to the other side of the street, where he stopped in front of a man and woman. "Mose Simpson, I'll be taking what's rightfully mine."

The man had to have been scared out of his wits, but he managed not to let on. "I don't know what you're talkin' about. I ain't got nothin' of yor'n. Hell, I'm too poor to change my own name."

"Maybe you don't know you got what's mine. But I'm a takin' it this morning. Tuck smiled as though he had just outsmarted the whole town. He held out his hand. "All right, Mose, gimme what's mine."

Mose looked at him like he was crazy. "I ain't got but two nickels in my pocket. Is that what you'ns are after?"

Tuck shifted his attention to Mose Simpson's young wife. "C'mon Dolly. I'm tired of waiting. You're going with me now."

The woman looked at Mose, then back and forth at all the people gathered around them, then pleadingly at the horseman. "Please, Tuck, don't do this now."

Mose stared at her. "You know this here bandit?"

Tuck replied for her. "She knows me real well, Mose. She's too much woman for an old man like you. She's going with me." He bent down and with one swift motion, put his arm through hers, pulling her up on the saddle in front of him.

Dolly looked at her husband. "I'm sure sorry, Mose." And with that farewell hanging in the air like the wind off a chicken coop, Tuck spurred his horse and they headed south down Main Street.

But the pain of the insult was too great to stay silent. Mose hollered after them. "Yer nothin' but a lowdown whore, Dolly."

Tuck brought his horse up short in the middle of the street and turned around. "Mose, I got my hands full right now. But you're gonna regret that remark one day real soon." He wheeled his horse about again and was immediately followed by the five other horsemen, still wearing their masks.

Before they were completely out of sight, B. F. began hearing comments from the crowd. "We got cheated out of that raffle." "I just come to town for the drawing." "Not our fault the raffle money got stole."

Old Swede piped up, "Ya, my wife raise Holy Ned to come to this raffle."

B. F. quickly went inside his store and retrieved seven dollars from his cash box, then came back out on the porch, grabbed Squire Cave, put the money in his hand, and spoke in his ear. "Tell them the raffle is still on. Don't let them leave without the drawing."

Before the end of the day, Cave came over to see B. F. and handed him five dollars. "All but Peevey and George put in a dollar to pay you back. They all said you done some fast thinkin' this morning. We wouldn't wanta do nothing to mess up this raffle. We're doing more business now than we were before the war."

"Thanks. I didn't figure on the raffle working as well as it has for me, either. I'm glad to work with you." B. F. extended his hand. "Say, Mr. Cave, has anybody ever talked about these bushwhackers or guerillas or whatever you want to call them, in terms of putting them completely out of business in Barry County?"

"Not before today, at least not to me, but we sure don't want that happening again in Keetsville. Course, mebbe they won't be back now that Tuck Smith got Mose's wife."

"I hear that gang has some kind of a hideout between here and Roaring River."

"I heard that too, but they got lots of friends around here. You oughta ask yourself if there might be another reason besides bein' cheap as to why Peevey and George didn't put no money in the kitty."

He described what he knew about the Honest Men's League, but Cave just shook his head. "For that to happen here, they'd have to be more dirty dealin' going on than stealing seven dollars and hijacking a girl that everybody knows is a no-count tart."

"I understand. Thanks for the five dollars. I appreciate the friendship."

On Wednesday afternoon, Squire Cave was back to see B. F. "Did you hear about Mose Simpson?"

"You mean the man that lost his wife last Saturday?" Cave nodded. "No, nothing since then."

"His brother Lem found him this morning, dead. The killers shot him in both knees and both his elbows. Lem said it looked like after they shot him up, they drug him over to a big walnut tree and hung him. His neck wasn't broke. Looks like they just strung him up and let him choke to death."

"I saw three men die that way in California. Hard to forget a thing like that." B. F. shook his head as if to clear his vision. "Anybody see who did it?"

"Lem says there were three sets of horse tracks that left there. And it looks like all of Mose's wife's belongings are gone from the cabin. But nobody saw a thing, and if they did, they'd probably be smart enough to keep their mouth shut."

"So now it's more than seven dollars and a tart, as you put it. Now it's murder."

"Maybe we need to have a meeting like you said. But we'll have to be real careful who we invite. That gang is probably made up of twenty-five different men, but they don't all ride at the same time. So lots of people got friends and relatives who're connected."

"I'll leave it to you to decide who we can trust. I don't have any way of knowing who's connected to who."

In his letter to Crocia that week, he wrote, "Right now is not a good time for you and your ma to come to visit. There's a gang of bushwhackers in the area, and I wouldn't want the two of you to be riding on the stage while they're still around. They are men of the lowest kind and capable of most anything. I'll let you know when it's safe."

Forty-Six

You're Gonna Get Everybody Kilt

Keetsville, Missouri 1865

That Saturday, the raffle went off as usual, with no unexpected interruption. The crowd and the ticket count were a bit smaller than the previous week but still respectable. All of the businesses were feeling a little better about their situation.

At almost five o'clock, B. F. had already secured the majority of his money in the safe and was ready for the day to wind to a close. A man entered the store, or at least an older boy entered, but it was doubtful he could have been more than seventeen or eighteen years old. He appeared to be unshaven, but mainly because he didn't have enough facial hair to make it worth his while to even try to shave. Like a majority of men in the county, he wore a pistol on his leg, but he also carried a rifle inside the store. B. F. instinctively put his hand on his own pistol underneath his jacket, wondering if he was about to be robbed. "What can I do for you?"

The boy put the rifle on the counter. "I'm looking for a scabbard to fit this rifle. It's shaped sorta different from most, and I suppose it needs its own."

It was a Spencer rifle. "Yes, sir. This rifle requires a Spencer-made scabbard. I used to own one or two of these myself. Mind if I look at it?"

"No, go ahead. It's practically brand new, but I'm gettin' it all scuffed up with no proper scabbard."

B. F. was looking at the serial number—#24027. His hand shook for a second. His initial instinct was to pull out his pistol. This very rifle had been aboard the *Rei* on its last voyage. He saw his fingers turning white as he squeezed the stock and tried to compose himself to speak casually. "Yeah, I see where the brass is really starting to scuff up—particularly around the trigger guard—and then at the base of the stock too. I think I can get a scabbard for you within two weeks with no problem."

"Well, I reckon that's all right."

"Say, you wouldn't know where I could buy a brand new Spencer would you? I'd like to have one of these again."

The boy looked thoughtfully at the store owner for a moment. "I think I just might know somebody. I'll try and bring one in when I pick up that scabbard."

"That would be real fine. What's your name so I can hold it for you?"

"Bob . . . uh, Bob Watson."

"OK Bob. I'll see you in two weeks."

B. F. noticed when the boy left that his pant legs and boots appeared to have fresh mud on them. He thought that a bit strange. It had not rained in at least two weeks. He watched the kid untie his horse and ride south down Main Street. On the spur of the moment, he locked up the store, ran across the street to the stable, threw a bridle and saddle on his horse, and took off after the boy.

When he reached the Wire Road he looked to the south and could see no sign of a horse for three-quarters of a mile, so he turned to the north. He passed the Durham house, but saw nobody in the yard who he might at least tell what he was doing, so he kept riding. Again, he saw no sign of the horse and rider, but when he reached the cross-roads with the Cemetery Road, he noticed what looked like dust in the air at the top of the hill. That was his only hope, so he turned to the east toward the burial ground.

As he topped the hill, he saw a horse and the kid turning to the southeast down a rutted wagon track. He had not been down that way before, but remembered Matt Durham telling him there was a road down this way leading to Roaring River by way of Dry Hollow. B. F. kicked his horse. He couldn't afford to get so far behind that he couldn't keep the kid in sight, particularly since there was little light left in the sky. Suddenly Mr. Finnerty's voice came out of nowhere. "Best not interfere with somethin' that ain't botherin' you none."

After about a half mile, the track turned downhill to a significant degree, so B. F. held his horse back a bit, realizing that the rider ahead would probably not try to ride at any speed down this grade. The woods on both sides of the road seemed to close in on the narrow track, and going down into a valley meant that what sunlight there had been on the hilltop would be obscured the further down the hill he traveled.

He saw a light on the left at the bottom of the hill, coming from a cabin back in the trees, and wondered if the rider had stopped there. But he looked ahead, and there, crossing a rocky creek bed out in the narrow valley, was the rider again, still headed in a southeasterly direction. He seemed to be staying in the valley on the wagon track, but the light was so faint now that he felt sure he would lose the connection before the rider stopped.

This time he heard the horse ahead, making racket as he crossed the dry creek again. He couldn't have been more than fifty or sixty yards away from the rider. B. F. knew he couldn't afford to cross that same creek bed on his horse, as the noise would surely give him away. He found a place in the trees, away from the track, tied his horse, and continued on foot. He just hoped the destination was not too far ahead. He didn't want to try and keep up with the horse for any distance.

He walked for about twenty-five steps, then paused to listen, then walked again, and listened again. But no more than two hundred yards from where he left his horse, he saw a small light about half way up the ridge on his left, and then the light flared into what appeared to be a lantern. He crept close enough that he could see the kid holding the lantern in front of him as he walked.

The kid stopped. "Say Mac . . . you down there? It's me, Bob."

"Put out that damned light."

Bob blew out the lantern. "I'm scared of falling in this hole in the dark."

"Hold your water. I'll put the ladder up."

Within a minute, B. F. could see that Bob had disappeared into some kind of hole in the ground. He decided to move closer to see if he could hear anything. He had a general idea of where the hole was, based on where Bob had been standing when he blew out his lantern, but he decided to get on his hands and knees just in case he had miscalculated.

Just before he put his right hand out into bare space, he recovered in time to lean back on his knees. He was looking at a hole in the ground that was about eight or ten feet across, and encircled a ladder sticking up out of the earth. He had no way of knowing how deep the hole was, nor what was down there. However, there was a faint glow of light when he looked into the cave. Undoubtedly, they had no fear of a lantern giving them away down there. He guessed that the bottom must be at least fifteen feet below where he now knelt.

He could barely hear conversation, but it was too indistinct to make out any more than bits and pieces of what was being said. About all that was understandable was "Tuck . . . Keetsville . . . tomorrow . . . Yankee lovers . . . gunpowder . . . safe"

He just couldn't fill in the empty spaces except with guesses. All of a sudden, the voices became more distinct, and the light was brighter. The men were moving close to the base of the ladder. B. F. backed slowly away from the cave.

"Just be sure ye get Tuck and the boys here at daybreak—then we'll see about that town."

"You sure about all that black powder?"

"Don't you worry none about me doin' what needs doin'."

Bob emerged from the hole, got his bearings, and moved off toward his horse. B. F. noticed that the end of the ladder then disappeared down into the hole. Apparently, they only raised the ladder when they had company. Something about the man in the hole sounded familiar to B. F., but he just couldn't figure out why.

One thing was certain, he wasn't about to try to follow Bob any further in the dark, particularly if he was headed to meet Tuck Smith and his gang. Mr. Finnerty spoke to him again. "Don't corner somethin' that you know is meaner than you." Despite this added advice, he decided his best chance to figure this out was to get down that ladder.

He waited a good ten minutes until he could no longer hear Bob's horse clattering away down Dry Hollow Creek, then walked back over to the opening in the ground. He hoped he could pull this off. "Hey Mac . . . it's Bob again."

"What the hell you want?"

"Forgot to tell ye something."

"Dammit."

There was a scraping sound as the end of the ladder rose up out of the hole. B. F. pulled the collar up on his coat. He would have his back to the man when he climbed down the ladder, but he needed the element of surprise if possible. He made sure his pistol was resting loosely in its holster, took a deep breath, and started down the ladder.

When he was still two steps from the floor below, he could tell the man was no more than eight or ten feet behind him when he said. "What the shite is it?"

B. F. took one more step, held on with his left hand, and turned his body halfway around. The hammer on his pistol suddenly sounded very loud when he cocked it back. "Don't move your hands, Mister."

"Who the hell are . . . Mistuh Windes! What're you doin' here?"

B. F. stared at the man, and realization took hold. "John McCorkle. I'll be asking you the same question!"

McCorkle glanced behind him, calculating the distance to cover. "Why, I'm hiding out from the Yankees. They're still trying to catch some of us."

"McCorkle. Don't waste your breath. You're going to have to convince me not to shoot you tonight." He took the final step off the ladder and squared himself away, with the big pistol pointed dead level at the man's chest.

"Why would you want to do a thing like that? We're on the same side."

"Tell me about my shipload of rifles and ammunition."

"Major Anderson told me your ship was sunk."

"If you lie to me again, I'm going to shoot you in the knee. Kind of like you did to Mose Simpson."

McCorkle's eyes went wide. "I didn't have nothing to do with that."

"My ship and the rifles."

"It was Major Anderson. He cut a deal with that ship captain. He took the guns and the captain got the ship."

"Where are the guns?"

"I reckon with the Texas Third Cavalry."

B. F. took a step forward and sighted the pistol at the man's knee. "That's a lie."

"No, no. Don't do that. Anderson sold some of the rifles and car-tridges to Colonel Quantril, some to Captain Todd, and he kept the rest for his own troops."

"Quantril—that makes me sick just to think about it. And Todd . . . he was in it too! How many guns are left, and where are they?"

"I expect they're all gone. Major Anderson been dead over a year now, and Captain Todd was kilt the week before when he was up in Independence."

B. F. redirected his pistol toward his knee again. "Where are they?"

"I don't know, honest. I don't know."

"Tell me exactly what you and Tuck Smith are planning tomorrow."

"We're just gonna go scare some boys over at Keetsville that's done turned into Yankees."

"McCorkle. That's not right either. I make that at least three lies. You're going to be walking with a crutch for the rest of your life."

The man jerked his head quickly to the left, and B. F. took the bait, turning to look himself. At that instant, McCorkle lunged for his gun hand, something flashing bright in his own hand. B. F. blocked him with his left arm, feeling a sudden burning sensation in his forearm, but was able to swing his pistol at McCorkle's head as hard as he could, considering he had limited room to maneuver. He heard and felt the trigger guard as it smashed into the cartilage on the bridge of the man's nose. McCorkle hit the ground and did not move, a bright pool of blood forming under his head.

B. F. held the pistol in readiness and turned him over. Blood was running down his face, and his nose was angled in an almost complete right turn. He was still breathing—though in a decidedly sideways direction. B. F. holstered his gun and searched him for weapons. He pulled a pistol from McCorkle's boot and picked up a knife on the floor. When he bent over, he saw a dark liquid dripping down his own left sleeve and into the palm of his hand. Blood. His coat was wet with it.

There was a roll of baling twine on a wooden chest, and B. F. tied McCorkle securely, making no apologies for the rope cutting into his flesh. First his hands, then his feet, and finally hog tying him face down. He drug him out of the way, and smelling an extremely strong, acrid area directly under the highest ceiling in the cave, he placed him on his stomach in the middle of what was hundreds of years of accumulation of bat guano.

B. F. took off his jacket and tore his shirt sleeve into strips and tied them over the long gash on his arm, then began systematically looking through the gear and supplies in the cave. It really only consisted of one large room of about forty by fifty feet. There were three tunnels leading off in different directions, but they quickly appeared to peter out to impassable crawl space.

He thought he recognized a long wooden box, and was glad to see twelve new Spencer rifles nesting inside. They were still greased and apparently had not been disturbed since he saw them last on the *Reis*. Another wooden case held 2500 cartridges, and a box about eighteen inches square contained a fifty-pound canvas bag of gunpowder. They were certainly capable of blowing up something very substantial the next morning.

He also found boxes of Union Army uniforms, tentage, cooking gear, and a small amount of food. Stuffed under this gear were two sets of saddlebags, one contained some written messages, a hand-drawn map of Pittsburg, Kansas, and some moldy hardtack. The other had several thousand dollars in Confederate currency and just over six hundred dollars in U.S. greenbacks. B. F. stuffed the American money in his pockets, assuming that it was all he was ever going to see of the $70,000 in goods and $20,000 ship he had lost to McCorkle, Anderson, and Captain Pesca in Texas.

Then he began carrying the Spencer rifles up the ladder in sets of three, followed by the case of ammunition and then the black powder. With this exertion, he could tell his bandage had become soaked with blood. When he went back down into the cave, he found that McCorkle had roused and rolled over on his side.

"Say, what is this stuff? I cain't hardly breathe."

"If you're lucky, I'll let you loose in a little while."

"You know you ain't gonna get away with this. You cain't run far enough."

B. F. knelt beside the man and pulled his old Army knife from the scabbard in his boot. But rather than cut the rope, he cut off a large piece of McCorkle's shirt. He then dropped it in the bat guano and looked at McCorkle. "Now look what you made me do." He picked up the now-fouled cloth, wadded it up, and forced it in McCorkle's mouth between his teeth and the side of his cheek. Then he cut another piece of shirt and tied the gag securely around his head. He paused for a minute, satisfied to see the man's eyes starting to water before he stood up. "Be glad you're still alive."

He stopped at the foot of the ladder, thinking about the implication that Todd had been part of the charade. That would mean that around half of his trade had been for the benefit of bushwhackers. It shook him to realize what he had been involved in. He resolved to never mention his blockade running again, as long as he lived.

He blew out the lantern, climbed back up to moonlight, pulled the ladder up after him, and hid it well away from the entrance in brush. Then he carried the rifles, ammunition, and powder half way down the hill and concealed them as best he could in a honeysuckle thicket in the darkness. He took one of the Spencers with him back to town.

As he walked back toward where he had tied his horse, it struck him that he was now in an extremely precarious position. He had left an eyewitness back in the cave that could identify him to Tuck Smith and his gang. McCorkle was right about one thing, there really was no place he could run to.

He stopped walking and stood there thinking in the middle of the creek bed for almost five minutes. If McCorkle were dead, there would be no witness, no identification, no way to connect him to this, and no reason to hide. He fingered the hammer on the Spencer as he mulled over his only two options.

He found his horse quickly enough with the moon now just above the tree line and rode back to Keetsville. It was already after eight o'clock when he knocked on the Durham door. Both John and Matt answered the door, each with a pistol in hand. "Oh, sorry B. F. You can't be too careful these days. Come on in."

"I need your help. I. . . ."

John Durham stepped forward and grabbed his arm. "Is that blood? Minnie, bring a pan of water and some rags in here, quick. Sit down, boy. What happened to you?"

He told them the basics of what had happened. "I need to round up Squire Cave, A.J. Stewart, John Burton, John Cureton, James Andrews, and maybe Lem Simpson, but I don't know where they live. I need them before dawn, and I need to ask them to go back down to that cave and get the drop on Tuck Smith and his gang. It sounds like they're planning to blow up the whole town tomorrow morning."

"Only three of those men saw any duty in the war. The rest are just shopkeepers. They won't stand a chance against Tuck and his boys."

"If we catch them by surprise and we're armed with repeating rifles, I think we can do it. They've got to be stopped. We'll never have a safe town with those men on the loose."

"You need to get the law from over at Cassville."

"It's too far to get there and back before dawn. Besides, there's only two lawmen up there, and I'd have to find them."

"You're liable to get everybody kilt."

"If we don't do this, they're gonna destroy this town, then there's no telling how many innocent people will get hurt. And if we don't do it at daybreak, the man I left tied up in the cave will make sure they know who took their weapons." He looked at the two men. "I'm not asking you to fight them. But I need help finding where the store-keepers—and Simpson—live."

John Durham shrugged his shoulders and waved him off. "I always wanted to shoot one of those repeaters." He turned to Matt. "You go get Andrews and Simpson. We'll get the others and meet you back here by four o'clock. Don't take no for an answer."

Just after four o'clock in the morning, seven men met in the Durham kitchen, nursing hot coffee that Sue and her mother-in-law brought them. They listened to B. F. describe the situation, the location of the hideout, and how they should arrange themselves on the north side of the cave opening. He also demonstrated how to load the Spencer and the necessity of pulling the hammer back each time before pulling the trigger.

As they stepped out in the yard, the moon was rapidly falling out of the sky, leaving the men only star light to guide them. All were bundled up and hunched over in their saddles against the cold. Thankfully, there was no wind, but B. F. guessed the temperature at no better than the mid-twenties. It was the kind of night where sounds carried a long distance, so there would be no way to ride down this rocky road and sneak up on anybody. They needed to be in place well before the guerillas arrived after daybreak.

They tied their horses in the trees a half-mile from the cave, after hearing Lem Simpson caution that on a still night like this, the horses might act up if they heard or winded the gang's horses. The moon was long gone as they walked the final stretch to the cave. It was difficult to see someone more than six feet away, so they stayed close together.

B. F. located the case of rifles and distributed thirty-five rounds of ammunition to each man. He stood by and observed every gun being loaded, then turned to Simpson and Matt Durham for their war-time experience in placing men in an offensive configuration near the mouth of the cave—all behind good cover. Each man crouched no more than twenty-five steps from the cave opening.

It was still a half-hour until daylight. They had all been told no moving, no matches, and no tobacco. It was hard to do, sitting at odd angles on the side of the hill and trying not to think about how cold they were. As the darkness turned to that gray time just before dawn, all of them saw things emerging from the dim light that looked like targets, but with continued inspection proved only to be an odd stump or bush.

With the sunrise just beginning to splotch the treetops above their heads, a pair of fox squirrels hopping through dry leaves off in the distance got them all on edge. B. F. repositioned himself to relieve his numb feet and to try and get his back aligned with a beam of sunlight. It didn't help—he was still cold.

About twenty crows set up a ruckus in the valley off to the south, and they could see them lifting above the tree line and flying to the east. Simpson looked at the men on either side of him and pointed at his rifle. They each passed a similar sign to the others, and the men made sure yet again that they were well concealed in the shadows.

In ten minutes, they heard the sound of horse hooves on the rocks below, then somebody climbing up the side of the hill. B. F. thought he could identify Bob from the night before, but there was no sign of anyone else. Bob walked up to the cave.

"McCorkle. It's me, Bob. Push that ladder up here." He waited almost a minute before calling again. "McCorkle. Wake up down there!" He looked around the cave opening, didn't seem to find what he was seeking, and walked back the way he had come about thirty yards.

He called down the hill. "Hey, Tuck. McCorkle ain't answering. And there ain't no sign of the ladder."

More steps coming up the hill—five of them including Bob. "You tell that sumbitch to get that ladder up."

Bob was back at the entrance, this time louder. "McCorkle! Tuck is here. Wake up!"

Tuck and the others were close behind. "Stuart, you and Best look hard for that ladder. The damned fool mighta gone in town to Peevey's last night."

John Durham's voice cut through the cold. "Get your hands up or we shoot."

Ignoring the warning, the guerillas all drew their sidearms, firing toward the voice, and simultaneously trying to find cover. B. F. pulled the trigger, dropping one of the men, and the hillside was immediately filled with smoke and the sing of lead. Their vision was occluded almost completely with a dense cloud of gun smoke.

B. F. was able to see another guerilla that seemed to be aiming his pistol directly at him and he quickly fired at about the same time the man's gun spouted a puff of smoke. He was fairly sure he had hit him but not positive the shot had finished him. He moved a few feet to his left to find a hole in the smoke and saw the man again, lying on the ground, but sighting on him a second time. B. F. fired again, but then spotted Tuck in his peripheral vision, scrambling for the cave entrance.

Due to the cloud of smoke, most of the others blindly emptied their guns in the direction of where the guerillas had been. Lem Simpson took off at a dead run down the hill the way the men had come, arriving among their horses in time to get off a shot at a man getting away on his horse. His target pitched backward, falling hard to the ground. Simpson ran up to where he landed, cocked another shell in the chamber, and fired at point blank range, then everything was still.

Back on the side of the hill, B. F. called out to the men. "Anybody hurt?"

John Durham looked at his friends. "I think we're all in one piece." He turned to B.F and smiled. "That hat of yours has seen better days, though."

B. F. pulled it off and found two holes about an inch apart through the brim of his almost-new silk hat. Apparently the guerilla's aim had been distracted just enough. It was far too cold to sweat, but nevertheless, he wiped his brow with the hat. That was about as close as he wanted to come to a bullet. He walked closer to the cave, stopped about ten feet from the hole, and called out, "Come on out, Smith. We know you're down there."

The voice was strained. "Come and get me, ye damned Yankee lovers."

B. F. signaled the men together and spoke quietly to them. "He probably hurt himself when he jumped into the cave. But don't get near the opening. He'd like nothing better than to pick us off!"

"How are we gonna get him outa there?"

"He's got enough rations down there to last several days. There is a way for us to get him without any of us getting hurt." B. F. looked around the gathered circle at each of them. "But it'll mean he won't live to go to jail."

Squire Cave shook his head. "If he went to jail in this county, he'd get loose in a week. He's got too many friends around for him to stay locked up. The only way to protect us all is to do this final."

B. F. laid it out for them. "Let's drag these boys over and pitch them in the cave. Then we'll give them a dose of what they were going to do to our town. They had enough black powder to blow up every store in Keetsville. What would you say if we blew up their hideout? Who would know they didn't accidently blow themselves up?"

Lem Simpson looked at him. "We done already gave them a better chance than they gave my brother. I say do it."

B. F. looked at the others. "What do you say?"

None of them had any desire to try and take on Tuck Smith. B. F. retrieved the box of hidden black powder and Lem took it from him. "This here job belongs to me."

The bodies were thrown into the hole, bouncing on the vertical walls of the cave until they landed with a final thud at the bottom. Then the ladder was retrieved from the brush, and thrown into the entrance as well. Tuck's voice from the cave. "What the hell you tryin' to do up there?"

John Durham spoke up. "One last chance, Tuck. Come up that ladder with your hands showing."

"Why don't you whores' sons come on down here?"

Lem made a wick of a strip taken from a dead gang member's shirt, pouring a line of black powder into the piece of cloth before twisting it together and tying it at both ends. He secured it to the cloth bag of powder in the box, pouring extra powder around the base of the cloth where it was affixed to the bag.

He waved them all back, kneeled close to the side of the hole, lit the fuse until it had less than three inches to burn, pitched it into the cave, and ran hard away from the entrance. Even fifteen feet underground, the explosion of fifty pounds of powder was louder than anything any of them had ever heard before. A huge cloud of black smoke, rock, and dirt belched out of the ground and rose above the trees, while an area of hillside at least eighty feet in diameter fell into the cave.

The men tentatively looked into the gaping depression in the ground. As the dust cleared, they could see no evidence that any entrance had ever existed. It was simply a huge indentation in the hill. John Durham looked every man straight in the eyes when he spoke. "Nothing happened here. None of us are gonna speak about this to anybody. Even our wives! Letting the cat out of the bag is a lot easier than putting it back in."

B. F. spoke then. "All of you—keep your Spencer rifle. You earned it this morning. But put it away somewhere for a few years. There may be others in their gang who know they had these guns. We don't want to be connected to this in any way."

John Durham again. "We don't want to ride back up the road in broad daylight in a group. Let's split up here by ones and twos and cut across these hills toward home.

"Let me just say one more thing. What you men done here this morning probably saved our town—and maybe a good many innocent people. You can feel proud of the courage you showed today. Don't never give them boys in that hole another thought. They all deserved to be dead—ever last one of them. As your former Magistrate, I just want to say I was proud to stand beside you today."

Forty-Seven

The Maid Of The Mountain

Blockade Hollow, Missouri 1865

The blast threw John McCorkle's body violently against a limestone stanchion in the tunnel, tearing his left ear almost completely away from his head and breaking his shoulder. The pain was excruciating. By the time he realized he couldn't hear anything in either ear, he didn't know whether he had screamed aloud or not. He was certainly in no position to fight if they had heard him and came looking.

He lay there for what seemed like an hour before he could get himself together enough to resume crawling forward—or at least he hoped he was crawling in the same direction he had been. It was impossible to use his left arm at all, so he awkwardly used his belt to hold his left wrist against his chest to prevent as much movement of the arm as possible. All he could do was pull himself along a few inches at a time with his right arm.

He began to think the tunnel was leading nowhere. In several places, it had narrowed to no more than eighteen inches in height before growing somewhat larger after a few yards. He wondered if he had simply crawled back here to get stuck and die because he certainly had no idea if the tunnel actually led anywhere. His right hip and his elbow felt as though they were rubbed raw by the floor of the tunnel, and he had lost count of the times the top of his head had cracked on the low ceiling.

He'd not been able to locate a lantern in the cave before he started down the tunnel, and the few matches he had were long since used up. So he had no light whatsoever and was struggling in complete and utter darkness. In fact, he wondered a couple of times if his eyes were even open.

He began to hear some sort of faint, but constant sound that seemed to be coming from just ahead of him, or maybe a bit off to the left. In another fifteen minutes of crawling, he realized it had to be water dripping. The bottom of the tunnel got muddy and then quickly dropped away into shallow water. When water droplets landed on the top of his head, he turned his face upward to catch the water in his mouth. Although he still couldn't see anything, it seemed that the water was coming from a gray area rather than pitch black.

He half stood in the tunnel, reaching toward the grayness. His hand touched something slick, and it smelled moldy. He jerked his hand back but finally determined that what he felt was wet leaves. There was no explanation for leaves being in a cave unless there was some sort of opening to the woods! He began to tear at the leaves with his good hand, throwing them into the water at his feet. Within a few minutes the light in the tunnel was sufficient for him to actually see the blurred outline of his hand in front of his face.

Along with a particularly large handful of leaves came a shaft of sunlight, forcing him to squeeze his eyes shut in pain. More leaves begat more light, and McCorkle was able to find hand and footholds on rocks and tree roots along the sides of the sink hole that finally brought him, exhausted and shaking with the pain in his shoulder, to the surface. He quickly recognized the huge difference in temperature between the cave and the outside air. His wet legs and feet were immediately almost unbearably cold.

After a time, he was able to stand and walk to the top of the hill to get his bearings. He was disoriented as to where he was until he realized that the huge depression in the side of the hill was the remains of the cave, and then it was possible to locate his horse. He had no idea how he was able to climb into the saddle and get the animal started toward Roaring River, but he must have passed out after traveling less than a couple of miles. He slid off the horse as the animal negotiated a dry creek bed, landing on his right side in the rocks, and that's the way the Maid found him in the early afternoon.

McCorkle awakened in agony. It took him a few minutes to realize he was lying on a makeshift travois, consisting of no more than a blanket tied between two poles, which was being dragged along by his horse. The frame of the travois bounced over every rock on the trail, sending shivers of pain down his shoulder and arm. He became aware of a light snow falling and suddenly thought of how cold he was. He tried wiggling his toes to get some circulation going, but his feet seemed to be well past the burning and stinging stage, and were now so numb he was barely aware they were attached to his body.

He attempted to twist himself around to see who was leading him, but the movement caused more pain in his shoulder. He tried to orient himself, but without being able to see anything more than his limited field of vision, he had no idea where he was or what direction he was traveling. Given the large number of downed trees they were passing, he was fairly sure that he was somewhere in Blockade Hollow, but from his vantage point there were no recognizable landmarks to help with his bearings.

Blockade Hollow was a two-mile-long, steep valley situated between Keetsville and the Arkansas border, which had earned its name during the Civil War when General Sterling Price's Confederate troops, who were being pursued by the Union Army, felled a large number of trees across the wagon road in order to delay the progress of the enemy. In late 1865, it still remained impassable to any conveyance larger than a narrow wagon.

McCorkle's ears continued to ring, but he did hear the sound of a hoarse voice as they came to a stop. "I knowed ye warn't dead, but I seen corpses that look a sight better. It's a good thing I was headed over to Keetsville, or you mighta been froze solid by now."

The slightly-built figure walked to the rear of the travois so they could talk. "Them clothes is tore to pieces, an ye got cuts all over. Did one of them panthers get to ye?"

He decided to keep close-mouthed. "I don't rightly know what happened. I think I fell off my horse."

"Well, he musta stomped on ye onct or twict for good measure. Yer nose is broke and yer ear's about tore off. Them knees is bloodied up bad, and the way you act, I believe that arm is broke too. Just stay still and we'll be at the cabin afore dark."

McCorkle blinked at the person standing in front of him, finally realizing that very probably it was a she, despite the fact that the clothes were those of a man. She had a belt wrapped tightly around a pair of very baggy pants that appeared ready to fall down if the belt failed in its assignment, and a red and white bandanna entwined around her head, so it was impossible to see her hair. It was likely that she had no more than a dozen good teeth in her head, despite the fact that her face was completely unwrinkled and her eyes were strikingly sky-blue.

"What's your name, ma'am?"

She turned to the side and spit a wad of tobacco. "Mattie Lansdown—but most folk calls me the Maid of the Mountain."

That got his attention. "I heard of you! They say you got special powers."

"Mebbe I do, and mebbe I don't. Depends on what a body's lookin' for."

The cabin could not have been larger than twelve feet square. She got a fire started and made sure McCorkle was settled on her pallet in front of the fireplace so he could get warm, then helped him get his boots off so he could get circulation started in his feet. "Two of them toes is shiny white. We hafta watch 'em close—could be frostbit."

She bent down and gave him a close inspection in the dim light. "I'm givin' ye a choice. I can sew that ear back on yore head, or I can cut it off. You ain't gonna be too purty whichever one I do, and either one is gonna smart."

"I'd like to keep my ear."

"You'll hafta keep still, and that ain't gonna be easy when I start stitchin'."

"Have you got any whisky?"

"I cain't abide no spirits. My pa had a terrible weakness for it."

"I suppose I can stand it. Go ahead when you're ready."

"Don't rightly know if that ear'll take or not. It's purty dried out. Looks almost like one of them dried peaches." She poured water on a piece of cloth and began to dab away the dried blood and dirt.

He jerked his head backward. "Feels like you're tearing it off."

"I ain't even picked up my needle yet. Are ye sure yer tough enough for this?"

"I can grit my teeth with the best of them."

She handed him a piece of kindling about eight inches long. "Bite on this so's ye won't get yer tongue. And once I start, you best not be jerkin' around."

The first two stitches, McCorkle dug his teeth deep into the piece of hickory, but with the third stitch, a big tear rolled down his cheeks. By the time the Maid tied off the twelfth stitch, his shirt was damp with tears and sweat, and he was almost panting.

She put her hand on his chin and pushed his face to the right, then the left. "Well, it sorta looks like an ear. Still may hafta cut it off if it don't get no color back."

"Have you got a mirror?"

She shook her head. "Vanity is one of them seven sins."

"I never knew a woman that didn't have a mirror."

"Still got some work to do. Gotta straighten that nose out. Never seen one broke that bad."

"It couldn't hurt any worse than that ear."

She just smiled, stepped behind him, reached around his head, and put her hands on either side of his nose. "You ready?"

"I guess so."

He wasn't. He expected her to gently and slowly re-position his nose. The sudden jerk of her movement surprised him, and the excruciating pain made him cry out. His eyes leaked more tears, while his nose poured blood onto his chest. "Why'd you do that?"

"Thet's the only way I know to do it." She looked at him again. "It's fair to middlin'. Not too crooked." She stood in front of him, studying some more. "Reckon it's not as straight as I figgered. Ye want me to give it another go?"

He gingerly touched his throbbing nose. "It feels fairly straight. Let's leave it be."

"That ain't the end of it." She put her hands on his upper left arm and gently worked her hands down the limb.

Her work quickly drew a response of pain from him, so she used a knife to cut his shirt sleeve open. "Don't see no sign of no bone. But it shore is swole up. Gotta put a splint on ye and then rig up a sling. You cain't be usin' that arm for a couple months if you expect it to heal."

When she was finally finished, they split a potato and some cold cornbread, and McCorkle felt the bile rise in his throat when he re-tasted the bat guano from some twelve hours earlier. He gagged but managed to swallow the potato.

The Maid looked at him. "Somethin' wrong with that spud?"

"No, no. It just stuck in my throat." He couldn't help but notice before going to sleep that she opened a leather pouch in the light of a candle, unfolded a piece of paper she retrieved from the pouch, and seemed to read it before blowing out the light.

McCorkle awoke to the sound of a gunshot. He automatically reacted and reached for where his sidearm should be, and at the same time the sudden movement caused a stabbing pain in his left shoulder and arm. The whole left side of his head was throbbing, and his nose was so swollen that he could neither inhale nor exhale except through his mouth. He looked around the small cabin, and finally the goings on of the previous day came to him, and he remembered he was no longer armed.

Pulling himself upright, it was obvious that the Maid was not in the cabin. He realized how cold it was, and decided he'd better get a fire going, as he had no idea how long she'd be gone. But just about the time he started adding kindling to the remaining embers, he heard her scuffing her boots on the front step. She had an old musket in one hand, a skinned squirrel in the other, and a grin on her face. "Get the skillet. We'll be havin' a fox squirrel and a little gravy for breakfast."

"Sounds good to me. You got any coffee?"

"Just mountain coffee."

"Parched corn?"

"Yep. Some in that bag there. "That's why I was headed into Keetsville yesterday—out of vittles."

McCorkle reached in his pocket. "I ain't got much to contribute—just a half a dollar."

"I got three dozen eggs I aim to trade at the store. It's better'n a four-mile walk to town. Can I take yer hoss?"

"Of course."

B. F. had spent a fitful night sleeping—or rather not sleeping—going over the events in Dry Hollow at least ten times in his head. He could think of nothing that would connect him and the other men to the shootout and the explosion, but he couldn't shake the uneasiness. So it was good to have the distraction of a customer in the store after the two inches of snow that had fallen overnight.

"Morning, Miss Lansdown. You're out on a cold morning."

"Hullo, Mister Windes. I got three dozen nice eggs here. Can I sell 'em to ye?"

B. F. thought briefly about the six dozen he already had on the counter, but it was seldom that the woman ever had any real money, so he didn't hesitate. "Glad to have them, Miss Lansdown. Twenty cents a dozen all right with you?"

"Thank ye, Mister Windes."

The woman puttered around, finding what she wanted, and finally placed rice, beans, salt, flour, potatoes, bacon and tincture of iodine on the counter. B. F. knew she had more than sixty cents worth of groceries on the counter, but before he had to speak up, she produced two quarters from a rag in her pocket. "How much is coffee, Mister Windes?"

"It's fifteen cents a pound."

"How much is all this?"

"It's exactly one dollar ten cents, Miss Lansdown."

She shook her head. "That ain't gonna do. I got me a gentleman caller at my cabin, and he was askin' after coffee."

B. F. looked around the store. "Say, Miss Lansdown, maybe we can work this out."

She backed up from the counter and gave him a dubious look.

"No, please, hear me out. I understand that you have the power to see into the future, is that right?"

"Some folks says I can."

"Would you tell me my future for three pounds of coffee?"

"Much as I want that coffee, I cain't rightly promise. This here power don't always work."

"I'd like to try if you will."

"Bend down here and let me pull a hair off the top of yer head." B. F. did as he was told and the Maid harvested a hair, then placed it in his open palm. "Now squeeze yer fist real tight and then open yer hand with the palm up." Again, B. F. followed her directions. The Maid leaned over and spit on the hair in his palm. Thankfully, it had been some hours since her last chaw. "Now what do ye want to know?"

"There's a young lady. I want to know if there's a future for me with her."

The Maid didn't take her eyes off his hand. "Mister Windes, this here palm looks like you ain't had much in the way of happiness. This appears to be yer chance. Don't let it get away from ye whilst ye parse every last little problem."

She raised her eyes, blinked a couple of times, and met his gaze. "This was one of them times when it worked." She broke into a smile, and so did he.

He had to ask her. "How do you do that, Miss Lansdown?"

"Waal, it's like walkin' along a road. I can see a ways behind me, and I can see a ways ahead. But the further I look—both back and forward—the dimmer things gets. I can see tomorry real fine, but twenty years from now is awful blurry. And sometimes, if things is just right, I hear the voice. My great-grandaddy from Scotland had the gift, and my mam said I got it from him."

He nodded in acceptance. "If it's allright with you, I'd like to talk to you again one day about some old times I just never could understand."

"Anytime, Mistuh Windes."

B. F. weighed a full five pounds of coffee beans on the scale. "Thank you, Miss Lansdown. I hope you and your friend enjoy the coffee." He watched her depart out the front window, and was surprised to see her mount a fine looking Appaloosa mare. Must belong to the gentleman friend, he thought.

By the time the Maid got back to the cabin, McCorkle had searched every sack, every pot, and every cubby hole in the place. One thing was sure, she wasn't hiding any money in the place. He was surprised to discover that she had a library of sorts. He didn't figure her to be able to read, let alone be a regular book collector.

He had quickly located the pouch she had opened the night before, hoping it might hold something of value, but it only contained the letter, a photograph of a lanky boy in the uniform of a rebel corporal, a buckeye, and what looked like a bear tooth with a primitive design etched on it. Although he could have cared less about her personal situation, he decided to read the letter in case it contained something he could use.

> *Dear Matilda,*
> *This here will be a short letter, as they only give us 5 minites to write. I got shot over here at Shiloh Church in Tenesee. Not too bad. Just a scratch. But the Yanks done capshured me an a bunch of boys, an they put me on a steam boat on the Tenesee River thet's headed to Illinoy. They says we gonna spend the rest of this war at Camp Douglas. Don't you worry no more bout me gittin kilt. Soon as I get back home we gonna git married. I think about you ever night an ever day.*
>
> *Your friend an servant*
> *Henry Sedgwick*

McCorkle shook his head as he put away the letter. Camp Douglas! She'll be an old maid for sure if he got put in that hell hole.

When the Maid returned, he decided to push a little bit for information. "Say, it must get lonely out here away from town. How long you lived way out here?"

"Since my place got burned down in town."

"I'm looking for a feller . . . a friend of mine . . . name of Windes. You know anybody by that name around Keetsville?"

Something in the way he said it made her hesitate for just a second. McCorkle saw it, and she knew he did. He'd caught her completely off guard. "Why, sure, I know Mister Windes. I believe he has one of the stores in town."

"Does he live in town?"

"I don't rightly know. He ain't been here long. Just since the war."

"Well, I'll get to town one of these days and look him up."

She changed the subject. "Lemme see them two toes of yorn."

He took off his boots and was surprised when a large piece of skin sloughed off the top of one of his toes. His little toe and its neighbor were a purplish-black. He couldn't understand why he hadn't felt any pain from them all day if they looked like that. Most of the pain seemed to be along the side of his foot instead of in his toes.

"Ye probably need to see that doctor in Cassville. I believe he's gonna take them toes off, else you likely to lose that whole foot."

"I don't believe I'm up to a ride like that. Maybe in a couple days."

"In a couple days it'll be yer whole foot. By then he'll be figgerin' he might oughta cut up to yer knee."

"What with sewin' me up yesterday, and you telling me this, you sound like you been doin' some doctoring yourself."

"After Pea Ridge I helped a doctor for a while. Seen lots of gangrene. Once it gets to goin' it's hard to catch up with it."

"Can I wait 'til tomorrow morning to see if they get better?"

"I don't rightly know. But it's about too late to go into Cassville now anyhow. I fetched some iodine from town, and I need to put some on that ear of yorn so's it won't hafta get cut off too." She inspected his ear and found that several of the stitches were festered up. "Now don't you jerk none. This'll burn just a touch."

He squealed like a young shoat when she drizzled the iodine and alcohol mixture on his ear. "This here'll stain yer ear and neck a reddish-brown color, but it's gonna wear off in a couple o' weeks."

The next morning the Maid pulled the blanket off his foot, sniffed of it, felt of his ankle and calf, and sat down in front of the fire with a whetstone and a hand axe. "I ain't got no fine doctor tools, but you about waited too long. Time you ride to Cassville, that poison gonna cause ye to lose that foot—mebbe worse. We're doin' it now."

McCorkle gazed at his foot. There was really no doubt about his toes. He'd seen battlefield doctors cut off plenty of legs and arms that didn't look any worse. He just looked at the Maid and nodded his head.

She finished her task with the stone and placed a large piece of firewood next to his foot. Then she poured water over the area and wrapped his three larger toes tightly together and turned them under his foot so that she had a clear shot at the affected toes. "Now listen here. Whatever ye do, don't do no movin'. I aim to just get them two toes. But if ye move, who knows what kinda stub you'll end up with."

She positioned his foot as flat as possible on the firewood, made sure his three good toes were out of the way, and struck the blow as straight as she could. McCorkle screamed again as the two severed toes slid off the piece of wood and on to the floor in a puddle of blood. He hollered almost as loud when she poured iodine on the fresh wounds, then watched as she broke open two eggs and carefully extracted the membrane lining from the egg shells, which she placed over the two raw stumps. The last step was to bind his foot with a cloth. In less than five minutes, the wound stopped seeping blood.

"It was a good cut. If ye can stay still, it's likely not to bleed too much. But if that foot starts to get black, ye got to get to the doctor. I ain't got the tools to cut no foot off. It was all I could do to get them toes." She surveyed her handiwork. "Now let's fry up what's left of them eggs."

The next two weeks were not easy for either of them. McCorkle was out of his head with a fever off and on for at least three days, and she didn't know whether to leave him and ride to Cassville for the doctor, or stay with him and try to keep his fever down by sponging him with cool water. She found a little bit of ground up asaphoetida root in her herb box, tied it up in a piece of cloth, and hung it on a string around his neck; but it was a long way from fresh, and had almost lost its stink. She had little faith in it.

What undoubtedly saved him was a poultice that her Scottish grannie had taught her to make when she was just a girl. She boiled a good double handful of slippery elm bark in a pot of water, and then allowed it to simmer until most of the water evaporated. Next, she soaked a rag in the mixture and bound his foot with the poultice. By morning, his fever had broken and most of the red streaks had disappeared from his foot and ankle. Sometimes she *did* have special powers.

Forty-Eight

Do You Know Anything About A Family?

Keetsville, Missouri 1866

Journal Entry—April 18, 1866

There are signs that Keetsville is making progress. Maybe it's because spring has begun and the hills are full of blooming dogwoods, but Squire Cave told me just yesterday that around fifteen families have moved back to the area after hearing from old friends that life is returning to something close to normal. To be sure, there are still few people with money, jobs are hard to find, and many homes have been so damaged by the war or the bushwhackers that they can't be lived in. But things are truly improving.

Since we took drastic action in Dry Hollow, there has been no guerilla activity in our area in over four months. People are beginning to feel like there is an actual community again in Keetsville. The Methodists and Baptists are sharing a meeting house, and alternating services every week. There's hope that a school might start in the fall, and some are even talking about giving the town a new name. Most people want to call it Washburn, after old Samuel Washburn, the area's first settler.

I spoke to my neighbor, Wilbur Stephens, who lives directly to the north of the farm, about sharecropping my 160 acres.

Mr. Stephens has four sons helping him on his own acreage,
but they need more work in order to keep them all fed. There's
certainly more than enough to do in the mercantile store, and
I have no desire to get behind a plow myself. All I asked of
Mr. Stephens was that he leave me about two acres around
the house.

After a flurry of letters between Crocia, B. F., and Sue, there was general agreement that a visit was about to occur, and this had been confirmed with the arrival of a telegram a week earlier. So for the last three days, B. F. closed his store just before four o'clock and drove his wagon over to meet the arriving stagecoach in case Crocia and her mother were on board. Each day he watched the stage arrive, no passengers disembarked, and the stage rolled on to the south. Although there was no way to know when they might arrive, he was disappointed every day, and had gone back to town to reopen his store for the remainder of the afternoon—just as though he wasn't miserable.

Unfortunately, he had made a serious error in judgment after his third unrewarding trip, by confiding in Squire Cave that he was expecting a young lady and her mother on the afternoon stage. So the next day, adhering to his previous schedule, he harnessed his horse to the wagon around three o'clock during a break in his customers. This would allow him to leave the store only a few minutes before the stage was scheduled to arrive.

True to form, he ran out of the store at the last minute and quickly departed down the street. He saw there was a small box in the bed of the wagon that he had not noticed before, but was in too much of a hurry to stop. He arrived at the stage station at almost the same time as the coach itself, and he was thrilled to see Crocia and Missus Rayl stepping off the stage.

He wanted to rush over and give Crocia a truly worthwhile greeting, but he remembered his manners, tipped his hat, retrieved their baggage, and led them to the wagon. It was only then that he noticed the rear of his wagon was full of green flies, and they seemed to be mostly interested in the small wooden box in the back of the wagon bed.

His next mistake was opening the box, which was full of a surprisingly fresh cow pattie that was completely engulfed in hungry insects. He slapped the top back on the box as quickly as he could, but that only served to stir the mass of flies into a swirling dervish, first around his head, and then quickly around Crocia and her mother.

His arms were full of suitcases, but he began to wildly wave the bags in the air, trying to get the flies away from them. The two women slapped at the offensive insects to no avail and retreated inside the small house that represented the stage stop.

Finally, he saw no solution but to drive his wagon down the road a hundred yards or so, knock the box out of the wagon into the roadside ditch, and then ride back to the station, finally free of all but the most stubborn of hangers-on, but dripping with humiliation. He dismounted the wagon and, entirely subdued, walked over to the women. "I'm sorry. I think one of my so-called friends has pulled a joke on me."

He was so red-faced and discomfited that Elizabeth Rayl couldn't help but laugh. "I don't believe I ever had a welcome like that before. You must have a friend with a strange sense of humor."

Crocia piled on as well with a straight face. "Mama and I'll sit up front. Why don't you sit in the back with your little green friends?"

All his plans for conversation went out the window, and it was all he could do to take them to the Durham home and deliver their bags inside the door. Minnie Durham turned her attention from Elizabeth Rayl to him. "We'll be expecting you for dinner soon as you close the store, B. F."

As he rode back to town, he couldn't help but wonder why in the world every time he saw Crocia Rayl he ended up looking like a fool. He had been in all sorts of difficult situations in his life and most of the time had been able to see clearly what needed to be done. Here she was, a girl of eighteen, but every time she entered the picture, all his planning seemed to be wasted, and his conversation skills were nowhere to be found.

The next morning the four women responded to his invitation and came to visit the store. He had arrived early and almost wore out his straw broom making sure the place was clean. The four front store windows had a woman's dress displayed, four different bolts of cloth, kitchen implements, and clothing for small children. To his eye, the place looked better than it ever had before.

When they arrived, one of his first acts was to direct their attention to the front of Squire Cave's Saddlery and Bridle Shop directly across the street. B. F. explained to them that he had undoubtedly been the "friend" that had put the special box in his wagon the day before. Hanging on the doorknob of Cave's store was a hand-lettered sign that read, "Store Closed—Out Carousing All Night." B. F. smirked. "I don't believe he's had a customer all morning. Maybe I ought to take the sign off around noon."

His guests spent a little while in the store, then the older women left Crocia and Sue behind. B. F. asked for their suggestions, but he wasn't really ready for all the advice that came his way.

"These shoes are fine for old women, but put something newer in your window."

"Everybody already has a sausage grinder—why don't you show off some decent dishes, or maybe something most people don't have—a wringer washer, a cherry pitter—maybe one of those new stereopticons."

"Buy a couple of seamstress' dummies and put the dresses on them—don't just lay the dress on the windowsill."

"Change these bolts of cloth every week. These are the same ones you had in the window when you opened the store."

"When the strawberries start coming in next month, put some in the window."

"Put that new wringer washer out in the store so people can see it."

"Leaving hats in the hatbox is a waste of time and space."

"Put some of these cameo pins and hat pins in your display case."

"How about some nice ladies' fans?"

"Buy a spool cabinet and put all your thread and needles and knitting things in there so ladies won't have to hunt all over the store for what they need. It's fine to put functional things in the store, but put pretty things in the window."

He filled up two pages with their comments and different items to be ordered. "Thank you for all your help."

Crocia looked at him, then pointed to a glass jar on his counter. "That's going to cost you two peppermint sticks and a ride home."

"Can I talk you into riding out to the house with me about five o'clock? It's only about a mile from here . . . and you're invited too, Sue."

Sue half-smiled at Crocia. "Why don't you two go without me, and I'll help Mama with supper."

When he stopped at the Durham home that afternoon, Crocia was waiting on him at the front door. "Do I need to ask your mother to go with us?" B. F. asked.

She turned her head to him with a questioning look. "Do you *want* my mother to go with us?"

He looked behind her to be sure no one was listening, then smiled. "Not really. I just wondered if she might feel like she needed to be along."

"Let's go before she decides she does."

Within a few minutes, they had reached the southern boundary of the farm, and he pointed out the spring branch as well as tried to give her an idea of where the property lines were. The sugar cane was as green as a gourd, and the lespedeza was already at least six inches in height. The other fields had been recently planted, and they could see the evidence of corn and oats breaking the surface.

When they pulled into the lane and she had a good view of the farm house, he could tell she was disappointed. After all, it was small and very plain. "I bought this property for a good price, which will give me an opportunity to spend some money on the house. It's not much to look at—inside or out—but it could be a nice place with a little money and a good carpenter."

"Let's go inside."

The place was in no better shape than when B. F. had first purchased the property. The spiders and mice obviously had full run of the place. As he looked at it again, he saw it with a different set of eyes, and he realized that Crocia was simply looking at a glorified one-room cabin with a yard full of unkempt grass and weeds. He fumbled for an excuse. "I haven't done anything in here since I bought the place. To tell you the truth, I've been waiting on you to tell me what it would need to make it a decent home."

"I'm sure there are plenty of girls around here who would be glad to help with that."

"Well, I don't know about that. I was more interested in what you might have to say."

"Are you sure you really want to hear it?"

"That's why we're here."

She kept an eye on him while she talked to gauge his reaction. "It's not half as big as it needs to be. The existing house could be used as a kitchen and sitting room, but it needs at least two full size bedrooms built on the back of the house. The flooring needs to be replaced or covered. It needs interior walls rather than just chinked boards if it's to be a snug home. You have to get a decent cookstove, a kitchen table and chairs, cabinets, a dry sink, an icebox, and you'll need to dig a well so you can have a pump inside the house. Nobody wants to carry water in a bucket from a spring branch.

"The sitting room needs a mantle over the fireplace, a couple of comfortable chairs, maybe one of those black, Lincoln rockers I saw in a catalog at Pa's store, a bookcase, a desk for you to do your work at home, and pictures on the walls. The bedrooms should be separated by a central hallway, and they'll need comfortable beds and chiffarobes, with maybe a nice big mirror in one room. Each of the bedrooms should have two windows for good circulation.

"The yard is in need of shade trees. You should put a porch across the front with one of those gliders, a flower garden in front of the house, a vegetable garden in the back yard, and a stone walk from the lane to the front door and from the back door to the necessary so a body wouldn't have to get her feet wet. The only thing holding up that rickety fence is the poison ivy. Papa says a fence should be horse high, pig tight and bull strong. A back porch would be a nice place to put a wringer washer. And you need a decent storm cellar, no matter what!"

His eyes had gotten steadily bigger as she talked. "I surely under-estimated what it would take to turn this house around. I didn't think of more than a fourth of all that."

"I told you that you might not want to hear it."

"And I told you that's why we're here."

She walked over to him. "Is that why you invited me to come to Keetsville, Mister Windes—to give you advice on your house?"

"Among other things." He put her hand in his.

She looked at their hands, then back at him. "What other things?"

"Right this minute, I can only think of one thing." He kissed her on the lips, then her ear, her neck, and finally back to the lips. It lasted long enough that he forgot to breathe. She put one hand behind his back and pressed herself close to him. This time, she kissed him. Despite her modest clothing, the closeness made him very aware of her figure.

Finally, they pushed away from one another, and B. F. said in a voice that sounded strange, even to him. "I think we'd better leave."

She looked at him, smiled ever so slightly, and nodded. "I think maybe you're right."

Crocia spent most of the next day in the mercantile store with him, writing down more recommended changes and actually moving things around a bit to accommodate some of the suggestions she and Sue had made earlier. B. F. suddenly realized how much he appreciated her company in the store, and told her so. She returned a smile to him that affected him so much it made him almost feel uneasy with the emotion.

About noon, Squire Cave came in the store, didn't see any custom-ers, and said indignantly, "Out carousing all night? You low down son-of-a-gun, I didn't have any business at all yesterday morning. No telling what folks thought."

Crocia was bent over her work behind some shelving, and hearing Cave, she stood up with an innocent look. "I think it's terrible that an upstanding business man would close his store because he'd been out having a high old time the night before."

Cave was embarrassed. "Excuse me, Miss. I didn't know anyone was in the store, but I can assure you that I didn't go out carousing."

He paused for effect, casting his eyes downward. "Actually I spent the evening in private bible study."

She looked at him. "Now that just doesn't sound like the kind of man who would play with cow pies one day and go out carousing the next!"

Cave tipped his hat. "Sorry ma'am. It's just that I have an uncontrollable desire to improve on the truth."

Cave looked at B. F., who was about to bust his collar to keep from laughing, then at Crocia, still with a straight face, and it finally hit him. "You gotta be the girl B. F. talks about." Then he smiled. "Reckon I see why."

Early Sunday morning, the Durhams, Rayls, and B. F. took two wagons down to Roaring River for an all day picnic. As they passed through Dry Hollow, none of the men said a word about their experience there some four months earlier, let alone anything about the cave that was no more. All three were armed, for even though illegal activities in the area were much reduced lately, you could never take safety for granted—particularly when beautiful women were involved.

There was a good foot of water at the crossing in Dry Hollow Creek, but they progressed well enough. The second time they stopped to cross the creek, B. F. could have sworn he heard a horse making noise on the rocks well behind them, but there was nobody within sight.

They arrived at the confluence of the creek and the river in about two hours, then headed up the river a short distance to its source, where it poured out of a huge cave at the base of a mountain. There was a grain mill and a carding mill on the river, and from the looks of the water and the way the millwheels were turning, the owners had picked fine sites for their businesses.

Roaring River had scoured a large lake out where it rushed out of the cave, and the water was crystal clear. Crocia stuck her hand in the water and exclaimed at how cold it was. In fact, with the combination of the roiling spring and the large cave, the air temperature seemed to have dropped at least ten degrees near the opening in the mountain.

Two men were fishing along the bank of the lake, and another directly below where the lake emptied into the riverbed in a white, frothing torrent. All of them had caught speckled trout that morning. As they watched one of the fishermen struggling with yet another fish on his line, B. F. asked Matt and John if they had ever tried it. "No, but it might be enjoyable to come down here and catch our picnic lunch."

Minnie Durham looked at her husband and laughed. "We might all go home hungry if we depended on your fishing."

B. F. and Crocia wandered downstream a ways and sat on a large stone by the edge of the river, dangling their bare feet in the cold water. They sat close together, holding hands. "Crocia, I wonder how long it might take to get all that work done on the house."

She smiled and snuggled up to him. "If you put things off like my pa, maybe five years."

"I was thinking maybe five months."

"There's a lot to be done."

"I'm tired of living in the back of my store. I'm ready to start having a real life."

She raised her head off his shoulder. "What does having a real life mean?"

"It means something besides just work. It means a home and a family."

She pulled her hand away from him and wrapped her arms around her knees. "Do you really know anything about a family?"

"I've never had one, if that's what you mean. I sure don't count my pa and my stepmother. But I've seen the way I don't want it to be, and I've seen the way I want it to be." He looked at her. "What about you? Your folks look like they care about each other, and they surely care about you. What kind of life do you want?"

"I want to be happy. I want a husband who loves me and I love him. I want a family. I miss my brothers, so I'd really like to have two boys—and girls too. I'd like to have a nice home. And I'd like to be part of a community—church, friends, school." She looked at him. "Maybe I want too much."

"One of the best men I ever knew was a farmer from Tennessee named Fitzwater. We crossed most of the country together before he got killed. He could just barely read, but he knew exactly how to be a good man, a good husband, a good pa, and a good friend. I asked him one time what made him decide he should get married. He told me he got married because he found somebody he just couldn't live without." He looked at Crocia. "I've never forgotten that."

She looked away again and threw a small rock into the river. "Have you ever found anyone you felt that way about?"

"Yes."

Her voice was quieter. "You have? What did you do about it?"

"Mostly just thought about her every day and every night. What about you—have you found anybody you felt that way about?"

"I think so."

"And what did you do about it?"

"Tried to make him see that I do."

He stared at the foaming river, arguing with himself as to whether or not she meant him or someone else. He finally looked behind them at the Durhams and Elizabeth Rayl laying out a picnic lunch. "Come with me back to the cave again." They put their shoes on and walked upstream a bit out of sight of the group to where the river surged out of the mountain. The water came out with such force that it created a mist in the air that instantly cooled them off.

They stood there for a minute, while he took some time to work up his courage. He put his hands on her shoulders and turned her around to face him. "Crocia—surely you know it's you. I don't think I can do without you."

A tear ran down her cheek. "I feel the same way, B. F. Mama and I have to start back to Waynesville Wednesday, and to tell you the truth, I want to stay right here."

He kissed her. "I want to ask your folks for your hand."

"When?"

"I'm going to ask your Ma in about two minutes. I'll have to send a letter to your Pa."

"A telegram—so he'll know before we get home."

"Even better."

They walked back to where the group was sitting in the shade. "Missus Rayl, could I speak to you for a few minutes?

Elizabeth Rayl looked at her daughter, saw her flush, and knew down deep exactly what was coming. The others speculated as they watched her and B. F. walk down to the river together, stand talking for a few minutes, and then saw Elizabeth hug B. F. and kiss him. They walked back arm in arm and Missus Rayl grinned at her friends.

"Minnie, Sue—you're invited to Waynesville sometime soon."

"Wonderful. What's the occasion?"

"We're havin' ourselves a wedding."

McCorkle lay on a steep bluff that extended out over the river, about two hundred feet directly above the picnic, talking to himself. "Now ain't they the happy couple. I think I'd like to give that girl a proper wedding present myself." He smiled at his joke.

He had to have a decent gun, and he definitely needed more information. There would be no way to do anything when the three men were around, as all of them were armed. He could only catch bits and pieces of conversation, but apparently, the girl and the woman didn't live in Keetsville. That had to mean they would be traveling soon.

Forty-Nine

I Believe You Kilt
Me This Time

Keetsville, Missouri 1866

Henry Sedgwick was as sore as he'd ever been, having ridden the bony old mare almost five hundred miles in the last two weeks. His bad leg burned like fire from trying to stay in the cheap saddle, and his backside was raw from all the bouncing around he had done on the backbone of the horse. It had taken almost six-month's work in the Chicago railyards just to save enough money to buy the horse and saddle. But finally, he was a few miles north of Springfield and less than three days from home. Home and his Matilda.

It worried him that she had not answered either of his two letters since the end of the war and his release from prison. But he'd heard stories about stolen mail, and even hints that some Yankees destroyed all letters going south, just to be mean-spirited. One thing was sure, in the last four years he had found there was no shortage of meanness in his fellow man. But he had to keep believing she was safe and still waiting for him.

He hardly looked like the boy who had left Keetsville in January of 1862. He was at least twenty pounds lighter now, although a sight heavier than he had been during three miserable years of confinement at Camp Douglas. Between the horrible food and the frequent bouts of dysentery, he had only weighed around a hundred and ten pounds at the end of the war—hardly enough to cover the bones of a man six feet tall. He'd seen a lot of good men just wither away to nothing in that prison. He hated to guess how many had walked in the prison camp healthy as could be but were carried out feet first in no time at all. Frankly, he didn't know why he had lived through it, while so many others had not.

The gunshot wound that had gotten him captured in the first place had taken quite a plug out of his left calf, but it was the lack of medical treatment that had resulted in his leg drawing up so that he had to get around with a pronounced limp. The leg pained him most days, particularly when he was handling freight, so it was likely his farming days were over. He'd already resigned himself to the fact that he would have to find a job in a store. Working inside for the rest of his life . . . he'd sure never planned on that.

The important thing was he could almost smell the Ozark Mountains the further south he rode. And at the end of the journey he'd find his Matilda.

———————————————

Lydel Suggs managed to eke out a living, even during the war, by selling a little 'shine at the head of Blockade Hollow. His still was down a spring branch from his home, located so that he could take advantage of the cool water twice—once for his recipe and once more to keep a jug or two good and cold. There was a big flat rock that jutted out over a deep pool in the spring, which afforded Lydel a good place to hide his cooled, fine liquor.

He was just naturally suspicious, having been hoodwinked more than once by friendly drunks. Maybe they meant well, but their promises to "pay ye later" never seemed to go his way. So he was careful about his customers; but even when they were regulars, he never disclosed his ready-made cold storage site. Nor did he make any sales down at his still or at the spring branch, as all transactions were carried out on the front step of his cabin, and only between the hours of five and eight o'clock in the evening. It was his practice to retrieve three or four jugs from his stash each afternoon and have them ready for sale at five o'clock. If a customer was interested in a cooled version of his shine, they would be expected to pay an extra fifty cents for the privilege.

Sundays were generally slow days in his line of work, as his loyal customers usually bought a jug on Friday or Saturday and commonly reserved Sunday, and even Monday, to recover from their purchase. So Lydel was surprised to hear a knock on his door at five o'clock on Sunday.

The fellow standing on his step was not someone he had seen before, and he was not keen to change his recent practice of knowing everybody he dealt with. He put his hand on the butt of his revolver. "Are ye lost, friend?"

"No sir. I hear down at Roaring River that you might be able to quench a man's thirst—particularly since Peevey's closed on Sundays."

"There's a fine spring behind the house if yer thirsty."

"I was thinking more about some of that liquid corn you make."

"Just enough for my personal use. It's too precious to sell."

"Maybe ye'd consider sellin' just a short jug?"

"Sounds like yer in need of a dram or two."

"I sure am, friend. I got the quivers somethin' awful."

"One drop of this here shine will make a bullfrog spit in a black snake's eye. It's pure as the driven snow. Why, the first sip will heat you up all over like a hot bonfire."

McCorkle licked his lips. "I'm a thirsty man, friend." He watched Suggs take his hand off his revolver and turn to pick up the jug behind the door. When Suggs looked back around, there was a musket staring him between the eyes. McCorkle kicked the door open and stepped inside the cabin. "Touch that pistol and you're dead."

In five minutes he was gone and Suggs was short the three dollars he'd had in his pocket, a jug of moonshine, half a ham, and a loaded pistol, not to mention being trussed up on the floor with his own bootlaces. As he lay there, trying to untie himself, he resolved that from now on he'd just go ahead and shoot anybody he didn't know.

The Maid was glad to see the ham coming in the door, however she had a pretty good idea what it had taken to get it when he stood her musket in the corner and then spied the revolver tucked into his waistband. But when he stumbled as he turned toward her and she smelled the liquor on him, she knew things were about to change for the worse. She had known something was coming for several weeks but had forced herself not to pay any mind to the voice. She wanted to believe he cared about her and that the months of taking care of him and nursing him was something he would reciprocate.

Not that he had said it in so many words, but surely he felt something for her. Tonight, though, she began to lose faith. "Mac, ye know I don't allow no spirits in the house."

"Don't you worry none about that." He turned around and walked back outside, only to re-enter in a couple of minutes. "I took care of that little problem. They ain't gonna be no spirits in the house. I just drunk 'em all up in the yard." There was no mirth in his face. All she could see was that kind of mean sarcasm she used to see with her pap.

"Let's have us some of that ham and maybe a couple of fried eggs."

She turned to the fire and stoked the coals. "Won't take but a few minutes." She kept a sharp eye out for him, knowing how quick a drunk could strike. But at the moment, he seemed more intent on looking at his foot. It had healed fairly well but continued to cause him to feel like his missing toes were still there, and still hurting. She had tried to talk him out of that before, but tonight was no time to get into any kind of discussion, let alone an argument. She glanced at him rubbing the stumps on his foot, but looked away so he wouldn't interpret her looking as though it was some kind of silent disapproval.

She put the two plates on the wooden plank they used for a table, and he shuffled over and began to eat hungrily. She ate as fast as she could, as it was important that she finish before he did. "I'll be right back. I'm going to the necessary." He barely looked up from his plate.

As soon as she left the cabin, she ran out in the woods and hid herself behind a big red oak. She wasn't sure what to do, but she had sensed there was real danger in the cabin. Maybe she would just wait until he passed out, but then again, the danger might still be there when he woke up. She decided to sit tight and wait on another sign.

In about ten minutes she heard him holler for her, then he came out on the cabin step with the coal oil lamp in his hand. "Woman, get on back in here." He pulled on his boot, walked over to the privy and slapped the door. "Mattie, come outa there." The lack of an answer seemed to set him off and he jerked the door open. "Mattie, you best come on back here." He held the lamp in the doorway to the privy. Empty. Where in thunder?

He walked back to the cabin and stood on the step for a few minutes, realized she wasn't going to take the bait, and pulled his new pistol from the holster. The door slammed behind him, there was a pause of no more than a couple of minutes, and she heard a single shot, then silence.

She wondered if he had accidently shot himself, or maybe even did it on purpose. She had an overwhelming urge to run back to the cabin to see if he was hurt, but after taking no more than three steps, it was almost like an invisible hand reached out and stopped her in her tracks. Only a couple of other times in her life had her special power intervened so forcefully. But she recognized it for what it was and obeyed.

She retreated further up the hill from the cabin, fluffed up some pine needles, and slept as best she could. She awoke at daybreak but speculated he would likely not stir for two or three more hours considering his time with the jug the evening before. She sat there with her arms around her ankles and her chin on her knees, waiting for him to waken.

Finally, at nine o'clock, she watched as the front door opened, but blinked in confusion as a blurred voice reached out from her past. "Mattie, little Mattie girl—ye'd best git over here. I ain't a gonna hurt ye, jest come an set a while on yer old Pap's lap." As she strained her eyes toward the ghost image standing in the cabin doorway, relieving hisself on just about the only extravagance she had—her four peony bushes that were pushing new buds up through the earth—her sight became clear and she knew the invisible hand was that of her Mam, guiding her away from accepting the same fate of her childhood.

When this action elicited no response, he hollered out, "Come on down here, Mattie. I wanta talk to ye." Silence. "Come on Mattie, I know you're out there." Still silence.

He went back in the house for a few minutes and reappeared with his boots on and gnawing on a good-sized hunk of ham. After spending a few minutes in the shed, he rode off to the northeast on his horse.

Still she waited. She could just make out the silhouette of his horse, halfway up the hill and standing behind a big hickory. After fifteen minutes he gave up—apparently deciding that she was no longer in the vicinity—and rode on over the hill. She waited another fifteen minutes and walked down to the cabin.

Her leather pouch was on the table. The letter she had read a thousand times was torn into tiny bits, and Henry's picture had a bullet hole straight through the face. She stood there looking at it for a long time. Finally, she picked it up and tried to push the jagged edges together, but no matter how hard she tried, it was impossible to recognize the picture as her Henry. *Her* Henry. She realized she hadn't thought of him that way for a long time.

Why had McCorkle done such a thing? Was it because he was mad at her—or could it possibly be that he was jealous of Henry? Maybe he did care about her after all, and the alcohol pushed him to show it. Mattie had wanted to talk to him about it, but she knew she'd get no satisfactory response. Rather than remain in the cabin and wait for him to return, she figured it would be safer if she made herself a kit and stayed up in the woods for a day or so—at least until she had time to puzzle on the message from her Mam.

She was careful to leave the letter and the picture right where they had been but took enough food and supplies to last for about three days. As she was about to leave, she decided to retrieve her musket from the corner, as well as some powder and shot. No sense being stupid.

McCorkle got to the Keetsville stage stop just after ten-thirty and found that the north-bound stage departed at ten o'clock, while the south-bound left at four in the afternoon. He realized not only did he not know what day they would be traveling, but he had no idea whether Windes' girl and the woman were headed north or south.

He grinned conspiratorily at the ticket agent. "Say, friend, was there two pretty women on that stage this morning? I was hoping to be on it with 'em."

"I don't know what you call purty, but they was an old granny and her colored maid on board. Didn't see no other women."

He snorted. "Nope. That sure as hell wasn't them." He didn't want to raise any suspicions, so didn't inquire further about the women. He felt the three dollars in his pocket. "You reckon Peevey is open for business this time of day?"

"If he was breathin' when he woke up this mornin', he's open."

He drank up half his loot before four o'clock and rode back to the Wire Road to a position where he could see who got on the south-bound stage, but was concealed enough that he was out of sight of the ticket agent. Only a middle-aged man got on board.

McCorkle had a strong hankering to go back to Peevey's, but he had enough sense to realize that he might miss the morning stage again if he spent the rest of his money. Instead, he rode south out of town until he found an unoccupied barn, ate the rest of his ham, and let the alcohol haze put him to sleep for the night.

He was in place the next morning as the north-bound stage pulled in, but with the same result—no sign of either of the women. It was just as well. The other six quarters were eating a hole in his pocket, and once again he spent the middle of the day at Peevey's.

B. F. closed his store at noon and rode over to the Durham home to spend as much time as he could with Crocia before she left the next day. His mind was a hundred miles away, and he wouldn't have noticed the horse tied up in front of the dram shop, except that an Appaloosa is a striking animal. He was almost positive it was the same one he had seen Mattie Lansdown on a few months earlier. Apparently, her friend was still around, and it looked like he was the kind of fellow who drank hard liquor in the middle of the day. This was confirmed when he came back an hour later to reopen his store and the horse was still there. Too bad. Mattie deserved better than that.

At just about quitting time a stranger stuck his head in the front door and looked around. "Can I help you, mister?"

The man removed his hat and slapped it against his leg. He'd obviously been on the road for some distance, as he was covered in dust. With his hat off, the only part of him that wasn't gritty brown was the top of his head. "I'm lookin' for Norwood Barefoot. He used to have a seed store here."

"Come in out of the sun." B. F. poured some water out of a jug and handed the man the tin cup. "Looks like you could use some water."

"I sure could, mistuh. Do ye know where I can find Norwood Barefoot?"

"Are you a friend of his?"

"I worked for him a bit afore the war. I ain't seen him in about four years."

"I'm sorry to tell you Barefoot was killed in a stagecoach hold-up over a year ago."

The man looked away for a minute. "I seen many a good man die these last years. Guess I still ain't got used to it."

B. F. picked up a chair and pushed it toward him. "I hope none of us get to the point that we get used to it. My name's B. F. Windes. Is there anything I can help you with?"

"Name's Henry Sedgwick. I'm looking for my girl, too. I went by her house, but it appears that it burned down. Her name's Matilda Lansdown. Do ye know her?"

B. F. thought for a second. "You must mean Mattie Lansdown. Sure, I know her. She comes in here to get groceries every month or so."

The tears came without warning to his cheeks. "I'm sorry, Mistuh Windes. It's just that I been prayin' she was safe since I left here in sixty-two. There's so many people died, I just had to keep hopin'. Do ye know where she lives now?"

"She told me she lives in Blockade Hollow. But I've just been here a few months, and I don't know where that is." B. F. thought about the Appaloosa down at Peevey's, and could only imagine the scene if Henry and the owner of that horse found themselves at Mattie's cabin at the same time.

"I ain't heard of Blockade Holler neither."

"Tell you what—I was just about to go over to the Durham's house. Maybe you know Matt and John Durham?"

"Matt and I are the same age. But I cain't go over there to that fine house, dirty as I am."

"I've got a shirt about your size, and you can wash up here in the back of the store. Maybe John or Matt can tell you where to find Blockade Hollow."

"I reckon they'd know if anybody would. Maybe I can just stop by for a minute."

As B. F. expected, Minnie Durham told Henry Sedgwick that he absolutely had to stay for supper, and they spent the next couple of hours listening to him describe the hellish environment at Camp Douglas, and in turn, telling him as much as they could recall that had happened in Keetsville since he left for the war.

When Henry asked about Blockade Hollow, John Durham spoke up. "You probably know the place as Simms Holler. Everybody started calling it Blockade after the battle down at Pea Ridge. I'll take you there in the morning Henry. I know where Mattie lives, but the road is so bad, I'd get us lost for sure in the dark."

"What time can we go, Mistuh Durham?"

Minnie spoke up. "How about just after ten o'clock? Elizabeth and Crocia are leaving on the stage in the morning, and we aim to see them off."

"Yes, ma'am, I'll be here." He smiled at her. "Thank ye so much for that supper. It's been a long time since I ate so good."

McCorkle was sick of waiting on the two women to travel. Worse, he didn't have a cent to his name, having spent it all the last two days at Peevey's. Now he was faced with another day waiting at the stage stop and not even the wherewithal to wet his whistle. Of course, there was that moonshiner down in the holler, but there wouldn't be any chance to do it the easy way this time. Whatever, he might get lucky again and get money, shine, and grub.

He reached Suggs' place right after dark. There was no sign of the man, but a light in the cabin confirmed that he was probably inside. He tied his horse well away from the house and crept up to the front door. There were two small windows in the front of the cabin and he eased over to one of them and looked in. The window was so dirty he could hardly see through it. He crossed to the other window and found a corner in one pane where he could just make out the figure of a man on the far side of the cabin.

He had no real desire to hurt the old fellow, but what was a man to do? Besides, he was gonna get awful thirsty tomorrow. McCorkle knocked loudly on the front door and quickly resumed his position at the window.

"Yeah. Who is it?"

McCorkle didn't answer him but watched him cross the room and come to within five feet of the door. He shot him through the window and watched Suggs fall to the floor in a heap. Then he picked up the biggest piece of firewood he could find and, with three licks, knocked the handle off the door.

When he entered, Suggs looked up at him, clutching his stomach in agony. "You! Why didn't ye just tie me up again? Ye done gut shot me—and with my own damned gun!" He looked down at the blood and bile in his lap. "I do believe ye kilt me this time."

"Sorry. I couldn't figure no other way to get in."

"The hell you say!"

"You'd best hand over your money. I don't want to shoot ye again."

"I cain't hardly take my hand off my guts." Suggs took his left hand away and reached into his pant pocket. "I ain't got but two dollars."

McCorkle stepped forward and leaned down to take the money from Suggs. The knife slashed at his face, missing by no more than an inch. But when he leaped back out of the way, McCorkle bumped the table and a full gallon jug of shine fell and broke on his foot—his bad foot. The pain sent a fiery jolt through his foot and all the way up his leg. "Ahhh! You old bastard! I ain't one bit sorry I done shot ye."

Once the pain allowed him to limp a little bit, he retrieved the one remaining jug of shine and took a decent dosage. Then he began rooting through the place, finding some bacon and coffee, before he came back to Suggs. "You gonna hand over your money, or do I shoot ye in your damn knee?"

Suggs reached into his pocket again. "This here is all I got."

"Pitch it over here. I ain't giving you another chance at me." Two quarters and a silver dollar rolled across the room.

Suggs was surprised that he didn't get another bullet before the man left, but he'd seen enough gut shots in the early part of the war—at least before he gave up the cause and came home—to know that he'd be dead tomorrow anyway. As soon as he could be sure his visitor was gone, he pulled the table over so he could reach the top of it, and began to use his finger to write a note in his own blood to whoever found him.

Merdered by man with cruked ear an nose.

He sat back to wait.

McCorkle's foot was throbbing like mad by the time he reached the Maid's cabin, and he almost had to drag his leg along when he got off his horse. He decided it hurt worse now than it had when she chopped it off! Finally he got a lantern going, having fully expected her to be there, but the place looked like she'd cleared out. Well, that could work too.

Mattie heard the horse coming up the trail and made sure she was well concealed up in the woods. She figured it must be McCorkle but couldn't tell in the dim moonlight. Once she saw the light in the cabin, she snuck down and took a look in the window. It made her heartsick to see him sitting there, working on another jug. She retreated back up the hill and crawled into her little lean-to. It was late before she finally went to sleep.

He left earlier than expected the next morning, and when she was satisfied he was truly gone, she went back down the hill and entered the cabin. His jug was still on the table, and she was surprised when she picked it up to find that it was at least two-thirds full. Maybe that's how he was able to get up so early. One thing was certain, he was planning to come back if he left his liquor. She made a decision to help him with his problem, took the jug outside, and poured the rest of the contents on the ground. Then she spied the remaining coffee and took it back up the hill to make herself a pot.

Fifty

I Got a Lot Of Paying Back To Do

Keetsville, Missouri 1866

B. F. hated to see Crocia go, if only for three months. Things were so different when she was around. He had looked forward to every day because he knew at least part of it would be spent with her. The alternative—sitting by himself beside a coal oil lamp every night until he nodded off to sleep—was not appealing at all.

The two of them had very little opportunity to be alone, despite B. F. looking for any chance to take Crocia aside one last time. Whatever they could say to one another would have to last until the wedding in September. About all they could do was hold hands one last time at the stage stop and whisper a quick affection to each other. B. F. looked for the right thing to say as the driver hollered "All Aboard"—but with sentiments left unsaid, save a last squeeze of her hand, she was gone.

When he sighted B. F. Windes at the stage stop, McCorkle knew he'd finally hit his mark. He was close enough to see the two women being helped down from a wagon, and this was enough evidence for him to mount his horse and ride hard out of town, a few minutes ahead of the stage, on the road toward Cassville.

He had picked a narrow spot in the roadway where the stage would be forced to cross a low bridge about two miles from Keetsville. He got there soon enough and pulled a log into the road that he had found a couple of days earlier. Then he took his horse about two hundred yards further north up the road and waited on the stage to make an appearance from the south. He caught himself reverting to his old habit of licking his lips in anticipation of what might follow. When the stage was still a quarter mile from the bridge, he started his horse on a slow trot from the opposite direction in order to arrive at the log blockade at about the same time.

McCorkle could see the driver beginning to slow his team of horses as he dismounted from the saddle, bent over the obstacle, and gave an exaggerated tug to the log. He looked back at the two men on the stagecoach seat. "Say, can I get a hand here?

The man sitting beside the driver pulled the brake back hard, leaned his rifle against the seat, climbed down to the roadway, and stepped around the four horses. McCorkle could see he was not wearing a sidearm, so he drew his gun and pointed it at the driver up on the seat. "Pitch that rifle and your pistol down here." The driver hesitated. "I ain't funnin' ye now. Do it quick or yer a dead man. Don't really make no difference to me which it is." The two guns landed at the side of the road. "Now drop them reins and get down here." He eyed the man on the ground and waved him around on the left side of the stage with the driver.

He called out into the coach. "Anybody armed in there, I better see guns pitched out the window." Nothing. Then to the stage driver. "What's wrong with your manners, friend? Open the door for the ladies."

He pointed his pistol at Crocia and Elizabeth as they stepped down. "Ya'll come right over here and stand by me."

Elizabeth looked at him with contempt. "We'll do nothing of the kind. We have very little money. I believe you've stopped the wrong stage."

McCorkle smirked. "You got somethin' almost as good as money." He took three quick steps, grabbed Crocia's wrist, and pulled her toward him. Elizabeth reflexively grabbed her daughter by the other arm and held on. The stage driver thought he saw his chance and he made a quick move to grab the rifle on the ground. McCorkle let go of Crocia, took a step back, and shot him in the knee. "Dadgum it—see what you made me do? Ye provoked me!" He waved his gun at the four of them. "The next bullet ain't gonna be at no knee. That goes for all of ya'll."

He grabbed Crocia again. "C'mon girlie. You're goin' with me." She fought against him, but he simply let go of her and pointed his pistol at her mother. "Your choice, girlie." Crocia looked at Elizabeth and immediately ceased to struggle. He backed up to his horse, picked her up by the waist, and pitched her halfway over the horse, with her stomach across the front of the saddle and her legs dangling on one side and arms on the other. Then he stepped into his stirrup on the right side of the horse, sat behind her, and clicked his horse over in front of the man who had been riding shotgun. "Just so you'll not be shootin' me in the back, I'll be taking that carbine."

Elizabeth ran at the horse and riders, tears running down her cheeks. "If you want a hostage, take me. Leave my daughter be." She pulled at Crocia's feet while McCorkle held on, finally pushing her away with the barrel of the rifle.

McCorkle looked at her and smiled. "Don't have room for you today, Mama." He winked at her. "Mebbe some other time." He kicked his horse and they left the road, riding to the east across a knee-high field of corn. By the time they got the stage and team turned around in the road, the horse and riders had passed completely out of sight in the woods at the far end of the field.

Henry Sedgwick met John Durham at his front door as soon as they returned from the stage stop, and they departed immediately, riding a mile south on the Wire Road before heading back to the southeast on a narrow wagon road toward Blockade Hollow. In no more than a mile and a half, they entered the hollow, and had to soon begin picking their way around the remains of felled trees and brush every hundred yards or so along the wagon track. At many places, the incline on the sides of the road was so steep that it was difficult for the horses to negotiate around the obstacles with any assurance of surefootedness.

After a half hour of slow progress, John held up his hand. "This is the draw up to Mattie's cabin. Shouldn't be any more than half a mile. But there's no wagon road up to her place—just a foot path."

The huge oak and chestnut trees on the sides of the steep draw appeared to have never been cut, as many were at least four feet in diameter. Henry was peering closely at the ground as he rode, and spoke up. "Looks like there's been a horse up and down this trail purty recent."

"Mattie doesn't have a horse. Probably somebody coming to get their fortune told."

"I was hoping she warn't doin' that no more."

"Times are might hard, Henry. Like a lot of folks, she's just trying to keep fed. Besides, she does a heap of good for people—me included."

Henry looked down. "You're right, Mistuh Durham. Matilda's the best girl they is."

In less than ten minutes, Durham pointed ahead to a small clearing. "There's her cabin. You want me to wait with you to be sure she's here, or you want to do this yourself?"

Henry's eyes were shining. "Mistuh Durham, I sure appreciate ye comin' all this way with me. But I been dreamin' about today for four long years—thinkin' about what I'd say, and what she'd say, and just how things would be. I'd like to do this my own self."

"I understand, Henry. Come back to town after you get settled in. Maybe we can find work for you."

"Thank ye twice, Mistuh Durham. I sure appreciate that." He lifted his hand, giving a half salute-half wave, and turned his old horse toward the cabin.

John Durham hadn't gone more than a hundred yards when he heard a shout echoing through the hills. "Matilda. Matilda. It's me, Henry Sedgwick, come home to ye!"

The stagecoach charged up the hill back into Keetsville. The injured driver was in the cab with Elizabeth Rayl and the second man was driving, using the whip without let up. Elizabeth cried to him. "Stop at the house on the left. That's where we've been staying."

The stage careened into the front yard and finally pulled to a stop, the horses nervous and unsettled. Elizabeth began hollering for the Durhams as she ran to the door. Minnie and Sue got there simultaneously, surprised to see her again. "What's wrong, Elizabeth?"

"Are Matt and John here? A man just took Crocia off the stage and rode off with her. If they hurry maybe they can catch them."

Minnie took charge. "Sue, Matt is out in the garden in the field behind the house. Get him quick and I'll get his horse saddled. Tell him what's happened, and that he's to go get B. F. and anybody else that can ride. Run, girl!"

In no more than fifteen minutes, Matt, B. F. and Squire Cave were back at the house, trying to get as much information as possible from Elizabeth.

"Had you ever seen the man before?"

"No."

"What did he look like?"

"He was about thirty. Average size. His left ear was all scarred up, and his nose looked like it had been broken."

"Why do you say that?"

"It was crooked."

"Did you see any sign of anybody else?"

"No. But it didn't look like he needed any help. He seemed pretty sure with a gun. He didn't hesitate to shoot one of the men on the stage."

"Did he kill him?"

"No. He shot him in the leg."

"What kind of horse was he riding?"

"I don't know. It was brown and white—but had brown spots all over the white on its head and neck."

B. F. spoke up. "Was it a mare?"

"I didn't pay any attention."

"Which way were they headed?"

"There's a log in the road north of town by a little bridge. He stopped the stage there, and he took Crocia straight across the corn field on the right. There's something else. It seemed like taking Crocia was all he was after. Didn't even attempt to rob anybody—just grabbed her first thing. I tried to get him to take me instead, but he was dead set on taking Crocia."

B. F. put his hands on Elizabeth's shoulders. "You stay here in case the sheriff comes down from Cassville. "Don't you worry. We'll get her back." He held the woman firmly, making sure she was looking at him. "I promise you." Then he called to Minnie. "If John gets back here before we see him, tell him come back to Blockade Hollow—I think that's where they're headed." He turned to Matt and Squire. "Let's get going."

In the yard he explained himself. "I didn't want to worry Minnie. I believe I've seen that horse before. It belongs to a man that was staying with Mattie Lansdown. I saw the horse just this week at Peevey's, so the fellow is still around." He looked at Matt. "I'm afraid John Durham is headed right into trouble with Henry this morning.

"In case I'm wrong, Squire, you go get Lem Simpson—the man can track anybody, anywhere. You two head up the Wire Road to where Crocia got taken and start tracking from there. Matt and I are headed for Blockade Hollow, and I hope we catch up with his pa before something bad happens."

Mattie heard, but she could not believe. She stared at the tall, skinny man getting off his horse and realized it just might be true. She ran down the hill to the clearing in front of her cabin and stopped a few feet from him, looking him over from head to toe. "Henry, is that truly you? I thought you was dead. I couldn't see ye no more in my visions, and I just know'd you was gone."

"It's me, Matilda. I don't look like much—but it's me. Can we go in the cabin and get outa this sun?"

"Henry, it's a long story. But I been livin' in a lean-to up on the hill yonder. There's a man that run me outa my cabin, and I'm scared of him."

"Where is he? I'll get rid of him!"

"He rode off this mornin'. I never know when he's comin' back, and I'm afraid to be down here at the cabin if he shows up. He's armed, and he's a drinkin' man—mean when he's had too much."

"Who is this man?"

"His name's McCorkle. I found him on the trail some time back and nursed him—sewed him up an all. But of a sudden he took to bein' mean—real mean."

Henry cast his eyes down before he asked the question, not sure if he could stand the answer. "How long has he been here?"

"A couple months. I had to cut off two of his toes, do quite a bit of stitchin' on him, and he was sick for quite a while. Just started gettin' around a week or so ago. That's when he took off and come back drunk and mean."

He looked down again. "Do you care for this man?"

To see how much it pained him to ask her that question made her remember all over again why she had cared so long for this gentle man. "Henry—yer my true love. Ye oughta know that."

He reached out and took her hand, pulled her to him, and looked in her eyes. "That's good enough for me."

John Durham didn't realize it at the time, but he had his thirst to thank for staying alive. As he neared the head of Blockade Hollow, he kept thinking about the cool moonshine manufactured by Lydel Suggs. Sure, he'd made a promise to his wife he wouldn't go over there anymore, but it was just so *hot*—what was a man expected to do on a day like this? And if he wasn't mistaken, Suggs' place was no more than a quarter mile up the last deep draw before leaving the hollow.

He convinced himself he wouldn't stay long, but the sun was just too intense to be out in the middle of the day. He stuck his hand in his pocket to be sure he had a little money, and satisfied, he turned his horse to the east, following Simms Creek upstream. As he came within sight of the cabin, he was surprised to see the front door standing open and sort of hanging at an angle.

At almost exactly the time he got off his horse, passing behind him along the main trail of the hollow was McCorkle and his captive. Had Durham and McCorkle met face-to-face on that road, in all likelihood McCorkle's killer instinct would have prevailed. Thankfully, they were completely unaware of each other's presence.

Durham walked up to the cabin and felt apprehensive enough that he drew his pistol. "Mr. Suggs? It's John Durham. Mr. Suggs?" He recognized the smell before he reached the front step, and heard the flies working their victim. He stepped sidewise around the half open door, allowing his eyes time to adjust to the muted light in the cabin. He shook his head when he saw Suggs lying there in his own gore.

Someone must have been a lot thirstier than he was to do something like that. In his hurry to get away from the stench, he almost left without seeing the note. He marveled that Suggs could be so calm as to describe the man who shot him as he was dying. He didn't look around for anything to drink. His thirst had seemed to disappear somehow.

There was nothing to do but head back to Keetsville and send someone into Cassville to fetch the sheriff. He was on the wagon road, headed back to the northwest toward the Wire Road when he spied two riders headed his way in a big hurry. Unless he was mistaken, the one on the left rode just like his son Matt.

Crocia struggled again to get his hands off of her, but she had to spend most of her efforts just holding on to the horse. "Why are you doing this to me?"

"I got a lot of payin' back that needs doin."

Once they had reached the relative safety of the woods, McCorkle had allowed her to sit in front of him. She was trying to keep from straddling the saddle horn, but the road was so rough she couldn't seem to get her balance for more than a few seconds at a time. Twice she had almost fallen off, and he had man-handled her back to an upright position in front of him. "I don't even know you. What are you paying me back for?"

"I'm payin' back a bunch of people. Them Yankees that kilt my little sis, Charity, in Kansas City three years ago for starters."

"I've never even been to Kansas City!"

"That damned General Ewing locked a bunch of innocent women and girls in an old building in Kansas City, usin' it as a prison. The Yankees say the building just fell down, but I got good information that they blowed it up. Kilt my sister dead. Kilt one sister of my commandin' officer and his other two sisters was all broken up."

"My two brothers died for the South at Wilson's Creek. Everybody suffered during that war. You've got no call blaming me for your sister."

"What about that Yankee-lovin' B. F. Windes?"

She almost lost her grip on the horse's mane. "B. F.? B. F. is no Yankee!"

"He kilt all my fellers. Just missed killin' me, too. He'll be downright displeased to find out I ain't dead!"

"You're crazy! B. F. is just a storekeeper!"

"He may be a storekeeper, but he's a sure-fire killer." He grabbed her chest again, kneading her as though she were bread dough. "And I'm gonna enjoy gettin' even."

She didn't want him to know that he was hurting her. She bit her lip. "Get your hands off of me!"

"You ain't seen nothin' yet, girlie."

Fifty-One

In The Bye And Bye

Blockade Hollow, Missouri 1866

Henry held her at arm's length, taking in the sight of her. "Mattie, I ain't kissed ye in four long years."

"I read that letter ye wrote me from when ye got captured by the Yankees every night for them four terrible years. Fact, this here McCorkle tore it to pieces when he was drunk."

"Why would he . . . Mattie, I hear a hoss comin'."

"Quick, let's get up in the woods. It must be McCorkle comin' back." Both of them hurried out of the clearing, with Henry's injury and his horse slowing him down. But they were out of sight when the pair came up the trail.

"Quiet, Henry. That's him. Looks like he brung a woman with him."

McCorkle called out. "Mattie, I heard you goin' up the side of that hill yonder. Get on down here and fix me some dinner." She kept silent, hoping he was bluffing.

"Don't make me come up there and get you. You won't like it if I do."

She whispered to Henry, "I don't want him coming up here. He'll likely kill you if he sees you. I'll go on down there. Don't worry about me. I'll run off soon as I can."

"I don't want you goin' down there. Say, that girl . . ." Henry squinted against the sun, "she looks familiar."

She noticed that McCorkle had turned his horse in their direction, so she stood up, and tried to keep her voice from revealing just how scared she was. "I'm a comin'. They ain't much to eat though."

Mattie realized he was tying one end of a rope around the woman's neck, and the other end around his waist. "What's goin' on here? Why is that woman tied up?"

"Ain't none of yer business. I ain't had nothin' to eat today. Put a meal together."

Crocia thought the rope was going to gag her. She put her hand around the knot to try and take pressure off her neck. "He took me off the stage coach. He shot. . . ." The rope was yanked even tighter and she had to fight to keep from choking.

"Keep yer mouth shut if you know what's good for you."

"Say, she's just a young girl. What are ye tryin' to do?"

McCorkle drew his gun. "What's it gonna take for the two of you to shut up?"

The three of them went into the cabin, and in a few minutes, Henry saw smoke coming from the chimney. He was torn between riding back to town to tell where Crocia was and staying close. The man seemed to be on the verge of doing something violent, and he had to be there to help if he could. He wished he had a weapon.

Back up the road, John Durham told B. F. and Matt what he had found in the cabin and described the note Suggs had written in his own blood before he died. "They don't make folks any tougher than the people livin' in these hollers."

B. F. then described what had happened on the stage that morning and the description of the hold-up man. "It sounds like we may have the same man, and now we know he's capable of murder." He then told them about the Appaloosa that Mattie had been riding a few months ago and how the same horse could have been ridden by the low-down scum that had taken Crocia. "You didn't see a horse up in the hollow did you?"

"No, but we did see some fresh sign of a horse. Seems like I would have seen him though—unless he passed me by when I went to Suggs' cabin. Course, he could be headed for Arkansas for all we know."

"Only one way to find out. Can you take us to Mattie's place? We'll probably need to go on foot the last stretch."

Crocia kept telling herself to stay calm and look for a way to escape. But the cabin was small, with only a single window, and the knot at her throat was resistant to her quick attempts to loosen it when McCorkle wasn't looking. He realized how restrictive it was to have Crocia tied to him, so he simply untied the knot at his waist and reattached his end of the rope around Mattie's neck, making sure it was tight enough to make her cough. "Maybe I'll just keep the two of ya'll like that. We're just one big happy family. Fact, we're gonna practice bein' a family right after dinner." He leered at the younger woman, laughing at her reaction to his remark. "I reckon ya'll ain't gonna get far hitched together like that."

He sat down and began to remove the boot from his throbbing foot. Crocia couldn't believe this was happening. She stared at this evil man with the misshapen ear, then looked to the woman on the other end of the rope for some sign of mutual comfort. Mattie was at the fire, bent over a dutch oven with her biscuits. How could she be so calm at a time like this? Since she was tied up too, surely she felt just as threatened as Crocia did.

Mattie finally raised an eyebrow, looked sidewise at Crocia, and tugged ever so slightly on her end of the rope to be sure she had her attention. She eyed McCorkle to be sure he wasn't watching, and mouthed "Get ready." Crocia glanced at the man, then at Mattie, and slightly moved her head down to affirm she understood.

The biscuits finished, Mattie made some gravy with what bacon scraps could be found and presented a plate to McCorkle. He eyed both women and made sure they saw him set his pistol on the table beside his dinner. She had hoped he would holster it. That meant she had to be right on the mark.

She let him get through with one biscuit and start on a second before she asked, "You want some water?"

He looked around. "Where's my jug?"

She flinched. Why hadn't she remembered that before she asked? "It's not here no more."

"Where is it?"

"I put it in a shady spot down yonder in the spring branch."

McCorkle hesitated to calculate the situation, but he couldn't very well let them out of his sight. He'd just have to get the jug later, after he'd had some fun. "Gimme some water."

Mattie looked hard at Crocia to be sure she was watching, then dippered a tin cup full of water and set it on the table, well away from his pistol. When he picked it up and turned his head up to drink, she stomped his bad foot with all the force she could muster in her hundred pounds.

McCorkle screamed. The tin cup went flying and he grabbed for his foot, then thought better of it and reached for his pistol. Before he could get to it, Mattie swung as hard as she could, hitting him on the back of the head with a glowing log from the fire. He crumpled up like a wet rag and fell over on the floor, while the burning stick rolled toward his sleeping pallet.

She hollered at Crocia, "Come on, let's get outa here before he comes to himself." Crocia fumbled with the knot at her neck. "Don't worry with that in here. Let's git." They headed for the exit, but both were yanked up short by their tether. McCorkle had fallen on the middle of the rope and they were held fast by his weight.

Mattie started to try and lift him up, but Crocia held up a hand. "Wait a minute." She picked up the cast iron lid to the Dutch oven, swung it over her head, and hit him as hard as she could, just above his bad ear. The almost healed wound began to bleed profusely. "All right—now let's get the rope."

It took both of them—one pushing the limp McCorkle and the other pulling on the crimped rope—for them to be freed. Finally, the two women stumbled through the door and out into the yard. "Henry," Mattie hollered, "Bring your horse, quick." She and Crocia began to struggle to untie the knot around each other's neck. "He got this so dadburn tight I cain't budge this here knot."

Henry appeared with a knife and began to saw on the heavy hemp rope. It seemed to take forever, but they were both free in a couple of minutes.

"Let's get outa here!" hollered Mattie.

"Wait. Matilda—yer cabin's on fire!"

She stopped and stared at the flames coming out from under the eaves. "I hate to lose my herbs . . . an all them books." She shook her head. "But it cain't be helped. McCorkle might come awake if we went back."

Henry looked at her, then the cabin. "We cain't just ride off and let a man burn alive."

"Ain't nobody in there fit to be called a man." Mattie grabbed his hand to tell him not to do it, but she jumped back as though a shock had struck her. "Henry, don't ye do it. I seen what happens if ye do. I seen ye lyin' dead. Leave him be, Henry."

"I cain't do that, Matilda."

"Henry!" She screamed. "Please." He started for the cabin and she tackled him from behind, throwing herself into his bad leg. He went down and she leapt to her feet, running past him. "Stay back. I'll go. It ain't me in the vision."

As she made it to the door, the front of the house was completely ablaze. The wave of heat forced her backward, and this gave Henry the opportunity to push her out of the way.

He grabbed for the door and the iron handle blistered the skin on his palm in less than a second. He tore off his hat and used it to protect his hand in order to get the door open. Immediately, flames shot out of the cabin doorway and pushed him back several feet. "Are ye in there, mister?" He put his arm in front of his eyes to shield them from the heat and took two steps toward the fiery doorway.

"Get outa my way ye bastard!" Came the shout from inside the burning cabin.

Crocia looked at Mattie. "Was that a gun shot?" In answer to her question, Henry stumbled forward, grabbed the door for support, and fell against it, his body forcing it shut, and sealing the door on the shooter.

"Henry!" The sound of her voice was horrible—a combination of desperation and cold dread. The cabin was completely ablaze. Mattie threw herself into the flames and tried to pull Henry out of the fire. She couldn't budge him an inch. She heard an animalistic scream from inside the cabin—McCorkle. She could hear him slamming his weight against the door, but the weight of Henry's body and the latch held it fast. There was another scream, and another, then nothing. She pulled against Henry's weight again, and suddenly he was moving backward. She realized that Crocia was beside her, in the fire, pulling Henry away from the cabin.

They dragged him at least forty feet from the cabin before Crocia realized the bottom of her dress was in flames. She swatted at the fire and tried in vain to rip it off, but then started to try to run away from the intense heat. Mattie caught her around the waist and rolled her in the dirt, slapping at the fire on her dress with her bare hands.

"Oh, Mattie—your hands! They're burned something awful."

"Don't worry about me. Look after Henry."

He was in bad shape—shot in his chest just above his right breast. When Crocia turned him over she could actually hear a gurgling in his chest, as though his lung was sucking air in through the hole. He seemed to be struggling to draw a breath, but was able to choke out, "Matilda . . . Matilda"

She was there on her knees, bending over close to him. She saw the chest wound, and placed her open palm over the hole. "I seen a doctor do this once to stop that gurglin'."

Despite the warm day, his teeth were chattering. "I'm cold . . . so cold . . . my coat. . . ."

Crocia retrieved the tattered old coat from his saddlebag, and she and Mattie tried to wrap him to provide a little bit of warmth. He looked at Mattie, his eyes brimming over. "I done loved ye forever." He choked and spit up a gush of blood.

Mattie had one hand on his chest and held his badly burned right hand in hers. She squeezed her eyes tight with the sudden agony of reality but knew she had to give him comfort in these last minutes. "Don't you worry none, Henry. Ye lived a righteous life. I done seen us together in paradise. I'll be there with ye in the bye and bye."

He choked again, finally caught his breath, and managed to get out one last sentence. "I'll be waitin' for ye." And just like that, his body was empty.

As if on cue, the afternoon sky turned black, lightning and thunder rent the little valley, the heavens opened in an extremely heavy downpour, and large tree branches were torn from trees. At this moment, B. F. and Matt, followed at a distance by John Durham, ran into the clearing with their guns drawn.

B. F. was so relieved when he saw her that he almost fell on his knees. "Crocia—are you hurt? Why, you've been afire! Mattie—are you? Oh, your hands are burned bad!" Then B. F. realized that what he had thought was just a pile of ragged clothes on the ground was actually a man. She was kneeling over Henry. "Mattie—is he?" He stepped closer, speaking quieter than before. "Is he gone?"

She nodded mutely. He put his hand on her shoulder. "I'm so sorry. He loved you."

She nodded again and whispered hoarsely toward the heavens. "This here storm is Lucifer and all his devils, celebratin' that one of the very best of us has passed on."

She began to rock back and forth on her knees, holding her arms around her shoulders, making the primitive sounds of grief she had first heard so long ago from her grandmother.

B. F. stepped away, giving her some privacy. He took Crocia aside and spoke to her. "We heard a shot."

She stared at the revolver in his hand. "Please put your gun away. Guns have already done enough today."

He looked at the weapon in his hand and holstered it. "Where's the man who took you?"

She pointed at the burning cabin, now completely engulfed despite the heavy rain. "In there. He killed Henry."

"Why did he do this? What was his name?"

"McCorkle."

"John McCorkle?" He was incredulous. "I could have killed him myself four months ago! In fact, all this time I thought he was dead!" He turned toward the grieving Maid. "Oh, Mattie. It's my fault—it was McCorkle who did this to Henry."

Crocia looked at B. F. "McCorkle said terrible things about you. You . . . you aren't who he said you were, are you? He . . . he said you were a killer." She looked away.

He put his arms on her shoulders, but she pulled back. "Are you a killer? Are you . . . are you like McCorkle?"

B. F. was stunned that she, of all people, could compare him to McCorkle. "I knew McCorkle during the war. He and a man he worked with stole my ship and seventy thousand dollars worth of cargo. They made me think it had been sunk by a Union gunboat."

"Why did you get mixed up with somebody like that?"

"They convinced me they were with the Texas Third Cavalry." He hung his head with the shame of it. "I found out too late that they were nothing but vigilantes."

"Why didn't you just stop dealing with them?"

"By the time I found out, they had already stolen my ship and cargo. So I was no longer in business."

"Is that why you bought property here—because you wanted to get even with them? Even kill them?"

"The man McCorkle followed was killed during the war by Union troops. I didn't even know McCorkle was in this part of the country until four months ago. Then I found out almost by accident that McCorkle and his gang were planning on blowing up Keetsville with dynamite. Some of us in the town were able to stop them. We thought we'd gotten rid of all of them. I don't have any idea how McCorkle got away. The next time I heard the name McCorkle was five minutes ago." He tried to take her hands in his, but she pulled back again. "McCorkle must have taken you to get back at me. You've got to believe me—I'd never do anything to put you in danger."

Crocia put her head down for a few moments, then found what she needed within herself, and squared her shoulders. "I'm not the one whose life was ruined today because both you and McCorkle had to get even with somebody." She knelt down and put her arm around Mattie, then looked up at B. F. "Mattie saved my life today, and she lost everything she owned, and everything she loved in doing it. Until she finds another place, she's coming into town with me. Tomorrow, hire someone to make that farm house of yours liveable. You sleep at your store, and I'll stay at the farm with Mattie for the time being. When she's ready, I'll go back to Waynesville."

B. F. looked at the two women in front of him. A mixture of soot and rainwater ran down their faces in rivulets. They each had bleeding rope burns around their necks. Their clothes were half burned away, their legs and faces blistered, and both of them had burns on their hands. All of a sudden he was filled with fear and love—but in his life, fear always had the upper hand.

Love was certainly important, because he knew beyond any doubt that he felt love for Crocia. Although he had thought about it in the abstract several times, he had begun to be aware of the deep and powerful feelings that could be initiated with the realization that a truly good woman was a wonderful and precious thing.

But then there was fear. Fear that he might have lost this woman because of the bad things that he had done, the business he had been in, the people he had run the blockade for, and maybe even the fear that came unbidden to his mind—an admittance that he could have been born to be this way—born under a bad sign. Down in the bottom of his gut, he couldn't get away from remembering all the people who had suffered, and even died, who had been closest to him—Mr. Fitzwater, Jane, Ethan, his own mother, and now poor Henry. All of them because of things he had done, or things he had failed to do. Could he be a murderer? Could it be true? Was this the pattern of his life?

By the time they got back to the Durham house with Henry's body, it was well past sundown. The sheriff had arrived from Cassville and was questioning Elizabeth Rayl when they rode into the yard. When Elizabeth saw her daughter safe, she couldn't stop crying. Minnie and Sue Durham were holding their husbands in a fast embrace, and B. F.,

Mattie, and the sheriff were bystanders. After a few minutes, Mattie turned Henry's old horse aside and started back out the lane toward the road. B. F. saw her going, and caught up to her.

"Miss Lansdown—you need to stay with us."

"No. You'ns got lots to share tonight. I'll get outa the way."

"Crocia meant what she said. I already know that about her. She means for you to stay for awhile."

"Maybe I'll see you'ns tomorrow."

"No, ma'am. That's not good enough." He gave her as warm a smile as he could muster under the circumstances. "Besides, we've both got a dinner invitation."

She smiled at his friendship, looked down at how bedraggled she was, and suddenly realized how long it had been since she had eaten a real meal. "I could use that right about now."

They walked their horses back to the yard. B. F. motioned to Crocia, said a few words to her, and she took Mattie by the arm to go get cleaned up.

B. F. rode into town, followed Crocia's instructions to find the smallest size in women's clothing he had in the store, and returned to the house. Sue helped them get cleaned up, bandaged their hands, and had to cut away quite a bit of their hair that was singed. By the time dinner was ready, both Mattie and Crocia had gotten into clean dresses and, despite their bandages and salve on their faces, were looking almost like themselves.

Mattie looked at the dining table. "Missus Durham, I ain't set at a table this nice since my Mam died. If my manners ain't quite right, I'm apologizin'."

Minnie and Elizabeth both came to her and hugged her. "The way we hear it, you saved our Crocia's life today—without regard for yourself. You're our hero, Mattie. You're welcome at our table anytime."

Although all of Crocia's suggested improvements on the farmhouse had not been completed, with five days of carpentry accomplished, Mattie and Crocia were able to set up housekeeping with most of the required conveniences. They spent much of their days in assembling the household, getting a late garden planted, and cooking for one another. But even with their busy schedule, every evening was spent in talking through each other's emotional turmoil regarding Henry and B. F.

Mattie was insistent that she intended, even in death, to spend the rest of her life being faithful to Henry. "After all, my mam and pap both passed on in their early forties. I figger I got fifteen, maybe twenty years left on this earth before I go to be with Henry. That's hardly any time at all.

"I'm a whole lot more worried about what you intend to do with your life. We both know you love B. F. Are you really serious about giving him up? That Civil War made killers out of hundreds of thousands of good men. B. F.'s problem is that the war followed him to Keetsville, and you were here when it caught up with him. That don't mean he's a killer."

"I know that's true, but I can't seem to stop thinking about how many people were put in danger because of him."

Mattie smiled at her friend. "Have you ever done something that you still regret—no matter how much time has passed?"

Crocia sighed. "Almost every day for the last five years, I wish I had begged Robert and William—my brothers—not to enlist in the Confederate Army. I was young and foolish, and thought they looked high and noble in their uniforms. They hadn't been gone from home a month before they were killed. I'll regret not trying to stop them for the rest of my life."

"Did your mother or father blame you for it?"

"Why, no. I don't think so."

"But you believe that you bear at least some of the burden for them gettin' killed?"

"I guess so."

"I feel that way about Henry, too."

"Why? It wasn't your fault. McCorkle is the one to be blamed."

Mattie smiled to herself. "I guess that's true. But I'll also be blamin' myself if you ride out of here in a week or so and don't come back to B. F."

"How is that your fault?"

"Because I know things you don't know. Have you ever wondered what your future is going to be like?"

Crocia thought a minute. "I remember on the day you lost Henry that before anything even happened, you told him you could see him lying dead. Does that mean you can see the future?"

"My great-grandpappy could. Sometimes I can too."

"Can you tell me what's going to happen to me?"

"Give me your hand."

With only the light from two coal oil lamps to illuminate the room, the two young women sat quietly for a full ten minutes. Finally, Mattie broke the silence. "I see two roads, and I cain't tell you which is your future. One road is plain as can be. You and a man with coal black hair and a big family. Your life is a simple one in Keetsville. A husband who stays true. But I see that same husband wearing a pistol for the rest of his life—in order to protect what's his.

"The other road seems to be in a haze or a mist. There's you and your ma and pa. Then there's a tall man with long, curly brown hair that takes you to a big city to live. I see two babies. There's no gun on his hip. But he strays sometimes. You stay with him.

You have to decide for yourself which road leads to the kind of regret you can't ever get away from, and which leads to a happy life. Then I can tell you which road truly belongs to you."

Well after dark, B. F. stood on the front steps of the Windes Mercantile, facing the southwest sky. He quickly found Orion, clear as could be, just waiting on him. "Mama—we haven't talked in a while. I've found the girl I want, but I made some mistakes that got a good man killed. And now I may lose her because she has her doubts about whether or not I'm a killer. I even wonder myself why almost everybody dear to me has died. Can you help me see the right way?"

He stood motionless for at least five minutes and then he could swear he heard his mother's voice just as clear as day. . . . *Fight for her.*

Abruptly he turned on his heel, walked back in the store, put on his hat and jacket, and hurried across the street to saddle his horse. He was at the farmhouse in less than ten minutes, tapping on the front door.

Both women answered the knock, with Mattie holding a rifle at the ready. "Sorry, Mistuh Windes. Have to be careful these days."

"That's alright, Mattie. Crocia, could I speak to you for a minute?"

The burns on her face had almost completely healed, and he was reminded again of just how pretty she was when she stepped out on the front porch in her house dress with the coal oil lantern inside the house providing a bit of light. "Crocia, I can't just let you go without a fight. I'd regret it for the rest of my days if I just stood by and watched you walk out of my life. Can you find a way to forgive me for putting everyone in danger, for getting you taken, and for poor Henry?"

"Mattie and I were just talking about regrets—particularly about regretting that you did nothing when you should have done something. I understand that very well."

"Would you still have me after all that's happened?"

She stood there for a full minute, staring into his eyes. Then she stepped closer and kissed him tenderly. "I believe I would." She turned, knocked on the door, and Mattie answered it with a quizzical look. Crocia smiled at her friend. "I just decided which road I'm going to take."

The next evening, they all convened at the Durham home. Before they sat down to the meal, Sue brought an envelope in the room. "B. F., this letter came today from Indiana for you. It was put in an envelope addressed to me."

B. F. opened the letter and Crocia stepped behind him, reading over his shoulder:

Dear Ben
We hear yer livin in mizzoori, an thet you got a fine bizness.
We are happy thet life has been good to you. We had a long spell

of bad luck. Life is hard here. Since we are yer blood kin, we hope you wil do the Crischun thing an share some of yer good fortun with yer famly.

Yer pa and ma

Crocia recalled many years later that B. F. had stood there with the letter in his hand, staring across the room at a blank wall for at least five minutes, remembering no telling what from those many years ago. He folded the letter and put it in the pocket of his jacket. Then he took no more than two steps, withdrew the letter, read it once more, squared his shoulders, tore the letter into pieces, and dropped them into the fireplace.

He looked at Crocia and pulled her to his side. "I do aim to share everything with my family . . . but my family is all right here." He put his arm around Crocia and touched Mattie on the shoulder. "Let's have some of that coffee!"

Acknowledgments

The main character of Orphan Hero—B. F. Windes—was my great-grandfather. Fantastic as it may seem in today's culture, the framework of the story is absolutely true. He ran away from a cruel stepmother at the age of eight, traveled to the California gold fields via wagon train, earned his own way as a barber and physician assistant, and then was a blockade-runner during the Civil War. He left Indiana in 1849 with nothing but a handful of dimes, yet when he arrived in Missouri in 1865, he had enough money to purchase a mercantile store, four rather large farms, and establish himself as the unofficial local banker. Yet his fight was not over in southwestern Missouri, as the bushwhackers terrorized the area for some time after the surrender at Appomattox Court House.

The novel is based on stories told to me by my grandmother, my aunt, and my father; as well as entries from B. F. Windes' personal journal, which he kept from 1849 until 1865. But as all historical novels must be, much of the specifics, all of the conversations, and many of the characters, are the author's own invention.

I have taken great care to be as historically accurate as possible, and have personally visited almost all of the sites mentioned in this book. Additionally, I was aided by wonderful people at a number of locations.

The Arabia Steamboat Museum in Kansas City is privately owned and is an exceptional source of information on the workings of an 1850s era steamboat on the Missouri River, as well as the make-up of the cargo it would have carried in order to bring supplies to the jumping-off point for the westward bound wagon trains.

The National Frontier Trails Museum in Independence, Missouri was very helpful in educating me about the earliest days of the Oregon and Santa Fe Trails, before Independence was replaced by the new town of Westport, Missouri, some twenty miles further west. It was not long after Westport had opened for business that the discovery of gold in California occurred, with the result that a much greater number of travelers headed west—this time diverging from the Oregon Trail to form a third major thoroughfare—the California Trail.

The Kansas Museum of History in Topeka was absolutely full of nineteenth century memorabilia—particularly all of the accouterments necessary to travel west on a wagon train.

The Hastings Museum in Hastings, Nebraska helped me have a good understanding of the various Plains Indian tribes, which may have been encountered on the trek west.

The Kansas City Public Library's Special Collections Room was the source of much of the information related to the old town of Westport, its citizens, street maps, and function as the jumping-off point in 1849.

The California Museum in Sacramento was a treasure trove of information related to the state's gold rush towns and their unique inhabitants between 1849 and 1860.

The Gold Museum in Dahlonega, Georgia was devoted to the brief gold rush experienced in the mountains of northern Georgia in 1829.

The Barry County Museum in Cassville, Missouri is an exceptional gem that any small town in America would be proud to host. Its many resources helped me to understand that much of the area was truly a no-man's land during and immediately after the Civil War. Additionally, they were the source of one of my characters, the Maid of the Mountain. Actually, B. F. Windes knew her, and personally utilized her skills as a seer, but only later in his life. Her insertion into my story in the 1860s was a fabrication on my part.

The Park Rangers at our National Military Parks are very well acquainted with all of the details related to the Civil War battles that took place at their current assignment. I visited National Military Parks in Pea Ridge, Arkansas, Shiloh, Tennessee, and Vicksburg, Mississippi, as well as the National Battlefield at Wilsons Creek, Missouri in order to have a better understanding of each of these locations mentioned in the novel.

I am forever grateful to JoAnn Collins from International Transactions, Inc., who was the first writer's agent to read, and even edit, my novel. Peter Riva of the same organization agreed to represent me, and Yucca Publishing has graciously published my work.

Joanne DeMichele, PhD, was unbelievably patient with me, as well as a myriad of my mistakes, in her undertaking to proof and format my manuscript. I had no idea that retired English professors could be so kind and understanding!

My father, BF Babb, was B. F. Windes' namesake. More than that, he undoubtedly inherited my great-grandfather's strength of character and personal courage. He was my personal hero, and it was only through his guidance, many anecdotes, editorial help, and faith in me, that this book was written. Sadly, he died at the age of ninety-three in 2013 before the book could be published.

My wife, Victoria Babb, and I lived less than a mile from the convergence of the California, Oregon, and Santa Fe Trails in Kansas City at my last duty station. After hearing my father and I talk about the exploits of old B. F. Windes for many years, it was she who finally said, "Why don't you write a book!" And I always listen to my wife.